Book Two
Firebird

MARINNA

Kathleen King

Kathleen King

ISBN: 978-0-578-73123-0

Cover art by Christine Rogers

Chickaloon Press

To my grandchildren
Seth, Parker, Ian, Alaina, Judah, James, and Abigail,
and to those who may yet join them.
It is my delight to watch you grow.
And to Dwayne's grandchildren
whom I am so glad to know.

May you find your deepest joy in our great Creator God
and share it one day with grandchildren of your own.

Acknowledgements

Thanks to so many of you who read Floxx (Book 1 of this series) and loved it and cheered me on to finish this sequel. Your enthusiasm was so encouraging!

Special gratitude to the gifted Dr. Christine Rogers for the book's cover and for her many hours of proofreading. And to Dr. Karen Williams, editor par excellence, whose insightful critique spurred me to deepen and strengthen the characters and the story.

I'm also grateful for these outstanding proofreaders: Talitha Daniels, Dennis Cochardo, Stasi Cochardo, and Lisa Jenkins. It's the little things, isn't it! Thank you for catching them.

And to Lee Rogers for sharing his publishing expertise; please know how appreciative I am.

Table of Contents

Chapter 1: Way Crazy

Rory laughed as her grandmother squeezed the last can of peaches onto the cold-room shelf.

"I did it! Full to bursting!" Gram beamed. "And not a day too soon; I can feel a snowstorm in these old bones."

"Yep, storm's coming tonight," Dad replied, looking back at his mother from the open fridge. He turned to Rory smiling. "I'm just glad you made it home in time to get all of this unloaded before it hits."

"Can't imagine what else we might need," Gram called, nudging a few cans back from their precarious perch. "Why, we could get by till spring if we rationed just a little. And all this fruit! I didn't think you'd have room for it in the airplane."

"But no rationing tonight," Dad proclaimed, reaching out to pat Rory's shoulder. "Tonight, we splurge!"

"How 'bout I whip up some chicken and biscuits and gravy?" Gram peered at them, daring them to say no.

"And can you also whip up a blueberry cobbler?" Dad winked at Rory.

Gram was already on her knees, scrabbling inside a cupboard for the right pots and pans. "Would be my great pleasure!" Her contagious laugh made them both smile.

"Rory." Dad turned to her. "You did so well flying the grocery run. I'm really proud of you; how focused you are on safety and on getting the job done so fast! You didn't forget a thing; you even added a few cases of canned fruit. You'll be flying supply runs before you know it!"

"Yeah, well, thanks, Dad," she said, squirming a little. She'd been able to stow the fruit in the right front seat only because Cue wasn't with her. Normally, his hairy 200 pounds was harnessed in; there was still dry slobber on the inside of the window from his last flight. A fresh wave of grief broke inside her. Cue. Her constant companion and protector. Gone. She remembered his last yelp as the wolf that had meant to kill her, killed him. Dad had asked where Cue had run off to but had gotten distracted with unpacking the supplies, so she hadn't had to answer.

She was so glad she'd thought to change into her jeans before she transported back to Alaska. If she'd come home in her palace gown, there would have been a whole lot of immediate explaining to do. But she looked normal, right down to her red sneakers. Ardith had brought them to her when they'd come for the King's funeral, brought everything Rory had left at the farm when they'd first struck out on their journey to meet her birth parents—her jeans and hoodie, even her cell phone, which was long dead.

She knew Dad wanted to debrief with her on how the flight had gone; this was a routine part of flight training. That would be her chance to explain she'd flown back from another world. Seriously, this was going to totally freak them out. It was way crazy, but she had to tell them. And soon. It would just get harder the longer she waited. How would they ever believe she'd crashed the airplane? The Cessna she'd just landed didn't have a scratch on it.

"So, um, I wanted to tell you about my trip. It, uh, wasn't exactly, ah..."

"As you planned?" Dad was nodding his head up and down in a way that said he'd expected no less. "I'm sure it had some challenges, Rory, and I want to hear about them. But you know, of course, that's normal. Good pilots always have a plan B in mind when Plan A isn't going as expected."

"It's not that," she said, her words wavering.

At the hitch in her voice, Dad riveted his eyes on her. "What?"

Gram had the infant gown turned inside out, studying the sewing. "It's beautifully made," she murmured, "each stitch is perfect." Her eyes were moist as she considered Rory, and the story she'd just told them. "This is incredible."

They'd talked for a solid three hours, all the way through dinner and long past the cobbler. Rory had given them a summary of her emergency landing in the strange world of Gamloden, of Floxx and Finn and the others, of moving the damaged airplane to Werner's farm. She'd brushed through their trip from Tomitarn to the castle, leaving out much of the death and destruction, as well as the dragon, the giant, the bloody royal ball, and her birth father's death. She'd get to that, but not right off. She was actually super surprised—and relieved—at how easily they believed her. Well, why wouldn't they with the things she'd brought home with her as proof? And then there was the fact she'd been delivered to their doorstep by a bird. Floxx, herself. Their own experiences proved the impossible could happen.

She could see Dad's mixed emotions as she told about her reunion with her birth parents. He seemed to be glad she'd found them, maybe even a little jealous, and definitely sad. His furrowed eyebrows gave away his worry that he'd lose her forever. They asked a lot of questions about her birth parents, the castle, society, physical looks, personalities, lifestyle, beliefs. But, finally, Dad had taken her hand and said royalty fit her perfectly. He was so gracious; he'd always been willing to help her face life's challenges and risks, yet his eyes held a pool of uncertainties about this. She let them savor their sweet princess thoughts for the moment, knowing how badly they would freak out later.

They'd thumbed through the book of her father's poems to her mother, enamored with his perfect swirly penmanship, his formal style and expressions, the parchment paper, and, of course, the sentiment. One thing led to another and she ended up telling them about Floxx and Finn and the Night of the Tennins. Actually, she talked about Finn more than a few times and couldn't help blushing. Though she mentioned Jakin, she left out his treachery. She'd get to it, maybe. Or maybe not, knowing how upset they'd be that she'd nearly gotten married.

It was late. Rory was exhausted. Finally, the questions stopped, and Dad sat quietly, his mouth set in a small smile that didn't hide the melancholy in his eyes. "A princess," he said nodding. "I can see that you have a grand life ahead of you."

She reached for his hand. "Seriously, Dad, I never wanted this. Never expected it, not in a million years. I thought of you and mom and Gram every day I was gone."

He squeezed her fingers. "I'm sure you did, Rory. It never crossed my mind you'd forget us." Dad was thoughtful. "But this is so bizarre. I mean, to us, it's just the evening of your cross-country flight to Fairbanks! It seemed so normal when you landed on the strip loaded with food, just as we'd expected." He sighed. "Life can spring surprises on us that change us forever." He flicked the bellasol on and off staring absently at it, then cleared his throat and sat up straighter.

Uh oh. Rory braced herself, knowing he was about to say something important.

"It seems you have a calling on your life, Rory. A really big one, both fantastic and daunting. And yet, you came home."

She nodded.

"Why?"

Rory sighed and looked at her lap. He knew there was more. She should have realized he'd see the holes in her story.

"Could it wait till tomorrow?"

"Certainly." He stood and stretched, setting the bellasol on the kitchen table next to her infant gown, the book of poems, and father's brooch, all so incongruous in her Alaskan log home.

Chapter 2: Syrean Sea

A breeze sighed through the trees and Finn glimpsed a few stars peeking through the clouds. The fire had burned to embers, brightening for a moment in the gust. Kalvara and Aric curled together, asleep on the other side of the firepit, a dark lump beneath her cloak. The blue orb that was Uriel hovered nearby. Finn poked at the coals, feeling the night chill, wanting to build the fire up. But his rustling would wake the others. Let them rest. Especially young Aric.

A small smile broke his consternation as he remembered Aric's hunting today. He'd gotten more birds than they could eat; they'd cooked them all, saving the six that were left over for breakfast. The boy was an astounding young marksman.

His thoughts turned to Rory as they often did. Had he done the right thing in leaving, likely ending their relationship? For the past few days as the three of them trekked through the woods, he'd agonized over his decision. He couldn't get her out of his mind; he missed her terribly. He feared he'd made a mistake he'd regret for the rest of his life. But their relationship was impossible. He was called to one purpose, and she to another. He couldn't have stayed one more day in that castle, cooped up in its stone walls amidst the grief and gloom, watching her move a little further from him each day as she faced her responsibilities there. She couldn't come with him. And he couldn't stay with her.

He let his mind wander to their occasional morning walks in the woods, hand in hand, talking sometimes, yet comfortable in silence. One morning, he'd made her a green, leafy crown and when he'd placed it on her head, she'd cried. He'd meant to please her, not make her sad! Then she'd told him about her mother's fireweed crowns and other special times they'd had together. But her mother had gotten sick and no doctors could make her better. She shared what had happened on her sixteenth birthday; how she'd found out her family had no idea where she'd come from, just that a great big beautiful bird had brought her. Her mother had given her the Firebird feather that night and died just a few months later. What a story! And here she was now; brought to this world by Floxx, herself. He wanted to spend the entire day with Rory, but her royal duty called. She had to return to the castle for a day's work.

Another time, she'd hidden a picnic under her cape: Crisp apples, a loaf of crusty bread, and a crock of tenninberry jam. They'd shared breakfast snuggled in the roots of a large tree deep in the woods. But again, way too soon, she'd had to leave. The Queen needed her; she had so much to do. His heart ached at their divergent callings, but he had no solution, just this desperate, impossible, irrational love, like a bird loving a tree. He had to fly, and she was rooted in place.

He stretched out on the ground facing the coals, one arm under his head, opposite Kalvara. She was impressive, especially when teamed with her little nephew. Their bond was unbreakable, and he admired her commitment to the child. She'd faced death many times on his behalf. She must have loved her brother deeply to risk everything for his son. She had been determined to escape the oppression of Droome and seek a better life. What courage it must have taken to run to an unknown world, a world she thought hated

7

her. Yet she'd done it. Would she ever have risked it for herself, he wondered, if Aric hadn't been the catalyst that sent her running?

She was smart, cunning, wild. Her instinct for survival was still stronger than her sense, with her shoot first, think later, response to a threat. But he'd seen a gentler side in the way she protected Aric, in her unguarded laugh at the antics of the dwarf children, Pelzar and his sister, Renaz. He remembered her tears at the news of young Pelzar's death and her genuine love of King Merek for his goodness and kindness to her and Aric. Rory's father may have been the first individual who accepted her for who she was and valued her life with much esteem. Finn had watched her anger cool to suspicion, then her defenses melted away as she trusted the King to love and protect her. He remembered her shock when he offered her and Aric a home in the castle for the rest of their lives.

And yet, she'd chosen to leave with him. She'd been ready weeks before he was, and it was no secret she was waiting for him to make up his mind. "You can't stay here, Finn," she'd said. "You are shrinking inside, your calling fading, weakening every day." She was so right. But could he go without Rory? He'd been blindly hoping she'd choose him. Madly dreaming she'd run off with him in the night. But Rory was more honorable than that. It was an unfair dream, a selfish wish. Kalvara bided her time and finally approached him. "I'll come with you," she said, "when you are ready. We will help each other."

They'd been gone five days, making good distance each day and suffering no delays, threats, or attacks in the woods. They'd stopped just before sunset, as had become their habit, so Aric could hunt their dinner. The boy had been high in the trees when they'd heard him shout, "Water! Look over there! Really big water!" Finn and Kalvara shimmied up the trunk and perched next to him. The southern horizon was blue for as far as they could see.

"What is it?" Aric wiggled with so much excitement, he nearly fell.

Kalvara recalled the stories the Queen had told. "Remember the picture window in the King's mausoleum?" she asked. "The one of their wedding by the sea?"

Finn laughed as he realized where they were. "So, we've reached the Syrean Sea already! It's beautiful! More beautiful than I ever would have imagined!" Small boats and sailing ships dotted the water and he wondered what it would feel like to be in one of them. He turned to look inland and noted dozens, maybe hundreds, of rooftops. "The edge of Syrea," he gestured. There was nothing to block the view of the city, as the forest abruptly ended just ahead of them and the sandy ground stretched flat to the horizon. Roads and paths tangled in all directions and a few weary horses struggled to get their wagons home before dark. Set off to the east was a cluster of tall, stately buildings, their shiny roofs glinting like jewels in the distance.

"See that?" Finn pointed. "I think that may be where Queen Raewyn lived as a child! I can't see much beyond it. Aric, can you see anything further?"

"Mountain peaks," he replied, glancing where Finn pointed. But Aric didn't elaborate, his attention riveted on the sea.

"We should stay out of sight," Kalvara warned. "No telling what humans might do to us."

"But I want to see the water! And the great ships the King talked about!" Aric pleaded.

Finn ruffled the boy's hair. "Yes, the King's father once had a whole shipyard here. I'd like to see what's left of it and walk on the shore of this enormous sea." He hesitated at Kalvara's frown. "I mean, look, we can't even see where it ends! Don't tell me you're not curious, too! Let's explore just for a little while."

Kalvara pressed her mouth into a tight line. "This is foolishness." But she said nothing more.

Early in the morning, concealed behind a cluster of sea grass, they studied the activity on the docks nearest them. Aric licked his lips, and Finn caught the surprise in his eyes.

"What?" Finn asked, licking his own lips. "Salt!" He grinned. "I've heard sea water is salty. Didn't expect to taste it on land, though."

Aric nodded and wrinkled his nose in distaste. "And the fishy smell—it's not as nice as the King's fish was."

Finn stifled a laugh. "The King's fish was cooked with delicious spices. This fish smell is raw, and maybe some of it is rotten."

The stench was nothing, though, compared to the noise—the clamor of sailors yelling and banging as they unloaded goods on the docks. And birds, so many of them, squawked and swooped over the water!

"Let's go," Finn said and stepped out into full view. No one noticed as they walked the short distance to the path and joined the multitude. It had been Finn's idea to mingle with the crowd in broad daylight. He'd studied the people from a distance as they'd approached the wharves, shocked to realize there were peoples he didn't recognize. Who were they?

Kalvara had tied her hair up and covered her head, hiding her face as much as possible. She carried Aric on her hip, continually wrestling with him as he wiggled to see what he could.

Finn was curious to get a closer look at these people he'd never seen before. They looked somewhat like human men, but were very tall and slender, built much like Kalvara. They shared her pale skin, but where her hair was white, theirs was dark and long, braided and caught in a twist of rope. Their necks were unusually long and their faces smooth, no beards, though their bushy eyebrows covered a good part of their foreheads. Their eyes were brown, not red, like Kalvara's and Aric's. One of each of their ears was pierced and hung with strings of tiny colorful shells that swung wildly as they moved. They worked silently and quickly, and it was clear they'd done this before, unloading, sorting, stacking, and they glanced around from time to time as if expecting someone. Finn gasped when he saw they had six fingers on each hand. He nudged Kalvara, wanting her to see them.

A dozen stocky dwarves worked with them, grunting and insulting one another, their muscles bulging as they carried heavy crates from the docks of the ship to the deck where the tall ones piled them in careful stacks. Ahead of them, large wagons weaved recklessly among those walking, their drivers shouting to clear the way. One wagon was parked on the side of the path near them, abandoned temporarily, and there they paused to watch the work on the ship.

Finn kept his voice low. "I never realized. I mean all I thought about was fish. Fishing. I didn't think about trade on the sea." He felt foolish. Of course! Trading goods with other countries by ship was completely logical! But what other countries? It was like he'd stepped into another world, and he felt a sudden kinship with Rory. She must have felt like this with each person she met and every place she visited here. His admiration for her soared as he realized more deeply her bewilderment, and the courage she had displayed in her short time here. Rory. His heart ached as he envisioned her.

"Ow!" Aric complained, and Finn was surprised at Kalvara's grip on the boy and the terror in her eyes as she studied the tall ones. Why was she so afraid? Were these eldrow relatives who had somehow escaped capture and lived free from the tortures of Draegin? Or were they enemies of her people?

Before he could say anything, there was a brief commotion on the dock. Then all activity ceased. The tall ones stood straight and still, eyes downcast; the dwarves stopped their bickering and slouched in silence. A wagon approached from the opposite direction. Two matching steeds pulled the carriage, and the driver and passenger sat under a shaded cover. Two men rode on horseback in front of the wagon, clearing the way through the foot traffic.

Finn wondered about these people of great importance, and instinctively moved in front of Kalvara and Aric, protecting them. But he needn't have worried; the carriage passed them without a glance and before it had come to a complete stop, the passenger jumped out, strode round the horses and leapt onto the dock.

Finn recognized him instantly. Jakin! He'd grown a beard, but Finn would have known him anywhere. Jakin, who'd been his best friend all of his life. Jakin, who'd stabbed him in the back, so jealous over Rory that he'd resorted to dark magic, giving her an enchanted bracelet that nearly resulted in Rory's marrying him. That cursed spell was partially responsible for the death of the King and many others at the ball. He watched slack jawed as Jakin spoke with the tall ones, then ordered the dwarves to load certain crates into the wagon. When the load was securely tied, Jakin hefted a lumpy sack to one of the tall ones, nodded curtly at the crew, boarded the wagon, and without a glance in Finn's direction, turned and drove away.

The entire transaction had taken just a few minutes, and no one had said a word. Their meeting had clearly been arranged; the goods ordered and delivered on schedule. Jakin! So, this is where that scoundrel had run! But what was he doing here?

Chapter 3: Conquest

Queen Marinna ran the long string of pearls through her fingers, relishing their perfect roundness. The lamp light brought out their luster, like moonlight glistening on snow. She tugged on the strand, testing the strength of the thread holding the beads together, pulling a little harder each time. Finally, she placed one end of the strand under her foot, mustered her strength and yanked as hard as she could. The strand held! Twice before, other threads had broken, scattering hundreds of Syrean pearls across the palace floor. Garbage, she'd raged at Prince Tozar, when he'd personally delivered the inadequately strung beads. Stronger thread, she'd fumed, or your own head.

"Never fear, Your Highness," he'd said, bowing in terror.

On his most recent visit, he brought her the strand of gems she now held. "I have heard of a long-forgotten gemological technique," he'd said, holding out the pearl rope.

When he'd told her what it was, even she had momentarily blanched. "And how did you hear of this barbaric practice?" she'd demanded.

"From our felinex," he'd replied, eyes downcast.

"I see. And I approve. It's brilliant, actually." She changed the subject. "And what of news from outside?"

"News, your Highness?"

Why was Tozar so guarded? "My father has not been well enough to speak much."

"I see. I am glad to hear he is recovering."

She could see the lie plainly in his eyes.

"There was a fight at the palace?"

"There was, your Highness." He trembled, clearly unwilling to continue.

"Were others injured?"

"Hundreds, your Highness. And many died."

"And the royal family? Are they well?"

"You have not heard?" Tozar was genuinely surprised.

She waited.

"King Merek was killed."

This was excellent news. "I see. How difficult for his wife and daughter." She hoped he would say more.

"Yes, your Highness. Difficult for all of us." He bowed. "Now, if you will excuse me."

She nodded and he spun on his heel and left without a look back.

So, the princess still lived! Her eyes narrowed. How is it she had escaped her father's attacks time after time? What forces protected her? Hundreds had died, but not her. Well, at least the girl's simpering father was dead. What a weak-minded King he'd been, so kind, so vulnerable; even allowing her to visit with his wife all those years ago. The fool. The princess must be ruling at the castle. Security would be high. Marinna would bide her time and wait for Draegin to recover. Then, they would attack together. Surely, one girl was no match for both of them.

The Queen stood and stretched, carrying a strand of pearls. They were perfect for what she had in mind. Though the beads were strung with the veins of her own eldrow captives, she didn't care. What clever ancient knowledge! There were plenty of eldrows to breed with ogres. More than enough to keep her army of inozak warriors well supplied with troops, even with Tozar's sizeable slice of her soldiers as part of the trade agreement. She pulled on the strand, again, twisting hard. Eldrow veins were stronger and more flexible than any fiber she'd ever handled. Once the long strings of pearls were braided, tripling their strength, and custom fit for her Pegasus, her harness and saddle gear would withstand the force of any battle. And it would be exquisitely beautiful! Tozar was handling all the arrangements, buying the bodies of the decapitated eldrows who would not breed, keeping their blood off her hands. How he did his gruesome work was his own business, and she really could care less. Several more crates of pearls were on their way to Orizin from Syrea; Tozar had promised to deliver them before the next full moon, and he knew better than to renege on their agreement. His price was high: two hundred Inozak to protect Orizin from attack, but it was worth it.

A Pegasus! She was thrilled with him! Though Draegin had promised her one when she was a child, she'd dismissed it over the years as nothing more than a wish. But her father had connections, wild and wondrous. It had been part of his plan for her world domination, the deal for the creature had been made more than a decade ago. But the magical flying steeds were so rare and matured so slowly that it had arrived untamed only months ago, not long after Draegin had stumbled in from the King's ball nearly dead.

Few dared face the fearsome Thaumaturge; how was it possible he'd been injured so severely? Would he live to tell her? She oversaw his care day and night, and the realization that he might not recover was terrifying. He lapsed in and out of consciousness and when he was lucid, she kept their conversations light, fearing the effect bad news might have. She wondered if she'd ever know what had happened. How could she take his place as ruler? She desperately needed his guidance, his strength, his magic, his wisdom.

She'd been shocked when she'd heard of the stallion's arrival, awed with its magnificence, and frightened by its fury. This steed is a killer, she'd realized; exactly what she'd need for war. Yet, she knew it could kill her as well. With the help of two Inozak, she'd managed to transport her father from his bed to the arena and show him the stallion. He'd raised his face to the ceiling, and laughed loud and long, celebrating the mighty beast as it snorted and tore at the ground, glaring across the arena at them.

"Now you will fly like me!" her father had rasped in his weakened state, "It's the only way to traverse these mountains, soaring and diving through their narrow passes, gliding to the flatter lands, seeing all who live below run from your shadow." The gleam in his eyes divulged his delight. He mustered his strength and continued, touching her hand in a rare display of affection. "Marinna, my dearest daughter, you were born for this. Train hard. Fly well. Fight to the end and win. Then you will reign as Queen forever and all the world shall bow to you and none other. As it is prophesied, so it shall be." His hand slid off hers as he gasped for breath, those few words having taken him to the end of his strength. They'd spoken little since then, as he had lapsed in and out of consciousness since that day. It was up to her. The great Thaumaturge might well die, and she was determined to rise to his challenge.

Wild and reckless, the Pegasus had already killed three trainers who had tried to break him with force, cunning, and trickery. Marinna refused to hire any others. In a rare spell of her father's consciousness, she'd confided this to him, but she'd regretted it. He had been outraged at the trainers' failures, and inconsolable that she, herself, was going to try to break the steed. But he could do nothing; just breathing took every bit of his strength. "I cannot lose you," he'd gasped. "You are my only hope; the hope of victory."

"I'm sure I can do it," she'd assured him. "And I promise I'll be careful," she'd murmured, calming him before he slipped back into darkness. She knew how to break the horse; her certainty was sure. Gentle, gentle. Woo him. Charm him. She would take her time and she would succeed.

The training arena was in a massive cave. Grasses, flowers, oats, even tennifel grew inside the cave by some enchantment from her father's hand. But the Pegasus ate little, and as the weeks had stretched into months and the training failed, so did the stallion's strength. He kept to the edges of the cave, snorting and huffing, nervously dancing, fluttering his wings. He'd taken flight only once in a panic, and barely gotten airborne before he'd run out of room, twisting and crashing into the opposite wall. Tall and muscular, and black as night, he tore at the dirt, often dashing in circles, frustrated at his captivity. Then he'd stand, sides heaving, glaring at the gate, daring any man or beast to walk through and face him.

Marinna did not try to enter the arena. She stood at the entrance, the gate's top half open, and leaned on the bottom half. For a week they watched each other. Then, Marinna tried tennifel, holding out a handful to the horse, tempting him with its bright blossoms. Another week and the steed move close enough to sniff it, then a few more days and he touched his nose to Marinna's palm. Marinna held her breath lest she spook him with even the slightest movement. She noticed his ribs protruding from his emaciated body. He must eat, or he would die.

That night as she'd fingered the pearls, a long-forgotten memory tried to surface. It had happened when the ghillies had been there. She replayed the scene in her mind; it was something they'd said. What was it? She concentrated, trying to recollect the conversation that day. The girl—that cursed princess who'd somehow survived all their attacks—yes, it had to do with her, in the very beginning when they'd first realized she was somehow still alive. Bile rose in her throat as her rage grew. Focus, she scolded herself. *We will yet win; it is prophesied. It would be my distinct pleasure to kill her myself. Woman to woman.* A smile grew on her face as she imagined flying over the princess, swooping low, and dealing her the fatal blow from the steed's saddle.

Enough daydreaming! The Pegasus must first survive. She pulled herself back to the memory. A farm, that was it, they'd sent the wolves to a farm by the banks of the Dryad River where an ancient apple tree grew. Apples! She'd heard rumors about those apples growing on that tree by the enchanted water. Irresistible fruit, flavor beyond description, bountiful in every season, and perhaps full of healing virtue. *Yes,* she thought, *those apples might be the perfect food for the steed.*

Two days later, a bushel of the fruit sat outside the entrance to the arena. Marinna picked one up, large, bright, and juicy and leaned casually on the bottom half of the gate, cooing to the horse. She held out the apple. He ignored her. She took a bite and at the sound of the crunch, the stallion's ears flicked. She took a second bite and the horse snorted, raising his nose at the tangy fragrance. Marinna placed the rest of the apple on her palm and held it out. "Come on, my winged conqueror. Come. Eat. You will find strength with each bite." She held the horse's gaze as it turned toward her. Slowly, he moved to her, hesitating, stopping to paw and shake his mane. Furious that he was being asked to eat from a human hand, yet desiring that fruit, he stepped closer. Finally, as Marinna purred encouragement, the steed reached out with wet, quivering nostrils to smell the fruit. Then, he wrapped his lips around the apple and lifted it from her palm, chewing it and never taking his eyes off Marinna. The Queen did not reach out, did not move. Just smiled and spoke softly, then quietly walked away.

They repeated this scene for the next two days, and by the third morning, the stallion was waiting near the door when Marinna opened the top half. Without hesitation, he lipped an apple from her hand, then another. They spent the day together, talking and touching and by the evening, Marinna could hold the steed's head in her hands and rub each side of his face. A week more and she dared to climb inside the arena. Two weeks and she stood on the bottom half of the gate running her hands over the horse's broad back, stroking his glorious wings, leaning over to put some weight on him. Soon she was sitting on his back, and he did not try to throw her off. That day, she named him Conquest. To mark her victory over him and to predict their victory over the world.

A couple of days later, Marinna slipped a bridle over Conquest's head. He snorted and bucked, thrashing his head. His eyes narrowed and bulged, and he turned to face her, betrayal written on his face. But after a couple of hours, he calmed.

"You just needed some time, didn't you? See, I told you it wouldn't hurt you." She reached up and stroked the side of his face and he did not blanch. They picked up where they'd left off, with Marinna sitting on Conquest's back. Of his own accord, he began walking, then with some gentle encouragement, trotting. Soon a cantor. After another week of riding in the arena, she knew they were ready to fly!

Marinna's heart pounded as the guards waited for her signal to pull the arena gates open. What if Conquest flew away with her and wouldn't bring her back? She might never see her father, again. She hadn't told him; it wasn't a topic to debate. She'd already made up her mind. Better, she reasoned, to tell him all about it when she returned. If she returned. If not, well, she wouldn't think of what that could mean to their kingdom, her disappearing and Draegin dying. It's worth the risk, she'd decided and there was no looking back.

She sat straight on the steed's back, gripping the rein, her red nails digging into her palms. Conquest sensed her excitement and tensed, flicking his tail. She nodded to the guards and they raised the gates. The stallion's nostrils flared at the scent of fresh air and he pawed the ground. He raised his head and shrieked at the sight of the sky and the snow-capped mountains. Before the gates were fully up, before it seemed there was room to fit under them, Conquest broke into a gallop and charged for the opening. Marinna screamed and pressed her head to his neck, burying her face in his thick mane. Her billowing cape brushed the gate as they swept through, and her heart nearly stopped when his feet left the earth and they careened into the air. This was madness. She was going to die. Her stomach lurched as the horse spread his wings, gracefully stopped their descent, and climbed above the trees, soon cresting the mountain tops. In among the clouds they flew, weaving, swirling, dancing as Conquest celebrated his freedom. Marinna hung on with all of her strength, surprised by the steed's grace and agility; his power surpassed her wildest imagination.

She dared lift her head for a glance. The mountain peaks looked like the bones of a giant's spine from up there. Her long black hair flew behind her, swooping with her cape in the wind. She sat up and shouted, loud and long. What a thrill! What ecstasy! The world was small below her. A thing to be conquered. And from this height, she could see it would be easy. Victory would be hers.

Far off in the distance, Marinna saw the edge of land and a thread of blue against the horizon! She caught her breath. The sea! The place her mother had called home! She yearned to have a closer look and leaned in that direction. Conquest understood her desire, turning toward the water and beginning a slow descent. Marinna gaped as they drew closer to its surface, marveling at its vastness, so big it disappeared into the horizon.

Conquest did not descend low until they were far from land, where it could not be seen on either horizon. Then, he swooped over the water, so close she could smell the sea and feel the salt on her face. Her heart surged! *Mother! You lived here! You swam in these waters with your people. My people! I never knew what you gave up for father; it's so beautiful! And you died so far from your home in the dark stone mountains. But, I'm here now mother. Home! I'm home!* She was captivated, struck with the wonder of the water! She'd not anticipated this; how could she have known? She knew her mother had been a siren and had left the watery depths to marry her magical lover. That made her half siren! Why had she not ever thought much about that? It explained why she felt so trapped in the mountains, a prisoner of sorts, always longing for something she could not describe. She belonged to the water!

Marinna threw her arms back and shouted to the sea, "I'm back! Your daughter has come home!" When she reigned, she would establish her throne at the edge of the sea! She threw her head back and laughed loud and long. Yes, that was it! She would rule both land and the sea and breathe salt air for the rest of her days!

She looked down and jolted in surprise, nearly slipping from Conquest's back. Just below the water's surface were mermaids and mermen watching her, reaching out with their arms, their great powerful tails keeping pace with the winged steed, above. They smiled at her, welcoming her, beckoning her to their underwater world. She laughed and waved but she knew she could not join them for it would mean death. Though her mother must have had gills, she did not, and she would surely drown in the sea. Yet, her heart was pulled to them, their silent siren song drawing her close, nearly irresistible. If Conquest had not shrieked at that moment and climbed toward the clouds, Marinna might have forgotten who she was and slipped from his back into the arms of the beguiling depths.

They flew high for a long time, but Marinna didn't notice; her mind was captured by the sea, and when she jolted back to the present, the horizon was edged with pink. The Pegasus started his descent. Nothing looked familiar to her; they were nowhere near home. Conquest swooped past the snow and descended into a narrow valley. The ground loomed quickly, and Marinna squeezed her thighs against the horse, burying her head in his neck, trying to find a balance between moving with him and not falling off. He pivoted his wings to slow himself just above the ground, folding them as his feet touched, then galloped a short distance before slowing to a stop. Flying was incredible! Thrilling. Spectacular. Terrifying. Exhilarating. Wondrous. They'd been one, gliding through the air, joyous together.

Conquest sauntered to a tree with low hanging branches, whinnied and shook his head, hinting for Marinna to drop the reins so he could graze. She leaned over and rubbed his neck. Then she reached for a branch and in one last burst of strength, swung herself off his back and dropped to the ground. She wrapped herself in her cape, leaned against a tree trunk, and closed her eyes.

Chapter 4: Runes

“This is without a doubt the most freaky, bizarre story I've ever heard.” Rosie frowned, her reaction vacillating between doubt and awe.

Rory, exhausted, just wanted her best friend to believe her. She'd only been back from Gamloden a few days and in Rosie's timeframe, they'd seen each other just a couple of weeks ago. Rosie couldn't put it together, how Rory could have been away for many months in the bizarre world she'd described. But she could tell something was different for sure. Something about your eyes, Rory, she'd said. You seem older. But then later, when she was tired, she'd lapsed into doubt. C'mon, Rory, quit the games, she'd accused.

Rosie had studied the photos of Finn, Jakin, Zad, and Floxx. Rory had actually forgotten about them till she found her phone in the bottom of her pack and charged it. She hadn't even shown them to Dad and Gram yet. Of course, they hadn't been as skeptical as Rosie; with them she hadn't needed proof of her story. After all, Rory had been left on their porch as a baby by the great bird. And it helped that she'd brought those things from Gamloden. She had wanted to bring them to show Rosie, too, but Gram and Dad had begged her not to. Treasures, they'd said. You have your necklace and your stories, Rory; Rosie will believe you, they were sure of it. But, nope, her best friend thought she was crazy. So much for telling all. Holding no secrets. Ever trusting.

It was way late; she'd guess three or four in the morning and they'd been talking since she'd landed in her village the afternoon before. Keep the visit short, Rory, Dad had said. A day or two, no more. When winter fully sets in, there's no telling when it will release its grip, and you don't want to be stuck there. She had to leave tomorrow; temperatures were dropping, and she could smell snow in the moistening air.

"Tell me about the bracelet, again," Rosie insisted. Apparently, that was her favorite part of the story. So, Rory did, but it broke her heart because it led to the blood bath and her father's death. She gave Rosie all the gory details this time, holding nothing back, and she was sobbing when Rosie's mother called them for breakfast.

"Okay," Rosie said, hugging her before they left her bedroom. "I believe you. I believe all of it. That was way too crazy to make up and besides, I can feel your grief. It's real." She'd held Rory at arm's length. "You can't go home yet; I wish you could stay for a month! There's so much more I want to know!"

By 10 o'clock, the winter sun cast a weak morning light making long shadows on the snow. It wasn't too cold, maybe 25 degrees and the wind had calmed to a breeze. With still a couple of hours before Rory had to leave, they put on snowshoes and headed for the woods, breaking trail till they got to the river. Once they were on its frozen surface, they slid on the ice, staying near the shore. Blue sky peeked between graying clouds in smaller and smaller patches, an ever-present reminder of the imminent weather change.

They'd been gliding along in silence listening to the rhythmic shushing of their snowshoes. Rory missed Cue, remembering the big dog had been with them the last time they'd been here. Suddenly she remembered something!

"Rosie!" Rory shouted so loud Rosie stumbled.

"Aw, c'mon, Rory, don't scare me like that!"

Rory cracked a smile. "Still scared of little people?" she teased.

"Not funny, my friend."

They picked up the shushing, again.

"That's what I wanted to tell you," Rory said. "I met some. In Gamloden."

Rosie looked at her, suspicious. "Sure, you did."

"I'm not making this up! I met a ghillie. I even know his name: Dew."

"So, why didn't you tell me about this before now? We just spent all night talking."

Why hadn't she? There was just so much to tell, and it was mostly about Finn and Jakin and the dragon and the King and Queen. "I don't know. It didn't seem all that important compared with the other stuff." It was hard talking and sliding over the ice, and they were getting breathless, so they stopped and sat on a frozen stump jutting out of the snow at the water's edge.

Rosie glanced at Rory, trying to hide a smile. "Dew. Okay, let's have it."

It didn't take Rory long to share what she remembered, and she fumed, again, that the tiny ghillie had climbed into her pocket and run off with her treasured feather. Especially now that she realized it had power to transport her between the two worlds.

Rosie hadn't said a word. She stared at Rory until she finished talking, then burst into hysterics. She laughed so hard, she fell off the stump and threw snow in her friend's face.

Rory jumped up and shushed away, annoyed, wondering what Rosie's problem was. She didn't have to be so mean.

"Fine. Don't believe me," she yelled over her shoulder and headed back to the village.

"Wait, Rory!" Rosie yelled and scrambled to catch up with her. "It's not that I don't believe you! I do. Well, sort of, anyway."

Rory glared at her.

"It's just your Dew is so tiny! Seven or eight inches! He doesn't sound scary at all; he sounds cute!"

"Not cute. Nope." Rory scowled. "Ugly. And meaner than a wolverine. And a thief besides. I hate him for taking my feather. The one Mom gave me, the one she caught from the Firebird on the night I was brought here. It's mine, Rosie. Maybe the most precious gift I've ever had." She swallowed hard.

Rosie reached over and grabbed Rory's jacket, pulling her to a stop. "I'm so sorry I laughed. Of course, you're upset. I'd be mad, too, if I'd lost something so precious. I wasn't really laughing at you. But all my life I've been terrified of the little people. It just hit me how ridiculous my fears have been if they are only seven inches tall." She stifled another laugh.

Rory saw she meant it. "Okay," she said beginning to feel embarrassed for being so emotional. She was suddenly drained. "Do you think I could catch a nap when we get back to the house?"

Rory was packing her stuff a couple hours later in the kitchen, talking with Rosie's mother, pumping her for details about the little people in the folk tales. She was not a big talker, at least not to her, and Rory had to work to pull anything from her.

"They are small," she said, "some say the size of a two-year-old; others put them more the size of an eight-year-old. Cunning. Magical. And vicious. The stories connect them with the disappearance of many children."

"So, they kidnap children?"

She nodded.

"And do the stories say what they do with the children?"

"Course they do. Grim. Very grim. They kill them and eat them."

"That is awful for sure." Rory let a few moments pass before she asked the question she was sure would end the discussion. "So, has there ever been proof, anything at all, of their existence? Anything found that could only belong to them?"

Rosie's mother was silent for a full thirty seconds, her lips pressed into a tight line. Finally, she nodded, turned and rummaged through a drawer, retrieved a small wooden box, and motioned for Rory to have a look. The box was beautiful though common, the scrimshaw artwork on its top carved by a local craftsman. They walked to the window where the light was best and opened it. Inside were three arrowheads, a small magnifying glass, and the broken quill of a feather. Rory vaguely remembered seeing similar arrowheads. She glanced at Rosie's mom and saw terror in her eyes.

"What?" she asked. "What is so frightening about these arrowheads?"

Rosie's mom reached into the box and handed her the magnifying glass and one of the arrowheads.

"Look," she said simply.

Rory studied it, turning it this way and that until the light caught something. It was engraved! She studied the tiny runes, and her blood went cold. She'd seen these symbols before. But not in this world. She remembered the day so clearly. A few days after Zad's funeral, they'd gone to stay with Tozar and Zirena. She recalled Floxx running her fingers tenderly over the markings on their ancient door, as if it were a thing of much worth to her. The markings were identical. The question was, how had they gotten to Alaska?

Chapter 5: Nizat

Finn stared at Jakin's coach as it disappeared into the distance. "Come on!" He swung Aric onto his shoulders. "Let's follow him."

Kalvara began to protest but drew a couple of glances from the tall ones, so she followed Finn, anger etched on her face. "Why are you putting us at risk for that worthless man?"

"Because I don't trust him. Because he's up to something, probably not good, and I want to know what it is."

"Why? You think it involves Rory?"

Finn looked chagrined, like a puppy caught with a shoe in its mouth. "Yes, Kalvara, it might. I worry about her at the castle. Floxx is there with her, of course, but I'm not—we're not—and Uriel is here with us." He glanced up at the blue circle of light. "She could so easily be the target of yet another attack. Please. I want to see what he's doing. Then we will continue on our way. We don't really know where we're going, anyway, but we know where we are, and I smell trouble."

Kalvara shook her head in disgust. "You still care for that girl even though you know you two can never amount to anything. You had to leave; she had to stay, remember?" She pierced him with the truth.

Finn slumped. "Of course, I remember. I've struggled with it since the day we left." He straightened. "But neither will I throw away our friendship or disregard her safety because of our different destinies." He stalked away, taking Aric with him.

"She's coming," Aric whispered from his shoulders.

He glanced back to see Kalvara begrudgingly follow some distance behind. He also caught one of the dwarves watching the scene intently.

Finn had little trouble keeping up with the carriage as more and more people crowded onto the road, impeding its progress. It veered sharply several times to avoid hitting a pedestrian. All the swerving and jostling loosened the crates from their ties, and they bumped around in the back of the carriage. In spite of the driver's efforts to avoid both people and ruts, one wheel struck a pothole and the coach careened sideways, nearly toppling. The driver managed to keep it right side up, but not before one of the crates bounced over the rim of the wagon bed and smashed open on the ground.

"Whoa, whoa!" The coach skidded to a stop. Jakin and the driver jumped off the front bench and hurried around to see the crate's contents strewn on the road. Thousands of pearls lay scattered in the dust, covering the ground like a summer hailstorm.

The two horsemen jumped off their steeds, trying to block people from grabbing handfuls of the gems, but many pearls were taken or trampled in the scuffle. Jakin yelled at the crowd to stay back as he and the driver hefted the broken crate back into the wagon. He stomped around to the front, daring anyone to get in his way, and caught sight of Aric sitting high on Finn's shoulders. He gawked for an instant, then turned to run. Kalvara snatched Aric as Finn hurled himself at Jakin just as he leapt on one of the horses. Catching him by the ankle, Finn yanked him to the ground; the startled horse rearing and nearly trampling them. Jakin punched Finn, sending him sprawling into the dirt and Finn fought back surrounded by a shocked crowd. Both of them were bloody before Jakin's men pulled them apart.

They glared at each other, panting. "You're up to no good, aren't you?" Finn accused.

"It's none o' your business, freak. I don't report to you." Jakin yanked free of the men who held him, turned and leapt on the horse. "Stay outta my life," he shouted as he galloped away.

Kalvara loosened her clutch on Aric to find a rag for Finn's bleeding face. The boy squirmed down to retrieve a few pearls nearly buried in the dirt by his feet. They were large, like Pelzar's marbles. He cleaned them off and dropped one in Kalvara's tunic, one in Finn's, and kept two for himself.

The three of them stepped off the road as the wagon moved on, to wait for the crowd to disperse. "We could follow it," Finn suggested, gingerly touching his cheek. "It's moving slow enough we could keep up and eventually Jakin will return for his goods."

"No, we don't want any more trouble. We should stay off the road and out of sight," Kalvara hissed. "There's no point in trying to track him. He could hide for days, and certainly will have his men watching our every move."

Finn scuffed his boot in the dirt. "He's got to be up to something. Why else would he run like that?"

"My guess is he's afraid you'd hunt him down to avenge both Rory and the King. And now his fears are confirmed."

"So, what's he doing here, then?"

"Running. Hiding. Trying to make a living. Looks to me like he's buying and selling pearls. As far as I know, that's not a crime."

"I wonder if he owns that ship – the one that delivered the crates."

"He is part owner," a rough voice answered, jarring the three of them.

They spun to see a dwarf standing behind them. "Ye don't recognize me?" He raised an eyebrow then broke into a gap-toothed smile. Neither Finn nor Kalvara had any idea who he was. But Aric did.

"You're Azatan's friend, aren't you?" the boy said shyly.

"Good for you!" the dwarf reached out and clapped Aric on the shoulder. "That I am! Azatan, Ezat, and me—we go back to childhood." He extended his hand to Finn. "Nizat's my name. Friend, not foe."

Finn shook his hand with a firm grip. "Nizat, a pleasure to meet you. How did you come to know the boy?"

"At Zad's funeral. He and young Pelzar spent much time together and I spoke with them on several occasions." He winked at Aric. "You using that slingshot he made you?"

"He is," Kalvara responded guardedly, putting her hand on the boy's head.

Nizat bowed to Kalvara. "I saw you, as well, in Orizin. A friend of Zad's is a friend o' mine." He looked at Finn. "May I ask what ye are doing in this part of the world?"

"I would ask the same of you," Finn stated.

"I work for Prince Tozar, me and the other dwarves on the ship. Any truth to the rumor the prince is Jakin's brother-in-law."

Finn side-stepped the question. "I had no idea Prince Tozar had dealings on the sea."

Nizar nodded. "Been at it a while now. Pearls, shells, and fish. Lots o' fish."

"I see. And Jakin's involved?"

"Went in on the ship. Sails sometimes. Thinks he's a big boss. The little scag betrayed ye to the dragon himself, didn't he?"

Finn did not respond.

"It's known all over these parts, it is. Word travels fast, especially when it's as tragic as 'at."

Finn nodded.

"Jakin works for Tozar, just like us, though he flaunts his relation to 'im. He makes the orders and delivers 'em to the prince. Sometimes he sails with us, more now 'n he used to. We try t'stay outa his way, nasty as his temper is."

An uncomfortable silence fell between them.

"Look, I, ah, thought ye might need some help. Mebbe as simple as some dinner, or a quiet place to bed down for the night. But I understand if ye have t'be on your way." Nizat hesitated, waiting for an answer and when none came, he turned to leave. He'd gotten some distance away when Finn caught up to him.

"Nizat, wait!" He stopped. "That's a kind offer you made and yes, we could use a good meal and a place to sleep."

Nizat grinned and waited for Kalvara and Aric. "C'mon then," he said, whistling and leading the way.

Finn woke with a terrible headache. He opened his eyes and couldn't see a thing; everything was black. He felt his face to see if he was blindfolded and flinched, remembering the fight he'd had with Jakin. He reached into the space around him and, satisfied he wouldn't smack into anything, sat up. That was a mistake. His stomach lurched, and dinner rose to the back of his throat. Dinner! Nizat had invited them to share roasted fish and potatoes his crew had cooked over an open fire near the dock. So, they'd eaten with the other sailors and the food had been delicious. But he didn't remember anything after dinner.

What had they done to them? Why couldn't he remember? Panicked, he called out for Kalvara and Aric. No one answered. He listened, concentrating on every sound. He heard no voices, just a soft, shooshing noise. He realized he was moving; not himself exactly, but the ground was moving. Was he in a wagon? No, it wasn't bumpy like a road and the sound wasn't right. Then he remembered the ship.

He was on the ship! The Syrean Sea was rocking beneath him.

He pushed himself slowly to his feet, feeling above his head until he touched rough beams. Why was it so dark? He must be in the center of the ship, thrown in some hold like a sack of rubbish. He found the door. Metal. He shook it, feeling for any weakness. He had to find a way out! He pulled and pushed until his hands were raw, but he couldn't budge it. He yelled for Kalvara and Aric. No answer. Had something terrible happened to them? Were they even alive? He yelled and banged and pounded until he collapsed, exhausted. Would he rot with the fish in the bowels of this filthy ship?

He fought panic with reason. If he was alive, then his friends likely were, too. He would not give up. And he knew they wouldn't either; they'd all escape somehow. Kalvara had escaped from Droome, surely, she would figure out a plan. He reached out for Eldurrin. *Help us! We need you now.* He focused on his calling. He needed to find the lost gems and recreate the Eldur Crown. How had he gotten so far off track? *Eldurrin, I'm so sorry. Please help us get back to our search. I had no idea we'd be captives on a ship. Please get us out of here. Put us on the path you want us on. Let me do the work you've called me to do. You promised to direct us. Show me the way.*

As his breathing calmed and his peace grew, he became aware of a faint sound, a tapping. He listened, holding his breath, counting the taps. And after a few times, he identified a pattern. Tap tap tap. Stop. Tap tap. Stop. Tap. Stop. Then it would begin over. It had to be his friends! Kalvara would think of this, making slight sounds heard only by elf ears.

He needed something to tap with. He groped around the slimy deck for his pack, for his bow and quiver, but couldn't find them. Patting his pockets for a miracle, he felt something round and reached in to find the pearl Aric had dropped there. *Thank you, Eldurrin! You will get us out; you will help us!* He wondered where Uriel was. Had he stayed with Kalvara? Was Aric with her, too? He tried the pearl on the door. Tap tap. It worked! He tapped out the pattern, twice, and waited. After a minute, he heard the answer. They were alive! They were probably locked in a cell not too far away. His hope rocketed. *Eldurrin, show us the way out!*

Every now and then, they would signal and encourage each other. In between tapping, Finn explored. His bow and quiver were in a corner, miraculously unbroken. His pack lay wet and crumpled nearby. He made an escape plan. He'd fight whoever came for him and lock him inside the hold. Then he'd find Kalvara. He thought through the possible scenarios, deciding on the best way to jump his captor. He would only have a split second. His concentration was broken by insistent tapping. It was different, harder, faster. A warning! He heard screaming and fighting, then the clanging of a metal door. He threw his pack and bow over his shoulder and crouched, tense, ready to pounce. His door flew open and he tackled his captor, rolling into the passageway.

"What are you doing?" Kalvara hissed. "It's me. Us. Let me go."

"Oh. Sorry," Finn said, squinting as his eyes adjusted to the dim light. He helped her up. "I thought the dwarf felt awfully skinny."

She punched him in the arm, muttering, "Some elf."

Aric locked the door and pocketed the key. Finn followed them through the dank passageway to the ladders connecting the floors. To Finn's surprise, Kalvara climbed down, not up.

"They'll miss the sailor and be chasing us," she whispered. "Expecting us to climb up." They sprinted toward a rusty door; its hinges so corroded it barely moved. Heaving it open, they crowded in behind the buckets and mops, breathless, listening. Footsteps echoed above them; dwarves shouted. As Kalvara had predicted, the crew climbed up until they couldn't hear them.

"Here, Finn, I saved this for you." Aric pushed a half-eaten apple into Finn's hand.

"Thank you, my young friend," Finn whispered, devouring it in three bites, core and all. "You two have saved my life."

"Well, now I've evened up," Kalvara said, nudging him with her elbow.

Finn nudged back, remembering how she'd nearly killed him when they'd first met.

"How did you get out?" Finn asked.

"I waited till a dwarf came to get us, then the two of us jumped him. Aric got the key and we locked him in."

"My plan as well," Finn said.

Kalvara glared at him. "So I found out!"

"Right." Finn chuckled. "Now what?"

"We wait till they've scoured the upper decks and when they head down, we head up."

"And when we meet them in the middle?"

"We trust Eldurrin."

Finn looked at her in amazement. Eldurrin! She trusted him, too! He leaned against a broken mop, crossed his arms over his chest, and waited. But, no one came down. Instead, the ship's motion slowed, and the rocking lessened to a gentle, nearly indecipherable movement.

Aric nudged Finn. "We've stopped."

Chapter 6: Rory's Return

Rory barely remembered flying back home. All she could think about were the runes on the arrowheads. How did they get here? What did they mean? How could the same ancient language be both in Orizin and in Alaska, two different worlds, with a barrier between them no one could cross except Floxx and her. Floxx had said the door to Tozar and Zirena's house was ancient. How ancient? She needed to talk to her.

Though she really wanted to go straight to her room and sleep, Gram had another big dinner waiting. She loved her grandmother's cooking; she'd yearned for it in Gamloden, but she just didn't have much of an appetite. She ate though, to make them happy, all the way to the apple pie. Dad was leaving next week. The airlines had him scheduled to fly another set of trips to Rio; he'd be gone two weeks, then he'd be home a week before the cycle began, again.

So, they talked, knowing their time was limited. They were drilling down for the details of what she'd already told them, filling in the gaps. Dad wanted to know all about the wolves. He couldn't believe their size! Even in Alaska, home of huge animals, wolves were way smaller. So, she dredged through the stories of the wolf attacks. They sat silent, shocked really, when they realized how the tables were turned; in Alaska, people hunted wolves, but these wolves were intelligent and had been hunting her. They wept with her when she told of Cue's death; they'd loved the gentle giant of a dog just as she had. He'd saved her life, but it had cost him everything. She also told them about the trows, whose caves were not far from where Cue had died, and how they'd probably given her the scars that raked the side of her face and neck. She recounted Zad's story about the huge dog he'd seen carrying a bloody baby and how they'd vanished with Floxx.

"Well that explains a lot, doesn't it." Dad's eyes were moist. They sat in silence for a while, imagining the whole horrible scene that had transpired just before Rory had appeared on their porch.

Gram was curious about the food and it was a relief to move off the terrible topics. Goodies like tenninberry jam delighted her, and she was amazed to hear about swiltingen, the huge, winged animal caught and roasted for Zad's funeral. "Kind of like a flying dinosaur," she suggested, pumping for all the details about how it was cooked and served. Rory described it right down to its dull brown eyes and gaping jaw on the platter, stuffed with small birds, apples, and flowers. Tastes a lot like moose, Rory recalled. Gram was thrilled by the mundane, as well, astounded they grew carrots, potatoes, and turnips in this other world, just like she did.

She and Dad laughed over the tomtee's tails and loved Ardith's reaction to blue jeans. "So practical." Rory laughed. "But she thought it was totally weird that a girl wore them. And the zipper! She ran it up and down a dozen times studying it as I changed into some of her clothes."

They studied the photos, expanding the ones of Finn to see the pointed tips of his ears. Dad was thoughtful as Rory described him, the way he spoke, his courtly manners, how he led the group and fought for her. Though Dad didn't say anything, she knew he noticed both the tenderness in her voice, and her flushed cheeks.

Unlike Rosie, both Gram and Dad accepted all she said as truth. Rory figured it was because her arrival as a baby had been so bizarre to begin with and the back story made so much sense. Dad couldn't get over the photo of Zad standing by his airplane and she shared that the dwarf had been so enthralled with it, she'd given him the airplane operating handbook to study. Since they had the airplane here now, was it still in Gamloden? Were Werner and Ezat and Azatan at the farm working on it? She doubted it could be in two places at once, but really didn't understand how time and circumstance worked between the two worlds.

Later that night, Rory lay on her side staring at the stars through the window, absently tapping the bellasol on and off, its wondrous light a comforting connection with the other world. What was mother doing? Was she having big problems ruling the kingdom without her? And Floxx, was she staying close to mother, helping her with the daunting challenge of leading the kingdom? And Finn? Her heart ached at the thought of him and Kalvara traveling together. Sure, Aric was there, but what kind of a chaperone was a child? In spite of their initial animosity, she could see they were suited for each other, both of them elves, even if they were from lineages who held ancient hostilities. They'd soon grow close. She sighed. She'd lost him forever; she was sure of it.

She was on the edge of sleep when she heard singing, faint at first then growing louder. It was so beautiful, stirring up sweet memories and a familiar yearning that she'd never quite understood. She didn't wake up fully, at least not as she later recalled, but was alert in a very real sense. Was it a vision? A trance? She really didn't know. But Floxx was there, singing in the night, hovering outside the window, shimmering in her lovely way with the stars at her back.

"Rory," she said. "I'm with you. I see you every second, even though you are unaware of me. Don't forget me, dear. I love you." And she was gone.

Then Rory jerked fully awake and rushed to the window. "Floxx!" she shouted. "Floxx, come back. I need you. I have some questions." But there was no answer.

The day after Dad left for work, a big snowstorm set in. Gram set to baking and cooking one thing after another, filling the cold room shelves with bread and muffins and pies. Moose stew simmered on one burner and spaghetti sauce on another. Never know when we might lose power, she said, and glanced out the window with a frown every time the wind howled.

Rory shoveled three times, keeping the snow machines swept off and the path to them open. They were her ride to the big woodpile to replenish the logs stacked near the house, as well as the way to the distant sheds and the airstrip. Once the snow stopped, she'd pack the runway as best she could with the bigger snow machine, so Dad could land. It was while she was shoveling the third time, her fingers frozen and arms weary, that she heard Floxx, again.

"Rory."

She stopped and strained to see into the darkness, sensing her near but seeing no shimmer, no colors. She heard nothing except the tiny noise snowflakes make when they touch down.

"Floxx?" she said in her heart to the silence. "I know you are here."

"Yes." Floxx's whisper came from inside Rory, like it had in Gamloden.

"I heard you the other night, singing," Rory said to the voice inside.

39

"I wanted you to know I was near," the voice answered with a smile that Rory sensed as clearly as if she could see it.

"How is mother? Is she getting along all right?"

"Yes, she's well, Rory. Strong in body and mind. Ruling with courage and wisdom. Grieving still. Missing your father." She paused. "And you."

"I miss her, too. I really do. And I miss you, too, of course." She was sure Floxx laughed.

"What?"

"You needn't miss me, Rory. I'm with you, even here. You just can't see me. You should reach out to me often, like this, or maybe it's reaching in. Talk to me. I will hear you."

"Okay. Yes. I will do that more often." She knew it was true. Floxx had told her so before she'd left Gamloden, but since she'd been back, she'd been so caught up with Dad and Gram and winter and Rosie, she'd forgotten. Oh, that's right—Rosie!

"Floxx! I saw something at Rosie's house. Arrowheads with runes on then. Runes like the ones on Zirena's door in Orizin."

Silence.

"Floxx?"

"I'm here." A long pause. "You have a good memory."

"What does it mean, Floxx?"

A sigh. "Eldurrin will reveal that when he's ready."

"But we're connected somehow? Our worlds?"

She laughed. "Of course, we're connected. I'm in both. You're in both."

"Yes, but there's more than that, isn't there?"

Floxx began humming and would say no more. The snowfall suddenly shimmered a bit like fairy dust in a Cinderella story, and Floxx was gone. How could she seem to leave and yet be inside her all the time? Rory didn't understand.

She had a dream that night. The elves had caught her and tied her up and no matter how she fought or twisted against them, she couldn't get free. They dragged her into the woods and the terror of her Inozak kidnapping gripped her again. She screamed and woke to Gram shaking her.

"Rory, it's okay, just a dream. You're all right." She held her granddaughter, rocking back and forth until she stopped shaking, just like her Alaskan mom had done when she was little. Finally, Rory calmed down, but she lay awake all night, unwilling to reenter that nightmare.

She refused to think about the dream, about the kidnapping. She had buried that terror deep and wanted to keep it down. She'd glossed over it in the stories she'd told. It was Gram who helped her face it the next day, sitting by the wood stove. Rory talked reluctantly at first, but as Gram listened with compassion, all the details spilled out, from the inozak's disgusting finger running down her body to the nauseating smell of Zad's burnt flesh. She relived all the horrors of that nightmarish time, how the dragon had stalked her until he'd found her and how, if not for Floxx and the tennins, and Finn and her friends, she would have certainly been killed that night. Gram frowned and nodded, asked a few questions and made no judgments.

When Rory finished, silence hung between them. Gram sighed and reached for the infant gown, spreading it on her lap, methodically smoothing out the wrinkles with her knobby old fingers. Rory waited for the consolation, for Gram to say it was okay, she was home now, God had spared her and kept her safe.

But Gram didn't dish out sentimentalities. "Some of us are meant for greatness, Rory. It takes faith to believe you were made to do something really special; courage to accept the challenge, and grit to talk down the fear that insists you are foolish."

Rory couldn't believe it. After that horror story Gram was saying she was meant for this?

"None of us chooses our calling. We don't think up our own gifts or the dreams that beckon us. Like the color of our eyes, we are born with them. What we do choose is our way, whether to say yes or no. For some of us, saying yes will cost us everything." Gram reached for Rory's hand, then continued. "You faced grave danger many times over. Yet your friends believed in you enough to put their lives on the line for you. Floxx encouraged you. They all fought to protect you. It seems to me you are somehow key to overcoming something very terrible in their world. Even the tennins fight with you."

Gram stood and disappeared into her room and came out holding her feather. She handed it to her granddaughter with tears in her eyes. "So you can go back and still use the necklace to come home, again." They hugged and wept, and Rory struggled with whether or not Gram was right.

That night in bed, still upset, she thought about the dream and it hit her. Despite the trauma of being captured and the terror it triggered, it had actually been elves who'd caught her, not Inozak! Little people, like Rosie's mother had described. It had taken several of them to tie her up and drag her away. And in all the terror, she'd overlooked some details: the woods were Alaskan, full of black spruce, not a plush Gamloden forest. And perhaps most significant of all, they'd carried quivers of arrows on their backs. Maybe it was just a convoluted dream, fragments of her consciousness mixing Rosie's mother's arrowheads and the kidnapping together, but somehow, it felt more like an omen to her.

Dad was detained due to weather. His two-week stint stretched to three. Rory stewed about what she should do. Go or stay. If she left for Gamloden, would she live to make it back to Alaska, again? It sounded like mother was doing fine. Finn was gone. So why, exactly, did she feel compelled to return? Hadn't she done what she was meant to do: kick off the prophecy and set it in motion? Did she have a further part to play? Gram never brought it up, never pushed, but Rory knew she was thinking about it, too, wondering what she'd do. Finally, the weather cleared, and Dad roared over the house letting them know he was back.

Never one for small talk, Dad sensed the tension in the house and had barely hung up his jacket before he asked them about it. Rory gave him the summary story, figuring Gram could fill in the details later.

"And so," Rory said, her cracking voice betraying her struggle, "I'm wondering if I ought to go back."

"Rory, look at me."

She did.

"If there was no danger, what would you do?"

She answered immediately. "I would definitely go back, knowing I could eventually return home."

"So, your heart wants to return to Gamloden. Fear—and believe me, I don't take it lightly—is holding you back."

That was it. Fear. She burst into tears, the reason for her reluctance suddenly clear. "Yep. I'm scared, Dad. Maybe I am needed there, but I don't want to die there. I want to see you and Gram, again. I love you both so much."

They sat in silence gathering their thoughts.

Finally, Gram spoke. "Rory, have you asked Floxx?"

She was ashamed to realize she had not. Of course, that was the answer.

That night, Rory leaned on her windowsill. "Floxx," she whispered, staring into the night. The moon on the snow made it light enough to see the silhouettes of the trees. "I need you."

"I'm here, Rory." A soft voice came from deep within her.

"You know the decision I'm struggling with?"

"Of course."

"What should I do? Am I needed? Do you want me to go back?"

"Finn is in trouble, Rory."

That was all she needed to know. She put on a simple dress, her boots and her wool cape, and threw a few things in her backpack. Gram and Dad were still up, reading by the woodstove. She gave them a quick explanation, hugged them, and, feather in hand, concentrating on Finn, vanished.

Chapter 7: Pearl Isle

F inn, Kalvara, and Aric had crept as far up the ladders as they dared, listening every few moments, but hearing nothing unusual. As they neared the top deck, though, the clamor grew. Finn peeked over the edge of the floor. They'd stopped all right, but not back at Syrea. They actually were not docked at all; they were anchored a short distance offshore. He wondered if the ship was too big to maneuver in the shallowest water. A narrow beach stood between the sea and a thick forest of unusual blue-leafed trees. Dwarves were hoisting crates to the tall ones, who chattered as they heaved them to shore though Finn couldn't make out their words. But he could hear the dwarves and he recognized Nizat.

"What about the prisoners?" one of them was saying to him.

"We'll find 'em after the others 'ave gone," he replied. "They'll bring a lot 'o gold, they will. 'Specially the woman and the child. The Tall King will be amazed to see them. Too bad she was so ornery; I would'a liked to a played with 'er a bit."

Finn warned Kalvara with a stern look. Don't react. They waited until the last crate was overboard and most of the dwarves had left for wherever they went on this island. Nizat kept three mean-looking dwarves back and they pulled out a hidden cask of ale and sat drinking in the hot sun. That's right, drink, Finn thought. Drink a lot. The three didn't make a sound, biding their time. As the sun sank toward the western horizon, Nizat stood a little unsteadily. The others sniggered as he stumbled.

"I'm jest missing the sea under these sea legs," he roared. "Let's go find us some prisoners!" The three yelled, "Hear hear" and staggered to their feet. Before they could get very far, Finn and his friends charged, throwing the dwarves into chaos. The ale had rendered their reflexes slow and before they could react, Kalvara had sprinted over the ship's bow, splashed through the shallow water and onto the sand, Aric in her arms. Finn was not so lucky.

"Get him," Nizat yelled and Finn was tackled by two of the thugs. They were sober enough to tie him up in seconds.

"What do we do with 'im, boss? Throw 'im over the deep side?"

Out of the corner of his eye, Finn saw something he couldn't believe! Was he dreaming?

"Rory!" he yelled, and the two thugs turned to see her charging them. They threw up their thick arms in mock horror as she demanded they untie him.

"Bahahaha!" one of them roared. "Aren't you a fiery one!" And he grabbed her roughly.

"Wait!" Nizat commanded. He grabbed Rory's chin, roughly turning her face to see her scars. "Jest as I thought. If it ain't the princess, herself. Look boys. No one else could be this ugly." He leered at her and Rory kneed him in the groin. He doubled over in pain. "Tie 'er up, too," he gasped. "Jakin's hussy. The one 'e double-crossed." He straightened and sneered at her. "Come to get even, did ya? Well, Jakin ain't here. He's back in Syrea. But this is from him." And he slapped her, nearly knocking her from the other sailor's grasp.

"Leave her alone!" Finn raged, struggling to get free.

Nizat mocked him. "Save her, Finn! Come on, save her!" And he slapped her, again.

Just then, a blue light exploded on board and Uriel roared into sight, lunging for the dwarves. Within seconds, he'd thrown them far into the deep water, and they were flailing for the shore.

Uriel helped Rory up and she hugged him fiercely. "Saved my life, again!" She said rubbing her bruised cheek. "Thanks, my friend."

"Welcome back," he rumbled.

Finn whooped and yelled. "Well, untie me, so I can hug you, too!" She knelt above him and he melted. She'd come back. To him. How had she found him here? He wrapped her in a fierce embrace.

Kalvara hollered a warning from the rocky shore. "Are you coming or not? There's not much time." They scrambled for their things and splashed to the shore, dashing into the forest, Finn and Rory hand in hand and Uriel bobbing blue above them. They ran for a long time putting as much distance between them and the ship as they could. Finally, they slowed to catch their breath and had a chance to observe their surroundings. Finn turned a full circle, gaping. These were not birch trees or oaks; most of them had tall bare trunks topped with a canopy of broad blue leaves that swayed high above.

"I've never seen trees like these before!" He grinned and turned to tease Aric. "Do you think you could scale these smooth trunks?" In a blink Aric had thrown down his pack and was wrapped around the tree, shimmying up a few feet at a time.

Kalvara frowned at Finn and stalked by him to climb after the boy. "It's very high for a child, alone, don't you think?" But by the time they'd reached the top, Finn could hear them poking about through the leaves, laughing and having a lot of fun.

"Taste this," Aric said. "It's delicious!"

"Ohhhh!" Kalvara replied. "Yes!"

Seconds later, a huge leaf came floating down and Aric and Kalvara slid down after it.

"The berries! Taste them!" Aric reached for the leaf, which was nearly as big as he was and turned it over. Growing along the thick, center vein were clusters of large berries, the size of grapes, but turquoise like the sea they'd just crossed. He dug out a handful and offered them to Finn and Rory. Finn was dubious.

"Just eat them!" Kalvara scoffed. "They're not poison. We're not dead."

Finn glanced at Rory. "What do you think?"

She gestured at Aric. He was clearly not suffering any ill effects. "I think they're okay. And I'm starved." She and Finn took a few berries from Aric's hand.

"Wow, these are really good!" Rory grinned.

Aric reached for another handful and pulled his hand back as if he'd been stung. "Ow!"

He gripped his hurt fingers with his good hand.

"Let me see," Kalvara insisted, prying open his hands. "Oh, this finger is red on the tip."

"I can feel it thumping," Aric said in a higher voice than usual, trying not to cry.

"Let's see what it was that stung you." Finn squatted next to the leaf.

"It's not another wicked ghillie, is it?" Rory said, instinctively feeling her pocket for Gram's feather.

"No. Not a ghillie. Just a bramble. See there?" She knelt next to him and he pointed to a tangle of thorns stuck in among the berries.

Aric, sucking on his sore finger, leaned over to look. He picked up a stick and carefully dug the bramble out, holding it close to study.

"Those thorns are sharp." He frowned, set the bramble on the ground, and studied the rest of the fruit intently. "Look."

He pointed with the stick. "Brambles are buried between each cluster."

"We'll have to be more careful from now on. You sit down and let me take over." Kalvara squeezed his shoulder and he curled up against a tree, studying his finger. One leaf provided handfuls of berries, and she piled them in front of Aric. There was enough to share. Kalvara tossed the brambles on the ground, and Rory gingerly picked them up and threw them under some foliage. "Wouldn't want to step on these spikes," she said.

"Missed one, Rory," Aric pointed next to him. Sure enough, there was a bramble an inch from his pants.

"Ah, good eye, Aric," she said. "Oh, that would've hurt if you'd sat on it!" At the thought, Aric dissolved into laughter, grabbing his rear and yelling 'owww' so loud Kalvara shushed him with a grin. Rory tossed the brier aside with the others. "I think that's all of them," she said, studying the ground to be sure. Satisfied, she joined Finn and Kalvara and ate.

"Let's see your finger, Aric," Finn said.

The child held his hand out.

A small blister was forming where the thorn had punctured the skin.

"That looks sore." Finn frowned.

"It hurts," the boy said grimacing.

"I've been poked by many a thorn, but none ever left a blister." He looked at Kalvara. "Any idea why?"

She shook her head as she dug in her pack. "No. But Floxx gave me some tennifel oil." She pulled out the small vial and let a drop fall on Aric's finger. "I'll keep an eye on it."

"What did you two see from the treetop?" Finn asked, trying to take their mind off the injury.

"Trees in all directions!" Aric laughed. "And a lot of birds. We'll eat good here!"

Finn laughed and ruffled the boy's hair. "Did you see any villages?"

"No, just trees."

He glanced at Kalvara and she nodded in agreement.

"The tall ones on the ship. I thought I heard them say they were from this island."

"I thought so, too," she said thoughtfully. "And the dwarves. But we saw no sign of a village. Could be we just aren't close enough."

"Strange. When the crew disembarked, they'd surely have gone home."

Rory shrugged. "Could be we ran right by their homes and never noticed. I can't imagine they live very far from shore. I mean, they have to walk to work every day."

Finn nodded but felt certain he'd have noticed. "Well, I think we are out of danger here," he said. "Aric, is your finger well enough for some exploring?"

Aric jumped up with a whoop and checked his pocket for his slingshot.

"Do we bring our gear, or will we come back?" he wanted to know.

"We should bring everything," Kalvara cautioned. "We may not find our way back."

They gathered their things and as Aric stood, Finn noticed a bramble on the leg of boy's britches.

"Uh oh, another one!" Finn pointed, and Aric reached for it.

"Careful!" Rory cautioned. "I can't believe I didn't see that one."

Aric slowly pried the sharp-edged bramble from his pants and held it up to study, turning it this way and that.

"Bring it over here with the others."

As Aric started to move, the thorny ball uncoiled and stood upright.

"You are pinching me!" it said.

"Aaaah!" Aric hollered and threw it in the air.

"Did you hear that?" he yelled. "It talked!"

The others were by him in an instant, scouring the ground for the talking tangle but they couldn't find it.

"I'm right here!" a small voice called, seeming to come from Aric's foot. Sure enough, there was the bramble, caught in his sock.

The boy reached down to pick it up.

"Stop!" it called. "Just hold out your hand and I'll jump onto it."

Aric did just that and the four of them found themselves staring at a tiny stick person who turned in a circle to stare boldly back at each of them.

"Well I'll be..." Finn said, scratching his head.

"Oh my!" Rory said.

Kalvara just stared, wide-eyed.

Aric let out his breath and smiled. "Hello," he said.

"Hello," it answered.

"You are not all prickly now," Aric observed, pointing at the creature with his blistered finger.

"The thorns poke out when I roll into a ball. That's how I travel. I stick to things."

"Oh," the boy said. "Or you poke things." He waggled his finger.

"I don't poke anything, but if something presses into my thorns, it drops me fast."

The boy nodded. "I'm Aric," he said and introduced the creature to each of the others. By then, even Kalvara was smiling.

"What's your name," Aric asked.

"I'm Parviflorus Rubus Rosales, seventh generation," it said with a bow.

"That's a hard name," Aric laughed. "And a long one."

The bramble held out his stick hands, explaining. "We all have the same name; it just means Bramble. But when my family wants me, they call me Spike."

Chapter 8: Spike

"Spike!" Aric laughed. "That's a perfect name for you!"

Finn knelt by Aric, eye level with Spike. "Are all those briers we tossed under the tree alive like you are?"

"Oh no, of course not," Spike was appalled. "There'd be billions of us. We are just a family of bramble sprites."

"Ah. Bramble sprites. So, you live in the treetops?"

Spike gestured, making a circle with his tiny arm. "We live everywhere. I caught a breeze that blew me up there and I stuck. I'm quite glad to be down on the ground again."

"Well, then, Spike," Finn said, "we will set you down, so you can be on your way."

Aric's face fell, but he squatted to let the sprite jump off.

"She is like the others who live here." Spike pointed to Kalvara. "Tall as the trees."

"Wait a minute!" Finn peered at the sprite. "You know the tall ones who live on this island?"

"I wouldn't say I know them, exactly. I've not been introduced like I have been to you. And I doubt they pay much attention to brambles. But I have noticed much about them."

"Spike, maybe you can help us. The tall ones, and some dwarves, were on the ship that brought us here. Where do they live; we haven't seen any homes."

Spike laughed. "You'll not see homes topside, of course!"
"Topside?"
"Up here. Topside." Spike grinned.
Finn frowned. "So, is there a bottom side?"
Spike chortled. "There is, indeed, my new friend! Underside. Down below. It's where the homes are, though I warn you they are not friendly."
Finn repeated, "Underside?"
"Under the ground," Spike clarified.
Aric piped in. "How do we get there?"
"It's a distance to walk; far faster to float on a breeze. But put me on your shoulder and I'll take you there." The sprite hesitated. "I'll take you close, at least, and show you the entrance."
"What do you think?" Finn asked the others. "Nizat and the others will be looking for us, angry that we've escaped and ruined their treacherous plans."
"What are our other choices?" Rory asked.
Finn thought a moment. "Well, we can't stay on this island for long, it's too risky. I suppose we could walk back to the beach and try to board another ship."
"The crews are probably all looking for us." Kalvara frowned. "The dwarves, at least Nizat, thinks he can profit from us. Sell us to the tall ones. Psshht. There's not much chance we'd find safe passage on any ship. I think we should spy out the villages, stay hidden, learn what we can. Perhaps we will find an ally."
Finn remembered how Kalvara had done exactly that to him and his friends, spying on them, stealing food, listening and using what they said to her advantage. Until they caught her.
He turned to Rory. "What do you think?"
She hesitated, looking a little embarrassed. Finn waited. "I'd like ask Floxx," she stammered. "She promised to be with me and said I'd hear her voice. But I have to take the time to listen."

Kalvara snorted.

"Okay," Finn said, scowling at Kalvara. "You take all the time you need. We'll climb up there and wait." He nodded to the treetops. He wanted to see for himself whatever he could.

Finn got comfortable in the high branches, enjoying the beauty of the swaying blue foliage, and studied the acreage in all directions. Why had he doubted Kalvara and Aric? Their vision was as good, even better than his. And they were right. He saw no indication of either dwarves or tall ones living anywhere below. No noise, no smoke, no smell of food, not a whisper. It was eerily quiet with just the wind tickling the large leaves. It didn't make sense. And something about it didn't feel right.

"Spike," Finn whispered, goosebumps on the back of his neck. "Why is it that everyone lives Underside?"

Spike's tiny face contorted with fear. "The vapors," Spike whispered, his eyes darting around as if the word, itself, brought danger.

"What are the vapors?" Aric asked.

"Thin fingers of death," Spike whispered, then curled into a ball and refused to say another word about it.

"Finn," Rory called. "Come down. I'm ready to talk."

"That was quick," Finn said, slightly breathless after his fast descent.

Kalvara dropped next to him. "So, what is it, Princess?" she asked, crossing her arms and smirking.

"Kalvara, please," Finn shook his head. "Give her a chance. She has the right to an opinion, just like each of us."

"Psshht." Kalvara walked away.

"Go on," Finn encouraged Rory.

"Well," she hesitated, glancing from Kalvara back to Finn. "I honestly thought Floxx said to go back to the ships, but now, well, I think I might have been mistaken. It makes no sense to go back. Kalvara is right about that. So, I think we should go Underside."

Finn raised an eyebrow. "You're sure about that?"

"I'm not totally sure, no, but it does seem to be the best of the two choices."

Finn picked up Spike. "Underside it is. Let's get as close as we safely can."

"Can he ride with me? Please?" Aric begged.

Finn settled Spike on Aric's shoulder so his barbs could grab the boy's cloak, then lifted them both to his own shoulders where they could see to lead the way.

Finn fell in stride with Kalvara. "Give her a break, will you. She's here to help us."

"You. She's here to help you," Kalvara corrected, her face stony.

He hadn't gone far when he turned around looking for Rory. She hung behind, walking slowly, watching them, and he caught her sad expression before she realized he was looking.

"Rory." He held out his hand to her.

She hurried to catch up, a smile plastered on her face. "Hey!"

"Hey," he said, reaching for her hand. He saw the flicker of surprise in her eyes, and he melted with affection. How could he make her understand how much he cared for her? He'd dreamed of this moment, hoping against all odds that she would care for him like he did for her. He squeezed her hand.

"You came," he said, realizing how lame it sounded. He noticed she wore Floxx's necklace. Why? What had happened?

"Yes. As soon as I heard you were in trouble."

He was shocked. "Who told you that?"

"Floxx, of course!" Rory laughed, tossing her hair over her shoulders.

"Oh, right. Yes, she would know that!" Silence hung between them. Then the fog that engulfed him when he was near her thinned a little. He realized she had shown up exactly at the moment he most needed her. "You left the palace? But how did you find me? How did you get to this island? I mean, we are in the middle of nowhere! What happened?"

Rory laughed. "Wow, so many questions! A whole lot has happened since you and Kalvara left." Finn saw the pain in her eyes, despite her smile. She told him about leaving the castle and returning to Alaska, about being able to roll back time to the moment she wanted, about how she'd struggled with the decision to come back to Gamloden, not being sure until Floxx had told her he was in trouble.

Finn couldn't believe it! Rory had come for him! She must care about him after all! It must have been a huge thing for her to leave her Alaskan family. But why had she left Gamloden in the first place? He knew she loved her birth mother and grieved the death of her father. And Floxx, Rory loved Floxx. They were as close as any two friends he'd ever known. Floxx had promised to help Rory and her mother transition to their role as rulers. Everything had seemed to be in order when he and Kalvara had left. He'd wanted Rory to go with him, to help him with his daunting quest. He needed her. He trusted her. But she was so deeply involved in government affairs, it was clear she couldn't go with him; her duties at the castle held her captive. And yet, here she was, on this forsaken island with him. Here she was holding his hand and he could tell she liked it. He risked a glance at her and saw she was staring at him.

"Finn?"

"Huh?" he snapped back to the moment.

"Did you hear what I said?"

He looked at her apologetically. "I think I may have missed a few things. Sorry, I'll try to stay with you." He grinned. "So, I missed how, exactly, you got here."

She held up the feather. "This was Gram's. All I had to do was focus on you and in an instant, I was here."

Finn stared at her. "Another feather! Let's keep this one safe!" He realized anew how pretty she was. She'd pushed her hair behind her ears, and he could plainly see the scars on the side of her face and neck, a constant reminder that she'd been mauled nearly to death as a baby. He loved those scars, he wanted to touch every inch of them. He blushed hot at the thought. She was not just a survivor, she was brave and courageous, born for greatness. And she'd come back to him. To him. Not to her mother, not to the castle. She'd come to him.

"Will you stop daydreaming and keep up," Kalvara scolded, breaking into Finn's thoughts. "Spike said it was a long way and at this rate, it'll be days before we get there."

Chapter 9: Nerida

Marinna woke refreshed and famished. She threw her cape back and stood to stretch. Conquest whinnied and ambled over, nudging her for a nose pat. "Good morning! Did you sleep well?" He raised his head up and down as if he understood. She was starving and her stomach was noisily complaining, but she saw no fruit trees or berries, or anything edible. "I wish I could eat grass like you." Then she remembered she'd tucked some apples in the saddle pocket, really for the stallion, but he could share! Though bruised in places from bouncing on their wild ride, her apple was delicious. She offered Conquest the core and he was grateful for it.

Marinna wandered a short way and explored the narrow canyon. She was likely the first person to have ever set foot here. Breathtaking in its raw beauty, she was surrounded by jagged snow-tipped mountains. Birds were abundant, and their song filled the air. She came upon some low, thick bushes she recognized and bent to separate the branches. Blueberries! She ate several handfuls of them and felt much better. This was a valley for the gods! How fitting! For she would soon take her place as the eternal world ruler, with power her parents had dreamed would be hers before she was even conceived.

The sun was soon high enough to warm the day and she yielded to its warmth on her face. She closed her eyes, dreaming of the sea, staring into the eyes of beckoning mermaids and mermen. She was under their spell and savoring it. Would the memory ever leave her, or would its magic pull her forever toward them? She hoped it would. There was something thrilling about them, tempting, beguiling. They were her people. But she must not give in to them completely. No, she must rule all the peoples in Gamloden, both under the sea and above! It was her destiny.

She set her gaze on the peaks above, knowing her father trusted her. He'd prepared her for this time, called her to this role, infused her with a call to conquer, rule, and lead. She recalled what he'd said: *It is why you were born; why your mother gave you life, though she knew your birth could mean her own death.* She wouldn't let her mother down. Her death would not be wasted. She would be Queen. Her seaside throne would be a tribute to her mother's memory.

She rose and beckoned Conquest. "Let's go home," she said, and he whinnied in agreement. Even the steed, though clearly elated by their long and wondrous flight, seemed to know there was much work to be done, and headed straight for the palace, landing gracefully in the arena. The guards moved to close the gates, but Marinna stopped them. "They stay open from now on, so we can come and go as we please."

Draegin raged in his bed as she stood by him. "You left without telling me!" His parietal eyelid quivered in the middle of his forehead.

Marinna had seldom seen it, and she'd been revulsed each time she had. She willed it to stay closed. "You were unconscious, father," she said calmly, trying to soothe him.

"You could have been killed!" he exploded.

"But here I stand, having trained the indomitable Pegasus. Isn't that what you hoped for, father?"

"Of course, it isss." His anger weakened just a bit. "But the risssk!" He revved up, again. "If you'd died, and you well might have, what would have become of usss? Me, unable to rule in my condition, and you dead? I have planned for this time in history for eonsss; the ancient prophecy you will fulfill. We will rule, or more accurately, you will rule. You with your royal blood. The price we've paid! The cost! Don't you understand?"

She shook her head. "Royal blood, father? You mean your blood. Mother was a siren."

He sighed at the mention of her mother, his eyes glazing as he remembered her. Eventually, he regained his composure and responded, "A siren, yesss, of course. But sirens have their own order of royalty. I've not discussed this with you, but perhapsss it isss time."

"Yes! Tell me everything! I know so little about her." Marinna half dreaded what he might reveal, and yet yearned to know.

He stared into the past. "Nerida was a treasure from the sssea. Exquisitely beautiful! Wild and seductive. Beautiful and untamable. A siren of sirensss, she was strong and powerful, fitting for the granddaughter of Sea King Llyr. Long life is typical for sirensss, not as long as mine, but far longer than most other racesss." He paused. "Unlesss the siren chooses to leave the water and live in the air. Then the life span shortensss significantly. Your mother chose that for herself because of our love."

Marinna could not contemplate a love like that. She couldn't imagine a feeling powerful enough to provoke even the thought of self-sacrifice, much less a willingness. It was unthinkable. She wondered for a dark moment if her father had enchanted her mother with some malevolent spell to achieve her devotion.

"We met often by the edge of the sea. For all of my magical powersss, I could not live under the water though I would have if I could. I loved her deeply, Marinna, and she returned my love. Those were the happiest days of my long life—a short burst of joy amid eons of war and bloodshed. We dreamed of a life together and decided to marry. We wondered if we could produce offspring. We studied the ancient prophecy and realized that if we could, our child would have the heritage to one day reign over the entire world. When you were conceived, we knew you were destined to be the one! There were other royal babiesss, of courssse, but they were nothing we couldn't deal with." His lipless smile spread.

With the exception of the human child who'd escaped, Marinna thought. And now Princess Rory ruled with her mother. She began to realize the importance of eliminating her, the only other living being who could steal her throne.

Her father was still talking about her mother. "Though she would have lived far longer had she stayed in the sea, she risked death in order to give you life, Marinna. And death took her when you were born, a tragedy we could not have foreseen."

Marinna felt the familiar lump in her throat when she thought of her mother. She wished she could thank her, see her just once, and tell her she loved her.

"And, of courssse, your royal heritage runs deep on my side, as well. You know the powersss I possess, Marinna, abilitiesss other races can't even imagine. But I am the last one, the sole survivor of the royal line of Thaumaturgesss. My dragon blood allows me to live at will in either form, making me the King of Thaumaturgesss. No one else alive has the blood of both sorcerer and dragon running in their veinsss. I have lived thousands of yearsss and if I can regain my strength, could live thousandsss more, but in my condition, it is possible my daysss may be shortened."

"Nonsense, father. Surely you will recover! I have no doubt."

He changed the subject. "We face a formidable foe in the Firebird. Do not underestimate her. She is the only creature who could face me with even a remote chance of winning, unlikely as it is." He shifted his position with difficulty, his weariness apparent. "Though this knife wound has dealt me a blow no enchantment of mine can reverse."

"How is that possible, father?"

He sighed. "There is a dangerous magic, Marinna, whose source is hidden from me. It is seldom seen, but those who wield it have unexplainable prowess." He considered his daughter. "Some of my powersss you have inherited, as well as some of your mother's, though they are yet to be discovered and developed. Your tact with the Pegasusss seems to be one of them. You are good at dominating magical creatures. And perhaps not just flying horsesss. This may fare you well in facing the Firebird. Woo her, coax her, earn her trust." He thought a moment. "Yesss, yesss, that may work far better than facing her with force as I did."

Magical powers? She hadn't thought of taming the Pegasus as anything magical. And yet, perhaps it was. She could see her father tiring. She had to lean close to hear him.

"And so, my dear daughter, the blood of kingsss flows in you, both from royal Thaumaturgesss and Kingsss of the Seas. Nerida and I brought forth the child of promise. You, Marinna. You were born to rule."

Marinna let out a breath she didn't know she'd been holding. It seemed Draegin really had loved her mother. At least she had that to hold on to. She wished she had at least a few of her own memories. What had Nerida looked like? What were her people like? She knew only that her father said she had inherited her looks from her mother.

"You have no equal," he rasped, "no one has ever been born with the unique and marvelous qualitiesss you have. No one will ever outrank you. Embrace your destiny, Marinna.

The world belongsss to you." Draegin, worn out from their conversation, collapsed against his pillow, waving her away, then slumped into a state of consciousness she could not penetrate.

Marinna walked to her throne room. She surveyed her throne, bejeweled with the gems of the sea, pearls and shells of all sizes and colors. In the center of the arch was an enormous chambered nautilus shell, as long as her arm, its lustrous nacre shiny in pastels and gold. It was set among large pearls and aquamarines the color of the water. The wealth of the sea. She climbed on her seat and stood, placing her ear on the nautilus shell, listening. There! The sound of the sea. She'd heard it before, but it hadn't meant anything to her, just a shell with a swooshing sound. Now it meant everything. She closed her eyes and recalled the fishy air, the salt on her lips; she stared into the faces of the mermaids and mermen below the surface, marveling at their shiny thick tails. They were exquisite, beguiling. Mother had been one of them. What magic allowed them to walk on legs? She knew their evil reputation, their powerful seduction over the human race, beguiling lovers into the sea at the cost of their lives.

But her parents didn't fit that mold. Draegin's magic must have been stronger than her mother's, for he was the one who captivated her, convincing her to leave her beloved sea and live in the mountains. That dark thought niggled, again. Had he spun some enchantment that had assured her love? He was the master of altering creatures to meet his needs. She thought of Dread, her beautiful Caladrius bird whose natural healing power he'd altered to bring curses on whoever beheld it. How she wanted to talk with her mother. What would she learn about her own destiny? Was she truly destined to greatness? Or was she just a pawn in the hands of the greatest lizard-skinned wizard who'd ever lived, who lusted for world dominion with every breath he took?

She sat on the seat of her throne, resting her hands on its elaborate arms, each carved in a dragon head and adorned with brilliant gems. The wealth of the land. The golden dragon horns reached toward the nautilus shell, symbolizing the union of land and sea, the marriage of Thaumaturge to siren, harnessing the magical prowess of both worlds. The dragon's scales were green beryl, emerald, and multicolored opal, subtly changing color as the light moved, just as her father's did when he shape-shifted. Both jaws were open revealing sharp, white moonstone teeth, and long tongues overlaid with red ruby.

The dragon's eyes, set with black star sapphires had an uncanny ability to focus on whoever stood before it, but now Marinna sensed they'd turned to challenge her. Could she do this? Could she rule with absolute power? What was this magic her father said dwelt inside her and would she know how to use it? When to use it? In his condition, he wasn't able to teach her. She needed him, now more than ever, but he was dying. She had so much to learn and no one to guide her. That pull of the sea, that force so powerful, what was it? She sensed it could either propel her to greatness or be her demise. She hoped she was wise enough to choose carefully.

Chapter 10: The Vapors

"Not too much farther now," Spike called down to Finn as late afternoon moved toward evening. They had stopped briefly to scoop some berries from one of the trees, eating as they walked. Finn had slowed to keep pace with Rory; he could see she was struggling to keep up. Conversation with her lapsed as she focused on breathing and matching his stride. She smiled as if everything was fine. No way was she going to admit her fatigue.

"I could use a break," Finn announced. "Just for a few minutes." He lifted Aric off his shoulders, tossed his pack on the ground and settled back against a smooth tree trunk. "Ahhh," he stretched his legs out, crossed his arms, and rested his head against the tree. "Aric, if I fall asleep, wake me when the sun has moved this much." He squinted at the boy, gesturing a half inch with his fingers.

"Okay," Aric said, studying the sky and holding his small fingers in front of the sun to anticipate about when wake up time should be. "I'm hungry," he said. "I'll climb up and get us some birds for dinner. You have my slingshot?" He looked at Kalvara.

She dug through her pack and tossed it to the boy. "Stay close. Just in the trees right here."

Finn caught Rory's eye and patted the ground next to him. She sat so their shoulders touched.

"A rest and meat for dinner," she said with a sigh. "Perfect."

Finn smiled and slipped his arm around her, pulling her close. In a blink, she was asleep, her breath warm against his neck. He'd keep an eye on things while she napped. But some time later, he woke from a sound sleep to Aric's jostling. The boy was grinning ear to ear, holding a string of six small birds.

"I'm starving, Finn! Can we eat them now?"

"Whoa, Aric, you're amazing!" Rory yawned. "I forgot how fast a hunter you are!"

"Help me get some wood, Rory, before it rains," he said.

"No problem," she said, brushing her clothes off.

"Rain?" Finn asked Aric, looking at the blue sky between the treetops. "Did you see rain clouds?"

The boy nodded. "Treetops are covered way far off. We have time if we hurry."

Kalvara and Rory scrounged for wood as Finn and Aric prepped the birds. In a half hour they had devoured all the juicy meat, sucking every bit off the roasting sticks and licking their fingers. The tops of the trees began to sway as a breeze picked up. A sour odor filled the air.

"Anyone smell that?" Finn asked.

"You mean the campfire or the meat roasting?" Rory laughed.

"No, not that." He sniffed, his senses on high alert.

"I do, and it's not good," Kalvara answered, exchanging a worried look with him.

"Time to go!" Finn hurried everyone. "Something's not right!" He lifted Aric to his shoulders and called up, "Lead on, Spike."

"Finn!" Aric yelled. "Spike's gone!"

Finn set the boy on the ground and checked all his clothes, then all their clothes and their packs, but the bramble was nowhere to be found. By then, the blue sky had vanished, and clouds hid the treetops. Oddly, the breeze had stopped. The air was as still as a cat poised to pounce. Thin tendrils of fog wisped down from the clouds, curling around the trees like snakes. The air burned their faces.

"This is not good!" Kalvara cried, lifting Aric to her hip.

"Run!" Finn yelled, grabbing Rory's hand.

They tore through the forest, horrified at the noxious serpents coiling down every tree. A large leaf fell near them, its berries sizzling as if they'd been fried. The leaf, itself, was eaten with holes, curling at the edges. The air burned their throats with each breath. More leaves tumbled down shriveled and smoking and they dodged them, zigzagging through the forest. This was no rain fall; this was a toxic storm. One touch and they'd be burned; if they were wrapped by a coiling wisp, they'd be fried alive. They desperately needed a place to hide.

Kalvara had sprinted ahead. "Here!" she yelled, just before she and Aric vanished.

Finn was several steps behind her, pacing himself with Rory. He saw no sign of where they'd gone but heard Aric's faint call.

"Down here! Slide down the hole!"

The vapors stretched just above their heads, their gaseous fingers grasping for them. Finn pushed Rory into the hole, then leapt for its safety just as a corrosive wisp brushed the tip of his ear. He cried out, covering it as he fell down a dark hole and landed with a thump in the blackness.

"My ear!" he moaned, feeling it burn terribly. Rory fumbled for the bellasol and touched its light on.

"Let's see," she said, pulling his hand away. Its tip was bubbling with blisters.

Kalvara dug a tennifel blossom from her pack and pressed the blossom to it. "Hold it there," she told him.

"Oh, already some relief." He exhaled. "This plant is wondrous!" He looked around. "We're in a tunnel. A back entrance to Underside, maybe."

Aric was sitting off by himself, his head on his knees.

"You okay?" Kalvara asked him.

The boy looked up with doleful eyes. "I know why Spike disappeared. I thought it was rain coming, but Spike knew it was the vapors. Remember how scared he was of them?"

"I do," Kalvara sat next to him. "Well, we can't blame him for leaving, can we Aric? We'd have run sooner, too, if we'd known what was coming."

"I guess," he said, scuffing the dirt. "But I sure did like him. Do you think we'll ever see him again?"

No one answered, not willing to dash Aric's hopes. They were startled by approaching footsteps. Rory tapped the bellasol off.

"Did ye hear something?" a rough voice echoed in the distance.

"Aye, I did. Might be some poor critter fell down our hole."

"Dinner, mebbe." They laughed. "Let's go check."

Noisy boots clumped in their direction. Finn and the others moved silently to the side where they were partially hidden by a stone protrusion. The dwarves carried torches and the tunnel filled with light as they approached. As the floor illuminated, Finn saw his mistake. In his haste to hide, he'd moved his hand from his ear and the purple blossom lay in the dirt like a lone star in the night sky.

"What's this?" one of the dwarves said, picking up the tennifel. "Never known a flower to make a racket, did you, Nizat?"

"Not before this," Nizat said, turning around to face Finn and the others. A smile spread across his face. "Well whadda ye know. Caught like rats in a ship."

"Run," Finn said, grabbing Rory's hand and pushing past the dwarves. He heard Kalvara shouting at Aric to go with Finn and the dwarves cursing and yelling.

"I got 'er!" Nizat yelled.

"And I got the boy!" The other dwarf snorted.

"The Tall King will pay us well for this pretty prize." Nizat laughed, but a second later, cried out in pain.

"Touch me, again, and I'll kill you," a furious Kalvara threatened.

Nizat slapped her. "Tie 'em up and gag 'em both," the angry dwarf ordered.

Seconds later, the dwarves stomped by Finn and Rory, never noticing them pressed against the rock wall. Nizat yanked a gagged Kalvara by a rope tight around her neck, her hands bound behind her.

"Wish we'da got the princess, too," he grumbled. "Not that the tall ones'd want her, but Jakin mighta. He hates 'er. Says she causes trouble wherever she goes. Mighta paid a handsome reward to be rid o' the wench."

The other dwarf followed behind with a gagged and bound Aric tossed over his shoulders, a blue ball of light barely visible above the boy's head. "She can't be far. We'll find 'er and the other one, too."

The boy glanced up and saw Finn and Rory follow in the shadows, and hope lit in his terrified eyes.

Chapter 11: Captured

Rory chastised herself as she and Finn slunk through the shadows. The tunnel eventually led to a maze of dirt paths. Although torchlight burned at intervals, it was very dark, but she could see they were in an underground village, similar in some ways to Orizin where dwarves had carved a city inside the mountains. But in Orizin, they'd been celebrated guests; here they were intruders. It was her fault they were in this mess. She knew full well what Floxx had told her when she'd taken the time to ask. *Go to the dock. You will find safe passage back to the mainland.* But in her eagerness to keep the peace, she'd agreed with Kalvara, lying to her friends about Floxx's guidance. No wonder Uriel had gone with Aric. He must know what she'd done in turning her back on Floxx. Her duplicity might cost them their lives. Why hadn't she had the guts to speak the truth, even if Kalvara had ridiculed her? Since when did she care so much about her, anyway? The thieving, murderous eldrow had spit in her face when she'd tried to be nice. And stolen Finn right out from under her nose at the castle, convincing him to leave with her.

Rory cleared her head. Wait. What was wrong with her? Kalvara had changed in a huge way. They were friends. She'd saved her life more than once on the trek to meet her birth parents. She'd proven her trustworthiness over and over, again. Kalvara had been scared and starving when they'd first met, with a child to care for—an understandable reason for stealing food to stay alive. And it was only apples, not valuables. It was this place, Rory thought, that gave her such dark thoughts. Murky corners everywhere. Hollow echoes. Damp and creepy. She wanted to get out of there. To risk the vapors and race back to the ships. Why hadn't she listened to Floxx? They could be on the sea right now, safe, and headed to the mainland. Her heart broke. She could never tell her friends, especially Finn. If anything happened to Kalvara and Aric, he'd never forgive her.

It was way too quiet; no one was out, except a few dwarves who appeared to be on guard duty. What were they protecting? Who were these tall ones and where were they? Where was anyone? Had they arrived while everyone slept? It was impossible to judge day or night, but it sure seemed like most everyone was sleeping.

They stalked Nizat down dark, hard-packed dirt paths, winding left then right, then back, again. They were in a labyrinth, a series of caves, low-ceilinged and clammy. They passed a door that resembled Tishkit's, and she was reminded of Zad. A wave of grief washed over her.

"Rory!" Finn hissed. She jolted from her reverie to see him motioning for her to follow. She'd nearly missed a turn.

"You okay?" he whispered when she caught up.

She nodded. Another lie.

"Stay with me!" Finn took her hand and led her soundlessly through the shadows, following the dwarves' heavy tread.

Finally, the footsteps stopped, and the dwarves pounded on a door.

"Stop!" a rough voice commanded. "Ye want to wake the King?"

"Aye, we do!" Nizat snapped back. "Prizes. We got prizes he'll want t'see."

Some scrabbling and mumbling followed as the guard must have come out to see for himself.

"Ah! Oho!" Then laughter. "Aye, this is worth waking 'im! But let's get 'em cleaned up and lookin' their best, first."

Rory and Finn crept close enough to see where the sentry led Nizat and the others. No one seemed to notice them as they followed, but the back of Rory's neck tingled. She sensed they were being watched, but glancing around, she saw no one. This part of the village was considerably nicer. The dirt walls were hard-packed and smooth and the ceilings much higher, no doubt to accommodate the tall ones. Torches lit the cavern at frequent intervals. They rounded a curve and Rory felt humidity and, daring a quick peek, saw the sheen of water.

Two dwarves approached Kalvara. One reached up to remove her cloak. Kalvara kicked her. Nizat roared with laughter.

"She's a feisty one, Riza!"

He yanked the rope around Kalvara's neck, nearly jerking her off her feet. "Do what she says, or I'll bathe ye myself. I'll be back in a few minutes to drag your soggy self to His Majesty, and it'd go best if ye cooperate." He glared at Aric who trembled next to her. "Both of ye. Now, I'll leave ye and the boy to the washing." As he and the other dwarf marched out, he turned back. "Make 'em pretty, Riza. Ye know what the Tall King likes, don't ye." And he hooted, again, chuckling as he disappeared into the shadows.

Rory pulled back next to Finn, only to realize he was gone. She spun around see a hairy hand clamped over his mouth. The dwarf who had carried Aric now pressed a knife to Finn's throat. Finn's wide eyes brimmed with sorrow that he hadn't been able to warn her.

"Nicely done," Nizat said, springing from the shadows and twisting Rory's arms behind her back to bind them.

"You rats followed the bait all the way in."

"Whadda we do with em?"

"No need to waste a bath on these two. We'll lock 'em up until we decide."

He yanked Rory's arms so hard she couldn't help crying out.

"Shut up," Nizat growled, pushing her along in front of him. Terrified Rory moved forward, trying to keep a half step ahead of his rough prods. He carried a torch, but light behind her did little good in the blackness ahead. They returned the way they'd come, leaving the tall tunnels behind. A painful shove to her left pitched her into a hole she hadn't seen. With no hands to catch herself, Rory landed with her face in the mud. Nizat yanked her up, blinding her with the light of his torch. When he saw her filthy face, he laughed. "Pretty princess!" he mocked and bowed.

In a blaze of anger Finn broke the grip of the other guard and lunged at Nizat, smashing him hard against the rock wall. Rory watched horrified as both dwarves leapt on him, punching him until he was bent over and bloody.

"If ye wasn't worth something, I'd kill ye right here. Right in front o' the princess. Try it again, and I may decide ye just ain't worth the pay." He kicked Finn, knocking him off his feet, then shoved Rory down the dark passage. Virtually blind, she stumbled ahead, somehow managing not to trip.

"Right here, Princess." Nizat pushed her sideways and she fell, cracking her cheek and her elbow on some big rocks. His flickering torch outlined a small cave. Finn was thrown on top of her.

"I'm so sorry, Rory," he mumbled, groaning as he rolled off.

An iron grate clanged shut behind them.

"Scream and I'll come back and gag ye," Nizat snarled. "And ye won't last long with a gag down 'ere in this bad air." The two dwarves turned and disappeared into the gloom.

As soon as the footsteps faded, Rory scooted next to Finn and whispered, "If I position my pocket just below your fingers, do you think you could lift out the bellasol?" She couldn't see his smile, but she guessed it was there.

"So smart, Rory!"

Soon the light from the wondrous rock gave them much comfort. Rory remembered the night the King had given it to Floxx. And Floxx had given it to her just as she'd left for Alaska. "A light for the dark places," Floxx had said, and so it was.

Rory's gasped when she saw Finn's swollen face. "I'm so sorry. And I can't even doctor you with my hands tied."

"I'll be fine," he said with a lop-sided smile. "What about you? You hurt bad?" He studied her face and even though he tried not to react, Rory could see his alarm.

"My face and my arm took the worst of it. But, Finn," her voice broke. "That's not it." She had to tell him. She couldn't bear the crushing guilt that she'd brought all this disaster on them.

Finn slid closer. "What do you mean, Rory?" His voice brimmed with concern.

She lost it, then. Sobbing, she told him how Floxx had told her to go back to the dock, but she'd done exactly the opposite because she'd wanted to make peace with Kalvara. "All of this – the vapors, our capture, all of it is my fault. Why couldn't I just have done what Floxx said? Even Uriel's left me for Aric. I'm so, so sorry, Finn."

He rested his head on hers as she wept, saying nothing.

When she'd calmed down, he whispered, "It's okay, Rory. We all make mistakes."

She burst into tears, again.

"Rory, listen to me."

Yes. She needed to listen. Get a grip on herself. He'd suffered enough, already.

"Floxx is our good friend. She hasn't abandoned us just because you didn't listen to her, just because you made a mistake. Have you told her, talked with her in your quiet place?"

"No, I've not had a chance. Besides, what if she's really mad? What if we all die? This wasn't a little mistake, Finn."

"Okay, Rory, quit beating yourself up. We're here now, and we'll deal with it. Look, it's quiet right now; no one's around. Take some time with Floxx. Tell her what's happened. Tell her you're sorry—I'm sure she's worried about you. She probably already knows something bad's happened. Ask her for help."

Rory tried. She started a few times, but couldn't get any words out without hysterics. "I'm sssorry, Finn." She hiccupped.

"Do you think it would help if I called to her?" Finn offered. "Do you think she'd hear me?"

Rory shrugged. "Try."

"Okay, then." Finn took a few steadying breaths and leaned close, pressing his shoulder against hers. She nestled her head under his. His touch steadied her more than words ever could. He hadn't yelled; he hadn't been angry. He was standing with her, in spite of the pain and the horrible mess they were in.

"Floxx," he said out loud. "If you can hear me, it's Finn. Rory's right here with me." He paused. "We are in trouble."

"Floxx," Rory whispered, bolstered by Finn's words. "I'm so sorry. I heard you when you said to go to the ships, but I didn't do it. I wanted Kalvara to like me; I didn't want to cause any arguments, so I went along with her. I told them I thought I'd misunderstood you and that it seemed best to go Underside. What a huge mistake I made. I've ruined everything. Are we going to die?"

Silence.

Rory wanted to curl up and sob. But she knew she had to be brave. Suddenly, she remembered she'd been born for a purpose. She'd survived a kidnapping and attempted murder a few weeks after birth. Floxx had fought for her then, when she wasn't even aware of what was going on. She thought of the journey to Masirika and how she'd been attacked over and over, again. Floxx had stayed with her, guiding her, risking her life to defend her. Floxx wasn't just a friend. No! She was the one Eldurrin had sent to help her realize her destiny, to help them all fulfill the ancient prophecy. Confidence rose inside Rory. Faith in Floxx. Trust in Eldurrin. Could even her mistakes be part of their larger plan? Would they forgive her? Give her another chance?

"Floxx," Rory said, louder this time. "Thank you for loving me. Thank you for protecting my life on so many occasions. Thank you for listening even though I've done this terrible thing. Please help us, all of us, to get out of here." Then, the strangest peace overtook her, she never could explain it. There, laying on ragged rocks in the dark with her cheek and arm throbbing, with caked blood all over her, she fell asleep curled awkwardly beside Finn, greatly comforted by his nearness. She couldn't guess how long she'd slept when Nizat returned, but she went with him in renewed strength, certain that somehow Floxx would take care of them.

Chapter 12: Captivated

Jakin watched the dwarves haul a net overboard, and dump a large catch of fish into the hold kept cool with seawater.

"Ha!" they slapped each other on the back. "That'll bring a good trade, won't it, boys!"

"Barrel o' ale, at least, mebbe two!" another shouted and they raised their fists in a toast.

Dwarves! Jakin harrumphed. Keep them in ale and they'll work till they can't stand up. It was true a good catch of fish was valuable; it would bring more money than a load of pearls. What did Tozar want with all the pearls he'd ordered? The prince had always been distant, not one to talk much and certainly not divulge his business contacts. And Jakin would never ask. It was enough Tozar had given him a job and gotten him away from Byerman when his life was in danger. That more than his Uncle Merek would ever have done for him.

He stared at the sea, wondering about its fathomless depth and the variety of creatures that lived in it, the ones that paid his way these days, the oysters, clams, and fish of all kinds. He wondered if there really were exotic beings down there. He figured the Syrean Sea had been named for sirens, but he'd never seen one. Oddly enough, the sea had caused him to focus on the sky. By day, he studied the weather, the movement of the sun and the impact of its heat, the formation of clouds, the effect of wind. And by night, he studied the stars. He'd plotted night sky maps, comparing them over a period of time, learning which celestial bodies held a constant position in the sky. From that, he'd figured out basic navigation. His father had been a great sailor before he'd been born; at one time, he'd owned a fleet of ships and overseen much of the royal fleet. King Merek and his father were two brothers called to divergent destinies, one a ruler, the other an adventurer. Jakin, with saltwater in his blood, was just realizing the life he could have on the sea.

"Jakin!" One of the dwarves interrupted his thoughts. "Can ye give us a hand? Tis a full net, more'n we can handle." He jolted back to reality, hurrying to help hoist another catch onboard.

But Jakin was preoccupied with something else. His mind was on Finn. What were he and Kalvara doing here? How had they managed to find him? Finn must be furious with him for the debacle in trying to marry Rory. Had they chased him down? Did they blame him for the King's death and were they out to capture him? If he was caught, he might spend the rest of his life in the dungeon, if he was lucky enough to live at all. But the whole horrible mess hadn't been his fault. Sure, he'd loved Rory, and he'd been so jealous of her affection for Finn. But that enchanted bracelet had not been his idea. The creepy specter he'd met in the woods had tricked him into giving it to her. This will make her love you, it had said, its pale fingers dropping the jewelry into his pack without his permission.

He'd been a pawn, he knew now. A fool. Completely oblivious to the devastation he would cause. How could he have known the bracelet would cast a love spell on Rory and make her love him? He'd thought her love was real, that she'd finally come to her senses and chosen him over Finn. That she really loved him; after all, they were going to be married! His feelings for her had been genuine; his affection was not the result of any spell!

It still stung every time he thought of Rory dumping him for Finn in front of everyone, casting him aside like a filthy cape as soon as the enchantment was broken. He hated Draegin for his treachery, and was elated the sorcerer's plan had backfired, even though the King and many others had died that bloody night. And now somehow it was all his fault. He could care less about the King, his uncle who'd never loved him anyway. Who'd been too busy to care for him when his parents had been killed. Who'd given him to the dwarves, instead of raising him in the castle.

Well, at least he knew who his friends were. He studied the burly crew, tossing fish into the hold, sloppy, loud and crass. These were his people. They'd always been his family. He watched the fun-loving crew, snorting at their antics. They still loved him, in spite of the terrible recent events. Tozar'd given him this job, a chance for a new start. Humans, though, they were a different story, so suspicious now of everything he did. Didn't matter that he'd killed Morfyn and saved their city from the giant's deadly ravishing. That was long forgotten. He was shunned now. Not that he cared what all those people thought. Except for Rory. And Finn, who'd once been his best friend. He really did care a lot about them. But now they both despised him. They were tracking him.

Jakin spit over the rail. They were out deep, deeper than usual, far from the sight of land. He was distracted by a dark speck in the cloudless sky, but when he looked, again, it was gone. Was a raven way out here? He shook his head. Couldn't be. Ravens never flew alone.

The captain had assured him he knew exactly where they were. Good fishin' out here. Big ones. From the bountiful catch, it seemed he'd been right. Still Jakin was uneasy with the deep sea. The shallow water was great, he loved it, there was something calming about it. Tide in, tide out. The rhythm of the breaking waves, the moodiness of its color. It drew him. Safe. Soothing. But way out here in the deep with no sight of land, he was edgy. He studied the sky, blue and clear. Ah, there it was, again, a black speck way out on the horizon. A terrifying thought spiked his adrenaline. The dragon! Was it possible? Could the dragon be hunting him?

He ran to the bridge. "Cap'n," Jakin shouted. "I need this. Saw something." He held up the spyglass.

"Just bring 'er back when you're done." The captain dismissed him without a glance, focused on holding the sloop steady on course.

Jakin climbed the high mast, his heart hammering, afraid to look, but petrified not to. He steadied himself, gripping the spyglass so tight his hand hurt. Bracing himself against the spar, he focused it on the horizon, sweeping it back and forth until he found the speck. What he saw caught his breath, stunned him. He reached around the spar to focus the lens, studying the image, captivated, not believing his eyes.

This was not a dragon at all; this was a wonder! Such beauty! Who would ever believe this? A flying horse, black as night, graceful, agile, strong and powerful dipped and swirled over the water. On his back, he carried a woman, her black hair blowing behind her like the tail of a kite, responding to every move like ribbon in the wind. He moved the scope aside and rubbed his eyes. This was the stuff of children's tales. Should he tell someone? No one would believe him. He raised the glass, again, peering, searching, squinting, holding his breath lest he miss them. He moved it an inch at a time across the sky. Where had they gone? His heart sunk as he realized he'd lost them. A Pegasus! He'd seen it with his own eyes! And the stunning woman! Who was she? He lingered on the mast, studying the sky, captivated by the vision he'd seen, unwilling to give up searching.

Finally, a bellow from the deck jolted him. "What'r ye doing up there? There's naught but blue sky far as the eye can see." The dwarves guffawed and lumbered away.

Jakin climbed down, crushed that the vision was gone. But he'd keep looking. Every day, he'd watch for them. The memory of them dancing in the air stamped itself on his soul with black ink. His heart galloped at the thought of seeing them, again.

Chapter 13: Tall King

Filthy and sore, they were dragged to a place dappled with light. Though they stood in the shadows, Finn blinked at the sudden brightness. He rubbed his eyes, squinting, trying to ignore the stabbing pain the light brought to his head. He saw how badly hurt Rory was, her face swollen with darkening bruises; dirt and blood matting her hair. But still, she stood tall and confident, an undeniable ruler. She will get us out, Finn, watch and see, she'd whispered as they'd scrambled to their feet under Nizat's jabs. What a woman of strength she was. Unshakable in her trust in Floxx, who had saved her life so many times before. And she loved him. Sudden heat burst from his heart, warming his neck, his face, reddening his ears. She'd come back for him, leaving so many she loved behind. He stood taller, new strength pulsing through his own battered body. Yes, Floxx would save them. She'd burst in here with an army of tennins and blow the Underside apart if she had to.

He saw Rory frown and followed her gaze. He barely stifled a gasp. The Tall King sat on a crescent-shaped stone bench in the center of a garden! It faced another identical bench, forming a circle. A round table sat between them. Trees, flowers, and shrubs of all kinds bloomed in profusion in the gardens around it. The sight was ludicrous, astounding! How could there possibly be a garden in the depths of an underground village? He looked for the source of light and couldn't keep his laugh quiet. An enormous round domed ceiling covered the King's courtyard, and the garden flourished in its light. The ceiling, itself, was carved in magnificent flowers, light dancing through flower petal prisms, giving the air a shimmering effect. What ingenuity! What imagination! He spotted a cluster of tennifel blossoms carved above and saw that some reflected pinks and others, purples and blues. How did these tall ones do this? What wondrous knowledge did they possess? He'd never seen such craftsmanship with light and color. Who were they?

The Tall King wore a simple tan tunic, sewn from fine fabric but devoid of any embroidery or embellishment. He'd pushed his red cape off his shoulders, apparently too warm for the sunny morning. It was clasped around his neck with a gold brooch that matched the golden circlet of leaves on his head. His long brown hair was tied back neatly. A long strand of gold beads swung from each of his ears. He was engrossed in a conversation with a tall, slender woman sitting next to him. Finn jolted when he realized it was Kalvara!

She was dressed in a one-shouldered spring green dress. Her waist length, white hair, was neatly caught in a single braid over her bare shoulder, woven and tied with a vine of small pink flowers. She looked small next to the King, demure almost. He'd never thought her beautiful until this moment. Her face was raised to the King and she listened carefully, nodding often, her expression sober. What was going on? After all of Nizat's threats, this was the outcome? He was bringing the King a treasure, he'd said as he'd poked them along, sure he'd be well rewarded for delivering his prizes. But Finn had never imagined this—a treasure of friendship, that the eldrows would be honored! He remembered Nizat had been unusually sullen on their trip here this morning. Perhaps even he was shocked.

Aric was not with Kalvara, nor anywhere in the garden that Finn could see. Kalvara didn't seem agitated, though, so the boy must not be in danger. He watched her talking to the King, his head bent toward her, intent on her words. Had she won his trust? They seemed comfortable with each other, as if they were old friends. He glanced at Rory, questions in his eyes. She shrugged, as incredulous as he was. To Finn's astonishment, the Tall King stood and held out his hand to Kalvara, and she stood next to him. A dozen guards that Finn had not seen in the shadows stepped into the light.

"Bring the other two," the King commanded, startling a flock of birds from the trees.

Four soldiers escorted them into the garden, and despite his fear, Finn felt a wave of satisfaction that Nizat was not one of them. Rory followed close behind.

"Untie them," the King commanded, and the guards cut the ropes from their wrists.

"Leave us," the King boomed and in moments, they were alone.

Kalvara was grim as she studied their bruised faces, but when she caught Finn's eye, she said nothing. Finn clenched his fists to still his trembling hands. Rory stood beside him, stalwart. Their fate was in Floxx's hands, but he resolved to protect her till his final breath.

But the King surprised them with a bow. "Please forgive us," the King said. "These dwarves. They do not understand. They think I want to harm you. But no. You have done a great service in bringing Kalvara and Aric. I have long searched for tall ones but never before have any been found. These are ancient family, long lost. We welcome them." He hesitated, then added, "And their friends."

Aric jumped from the branches of a nearby tree, springing like a kitten to Finn's side. "Can you believe it! He's a friend!" He laughed. "And we were so scared!"

But out of the corner of his eye, Finn saw Kalvara's composure falter. What was going on?

"Come. Bathe and eat," the King said and from out of nowhere, servants appeared. They hadn't been alone after all.

They were taken to separate baths, so Finn lost track of Rory for an hour. He fretted about her so much he scarcely relished his own bath and the oils that were rubbed on his cuts and bruises. The attending dwarves wrapped his chest tightly in a soft cloth, providing support for his sore ribs. His raw wrists were anointed with a thick salve and wrapped in clean bandages. He was given a blue sleeveless tunic to wear and a brown cape light and soft that hung down his back to his knees. His boots were cleaned and buffed to a shine. Finn marveled at the advanced culture, and the spectacular gardens thriving underground. Were these people really a surviving remnant of eldrows, related to Kalvara?

"Now, you eat." the dwarf said.

Suddenly famished, Finn followed him past the King's courtyard to an outdoor terrace facing the garden. Rory was already seated at a high table. No one else was there. Her hair, like Kalvara's, was braided with a flowering vine, but instead of hanging long, it was coiled around her head, giving it the appearance of a crown. Fitting for a princess, he thought. She wore a purple sleeveless tunic and a tan cape covered her shoulders. He smiled a crooked smile, the best he could do with his swollen lip, and sat next to her. Platters of fruit and flat breads were laid on the table, and a small bowl of something thick and milky was placed in front of each of them. Finn raised an eyebrow at the strange food.

"Yogurt," Rory said, tasting a small spoonful. "Sweetened with something delicious."

The two of them ate quietly, not daring to speak openly, quite sure that whatever they said would be reported to the Tall King. Instead they gulped deep breaths of fresh air and enjoyed the trilling of the birds. As soon as they finished, they were led through winding garden paths, marveling at the artistic landscaping.

"What a gifted people; Kalvara must be thrilled to have found them," Finn murmured.

The garden was much larger than Finn had realized, extending far beyond its manicured center. Birch, Ash, and Alder trees mixed with evergreens, reminded Finn of his home. The path meandered through a small stand of evergreens and ended at an arena. The guards stopped. A circle of stone benches surrounded a flat pit area. It was cooler and dimmer here, only thin light from the domed ceiling reached this far. Finn's delight suddenly gave way to dread. Arena's housed competitions, usually ending with only one victor. He turned to grab Rory's hand, and saw his fear mirrored in her eyes.

The King approached; his arms spread wide in welcome. Neither Kalvara nor Aric were with him.

"You are feeling better?" he asked.

"Indeed, we are. Thank you," Finn answered, coolly.

"Sit, please," the King motioned to a few flat rocks. The guards stepped into the shadows. Finn wondered how many more were hidden, watching, listening. It's a trap, he realized. We are not free at all. He's kept us for some scheme of his.

"I have heard from Kalvara of your great feats from lands beyond our island, places we have not traveled."

Neither Finn nor Rory said a word.

"Fighting wolves and Inozak, even facing a dragon! It is true, yes?"

Finn nodded.

"And you are a princess?" He looked at Rory.

She nodded.

"Brave indeed. Both of you. Heroes."

No one said anything, and the King let the silence settle. "I need heroes. Just one, really. One to face our greatest foe. One is enough. The other can go free."

Bile rose in Finn's throat.

"Kalvara is sure either one of you could defeat it. So sure, that she has agreed to stay with me if I allow the victor to leave."

"What?" Rory stood in alarm. A guard was instantly at her side, a menacing presence.

"Sit, please," the King clipped, warning in his eyes.

Rory sat.

"It is a good deal, as I'm sure you will see. More than generous. One of you goes free, and Kalvara and the boy stay with me in safety. Three of the four of you live."

"What foe?" Finn spat. They'd been tricked, manipulated by this tyrant. Duped into thinking his artistic nature covered a gentle soul. What treachery! *Floxx, we need you. Deliver us from this terrible fate.*

The King frowned. "Pests. Deadly little insects who eat our crops, our trees, our beautiful gardens, and especially crave the flesh of our young."

Finn and Rory stood in the center of the arena, encouraging one another with reminders of Floxx's imminent rescue. "We will be okay," Finn whispered, squeezing Rory's shoulder, but his words couldn't hide the tremor in his voice. A gong sounded in the distance and in minutes, the arena filled with spectators. Hundreds of dwarves crammed into the seats closest to the pit floor, noisy and jostling. Nizat was the loudest, boasting about his capturing the four prizes. A dozen tall ones gracefully climbed to the highest benches and sat. Finn wondered why they chose to watch from such a distance. Kalvara and Aric were ushered in, both heavily guarded.

The King entered last, and holding up both arms, turned to face the arena. He shouted, "Net!" and immediately, a finely woven mesh was stretched over the entire arena and fastened just below the seats, about twenty feet above Finn's head. Once it was secured, the crew dashed, running from the arena to claim their seats above.

"Insects are small," he said, "but these must fly!" He gazed up at the net.

"Or jump high," Rory added.

The heavy gate barring the tunnel entrance to the arena slowly lifted. Finn stood shoulder to shoulder with Rory.

"Listen to me, Rory. When I say run, you run. Got it?"

"Sure," Rory said, way too quickly for Finn to believe her.

The gate was all the way up and nothing emerged. Or had it? Was it something so small they couldn't even see it? Finn turned full circle, studying the empty arena. The spectators sat in hushed silence. With his eyesight, he should have seen whatever it was. Unless it was invisible. He stood perfectly still and heard a low rustling noise coming from the tunnel like leaves in a breeze. The cavern mouth darkened as something huge filled it, so tall it scraped the ceiling.

"Not small," Rory hissed.

Angry at the King's deception, Finn welcomed the new surge of adrenaline spiking his blood stream.

The creature emerged and stood, bumping the net twenty feet above, as it shook itself to full size.

"I don't believe it!" Rory whispered. "A tree?"

Finn calculated the legs of the tree trunk were five feet thick and 10 feet high, with branches spreading like muscled arms in a hundred-foot circumference. It would have been beautiful, actually, had it been rooted in a garden. But moving toward them with thudding steps, it was terrifying. It swiped at them with its lowest branches, tripping Rory. It would have picked her up with its vine-like fingers had Finn not shoved her out of its reach. He grabbed the branch and swung himself up. He'd climbed a thousand trees; he was comfortable fighting from the inside. But these branches tore at him from all directions, and their strength could rip him apart with little effort. He leapt from their grip, leaving his shredded cloak behind.

The spectators roared, cheering their approval!

"Go behind," Finn yelled to Rory, thinking they could divide the tree's attention, hoping they could confuse it. They made faux attacks, pulling loose twigs off and using them as feeble weapons. The tree turned in two complete circles, tangling itself, and Finn and Rory broke off branches as they were able. But they did little serious damage; they were stalling for time, searching for a weakness. The crowd was agitated and shouting, weary of their little game; the tree screeched and thrashed, angry at their jabs. Finn was out of ideas.

Floxx! We need you. Now.

"Stand still!" He heard the command clearly in his left ear. He stopped.

"That's it. Good! Tell Rory." He knew this voice.

"Rory," Finn yelled as loud as he could. "Rory, stop. Stand still."

She gaped at him, tossing down her branch, and stood, terrified.

"Spike?" Finn whispered.

"At your service," the sprite announced.

"What's the plan?"

"Rescue. Just stand still and leave it to us."

Us? Finn slowly understood as he watched Rory through the branches of the tree, seeing brambles quickly cover her body. He could feel them sticking their way up his own legs, around his torso, his shoulders, neck and head. They poked his skin and he struggled to remain as still as he could. Brambles caught in his eyebrows and covered his eyes, leaving only a slit through which he could peek.

Something was happening to the tree. He couldn't see why, but the tree was exploding. Leaves blew apart, then branches, then the trunk itself, burst into a million pieces, glittering in the dim light. The tiny pieces flew in all directions, latching onto anything edible, and ate. These were tiny creatures, after all! Some devoured grasses and weeds in the floor of the arena, others pushed and tore against the netted ceiling, frenzied at the greenery outside and the flesh in the stands.

Finn mistakenly opened his mouth to yell to Rory and one of the insects flew into it. He clamped his mouth shut, biting the pest in half and spitting it out, but not before it had bitten his tongue and drawn blood. Rory had her hands over her face. The part of her that Finn could see was covered with insects, gnawing at the brambles, trying to push past them to the warm flesh they could smell underneath. They clicked and screeched, their cacophony rising to a crescendo before tapering off, then rising, again, like a thousand cicadas on a summer night. The bramble on the tip of Finn's left ear slid, exposing just a little flesh and when he screamed at the painful bites, another bug flew into his mouth. He spit it out, his throat on fire from the stings.

Spike was counting out loud in Finn's good ear. "Nine, ten, NOW!" he yelled, and the bramble sprites exploded their thorns, piercing the thousands of bugs crawling on them. Ear-piercing screeches filled the area, drowning out the cries of the spectators. In an instant, the ground around Finn was thick with dying bugs. The air screamed in chaos as bramble sprites attacked the insects, piercing them with a deadly sting. The crowd cheered as they saw their nemesis destroyed, but when the bedlam settled, their cheering turned to outrage when they realized both Finn and Rory still lived.

"Now, run, Finn," Spike hissed into his ear. "Into the tunnel." Finn grabbed Rory's hand and sprinted for the opening from which the tree had emerged. The gatekeepers struggled to lower the gate to prevent their escape, but they slid under it just before it thudded to the ground.

Spike directed them through the labyrinth, left, then right, right, again, twice more, three lefts, right and a long straight uphill run at the end leading to daylight. With a surge of energy, Finn and Rory pumped for the opening and crossed into blinding daylight. Spike urged them on, "No time to stop. Not yet. Run!" They pushed hard, winding this way and that through the forest, racing through the burnt debris left from the Vapors. Finn's lungs seared with the exertion and he couldn't believe Rory was able to keep up.

Finally, at the base of the palms where they'd first met, Spike said, "Stop. Climb to the top and rest." The acidic smell still lingered, and a few of the leaves up top were singed, but up they shimmied, collapsing into the swaying bows.

"How did you know where we were?" Finn asked as soon as he caught his breath.

"When I saw you were missing above, I figured you'd fled Underside to escape the Vapors. Then Nizat came above to patrol, bragging to the other guards about your capture, so I rode down on him, hidden in a fold of his cloak."

"You saw everything?"

"I did," he said, grief in his voice. "And when I heard the Tall King's challenge and ultimatum in the arena, I knew he wanted you to demolish his worst foe, the omnivorous bugs—Skrack, they are called. They've eaten many of his gardens and once, in a hideous incident, attacked and killed a child who was playing unattended. Knowing they'd devour you if they had the chance, I flew for my family, knowing our spikes are poisonous to Skrack. The timing was perfect as we were able to catch rides on the spectators all the way to the arena. It took some doing to get into the tunnel, but when everyone was watching the net being hung, we found our way down. When we saw the tree deception the bugs had created, it was easy to latch onto the trunk and be nearly invisible. We just rode in quietly with the bugs; they were too excited about eating you to notice we were even there."

"Did you say all those brambles were your family?" Finn asked.

"Family and friends."

"I thought you said you had a small family!" Rory laughed, and Finn's heart leapt with joy at the sound of it.

"Small compared to all the brambles on the island!" Spike spread his tiny arms gesturing.

Rory sobered and looked at Finn. "Kalvara and Aric! Do we just leave them there?"

"I don't know," he said, uncertainty in his eyes. "But I don't think we should go back for them. It's too risky. I doubt they're in danger; the Tall King seemed quite taken with her, and children like Aric are, apparently, highly coveted."

Spike agreed. "The Tall King will treat them very well. But he will never let them leave."

"So, what do we do now? We can't stay Topside."

Finn heard the apprehension in her voice. "You're right. Nizat won't give up easy. He'll soon be after us."

"I was actually thinking about the Vapors. There's no escaping them up here."

"Well now, there is a bit of good news about the Vapors. No need to worry about them for a while," Spike told them. "They don't come often; only when the island's shifted enough. It's a good thing, too, because the forest needs time to recover."

Finn wasn't sure he'd heard right. "This island shifts?"

"It does. It moves fairly often, deep down, under the Underside—makes a low rumbling noise—and every time it does, it releases a tiny bit of lethal gas. Eventually, over time, the Vapors form."

"Wow. That is totally crazy!" Rory said. "But, actually, I'm super relieved to hear another acid storm isn't imminent." She relaxed, leaning back against the branches, wincing as she shifted to a comfortable position. She stifled a yawn. "I know we have to leave, but maybe not this minute. Can we rest just a little while?" She was asleep a few seconds later, and Finn soon joined her.

It was dark when Finn opened his eyes. "You awake?" he whispered.

"Mmmm, hmmm." Her eyes were still closed. "That was the best nap I've had in a long time."

"We need to go. Nizat loves skulking around in the dark."

She sat up in alarm. "It's dark? Oh no! We slept way too long!" She started to descend. "Wait. Go where?"

"To the docks. Spike, can you lead us? I'm hoping to find a ship leaving for Syrea."

They slid to the ground, and Spike hung on Finn's hood, whispering directions. It seemed to take forever as they crept through the shadows, but finally they came to the dock. The silhouette of a ship hulked in the water; the shore dimly lit with a few sputtering torches. Dwarves heaved and shoved cargo aboard.

"Faster!" someone hissed at them. "Get a move on! We've already pulled the anchor. Tozar's meeting us at dawn and we'd better be there."

Jakin! Finn was sure of it. "Rory, as soon as we can, we'll make a run for the cargo holds and hope no one sees us!"

"It's been my pleasure to meet you both," Spike whispered formally. "I hope to find you, again, wherever you go!"

"Werner's farm!" Rory murmured. "That's where I want to go."

Finn was not expecting that. "Why?"

"My airplane. I have to see if it's still there."

The dwarves slammed the cargo doors shut, knocked the torches over and stomped the flames out, then trudged for the ramp.

"Oh no!" Rory groaned, seeing their hiding place evaporate.

"No matter! Follow them. Run for the ramp!"

They dashed out, and fell in behind the last dwarf, tromped up the ramp, then slid into the first nook they saw on deck, hoping no one would notice them. The dwarves were arguing about the ale, and whether anyone had carried the barrel on board. Finn heard a lot of boots racing back down and a hearty shout that they'd found it. They clambered aboard, pulled the ramp on deck and dropped it with a boom not far from where they hid. In all the commotion, no one had noticed them, and they breathed easier as the ship began to move.

Chapter 14: Test Flight

Rory stood in the doorway of Werner's barn, grinning, the tears in her eyes making the Cessna blurry. Her airplane was here! How could that be if it had been back in Alaska? She didn't understand, but she'd sort it out later. She wiped her eyes and walked in. Ezat and Azatan turned when they heard her.

"Rory!" they cried in unison, rushing over to greet her. She hugged them. These were her friends, Zad's kids—here fixing her airplane!

Werner turned from sanding a wooden prop. "You came," he said. "How wonderful! It's great to see you, Rory." He held her gaze, his eyes deep pools of emotion. Grief, joy, hope—all surfacing as he grasped her hands. He cleared his throat to hold on to his composure and turned to the airplane.

The engine cowling had been removed; the aircraft manual lay open on top of the engine. They'd been studying.

"We've made three propellers, Rory. One will work, I think. Come see." Werner took her arm and showed her his work. "This was my first one, and though I got the length and weight right, it didn't have the right curve to it." He touched its smooth finish and walked to another worktable. "This one was closer, really perfect in terms of its weight and proportion."

"But?" Rory asked.

"But I found this hairline crack in the wood back here." He turned the blade over and walked outside with it, tilting it this way and that until he could find it. "Here," he pointed. "Aha."

"So, I used it as a pattern for the one I'm just finishing. We'll put it on today and pull the airplane outside. Would you do the honors of starting 'er up?"

"I'd be thrilled! Werner, this is so amazing! I'll never be able to thank you enough!" Her smile stretched from ear to ear.

"Sure you will. I'll take my pay in an airplane ride."

"Me, too!" Azatan laughed.

"And me!" Ezat agreed.

"Deal!" Rory shook their hands, sealing their agreement.

"You'll be able to fly through the mountain pass, over to Gamloden in such a short time. No more week-long treks through the forest," Ezat said, clearly awed at the thought.

Azatan jumped in. "Any chance you could fly it to Orizin? I'd like to see my family's faces when they see it!"

"Maybe," she hesitated. "Help me think of a place with a flat stretch long enough to land there."

"Ah. Right ye are. I'll watch ye from Werner's field to see how much room ye need. This airplane needs bird feet to land in the trees like the other flying creatures." He chuckled at the thought.

"Okay, good. But I'll need more distance in the mountains than I do here, double maybe."

"Why's 'at?"

"The air gets thinner, less dense, the higher you go. So the airplane takes longer to get airborne."

"Well, if that don't beat all!" Werner slapped his leg, laughing. "All right, boys, let's get back to work." He turned to Rory. "Who came with you?"

"Finn. He's with Ardith. He smelled apple pie and couldn't resist poking his head in."

"Well, I'm glad to hear it. Let's go see him."

"No need," a voice called from the doorway. "I'm right here!"

Rory's heart did a funny thump seeing him leaning against the doorway, one leg crossed over the other, hands in his pockets. How long had he been there?

Werner rushed him with a bear hug. "It's so very good to see you! Well, boys, that's it for the day. No sense trying to get any work done." He laughed. "Let's just go sit on the porch and catch up awhile, shall we?"

No one argued.

Rory blushed when they left the bench seat for her and Finn. Were they that transparent? Finn wiped away any doubt when he reached for her hand in front of everyone.

"So!" Werner blurted, looking from Finn to Rory and back, again, a face-splitting grin on his face.

Ardith, hearing the chatter, hurried out with a tray of cheeses and a basket of bread.

"Soups not quite ready, but so you don't all starve!" She handed the food to Finn and hugged Rory fiercely, pulling back to examine her face.

"What happened?"

Rory knew her bruises, though healing well, were obvious. "Met a mean sailor but made it out alive."

Ardith cupped Rory's face in her hands. "Tell me later, dear. All of it. Sit, now, and eat." Ardith crossed her arms and leaned against the door.

Werner waved a piece of bread at Finn, gesturing at him and Rory. "So?"

"What?" Finn teased.

Rory stifled a laugh. Men of few words. She looked at Finn, her eyebrows raised, daring him to put their fragile relationship into words.

He stalled, stuffing a piece of cheese into his mouth. Everyone waited, the extended silence not seeming to bother anyone but her.

Finn cleared his throat. "She came back," he finally said. "To me. She came back to find me."

They were all confused, so Ardith jumped in. "Came back? From where? To find you where?"

"We're missing all the middle parts of the story," Werner added.

So, they talked through the afternoon, telling them all that had transpired since Werner and Ardith had said good-bye to them in Masirika after the King's funeral.

"Bramble sprites?" Azatan was stunned. "I've heard of such creatures, but always thought them just a tale."

"I would never have believed it!" Rory laughed. "He knows we came here and maybe he'll follow. He can be shy and knows how to make himself invisible."

"I hope he ventures forth," Finn added, hoping Spike was within earshot, "so he can meet our new friends." But Spike didn't emerge.

They had a lot of questions about Alaska and Rory's family there. "How did your folks react to your stories of your time here? Did you tell them everything—wolf attacks and all?" Ardith referred to her husband's brush with death right there on their farm.

"Everything," Rory assured her.

"And they let you come back?" Ezat rumbled in his gravelly voice.

"They encouraged me to come back!"

"Why would they do that? What about all the danger!"

"They think I have a special calling to be here. A purpose. So, they didn't try to stop me. But I doubt that stops them from worrying."

Finn took her hand, moved by this answer. "And what do you think, Rory?"

She felt the heat rise to her cheeks as she reached for the right words to share with her little circle of friends. She met Finn's eyes and kept it simple, cutting to the heart of it.

"Live or die, it's clear to me I belong here."

By the next afternoon, the new prop was on the airplane, the cowling replaced, and Werner had rigged a hitch on the plane much like the one on his wagon, so his horses could pull it to the far end of the field. Rory used a bit of her precious phone battery to snap a picture of the bizarre moment—a horse-drawn airplane—so representative of her two worlds colliding.

Having warned everyone to stand a good distance away from the propeller, she sat in the left seat. Wow. Her airplane. Here in Gamloden. She pulled the yoke to her chest, looking back to see the aircraft's tail respond. She ran her fingers over the circuit breakers and instruments, familiar old friends. She pulled the checklist out and went through the preflight procedures, paying careful attention to each one. The airplane had not been started since the accident, much less flown. And she might not fly it today. First, she'd run the engine up a few times. Then, if everything seemed to be working okay, she'd taxi it. If that went well, she'd consider flying a few feet off the ground, then set it back down. She'd approximated the length of the field at about half a mile. Room enough to take off if the engine sounded good, and if the prop didn't vibrate in a weird way. If everything worked as it should, maybe she'd fly. She was a test pilot today and she would not allow another accident.

A half hour later, she sat at the end of the field, holding the toe brakes so firm her legs trembled. All the gauges had read normal. The airplane seemed airworthy. She had half a tank of fuel. Okay, she was going for it. She lowered ten degrees of flaps and gave it full power, releasing the brakes when the airplane was quivering. She did her best to keep the front wheel from getting too banged up in the turf. Picking up speed, the airplane gently lifted off, and Rory held it steady for a few moments just 10 feet off the ground before she pulled the power back to set it down safely at the other end of the field.

That went well. She was sure it would fly. She taxied back to the departure end of the field, where everyone was clapping and shouting. Then, she took off, again, this time climbing out and circling over the runway. The land opened up below her. Two hundred feet and she could see the nearby forest, picking out the birch trees. She wanted to find Finn's house, but she resisted. She'd bring him with her one day and show him his world from the air. The foothills mounded to the north leading to the snow-capped mountains and Rory's heart hammered with the prospect of exploring them. Not today, though.

She circled to a thousand feet, and her eye caught a moving dot just above the foothills. She'd seen a lot of wildlife from her airplane in the Alaska mountains and by the size of the spot, this was big, about the size of a moose. But flying? The speck climbed and turned and caught a ray of sun. It had wings! What? Her heart nearly stopped. The dragon! She could not let him see her—he'd turn to fight her, and she was no match for him by herself. She forced herself to remain calm, keeping the field under her as she began a descent. She squinted at the shape, studying it. Wait. Something was wrong. The dragon had a long, skinny tail and the tail on whatever this was, was shorter, thicker, softer. She let out the breath she'd been holding. What was it then? It climbed and dove, its wings pumping, then gliding. Graceful. Like a dancer. She saw sudden movement on its back. A rider! Long black hair waved like a windsock as she looked around. A woman! No doubt she'd heard the noise of the airplane and had turned to look. They studied each other for a few long moments before the woman turned the creature into the shadows. What was it? Who was she? Slowly, a dark foreboding registered in Rory as she remembered Draegin had a daughter. Queen Marinna.

Descending in spirals, she flew over the village of Tomitarn, seeing dozens of tomtees staring up and pointing at her. *You have no secrets now, sorry Werner; the whole town has seen the airplane.* She touched down gently just past the point where she'd started and slowed to a stop in the middle of the field. She shut the airplane down, seeing her friends across the field laugh and congratulate each other. They had an airplane that flew! And, with it, they could speed above the ground, bridge the distances between their lands, and give them great advantage over enemy attacks.

But Rory was focused on what she'd just seen, its significance slowly unfolding. What if that woman really was the Queen? The one who'd cursed her birth mother, trapping her in a dream-like prison for 16 years. If it hadn't been for Floxx, her mother would still be under that spell. Marinna was rarely seen; she ventured from her stone palace only to kill and destroy. So, what vile mission was she now on?

Chapter 15: Beautiful Lady

Marinna urged Conquest farther from shore, closer to the water's surface; she was drawn to it like a vampire to blood. The scent of the sea haunted her; she craved the taste of salt on her lips. The rhythmic sweep of the tides played in her mind in the night hours, soothing her to sleep. She'd been driven to come back to the sea, to risk being seen, to gamble the perils of the sirens in hope of another glimpse of them. She had a wild hope that maybe some of the sea people would know who she was. Surely her family knew she'd married Draegin. But did anyone know they'd been expecting a child? Marinna dared to dream there might be someone, a friend or a relative, who would see a family resemblance.

The stallion banked right, dipping his wing just above the water and Marinna leaned over to let its wetness splash through her fingers, up onto her wrist and arm. It was cool, but not as cold as she'd expected. She lifted herself up and Conquest flew straight and level a foot above the surface. Marinna studied the depths, laughing at the schools of fish darting from their shadow, marveling at the beauty she saw underneath. If only she had gills; she'd dive and twist and swim through that world, celebrating her heritage, fulfilling an insatiable desire to understand who she really was.

They'd flown a long way over the open water, much farther than before, skimming low, searching for faces. But no one came near. No mermaids, mermen, not even a porpoise. Where were they? Were they avoiding her? Did they know who she was and decided to shun her? Her heart sunk. Marinna slumped in the saddle, devastated.

Conquest began to climb. They hadn't gotten more than a hundred feet in the air when she was startled to see an island emerge from the sea. It appeared from out of nowhere, isolated in the great watery expanse. She urged Conquest closer, her curiosity overpowering her common sense, breaking her rule about remaining out of view. A few ships were anchored offshore on one side of the island, but they appeared to be empty of both crew and cargo. The island was small; it was no problem to see all of it from their height, perhaps 10 miles long and a few miles wide. It was entirely covered with tropical trees, their blue leafy tops blocking the view of the ground underneath. There were no clearings, and it looked as if no one lived there. But the ships? Maybe it was just a seafarer's refuge, a safe harbor in bad weather.

Her imagination ran wild. A deserted island! How perfect! This was the place of her dreams—she could rule from here! The thought made her laugh out loud, imagining a castle set in the midst of the blue canopy, defended by a fleet of her own ships. If she couldn't live under the water, she could certainly live in the middle of it.

As she turned Conquest back in the direction they'd come from, she was startled to see a ship moving toward the island. She scolded herself for being so careless as to be seen in broad daylight. She was low enough to watch the crew of dwarves concentrating on bringing the boat in safely. They hadn't noticed her at all; no one was looking up and she was sure she could pass unnoticed. The sun was on Marinna's back and she hadn't realized she'd throw a shadow on the ship's deck. The silhouette of a flying horse threw the sailors into panic. They yelled and pointed, taking cover behind anything they could find. Cowards. She smirked. Good for nothing, weak-hearted sailors.

Except one. One sailor stood alone, watching her. As she passed next to the ship, Marinna studied him, impressed with his countenance. Daring. Unafraid. To her surprise, he wasn't a dwarf at all; he was human, tall and handsome, and he did not take his eyes from her. What was he doing on a ship full of dwarves? She held his gaze as they passed, and heat rose to her face when he raised his arms to her.

"Hello," he called in a strong voice. "Welcome!"

Her heart was doing things it had never done before, lurching erratically. Her breath came in short gasps. What was happening to her? She hadn't meant to steer Conquest around the ship, but they circled, and the man turned with them, never breaking eye contact. He was saying something she couldn't quite understand, gesturing. He wanted them to land. No. Oh no, she couldn't do that; she'd completely lost her head. She urged Conquest to climb.

As they flew away from the ship, the man called, "What is your name, beautiful lady?"

She would not answer.

"Please?"

She dared not reply but couldn't resist turning around for one last look. She barely caught his words before she flew out of earshot.

"My name is Jakin."

Jakin. A strong name. He was a man of courage and daring. And he'd called her beautiful. No one had ever said that to her before. She turned her back on him, and despite her resolve to remain aloof, lifted an arm in farewell.

Night fell, and Marinna did not want to return to her palace. She couldn't bear the thought of sitting in her throne room, so dark and stuffy. She'd long been a prisoner within its walls, living in ignorance, in sheltered luxury. How could she possibly stay there after knowing the freedom outside, soaring through the sky, skimming the sea, meeting a man who called her beautiful? So, she guided Conquest to a mountain ravine, and they camped there. She leaned back on her hands, staring at the stars and contemplating Jakin. She'd heard his name before, recently, in fact. When was it? She'd mulled it over but couldn't place it. She tried to put him out of her mind as she spread her blanket to enjoy the brilliant canopy of stars.

Sleep had nearly overtaken her when she remembered. Jakin! The giant killer! Tozar had bragged about him—he was, apparently, a relative. She'd never seen the dwarf so bold, so proud. He usually groveled when he brought her pearls, but that time, he'd stood tall. Could her admirer possibly be the same Jakin? Could Tozar have a human relative? How odd, but what if it was so! A thrill coursed through her, making her giddy, and she relished the sensation. Had a famous hero—a giant killer—called her beautiful?

Marinna slept restlessly that night, dreaming fitfully and waking suddenly. She'd been running from a giant, fearing for her life, but going in circles. She couldn't get away. She saw some water in the distance and made a dash for it, diving under as soon as it was deep enough. How cool it felt, so smooth and refreshing on her skin. She swam faster than she'd ever imagined she could; it was almost like flying underwater. Then she looked at herself and realized she had a fish tail. She was a mermaid! She'd been underwater for what seemed like a long time and she could breathe! She must have gills! She swam for a long time, finally stopping to pop her head above the water's surface. The giant was nowhere in sight. In fact, there was no land in sight anywhere. She was alone in the middle of the sea. Then she saw a ship approaching. His ship. *Jakin*, she called out, *Jakin, I'm over here.* She waved her arms, calling to him again and again. But he didn't see her, and his ship passed her by. She felt a tug on her tail and looked down to see another mermaid.

"Nerida," the mermaid said, "Nerida, is that you?"

She thinks I'm my mother! Marinna dove to tell her who she was, but when she opened her mouth to speak, water rushed in and she choked. She couldn't breathe. What had happened to her gills? Frantically, she pushed for the surface, but she was so slow. She struggled, but the mermaid pulled her down. She kicked with all her strength. *Feet – I have feet, again.* She finally broke to the surface, gasping, choking, gulping air. Where was the closest shore? Which way should she swim? She saw no land, so began to swim, taking one stroke after another until exhaustion overtook her. She couldn't lift her arms and her legs were two logs dragging behind her. She looked in all directions, but all she saw was water. She was going to drown. Help! Help me! The waves grew around her, enormous, crashing over her head, muffling her screams.

She bolted upright under the stars, trembling long after she realized it had been a dream. Unwilling to close her eyes for the rest of the night, Marinna watched the sky dawn a leaden gray. A few fat raindrops splattered on her hair and she snugged in closer to the tree trunk. Conquest sauntered over, nudging her with his head.

"You want to go?" She stroked his long face. "Even in the rain?"

He whinnied.

"You understand me, don't you?" she cooed. "All right, then, let's go. What's a little rain?"

She swung onto his back, weary from the short night's sleep; the dream had left her feeling unsettled. She was glad to be heading home.

They'd no sooner left the ground when the wind picked up. They hadn't gone far before it howled around them, driving rain into their eyes, whipping Conquest's mane and her own hair in stinging swipes. She could feel her steed struggling against the wind as he descended over the sea. She knew it was sometimes less windy close to the surface, but the gale still buffeted and once a strong downdraft nearly forced them into the water. Her dream! Had it been a portent of evil; a warning of drowning in the sea today? She buried her head in his mane, giving him full rein.

"Take me home, Conquest," she pleaded. "Please, get me home safe."

He fought the wind. She feared for her life, clinging to him, despairing he could reach land before exhaustion overtook him. Suddenly she felt him descend and she dared a peek. His hooves skimmed the churning surface. They were going to crash into the sea.

"Conquest," she begged, "Keep going, you can do it! Keep flying!" Thunder crashed over her nearly jarring her from his back. She clung tighter, her head pressed against his neck, as the sea churned around her. Terrified, she gulped a last breath, squeezed her eyes shut, and prepared to sink into the cold black water.

But they didn't fall into the sea. Instead, the stallion touched down on land. Stunned, she saw they'd made it to an island. The island! Conquest was trudging through the storm to a grove of trees not far from where she'd seen Jakin on the ship yesterday. As soon as the horse found shelter, she slid from his back and collapsed in the wet undergrowth.

"Hello?" a voice called from somewhere far away.

That voice. It was from her dream. She drifted back into deep slumber, but then heard it, again.

"Hello? Where are you?"

She stirred. Where was she? She had no idea. And it was hard to move. Slowly she drifted awake, shivering in the cold. Like a flood, it all came back to her, the terrible storm and nearly crashing into the water. But she was alive! She pried one eye open, looking for Conquest. Ah, there he was, resting close by. She sighed in relief. They'd made it to the island. They were safe. How fortunate they'd found this tiny haven in the roiling expanse of the sea.

"Hello!" The voice was louder now. Wet leaves moved, throwing raindrops on her. She curled into a tighter ball. Perhaps whoever it was would not see her and go away. She was averse to being discovered, but she didn't have the strength to run. She heard footsteps, felt the movement of the foliage that covered her, then a cool hand touched her head.

"Beautiful lady!" the voice whispered.

Her eyes snapped open. Jakin! She struggled to sit up, but his hand pressed against her efforts.

"Rest, please. I will stay here with you and no one will bother you. Sleep, beautiful lady, under cover from the rain."

Sleep? Of course, she wouldn't sleep! It was impossible with a stranger next to her. She didn't stir as he settled against a tree a few feet away where he could see both Conquest and her. She heard the stallion snort, but he didn't move toward Jakin. She'd never known the horse to tolerate anyone but her. She felt betrayed by her Pegasus. Then she realized he, too, was weary, perhaps too exhausted to move. She was contemplating whether she could trust Jakin when she fell back asleep.

The rain had stopped by the time she awoke, though the sky was still low and gray. She sat abruptly, gasping as pain surged through her head. The next moment, Jakin was next to her, supporting her shoulders.

"Easy now."

She balked at his touch and stood, putting some distance between them. Could he see her blushing?

"You had quite a ride. I couldn't believe it when I saw your horse appear in the gloom. Fate has certainly smiled on me to bring you here. I'd been waiting on the ship all night, hoping for another glimpse of you."

He waited for her? In a storm? What did he want with her? "Do not be so familiar with me. If you knew who I was you would fear for your life."

He bowed before her, maintaining his distance. "I know you are the one who has captured my heart and if you should leave without a few words, I would, indeed, fear for my life for I would die of heartbreak."

Her heart trembled, and she avoided his eyes. He was casting a spell on her and yet she would willingly believe his sorcery. She should go. Conquest ambled over, nudging her as he did when he was hungry. "Fine protector you are," she scolded the steed under her breath. "I, too, am famished." She reached into the soggy saddlebag and retrieved two apples, holding one in her palm for the horse and raising one to her lips. She changed her mind at the last minute and tossed it to Jakin, saying primly, "In payment for your protection."

He caught it and took a bite, then held it at arm's length in wonder. He studied her, incredulous. "I've eaten these apples before, and know they are from a certain tree far from here. Tell me, please, how you came to have such fruit?" He took a second bite.

Did he know the tree the ghillie had spoken of? "I sought the best apples for my Pegasus, and these were what I found."

"By far, the best! I cannot argue that." He grinned and let the subject drop, studying her intensely.

She found it unnerving and turned to mount the stallion.

He held out his hand, imploring, "Must you leave so soon, beautiful lady? Before I even know your name?"

Her name? What would she tell him? Surely not the truth. "Nerida," she said, her mother's name the first to pop into her head.

"Nerida," he repeated and dropped to one knee, his hand over his heart. "I am at your service. Please stay a while longer."

She hesitated. A voice sounding like her father's warned that lingering would surely lead to trouble. But another voice, musical as she imagined her mother's had been, disagreed. What harm would it be to stay a moment with an admirer on a small island? No one would see her; and she faced no threats. She deserved someone special, even if just for a short time.

Jakin reached for her hand and her heart lurched. Heat flooded her face. "Come with me, Nerida. There's a dry, warm place on the ship where we can talk."

She took his hand, all arguments silenced by the rush of pleasure she felt. "My steed?" she asked, more to draw his attention away from her reddened face than out of concern.

"Will he stay here and not wander?"

"He will."

"Come then, we shall not be long."

Chapter 16: Berry Trees

Aric had been gone for hours, and he was hungry. He imagined Kalvara was looking for him, maybe even climbing some trees, checking all the places he might hide. *Please don't worry, Kalvara. I'm fine and I'll be home soon. I just had to get away from the Tall King.*

He remembered their conversation. "If I hunt birds in his gardens, the King gets angry," he'd complained to her. "And when he gets angry, he scares me."

Though she'd assured him he had nothing to be afraid of, that the King really liked him and wanted him to be part of his family, he didn't agree. And, anyway, he didn't want to be part of the Tall King's family. Nothing would be worse than having to live underground. Bile rose in his throat, remembering the King's hand on Kalvara's shoulder. He touched her too much. She acted like she was pleased, and he couldn't figure out why.

"Let's just stay here awhile," she'd said, as if they had a choice. "We don't have to stay forever."

"Can't you see we're caught?" He'd glared at her. "We can't leave; we're captives here just like in Droome." And he'd stalked off and didn't regret it one bit.

Aric stared into the pool, consoling himself with the beauty of the reflection. He focused on the waterfalls feeding it fresh water, three of them, all with different sounds. He could isolate each one and enjoy its rhythm, and then allow his ears to harmonize their sounds. He let in a bit of bird song and the croak of a frog and he had a mix that lifted his dejected soul. Maybe it wasn't so bad here. They weren't starving, and they weren't being beaten or worked to death.

But he despised the Tall King. He was mean on the inside, cold-hearted; he hadn't cared at all that Finn or Rory, or both, would die in that arena. In fact, the King was so furious when they'd both escaped, that Aric hadn't even smiled for fear of triggering his wrath. He'd been cheering on the inside, though, and bursting with pride for Spike—for his tiny friend had saved both Finn and Rory! He really wanted to see Spike; he'd looked everywhere for him, and finally realized the bramble had probably escaped, too. His heart sunk at the thought of never seeing any of them again.

He reached down and ruffled the water's surface, counting how long it took the ripples to still. He made a game of it; left hand against right, ruffle, wait, ruffle, wait. As he watched the water still for the last time, he studied his reflection. His face had changed; he wasn't as skinny. His white hair had been washed and tied back with a piece of vine. He and Kalvara were the only ones with white hair. The only ones with reddish eyes. The tall ones maybe were distant family, but they were dark haired and brown eyed. Kalvara said that was because they went above from time to time and the sun kept them from being as pale as the eldrows in Droome.

A movement interrupted his thoughts. A blue dot came from out of nowhere and hovered in the reflection right over his head. Aric rolled out from under it, springing up in alarm. After the vapors, he wasn't taking any chances. It bobbled there above the place where he had been, and he recognized it right away.

"Uriel!" he called, holding out his small hand.

The blue orb gently settled in his palm.

"A friend," Aric whispered, holding the light at eye level. "Now I have a friend." The glow brightened in response.

"I'm not scared with you!" Aric said, jumping up. "Let's go explore." And the two set off into the forest. He stayed off the paths, weaving through the trees, instead, and found a shallow stream to follow. He saw a few turquoise berries on the forest floor, like the ones he'd eaten above. He whooped and gobbled them up! They were not quite as juicy as the ones Topside, but they were delicious! He craned his neck to see what tree they'd fallen from and saw he'd stumbled into a small stand of blue-leafed tropical trees. What were they doing down here?

He shimmied up one of the smooth trunks in no time and sat there gorging on the fresh fruit, enjoying the view, pretending he was king of the world. He would make things better. He would let people go free and do what they wanted. When he couldn't eat even one more berry, he burped and studied the forest, mostly evergreens, but also some birch and other leafy trees. Much to his surprise, he realized the berry trees formed a circle, their leaves forming a wreathlike canopy. He peered over the edge. They'd grown so big the center of the wreath was nearly covered with leaves.

"Will you look at that, Uriel! I wonder if I could climb from one to the other through the tops!" And he found a sturdy branch and jumped to the next tree, laughing.

Uriel was floating in a slow loop just above the treetops.

"Who do you think planted these trees Underside?" Aric called to his friend. "And how come the tall ones don't eat the berries? Do you think they even know about them?"

Twigs snapped as someone approached the grove. Aric ducked. He soon caught the murmur of voices and it wasn't long before a pair of dwarves appeared toting empty buckets.

"Here we are now. Let's get to it," one dwarf said to the other.

"I'll wade into the stream and fill the pails and hand 'em to ye. You carry 'em back and pour 'em around these trees, see? Six of 'em, so three trips. They each get a whole bucket full."

"Why so much water?" the other dwarf complained. "Wouldn't half a bucket do?"

"Nope, orders is one full bucket for each tree, every day. Them tall ones want their tall trees filled up with water and growin' good." The dwarf glanced up but Aric had made himself as small as he could and wasn't seen. The two walked off and in their absence, the boy pulled himself behind a couple of big leaves. He watched the one dwarf lug the buckets back and forth, three trips, obediently watering each tree. He picked up every berry on the ground with a rag, careful not to touch it. Why didn't he eat the ones on the ground?

"Seems a lot o' work for trees 'at grow poison fruit," he muttered to himself. "Don't make no sense."

As soon as the watering was finished, the dwarves trudged back the way they'd come. Poison fruit? No way! Aric felt fine. He watched as they followed a small trail out of sight. He'd wondered where it led.

He wrapped a handful of berries in a piece of leaf for Kalvara, noting there were no brambles in these berry clusters. He sighed. Not a chance of making a new friend.

"C'mon, Uriel," the boy whispered. "Let's follow those dwarves."

The trail was little more than a trodden footpath worn through the trees probably by those two dwarves. Aric wound his way easily, in the silent, graceful movements of a young elf. When he heard the noise of dwarf children, he climbed a tree to observe before venturing closer.

Five small shacks leaned at crooked angles in a tight half circle, with one large firepit out front. Chunks of meat roasted on the coals, strips of raw fish hung from a tripod in the smoke, and a couple of dwarf women kept the smudgy fire going. Two dirty children raced around the camp and the women alternated between warning them about the fire and scolding them about kicking dirt onto the meat. Finally, an old gray dwarf climbed out of one of the huts and with one authoritative motion, shooed the rambunctious children away. The old one straightened as much as he could, stabbed a chunk of meat from the hot coals, and limped back inside. Insects buzzed lazily just outside the smoke, waiting for a chance to alight on the hanging fish.

Aric didn't see a vegetable in sight, and he grimaced at the thought of eating just meat and fish. No wonder dwarves were so grumpy all the time. No juicy berries, no crunchy vegetables. He stretched as high as he dared above the treetops, searching for the children and he would have missed them altogether had one not emerged, crying, out of a tunnel they had apparently been playing in. The larger child followed quickly, pulling on the smaller one's arm, begging him not to tell.

Aric was captivated by the tunnel. Where did it lead? Down or up? Was it guarded? He watched for so long he got hungry, again, and with a silent apology to Kalvara, ate her berries, shoving the leaf back into his pocket so at least he could show her that. He waited as the women checked the hanging fish, cooked a second batch of meat, then finally baked misshapen loaves of bread. Always the coals stayed red, always the smoke fogged the air.

He had nearly fallen asleep when commotion from the children brought him back to high alert. Four dwarves were climbing out of the tunnel; men coming home. Where had they been? Two carried strings of fresh fish. Fish! Were these dwarves, sailors? The two others hauled a small barrel and hollered hearty greetings to their families. The women rushed to collect the fresh fish and set them in the smoke, batting away flies. The other two men lowered their cask to a flat rock, unhooked metal cups from their belts and filled them. Aric caught the scent of ale. Laughter and cheers boomed through the little village as the women and children gathered to eat dinner. Maybe they weren't grumpy all the time.

This was Aric's chance. No one noticed as he tiptoed around the back of the shacks and ducked into the tunnel. After the first curve he squatted next to the wall, waiting for his eyes to adjust. But he needn't have bothered; Uriel went ahead, lighting the way with his blue glow. The voices of the dwarves faded as they walked, and Aric listened hard into the heavy silence.

They came to a fork in the tunnel. He heard scraping coming from the left fork, and was glad Uriel took the right. He didn't want to meet whatever was making that noise. Further on, another tunnel branched off from the main one, but they stuck with the wider space. If Aric's hunch was correct, it led above and was the route the dwarves used to go to work. But it was so long! Winding left, then right, sometimes up and sometimes down.

He shuddered as he remembered the caves of Droome and their horrors. Suddenly, a bang! He fell to a crouch, shielding his head instinctively. Then, another bang. Muffled voices in the distance. No! He couldn't get caught! He had to get to the outside before he met them. He sprinted along the tunnel, trusting Uriel to lead the way. Another few turns, and the darkness lightened; the voices grew distinct.

"Let's go, hurry it up, get them crates on, and be quick about it!" Nizat! He'd know that harsh voice anywhere.

The tunnel widened, and shadows danced on the walls. Its mouth was concealed with shrubs. Aric peeked through. He'd been right! The tunnel brought them within a short sprint of the docks! No wonder they'd not seen any dwarves Topside. They cut back and forth underground. Another loud crack drew Nizat's wrath as a crate slipped and splintered on the dock. Pearls spilled all over, just like they had in Syrea.

Some rolled as far as the tunnel entrance. In a rash move, Aric darted out, grabbed a few of the pearls and dashed back in. Kalvara would believe him when she saw the pearls. He could convince her escape would be easy. He would tell her no one guarded the entrance or the exit, and no one except dwarves used the tunnels.

He needed to get home. Kalvara must be really upset. He turned toward the darkness and silently followed Uriel back to the mouth of the cave, waiting until he was sure all the dwarves in the village were asleep. He was hungry enough to eat even stringy meat, but there wasn't a morsel left as he crept past the firepit. He'd stop at the berry trees and eat, again, and bring some fresh ones to Kalvara. It was very late by the time Aric had finally eaten his fill. He lay back in the nook on the branches, unable to keep his eyes open.

"You stand guard," he told Uriel, yawning. "I need a nap. Just a short one," he mumbled as he drifted off.

He woke with a jolt, knowing he'd slept a long time. Kalvara would be pacing, worrying so much, she might make him stay inside for days. Not now; not when they could escape! He looked around for Uriel but didn't see him. He called softly for him, but he wasn't there. He stood to slide down the trunk, studying the blue canopy. There he was, his soft light glowing in another berry tree.

"What are you doing over there? C'mon, Uriel, we have to go. I'm in so much trouble."

Aric started to descend, calling the orb, again and again. But Uriel would not budge. Puzzled at his bizarre behavior, Aric poked his head through the branches.

"What's the matter, Uriel? Are you stuck?"

Uriel didn't move. He stayed in one place, a good way out of Aric's reach.

"Have you got some really good berries?" Aric stretched himself to see. "They look like all the rest of 'em to me."

Uriel lifted just a little and Aric studied the cluster of berries. "Juicy ones, maybe? You think I should pick them?"

He wished Uriel could talk but he never did when he was just a light. He had a sudden, thrilling thought. "Spike? Have you found 'im?"

The branches were thin where Uriel was, but Aric was willing to risk a fall to find his friend. He climbed gingerly, feeling the branches bend dangerously, and stretched as far as he could to peer at the berries. No brambles. Not one. Disappointed, he started to climb back but the orb brightened and settled, again, on the berries, then rose a foot above them. What was Uriel trying to say? Aric studied the berries, picking one to sample. Delicious, just like the dozens he'd already eaten. The orb flickered, and in the light, Aric saw a glint among the berries. He would never have noticed it without Uriel's persistence. He leaned closer to have a look.

"What is that?" Aric asked. Gripping the branches with his legs, he reached for it, poking among the berries for the shiny thing. It was deeply hidden in layers of the fruit. He lost his balance as he dug, and flailing for something to hold on to, he clutched the leaf desperately and felt something hard in his hand. "I got it!" he said, wrapping it in his fist, then cautiously pulling himself to a more stable position. He held up a blue stone for Uriel to see. Even in the darkness, it was beautiful.

The orb shot high in the air and back, blinking in celebration.

"You're excited about this?" Aric examined it, turning it over and over, feeling its smoothness. "It's pretty, I'll give you that. Never saw a rock all shiny like this one. Okay, I'm putting it in my pocket with the pearls. See?" And he dropped the stone into his clothing. "Can we go now?"

Uriel shot to the bottom of the tree, beating Aric to the ground.

"Got it safe right here," Aric reassured his friend, patting his tunic. "Now, let's hurry up and get home."

Chapter 17: Reunion

Finn's heart swelled as he watched Rory fly. What a woman! So smart, so capable, so beautiful. She was a treasure. His treasure. Surely, she'd been sent to him from Eldurrin. Surely, Eldurrin had made him just for her. Who else could weave together two hearts like theirs? But their situation was impossible; here he was, tasked to reconstruct a mythical crown whose restoration would likely ignite a world war. And Rory was to rule as Queen of Byerman. How could they follow their hearts when their destinies were incompatible?

Rory rolled to a stop in the middle of Werner's pasture, and Finn was the first to reach her. He was laughing at her wondrous flight, thrilled to see the airplane fly. But she wasn't laughing. She wasn't even smiling. She didn't make a move to open the door and get out. He knocked on the window, and she jolted back to the present, threw the door open and gripped his arm.

"Marinna! I saw her, Finn. She was riding a flying horse. She saw me. She looked right at me and I know she knew who I was!"

He was stunned. "Queen Marinna? On a flying horse?"

Rory was close to hysterics. "Yes. She saw me, Finn. Now she knows I'm here and what I look like."

He pulled her close. This was huge. Would Marinna take up the deadly hunt her father had started? The hunt for Rory, the love of his life. To try to kill her. No way was he going to let this go on. The others were within earshot, laughing and carrying on, too noisy to overhear.

"Rory," he whispered into her ear. "I'm with you. Floxx is with us. All the tennins are on our side. We will protect you like we have been doing. It's going to be okay." He gently pried her fingers loose from the vise grip she had on his arm.

Ezat and Azatan burst into their conversation, oblivious to her trembling, lifted her into the air and paraded around the airplane. "Behold the flying princess!" they yelled, and the others boomed, "Here, here! The flying princess!"

Finn saw her manage a smile, but it was shaky and for good reason. There was a flying queen to face.

They stayed a few more days on the farm, filling in holes in the grass runway, working on the airplane and test flying it, again; this time with no sign of Marinna. They'd packed after dinner and walked to the ancient apple tree for a few minutes alone. If the weather was good, Rory planned to fly with Finn to the castle in the morning. She wanted to see her mother; she'd been away a long time.

"Maybe I was mistaken," Rory confessed to Finn as they sat by the water. "Is it unusual to see a Pegasus here? Is it possible someone else was flying it and I just overreacted?"

"Unusual, yes. Very rare. I've never seen one, though I have heard of sightings. And maybe it could have been someone else, though I've no idea who." He plucked a leaf from her hair. "It's a bigger world than I realized, Rory. I mean, I never knew about eldrows and tall ones and ghillies and bramble sprites and I've lived here all my life, thinking I knew all there was to know about Gamloden."

"I wonder what else there is," she murmured, leaning her head on his shoulder.

Finn wondered the same thing. But he wouldn't think of it now. He was content for the moment to sit close to her by his favorite apple tree, listening to the rippling Dryad River, and trust their future to Eldurrin.

A couple of days later, Rory mustered up the courage to make two short flights, one with Azatan and Ezat, and one with Werner and Ardith. Azatan, fearless dwarf that he was, was dizzy and sick by the time they landed. The other three loved flying; and enthused over and over about seeing Tomitarn and their farm from the air. They hoped they could go again, sometime. Rory hadn't told them about seeing Marinna. She didn't want to alarm Werner and Ardith for no reason, though she'd been constantly on edge about seeing her, again. Those two dear tomtees had been through enough for her sake. She was leaving partly to keep them safe from Droome's scrutiny.

Spike had finally arrived late the night before, just in time to join Rory and Finn as they took off for the castle early the next morning. He straddled the compass as they flew over the Birch Forest, exclaiming at everything below. "I'd never have believed it! I've flown all over my island but didn't realize how much more there was! I mean, look at all the different trees and not one is blue! And mountains and a river! This is so different!"

Finn agreed, amazed himself at the wonder of seeing his world from above. Rory banked right and flew over some familiar trees, grinning. Finn stared down in awe! "My house! Rory, it's my house!" She laughed and flew a circle around it, so he could see it from every angle. She pulled her phone out and snapped a picture of it, just one, then turned it off, saving the dwindling battery for other shots. Then, she rocked the wings of the airplane to say good-bye and they turned back on course.

"Thank you, Mi Laroz" he blurted, then blushed hot when he realized what he'd called her. Dearest one. His parents had called each other that, an affectionate Dwarvish phrase they'd learned from Zad's father. Well, it was true. She was his dearest one and it was time he said it. He stole a glance at her. She was smiling and blushing, somehow understanding the tenderness of his words.

"Look at those mountains!" Spike was bouncing on the compass, pointing. "Huge and pointed like the brambles on my back! What's that white stuff on their tops?"

"Snow," Finn laughed. "Frozen water."

Spike for once had no words. He just stared at Finn.

"You've never seen snow before?"

"Never." He turned to look, again. "Tell me about it, Finn."

"It's different from ice, but you probably don't know ice, either."

Spike shook his head.

"Snow falls from clouds in small flakes when it's cold outside. It's soft, not hard like ice, and it's beautiful to watch falling. It accumulates in frozen white piles and melts when the temperature warms enough to turn it back into water."

"Wondrous!" Spike marveled. "So, I may conclude that it's cold on the tops of those mountains?"

"Correct!" Finn replied, amazed, again, at the tiny creature's intelligence.

They flew over the Caladrius River flowing south to the Syrean Sea and Finn saw the bridge spanning the turbulent water. He remembered the terrible battles they'd faced near there, how Rory had been kidnapped, how they'd faced the dragon, and how Ezat and Azatan's Uncle Zad had been killed. He ached at the horrific memory. He missed his friend and grieved his tragic death; they'd been so close growing up. South of the bridge the water roiled as the Caladrius River met the Tennindrow and they battled for space in the narrow riverbed.

He turned to watch Rory flying. Her jaw was set as she watched outside continually, looking for birds and unexpected obstacles, especially a Pegasus. She'd shared with him how she judged wind direction and speed from the way the leaves blew. She peeked often at the aircraft panel, keeping an eye on the gauges. She seemed especially concerned with two of them and he asked her why.

"Fuel," she pointed to the indicator. "And engine temperature." She didn't elaborate. He hoped she wouldn't need to.

They crossed into Masirika, the capital of Byerman, the land of humans, on the other side of the river. People below pointed. Some ran for cover; others were too stunned to move. She roared right over city center and stirred up a huge commotion, then completed the checklist to land on the long road leading to the castle.

Finn held his breath as the ground loomed, holding himself so tense his knuckles whitened. But he shouldn't have worried. He barely felt the touch down. Rory was so gentle it took him a moment to realize they were actually on the ground. She taxied to the huge circular entrance, pulled to the side, and shut the airplane off.

Dozens of castle staff swarmed them before they could get out. Spike hid in the hood of Finn's cloak as they faced their greeters. Hugs and tears and warm welcomes poured over them both, laced with astonishment at the airplane. What was it? How did it fly? You really flew it? Where have you been? We've missed you.

Finn spotted Queen Raewyn before Rory did. She was on the balcony, watching everything. When she caught Rory's eye, she lifted her arm and Rory waved both arms in greeting.

"Let's go see mother!" she said, and they hurried to the castle.

Rory and the Queen swiped at their eyes, and hugged, again. They were sitting in the Queen's suite by the fireplace, enjoying its warmth.

"It's so good to see you, dear! I've missed you terribly. Floxx has been gone a lot, too, I don't know where and she won't tell. But I've managed quite well on my own, if I say so myself."

Rory laughed. "Of course, you have, mother. I never doubted you would!"

"But now that you're back," the Queen said with a conspiratorial smile, "it will be so much better!"

Rory said nothing.

"We will work together, and I'll show you everything I've done. Wait till you see the castle; we've restored the ballroom and planted a huge garden around your father's mausoleum—it's gorgeous! With no giant and no dragon to threaten us for the moment, we are operating in peace and our people are beginning to recover from the terrible shock of the attack."

The Queen finally realized her daughter hadn't said a word. "What is it, dear? Are you all right?"

Finn pulled his chair closer to Rory's and reached over to take her hand. He feared how her mother might react to the gesture, but he held tight and looked Queen Raewyn in the eye.

Her gaze flitted from Rory to Finn to their interlocked hands and back again. "Rory," she said firmly this time. She wanted an answer.

Rory looked at her mother and sighed. "Mother, you know I love you."

Raewyn put her hand over her heart, barely nodding.

Finn squeezed Rory's hand, encouraging her to go on.

"I think about you often; mostly worrying really, about your health, about the castle, about my responsibility to rule eventually as Queen." She let out a breath. "I miss father so much. It was all so horrible."

Neither said anything for a moment.

"But when I was in Alaska, I realized my heart wasn't focused on being Queen—I wasn't thinking about it, not planning for it, not excited about it. I don't see myself ruling. Mother, my heart is set on Finn. I came back for him."

Heat rushed through him.

"I couldn't stop thinking about him. I knew he was with Kalvara and Aric and I was resigned to let him go if he wanted to be with her, but it broke my heart. And I thought I'd lost him for good."

Finn's throat constricted. He was glad he didn't have to say a word; he wasn't sure he could.

Raewyn studied them in silence. Finn dreaded what she was thinking. Did she hate him for stealing her daughter's heart? Would she allow this relationship to persist? As if she could stop it. His heart hammered in his chest and he wondered if Rory could feel the pulse in his fingertips.

Rory continued, "One night I was at my window, thinking of Finn, and reaching out for Floxx. She surprised me with a visit and told me Finn was in trouble. Immediately, I told Gram and Dad and they encouraged me to come back, even though they knew how dangerous it might be. They feel very strongly that my place is here, at least for now, so they let me go. Gram had a Firebird feather that I used to get back, but I focused on Finn, to go where he was. And, sure enough he was in trouble."

Finn listened as she recounted the whole tale of the island. And right on cue, as she talked about their escape from the arena, Spike climbed out of his hood and down his arm to stand on top of their joined hands.

"If I may say, Your Majesty, I witnessed it all and she speaks the truth."

Queen Raewyn gaped at the tiny creature.

"Pardon me for my rudeness in interrupting, without even an introduction." He bowed grandly. "Parviflorus Rubus Rosales, seventh generation, at your service." He straightened and continued in the next breath. "But please, call me Spike."

A smile played at the corners of the Queen's mouth.

"Now," the tiny bramble continued, "your daughter is a brave young woman, bravest I've ever seen. And Finn! Well, there's none so loyal, nor so kind." Spike lifted both arms in a gesture of pleading. "I beg you, dear Queen and loving mother, give them your blessing."

Raewyn rose and walked to him, bending to take Spike's tiny hand in hers. "You, my new little friend, are very wise." Then she turned to Rory, a look of wonder on her face. "You have my blessing, dear daughter. You must follow your heart, and I will support you in your choices." She met Finn's gaze and said warmly, "Welcome, Finn. It's wonderful to see you, again. My daughter's heart is a great gift and I trust you will guard it well."

"With my life," he said and meant it sincerely.

Raewyn took Rory's free hand and pulled her up. "Come on, then, all of you. Let me show you what we've accomplished. Then, tonight, perhaps after dinner, we can talk about your plans. I hope they include at least a short stay here. Spike, would you do me the honor?" Raewyn extended her open palm.

"The honor is mine, Your Majesty!" And he gracefully leapt onto her hand.

Chapter 18: Poison

Kalvara leapt at the sound of Aric's footsteps. She raced outside and scooped him up, tears of relief stinging her eyes. "Where have you been?" she said, setting him down but keeping a firm grip on him.

"I'm sorry, Kalvara, truly I am," a contrite Aric said, fearing the consequences of his behavior. "Uriel and I went exploring. We found some berry trees, see?" He held out the crumpled blue leaf, wet with juice and bruised berries. "For some reason, the people here think they are poison berries, but I ate a lot of them, and they are fine." He caught his breath and plowed on, "But most important, Kalvara," he lowered his voice to a whisper. "We found a way out, an escape route! It goes all the way to the ships!"

Kalvara stared at him. "A way out? Slow down, Aric. Wait, did you say Uriel is here?"

"Up there!" Aric pointed above her head where the blue orb brightened in greeting.

"Well that's a relief. At least you weren't alone!"

"I wouldn't have gone so far by myself." Aric picked a berry from the leaf. "Try it; it's so delicious!"

Kalvara obliged. It was tangy and sweet. The burst of flavor brought back memories she'd shoved down, memories of forests and fresh air and freedom. She loosened her grip on the boy.

"Go to bed right now. It's nearly morning already."

Without another word, Aric placed the leaf in her hand and went straight to his room.

She lifted her head to Uriel. "Thank you. Thank you for keeping him safe. I was terribly worried."

The orb floated in front of her and blinked once, then followed Aric to his bed.

Kalvara was not sleepy, so she opened the door to sit outside, thinking starlight would be most welcome. Starlight! How foolish she was! She had momentarily forgotten she was underground. The darkness was thick and silent. Everyone slept. She picked another berry from the leaf and let its flavor explode in her mouth. Aric! How she loved him; he looked just like her brother had as a child and had the same fearlessness. Escape. Was it even possible? Should she risk her life and Aric's, again, when they were living here in peace?

It wasn't terrible here—much, much better than they'd had it in Droome. They faced no threats, the King was kind, they had plenty of food and a place to live. Why was the King treating them so well? He'd never hinted at any reason other than that they were distant family. Long lost and reunited kin. She believed him. She liked him. No one had ever treated her with such gentleness and respect. He listened to her stories, ideas, concerns. He'd assured her she need not worry about anything; he would take care of her. She'd never, ever had rest like this; she'd always feared for her life, scraping out a bare survival, wary of anyone she met. But did she really trust him? She wanted to. She tried to. She told Aric she did. But something gnawed at her deep down. She'd been reluctant to face it. Aric was right, the King was sly. He had ulterior motives for everything he did. She wondered what it was he wanted from her?

Approaching footsteps woke Kalvara from where she'd fallen asleep on the ground outside her door. She clambered up and brushed herself off, just in time to see breakfast arriving, carried on wooden trays by the two dwarves who'd been assigned to her.

"Good morning!" she greeted them, hoping they'd not noticed she'd been sleeping outside. "That smells wonderful!" She opened the door and motioned them in where they set the trays on the small table. "Just leave it, today, please. No need to stay and serve. Aric is still sleeping, so I will wait for him to wake." They bowed graciously without a word and left.

A cup of tea sounded wonderful, so Kalvara poured hot water over the tea leaves in her cup, savoring the minty fragrance that filled the room. She sat sipping, content, relishing the quiet before Aric awoke. Her thoughts turned to Rory and Finn. Did they get off the island? Where would they have gone? She pictured them together, Rory leaving her family—both families—to come to his aid; he so obviously fond of her. She sighed. It would never have worked for her and Finn. She had dreamed maybe it could have been the three of them, but he'd never looked at her the way he looked at Rory. She and Finn were friends, nothing more. She smiled wistfully as memories flooded her mind, remembering her terrible hatred of him initially, and how he'd not hated back, how he'd been generous and kind, saving her and Aric's life more than once in that tragic journey to get Rory to the castle.

Maybe there was someone Underside for her. Someone to look at her in that way. She dared hope it might be the Tall King, that love might soften his hardness. She heard Aric rustling in bed; he'd probably wake up hungry since he'd eaten nothing but berries yesterday. They were a real treat Underside and she wondered why the people thought they were poisonous.

"Oh!" she said aloud, scrambling out of the chair. She'd left the berries outside! She pulled the door open, eager to eat what was left of them. But they were gone! She looked everywhere, but there was no trace of them, not even a piece of blue leaf. Had they blown away? Had an animal come to eat them? Maybe the servants picked them up? Disappointment welled, but she consoled herself thinking Aric could bring more home.

She turned to go back inside but was surprised to hear the Tall King call to her. What was he doing here at this time of day? Why was he coming to her home? Adrenaline surged as she spun around. His dangling gold earrings swung wildly as he approached with quick, determined footsteps. Surely, he was on a mission. She bowed as she always did, and when he drew near, he took her hand to help her up.

"Kalvara," he said without a hint of his usual smile. He looked around to be sure no one was watching. "We must talk. Inside if possible."

She hesitated, feeling vulnerable inviting him into the privacy of her house, but reluctantly pushed the door open for him.

"After you," he murmured, and she nodded and went inside.

He surveyed the room in one glance and asked her whether she found her accommodations satisfactory.

"More than satisfactory," she assured him. "This is lovely, and Aric and I are deeply grateful.

"Aric." The King eyed the closed bedroom door. "He is here?"

"Yes, he came back late last night. He'd been exploring and fallen asleep in the woods." She laughed.

But the King did not laugh.

"Little boys!" She continued. "Such rascals. But eventually they come home!" She saw movement in the small opening between the bottom of Aric's door and the floor. He was awake and probably listening.

The King reached into his pocket and retrieved a crushed blue leaf and a half dozen mushy berries.

"Oh!" Kalvara was startled. "Where did you get those?"

The King said stiffly, "That is my question for you, Kalvara." His voice had an edge. What could possibly be wrong with picking and eating berries?

Her protective instinct took over. "I found them, sir, on the forest floor, when I was searching for Aric. We'd eaten them topside and knew how delicious they were, so I brought a few home."

"Did you eat any of them?"

"Yes, a few. Not many."

"Well, you are indeed very fortunate! These berries are terribly poisonous; even one is potent enough to be fatal! It is long-established knowledge that picking them is strictly forbidden, even off the forest floor."

Something about his overt lie unnerved her. Kalvara touched her throat with her fingers. "Oh! I did not know, Your Highness. I had no idea! I am indeed fortunate. Oh my, I will never risk it, again!"

"The servants saw these outside your door and feared perhaps someone had tried to kill you."

"No, Your Highness, though I apparently came close to doing the job myself."

"You give me your word that you will not return to those berry trees?"

She shook her head. "You have my promise."

He sat back, relieved. "Good. Well then, that is that." Then he had another thought. He leaned close and whispered. "Aric. Are you sure the boy wasn't anywhere near the area?"

Kalvara tensed. He needed to leave Aric out of this. "He was nowhere to be seen; I searched everywhere, calling, begging him to answer. I picked up a few berries, thinking to tempt him with them, but even that got no response. So, I returned home," she lied.

"I see." He seemed satisfied. He stood and bade her a stiff farewell, taking the berries with him and let himself out.

Kalvara sat in stunned silence. What was that all about? He's upset about berries? They most certainly are not poisonous, and he must know that, so why did he lie and forbid me to eat even one? And if the berries are deadly, as he claimed, why not cut the trees down and eliminate the risk?

Aric silently pulled the door open and tip-toed to her. "I heard everything," he whispered.

She glanced out the window and noticed a guard, partially hidden behind a tree. They were being watched. Her adrenaline spiked. With a mixture of fear and confusion in her voice, she said, "Tell me everything that happened with the berry trees. Don't leave anything out."

Aric crawled on her lap and spoke barely above a whisper. When he got to their trek back from the dwarf village, he remembered the pearls in his pocket and he reached for them, asking her to close her eyes because he had a surprise for her. He'd forgotten about the blue rock, but he felt it, mixed with the pearls.

Uriel hovered near the window, just out of sight. Kalvara picked up the pearls one by one, admiring them. She reached for the blue stone, but Uriel flew to her, flickering urgently. She quickly closed her fingers around it, frowning.

"Where did you get this, Aric?"

As he told her the story, Uriel returned to the window, watching outside, keeping his blue light from being seen.

"He wouldn't leave till I got it!" Aric whispered, nodding at the orb, "even though we were already so late." He reached up and took her face in his small hands. "Kalvara, this must be an important rock. Why else would a tennin be so excited to find it? Remember Floxx's song that night we were captured?"

She didn't. She'd been furious at being tied to the tree; frantic at being in the presence of an elf; fuming with hatred for Finn. She hadn't heard a thing.

"It was a star story about a war and a crown some ruler had lost a long, long time ago. There were three stones, and I think one was blue. Floxx sang about them and I imagined how beautiful that crown must have been. Finn's looking for the elves, Kalvara, to remake a crown. Right?"

She nodded. Yes, of course. She knew that.

"I think Uriel has found the blue stone that goes in it."

She caught her breath, stunned with the implications of what that might mean.

Kalvara kept Aric inside all day on the pretense of resting, asking the dwarves to bring their meals to them. It hadn't taken long for them to put the pieces together. The berries weren't poisonous at all; just the perfect hiding place for the invaluable blue gem that had been there perhaps for eons. The King's ruse about the berries being poisonous was just to protect this most precious asset. Had she not held his favor, they might have been killed with no explanation, just to ensure they told no one else about the grove of trees.

The more she pondered, the more worried she became. Surely, he would send a confidant to climb the trees to verify the stone was still safe; perhaps it was happening right now. Once he realized it was missing, she and Aric would be in grave danger; the favor they had enjoyed replaced by suspicion. They would be searched, questioned, and imprisoned until the stone was found. And if it was found in their possession, they'd be killed for deception and theft. They had to leave immediately; they had to deliver the stone to Finn. She began to make a plan.

An hour before dinner, Kalvara and Aric walked to the pools, fully aware they were being watched. It was customary to bathe and dress for dinner in the King's court and he had bidden their presence tonight. Kalvara had cleverly braided the gem into her hair and she felt sure it would not loosen or become visible even if they were chased. They'd brought clean clothes to wear, planning to roll their dirty ones into their satchels to retrieve after dinner. Kalvara was sure the bags would be searched while they ate, but she wasn't concerned. They did exactly what they normally did at the pools and the King's guards suspected nothing. Aric looped his slingshot into his belt, as usual; he was rarely seen without it hanging at his side. He couldn't pick up stones without arousing curiosity, but he'd tucked a few large pearls into his pocket. They're not as good as rocks, he'd told her, but they would sting.

Her heart hammered as they approached the dining area and saw it was empty, save for the King at his table. Where were the others who usually ate with him? She had desperately hoped they'd be seated at a table away from him. This was going to make escape far more difficult. Torches blazed in the garden and a slight breeze ruffled the leaves. Kalvara was nervous enough to sweat, which she never did, but she dared not wipe her moist forehead. She would not draw attention to her angst.

A beautiful bowl she'd never seen before sat on the side table, surrounded by fruits and cheeses, breads and rolls artfully arranged. The King stood and extended his arms to them.

"I've arranged a private dinner for us." He motioned the servers to begin. "We've a new cook and I thought you could help me sample his cuisine before he cooks for the others."

They began with a course of cold turnip soup, laced with a spice Kalvara had not tasted before. Delicious. Then came the platters of fruits and cheeses and different dips for them. This was different. She'd never seen elves dip their food in sauces of any kind. The server placed a spoonful of pink dip on each of their plates.

"Dips," the King said, raising one eyebrow. He touched the tip of an apple slice into the pink sauce, chewing tentatively, all the while watching Kalvara.

Hairs rose on the back of her neck. This was most unusual. Why was he paying so much attention to the food? Normally, his focus was on philosophy and history.

"Delicious, Kalvara. Try it."

She did. "Very nice," she agreed.

"Aric, you now," the King urged.

Aric dipped his apple into the pink sauce and ate.

Kalvara stared at her plate, trembling.

"Kalvara," the King persisted with far too much exuberance. "I've had some special fruit prepared for you two. I've heard it's particularly delicious with a yellow sauce." He motioned for the server to bring the elaborate bowl. It held berries—turquoise berries from the trees! They floated in a yellow sauce and the server spooned some onto her and Aric's plates.

"Oh, no, Your Highness, I'll not eat these!" Her voice wavered against her will. "They're poisonous, as you know!"

"So I have always thought," the King replied, a hint of regret in his eyes. "But, perhaps, you can prove me wrong. Eat," he commanded. "First you, then the boy. The sauce has a delightful flavor."

She was paralyzed, knowing with a terrifying certainty the sauce was poisoned. He wanted to kill them. To make an example of them, to reinforce how deadly the berries were. Kalvara took her spoon in her hand.

"No, Kalvara!" Aric shouted, shoving their plates off the table.

The King leapt to his feet, yelling for the guards just as a blue light exploded in the garden.

Uriel shoved the guards to the ground. "Run!" he growled.

135

Kalvara and Aric ran, chased by a few other troops who'd escaped Uriel. They snatched at their satchels as they sprinted past them, but the fabric snagged, so they left them dangling on the branches. Not important. Aric led the way through the woods, past the grove of berry trees, over the winding footpath to the dwarves' cluster of homes. The two dwarf children saw them, yelling and pointing, but they were gone before their parents came out of their huts. As they sprinted through the tunnel, darkness forced them to slow, but they pressed on, terrified they'd meet someone coming the other way. Eventually, they reached a section of utter blackness and were forced to stop. Kalvara saw a light coming from behind, not ahead and pulled Aric into a crevice.

"It's blue, Kalvara. Uriel."

The orb caught up to them moments later.

"I've delayed them for a while," he rumbled, then took the lead to the exit. Kalvara smelled the rain long before they reached the end of the tunnel. It was late afternoon and the fragrance of moist earth tantalized her senses. Aric carefully parted the branches that covered the tunnel hole. She was so proud of him. He'd saved their lives! Truly, her brother had fathered a wondrous eldrow child. Occasional drops fell from leaves high overhead, but mud and debris on the forest floor spoke of an earlier storm that must have been severe. Aric gasped, and she moved next to him to see why. This couldn't be! It was impossible! She shook her head, as if to clear the image from her mind. But there it was—a Pegasus, huge and proud, magnificent and strong, grazing about 20 feet from them.

They watched it in stunned silence. She was sure if they stepped out, it would react, and she didn't want to risk any noise. What was it doing here? Soon, they heard laughter and footsteps. They pulled back deeper into the shadows but could easily hear the conversation.

"So, you are Jakin, the giant killer!" A woman laughed shrill and giddy.

"I am," the man replied, his voice familiar to both Aric and Kalvara.

Jakin was here! That meant his ship was in port. Surely, he would help them escape. He walked into view with the woman.

"And your father?" she asked coyly, teasing him with a finger to his cheek.

Jakin sobered. "The giant Morfyn killed both my father and mother when I was a young child in the mountains near Orizin. I was raised by a dwarf family there."

The woman stopped, dropping some of her pretense. "I am so sorry to hear that, Jakin. And, you avenged their deaths, didn't you?"

He nodded.

"How brave of you!" She stepped closer to him, a striking woman. She flipped her long hair behind her and reached out to embrace him. Jakin hugged her back, holding her for a what seemed a long time. She pulled away and took his face in her hands, her long red fingernails bright spots in the dusky light. "I'm glad to have met you, Jakin the giant killer. I must go now."

"Nerida, please say we can meet again."

Kalvara's mouth dropped open. Jakin was smitten with her! Who was this Nerida? Had she come from another world like Rory?

"All right. Yes, I would like that, Jakin. I will look for you at twilight over the open sea." Then she walked to the Pegasus, stroked his face and murmured something Kalvara couldn't catch. Tossing the harness over his neck, she gracefully mounted the steed and without a look back, pranced out of the thicket. Moments later, Kalvara studied their silhouette against the dusky sky, the Pegasus' outstretched wings climbing above the trees, his lady rider sitting tall, her black hair blowing wild around her.

137

Chapter 19: Blue Stone

Finn had woken well before dawn and had stolen silently from the castle to the woods, as he had for the past couple of weeks. He needed to immerse himself in the quiet of the forest in order to manage the day ahead. Rory had been busy with her mother, holding court, making legal and administrative decisions, overseeing the country's militia in a time of peace, taking inventory of arms and ammunition, and building up supplies for the future. It took all the patience Finn had to sit by her side meeting after meeting, project after project, through political luncheons and dinners. He'd requested a day outside and she'd understood, though she couldn't come with him. How could Rory stand it?

It bothered him that he saw her thriving, witnessed her wisdom in solving both petty and largescale problems, and her tact with individuals and groups from all races and ranks in life. She was meant to rule. And he was taking her away. Did he have the right? Was this what Eldurrin wanted? Was he being selfish to want her with him? He needed to talk with Floxx. Needed her counsel. She had been his focus on many mornings. Floxx spoke with Rory from some place deep inside her. He wanted to connect with her the same way. He had raked his memory, reliving the Night of the Tennins, Floxx's words, his calling, the honor he was given. He had chosen this quest, been assured of Floxx's support and confidence in him. Why then, had he not heard from her? Why was she distant from him?

The sky was overcast, wisps of cloud touched the tops of the tallest trees. Birds warbled muted melodies, huddled in the leaves against the dampness. Finn pulled his hood up and tugged his cape around him, crossing his arms to capture his body heat, then called out silently. *Floxx, please hear me. I don't want to make a mistake here. You have honored me with a great quest, and I will not turn from it. But what about Rory? You know our hearts, our affection for each other. But is it meant for us for a later time? Will it disrupt our disparate callings? She's so gifted and a perfect fit to rule here in Byerman. Please, Floxx, help me here. I will go alone if that's what's best. I'm so torn; I just don't know.*

Finn heard whispering. "Floxx?" he called. "Floxx, is that you?" Silence. He peered through the woods from the low branch he sat on, seeing nothing. "Floxx?" he called, again.

Laughter burst from a treetop close to him, then a lot of leaves rustled. Finn jumped from the tree, staring at the jiggling branches near him. He'd know that laugh anywhere. And moments later, two small legs dangled and dropped to the ground.

"Aric!" he shouted, swinging him up for a hug. "You got away! I'm so glad to see you!"

Aric squeezed him back. "Me too. Wait till you hear everything!"

Finn held him so he could see his face. "Kalvara?" he asked, not seeing her, suddenly afraid.

"Right here!" she answered from behind him. He spun around and there she stood, more confident than he'd ever seen her, a wide grin on her face. They embraced, and Finn felt genuine warmth where there'd been coolness after Rory's return. They were friends, again.

"Rory will be so glad to see you two!" Finn laughed and the three of them headed back to the castle.

"Spike!" Aric spotted his tiny friend as soon as they reached the Queen's suite of rooms. The bramble was hanging on the window cord, engrossed in observing the world below.

"Aric, my dear boy!" Spike flung himself toward him, catching on his shoulder and planting a prickly kiss on his cheek. "We've worried ourselves sick over you and Kalvara. What a supreme treat it is to have you here with us!"

Aric touched Spike's head, a tender gesture he'd adopted in lieu of a hug.

"This castle is perhaps the most wondrous place I've ever visited," Spike enthused, turning a full circle, gesturing at his surroundings. "Even more wondrous than Underside! This world has all the beauty, plus sunshine and weather. And, the bonus? No vapors, never ever!" He bounced on Aric's shoulder, exulting.

Rory heard the commotion and ran into the room. "Aric! Kalvara!" She embraced them both. "We were so worried about you! How did you escape?" The blue orb floated across the room to Rory. She held out her hand and it settled on her palm. She lifted it to eye-level. "Uriel! So great to see you, again! You took care of them, didn't you?" The orb blinked. "I knew it! How could they lose with you on their side!"

"He did!" Aric exclaimed. "He helped me explore Underside and we found a way out!"

"I want to hear all about it! Everything!"

Kalvara smiled. "You won't believe this, but Jakin brought us from the island to Syrea."

"Jakin!" Rory was shocked. "You know, we actually came on his ship, too, but we snuck on and he never knew. He was so angry last time we saw him."

140

"Well, we made a run for his ship and definitely caught him off guard, but he could tell we were panicked and desperate. He didn't ask any questions; just got us on board and hidden until we were well out to sea."

Finn's face lit up. "Maybe he's changing," he said, hope in his voice. "Turning back into the Jakin I've known all my life."

"Hmmm. Maybe." Rory was dubious. But she could see Finn wanted to believe the best about his friend. "It was super nice of him to help," she conceded.

Kalvara's expression grew serious. "He was distracted. He'd been talking to…."

Queen Raewyn joined them, interrupting their conversation. "It is so thrilling to have you both here, again!" She gave them each a quick embrace. "Are you hungry? Breakfast is waiting; come, join us!"

"We're starved!" Aric jumped from the rocking horse.

"We have much to tell you that might best be shared in private," Kalvara whispered to Finn. He took the Queen aside to explain.

"We'll eat right here, then, where we have the most privacy," she told him.

No one said much during the meal, knowing the servants could hear their conversation in the nearby kitchen. Kalvara and Aric ate fast, gulping the food down. Finn wondered how long it had been since they'd last eaten. He couldn't wait to hear what had happened to them. Finally, after the plates were cleared and the servants gone, Raewyn closed the door to her suite, and they moved to the seats by the fireplace.

"So," Finn said. "We have complete privacy. Before you tell us what happened, though, I'd like to say how very much Rory and I have struggled over leaving you there." His voice cracked.

Rory took over. "Once we got Topside, we wrestled with whether we should try to go back for you. We thought we

141

had little chance of getting back in alive, much less escaping, again, with you. We would have tried, though, had we thought you were in danger. But we knew the Tall King showed you and Aric a lot of favor and doubted he'd hurt you. He didn't, did he?" she asked, fear and regret in her eyes.

Kalvara studied them for a moment. "Well, he actually didn't harm us, but at the end, he wanted us dead. I'll tell you all about it. But know that Aric and I were so glad you two got away. I was so enamored with the Tall King, I was blind to his true nature; though Aric saw it right away. He realized the King cared little about whether either of you survived, regardless of whether the bugs were destroyed. He was furious, though, when you both escaped, and we were careful to keep our distance from him. Since the bugs had, in fact, been abolished, I didn't understand his fury. But Aric did. We think he was threatened by you both; by the enemies you'd faced and defeated. It's possible he feared he could be the next." She hesitated, staring at the floor as she put her next thought together. "He did take good care of us, though, at least until the very end. He gave us a beautiful place to live and was generous with food. We had our freedom, I thought. I was content, happy even for a short time thinking perhaps I'd found someone special." Her voice trembled, betraying a fissure in her hard composure.

Finn felt her hurt and disappointment. She'd been on the run a long time, trusting few, deceived by many; hoping against reason she and Aric would find a safe place to live with people who loved them. And now her hopes had, again, been crushed. First by King Merek's death, then by Finn, himself, and now the Tall King. He felt a moment of guilt for choosing Rory instead of her. He hadn't meant to hurt her.

Kalvara cleared her throat and continued. "Aric was distrustful of him, suspicious even, and he was right. One day, he and Uriel went exploring and discovered a secret so crucial the King turned on us. We fled for our lives."

Finn caught his breath. "What secret?"

Aric dug in his pocket and pulled out a handful of pearls, then picked a dark stone from among them. "This," the boy said. "The Tall King wanted to kill us for finding this." He passed the blue rock to Rory who was sitting closest to him and proceeded to tell the entire story of the day they found it, the blue-leafed berry trees, the dwarves, the tunnel, and Uriel's refusal to leave the treetop where he'd discovered the hidden gem.

Kalvara picked up the story with the King's visit early the next morning and how he'd warned her the berries were deadly.

"Poison!" Finn exclaimed, incredulous. "Why would he lie like that?"

"We think he did it to keep everyone away from the stone's hiding place. If the berries were deadly, no one would venture near the berry trees. The gem was perfectly camouflaged in the leaves, an elaborate disguise to protect a great treasure."

Finn jolted as a thought hit him hard. "A great treasure? Let me see that rock, again, please." He examined it far more carefully than he had the first time he'd held it. He polished it on his cloak, then took it to the window and held it in the sunlight. Blue prisms shot all over the room.

"Wow," Rory exclaimed, "How beautiful! Can I see it, again?" She removed her star-sapphire necklace and compared the two stones. They were a similar color and about the same size and weight.

Her mother joined her to examine the stone. "This is a sapphire," the Queen said confidently. "A cabochon, shaped and polished, but not faceted. A beauty. We have several of them in the royal treasury, but none as large, nor as clear. Look at the brilliance inside it. I've never seen a cabochon emit a prism of light like this." She turned to Finn. "This stone is enormously valuable."

"We thought it might be one of the stones you're looking for, that maybe it belonged to the ancient crown," Kalvara shared.

Finn was grinning. "That's exactly what I was thinking! Why else would the Tall King go to all the trouble to hide it?"

Kalvara nodded.

"Can you remember the ballad, Finn?" Rory asked, grabbing a pencil. "There were three stones in the Eldur Crown. One was blue, right?"

Finn nodded. "A blue one, a yellow, and a red." He paused. "I wish I could remember the whole ballad, but I just recall pieces of it."

"Let's write down everything we can remember; it might be enough to be really helpful. So, three stones, red, yellow, blue. And I remember the refrain. Floxx explained it to me one night. It's about you and me, Finn. *The ruler will find her; and gently will bind her when that which was stolen is found.* That's me; I was kidnapped, and you found me when I returned to this world."

Spike stood on Aric's shoulder and whispered into his ear.

Aric hollered. "Spike thinks he knows the whole song. Come on, Spike, sing it loud." He held the sprite on his palm so everyone could hear.

Spike recited with great aplomb:

By the edge of the Tennin Sea
Eldurrin's hand did mold
The Eldur Crown, and in it, three
Jewels in a band of gold.
T'was delicate as tennifel
Grown there beside the Sea
And cast in light, a wondrous spell
Magnificent to see.

The stones it held in its circlet
Foretold of its great pow'r.
The stars affirm; we shan't forget
The coming of its hour.
The Eldur Stone sits at its core
Gem of eternity
Bright as the sun, the purest ore
That one shall ever see.
The red King Stone, bright as hot flame
For from a line of kings
This monarch comes, though no one names,
The family that brings.
Blue Stone of Valor shining strong
Brings pow'r to the fair throne.
Its might will overcome the wrong
Its force protects its own.
The ruler will find her; and gently will bind her
When that which was stolen is found.

They joined him on the refrain and finished together, then held their breath a moment before Spike bowed, and everyone applauded.

"How is it you know that all the way through, Spike?" Finn asked, amazed.

"Bramble sprites love songs, ballads, poems, and riddles, and are quick to remember them. Tis a song I learned as a young bud."

"How brilliant Eldurrin is to set his story in songs. It makes his messages so easy to remember!" Finn hesitated, thoughtful. "If Uriel thinks this blue stone is the Stone of Valor, I think we should trust him."

The orb blinked. No one disagreed.

"The Stone of Valor brings power. It overcomes wrong. Its force protects its own," Finn quoted from the song. He looked at the others. "Its own. That would be us. It protects us. Kalvara, this stone may be the reason you were able to escape the Underside against all odds."

"Makes perfect sense. We stood such little chance of getting away alive."

"Yes! Eldurrin is making the way for us, just as he promised."

"What will we do with it?" Rory asked.

"We need to keep it hidden, for sure!"

"Maybe we should hide it here at the castle."

"No," Rory was quick to say. "It'd just bring danger."

"I could keep it in my pocket, just like I did before," Aric said earnestly.

"Aric," Finn said smiling, "you did such a good job of keeping it safe. But we need a new place. Somewhere close to us; somewhere no one would think to look."

The orb floated to the stone and hovered above it, its blue color nearly the same as the stone. It flickered, then settled on it, encompassing it.

"Will you look at that!" Finn murmured. "The stone disappears when the light covers it." He bent to study it. "Uriel, can you pick it up?" The orb brightened and lifted off the table, carrying the stone inside. Everyone cheered.

"Wow!"

"That's perfect!"

"I can't believe it!"

"It's exactly what we need!"

Two days passed. Aric and Spike amused themselves playing hide and seek in the Queen's quarters. Kalvara, worried about the noise they were making, asked them to play in the woods. She followed them outside, convincing Finn to join them since Rory and her mother were tied up in diplomatic meetings.

"Some fresh air will do you good," Kalvara teased. "You can think about her while you walk."

Finn laughed. "You read me so well!"

They reached the place where they'd seen the bats fly over just before the King's ball and they remembered the moment. "I really loved Rory's father," Kalvara whispered. "Had we known what was coming, could we have altered the outcome?"

Finn saw the haunted look in her eyes. "We could have altered it, perhaps. But others would likely have died instead. Perhaps one of us. Or Aric, or Rory."

Kalvara heaved a great sigh. "How awful that would have been. There's just no choice but to trust Eldurrin. He numbers each of our days, as hard as it is to accept."

Up ahead, high in a tree, they heard Aric. "I've looked all over for you, Spike. You haven't gone to another tree, have you? You have to play by the rules and stay in the one we picked."

No answer.

Aric rustled higher up the tree where the branches were thin.

"That's far enough, Aric," Kalvara called.

Aric shook the thin branch in frustration. "Spike! I give up. Where are you?"

Finn heard a faint groan and glanced at Kalvara. "I heard it too," she said, and they sprinted for the tree.

But Aric was even faster. He'd jumped to the next tree. "Up here; this one!" he called.

The moaning grew louder. It didn't sound like Spike; it didn't sound familiar at all.

"Shhhhh," Aric warned as they poked their heads through the leaves. "She's hurt."

Finn couldn't believe it. He was face to face with a tiny ghillie. Not the wild bearded one who'd stolen Rory's feather, but a more delicate version, a female likely. She was clearly in a great deal of pain and it was easy to see why. Her head was grossly misshapen by a tight-fitting piece of jewelry. A gold band constricted her skull; her entire forehead hidden beneath a red gem, her swollen head bulging above it. Even her eyes were swollen, and they didn't seem to focus well.

"Ohhh," she moaned, swaying dizzily on a twig of a branch an arm's reach away. "Oh, I can't take it n'more. Dew, is that ye? Dew, ye've got t'help me. I can't barely see ye at all, the world's gone dark, it has, and the thumpin o'me head is makin' me so sick, I might fall out o' this tree."

Dew? That was the ghillie who'd stolen Rory's feather! He was around here somewhere? "Hello?" Finn whispered.

The ghillie squinted, trying to see. "Who's there?" she demanded. "Ye ain't Dew."

"No, but we won't hurt you. Dew. I've met him; is he around here?"

"He went for some help. Says there's a leaf in these woods that can take the swelling down and he's been searchin' for it. He'll be back anytime now." She moaned, swaying dangerously.

Finn reflexively reached his hand out to steady her.

Aric piped up. "Can we wait here with you? Just to make sure you don't fall out'a the tree before he gets here."

"I got no choice, I don't suppose, but anyway, that's kind of ye. If ye was going to hurt me, ye'd already a done it."

"That's right. We won't hurt you. And we'll help if we can."

The ghillie fell silent for several minutes, so long they thought she'd gone to sleep. They waited in silence, thinking the rest was good for her. But before long she began to thrash. "No! No, Dew! Don't let 'em get ye! Keep yer head down, right here, by me. Those bats, they can't see ye down here. Those red eyes, they look right over us. They want bigger victims, more blood than we got." She shuddered in her sleep.

"She knows about the bats. The vampire bats." Aric moved closer to Kalvara.

Dew arrived a half hour later. He was huffing and spewing all the way up the tree, furious that Cat had company.

"Don't ye touch her, d'ye hear me? I'll put a curse on ye, if ye do. Not a finger, d'ye hear." He leapt into view and punched Finn in the nose. Aric grabbed him, wrapping his small fist around the furious little man.

"Why'd you punch my friend?" he demanded, holding Dew in front of his face, but out of punching range.

"Who're ye?" the ghillie demanded. "And what're ye doing in my tree, botherin' me Catkin?" He turned to Catkin. "Are ye all right, me sweet?"

She nodded. "Did ye find the leaves, Dew? I can't hardly stand it n'more."

"They didn't hurt ye none, did they?"

"Not a bit. They stayed with me till ye came, dizzy as I am."

Dew looked at Finn, chagrined. "I beg ye pardon, then. I shouldn't a hit ye."

Finn rubbed his nose. The tiny man packed quite a punch. "Apology accepted, Dew." "Uh, your friend, Catkin, needs urgent care."

Dew didn't respond.

"That thing on her head needs to come off. And very soon."

"I know that, o'course. We tried as many ways as we could think t'get it off. But 'er head is too big—it's all swelled up on top there and the ring won't budge."

Finn looked closer and was amazed to realize that what squeezed Catkin's head was, in fact, a ring.

"The plant I'm searching for'll bring 'at swelling down so it'll slip off, nice like."

"I see." Finn was concerned that much more delay might kill Catkin.

"What does the leaf look like, Dew?" Kalvara asked. "Perhaps we can help find it."

Dew sighed. "Ain't none round here. Grows near water and the stream I thought was near, must'a dried up. It's a short, three-leafed green plant; nothin' special t'how it looks. Has little purple flowers in summer."

"Purple flowers?" Aric wiggled with excitement. "Tennifel?"

"How'd ye know that?" Dew said, eyes huge in surprise. "Ye got some?"

"We do," Kalvara smiled. "But not with us. It's at the castle, not too far from here. We could bring you both there if you'd like."

"Not on yer life," Dew frowned, his face instantly angry. "No way are we going with ye. We been trapped once in a castle and never again."

He turned to take Catkin's hand, casting wary glances at the elves. "C'mon, Catkin, me love. We have t' go now. We'll find that leaf soon, I promise ye. I swear with me life, I'll find it for ye and take care of ye."

She pulled her hand away. "No."

Dew grabbed her, more firmly this time. "Ye're out 'o your mind, Cat. It's the fever. Soon ye'll be better. C'mon now; we'll go slow, nothin' t'fear." He tried to pull her away, but she resisted.

"What is it, me love?" he whispered, confusion on his face.

"I can't go n'further, Dew. I can't hardly see a'tall, and I'm in terrible pain. These folks 'ave been kind t'me. I think we can trust 'em. And they have the leaf we want. Let them help us, Dew. I fear I'm about at the end."

"No, Cat! Don't say such a thing!"

Finn could hear the panic in Dew's voice. They waited, not saying a word, hoping their silence would be the best persuasion.

"I'd stake my life on these elves," a voice said from Finn's shoulder. Spike! Finn hadn't even felt him there. Dew leaned toward the stick man, not believing his eyes. "A bramble sprite! In these woods! Whatever are ye doin' here?"

"I'm with these elves, and I mean to say they can be trusted." Spike stood to his full height to look Dew in the eye. They studied each other for several seconds, respect and admiration on both of their faces.

Dew finally averted his eyes and something like shame filled his face. "All right," he said. "Guess there's no reason t'be angry. Ye're not like the wizard, I can see. Nicer. Way nicer." He sorted his thoughts aloud. "Me Catkin's just about wore out. All that searchin' and running' and riskin'—it can't be for nothin'. And ye've got the tennifel?" He looked at Kalvara and she affirmed she did. "Well, then, I guess 'tis best t'trust 'ye. Cat, ye want t'trust 'em, don't ye?"

But Catkin did not answer; her eyes were open but glazed over and she swayed dangerously.

"Cat!" Dew gasped, catching her. He looked at Kalvara, resignation in his eyes. "We're all yers."

Kalvara nestled them in her belt and climbed to the ground, barely jostling them. The others followed without a word.

Chapter 20: Bewitched

Jakin had lost count of the number of twilights he had watched for Nerida. Perhaps it had all been a tantalizing dream. He'd rather imagine that was true than think she had changed her mind, that she would never come back to him. He hadn't eaten in days. Dejected and weak, he slapped the end of a rope against the ship's rail. He had to sail in the morning. The crates were full of pearls; the deck crammed with barrels of fish, twice as large a load as he normally took back to Syrea. His crew had been grumbling for a week and were fed up with the delay, threatening to throw in with another ship if he didn't pull out at dawn. He'd stalled long enough, waiting for her.

As the last thread of sunset paled on the horizon, a harvest moon rose from the edge of the sea, orange and three times the size of a normal moonrise. The hair on the back of his neck prickled at the sight. Nights like this were legendary for mischief. He turned to descend to his hard bunk, thinking his scratchy blanket no match for the arms of the woman he pined for. That's when he heard her voice.

"Jakin."

He spun around, searching the darkness and caught her silhouette on the shore, her hair blowing across her face. She stood in front of the great Pegasus, nearly invisible in the night. Jakin leapt over the rails into his small boat, nearly

capsizing it and rowed to shore, jumping out too soon in his impatience to reach her.

"Is there no stealth about you?" she reprimanded.

"None needed. No one is anywhere near." He pulled her close, kissing her neck, her cheek, and brushing her lips with his. He shuddered. "Ah, Nerida; I've missed you so. Why were you gone so long?"

"Don't worry about me," she whispered. "I told you I would come back and so I have." She ran her red fingernails through his hair.

"Will you come on the ship with me? There is comfort down below." His heart flipped at the thought of draping his blanket over her.

"No, Jakin the giant killer. I prefer the open air."

He hugged her closer, fearful she meant she was leaving.

"Let's fly."

He was so shocked, he pulled away and held her at arm's length.

"On the horse? Together?"

"Exactly." She played with his ear. "You're not afraid, are you?"

"Of course not," he lied. Killing giants was one thing. Soaring through the sky was another. He hated heights. Even climbing the mast of the ship made him dizzy.

"Good," she purred. "I knew my hero would be brave."

Before he had time to think about it, Nerida had leapt on the steed's back and he had bounded up behind her. Nausea roiled in his stomach as he fought his rising panic.

"Hold on," she called, and he clutched her with a death grip as they left the ground.

A few torchlights blazed on ships on the other side of the island, but they flew in the opposite direction, away from the light of the huge moon. The dark sky melded with the opaque sea, and Jakin was completely disoriented. Which way was up? Where was the water? The rhythmic beat of the stallion's wings sent blasts of chilly air over him and he figured Nerida must be much colder. He ducked his head behind her, her hair flailing wildly above him, and gave himself over to the ride. How high were they?

They flew for a long time before he felt the horse slow and descend. The edges of mountains appeared on the horizon, white-tipped spikes against a gray sky. The moon cast shadows on the ground below. The Pegasus folded his wings and touched down on grass without so much as a sound.

Nerida slid from the horse's back and Jakin tumbled at her feet, sending her into a fit of laughter. She did not help him up. Surely, she wasn't laughing at him, was she? He hoped the darkness would hide his embarrassment. He straightened to his full height.

"Where are we?" he asked, brushing himself off. Though he tried to seem casual, as if this were an ordinary experience, a tremor in his voice betrayed him.

"In one of my favorite places. This valley is gorgeous in daylight, though, of course, we won't stay that long. But we can linger here awhile."

Linger. There went his thumping heart, again.

She took his hand and led him under a tree, coaxing him to sit. Her closeness was heady. He pressed his back against the tree trunk and pulled her to his lap. Her scent was alluring, and his hungry lips soon found hers. They lingered longer than he intended; he was powerless to resist her advances.

"Tell me I'm beautiful."

"You are beautiful. Enchanting. Irresistible."

She threw her head back and laughed. "You are so good for me! Exactly what I need." She kissed him again, teasing him, then pulled away. "Jakin, tell me, again!"

He added flattery to the mix, seeing how she loved it.

She responded with passion.

He was sinking fast, losing himself to her. Caution screamed as he struggled to control himself. He had to stop.

This was too fast, too powerful. Alarmed, he tore himself away and sat up, reaching for her hand. "Nerida," he ventured, "Tell me about yourself. Where are you from?"

She recoiled as if struck. "Questions? You have questions at a time like this?"

Jakin was mortified. He really did want to know who she was. And, besides, it was getting too steamy between them. Why was she so angry about him asking?

"Don't you want to kiss me anymore?" She pouted, her red lips glistening in the moonlight.

He relented. "Of course, I do! How could I resist a woman of your exquisite beauty?" He leaned closer.

"No!" she pushed him away and stood up. "You want to talk. You want to know my secrets." She stormed away.

Jakin was appalled. What kind of secrets did she have that she was so upset he might discover? Yes, he most certainly wanted to know who she was, thinking it would bring them closer, not distance them. He wanted to know everything about her. Why did she not trust him?

"Nerida," he called. "Where are you? Can we talk, please?"

"No, Jakin. I do not want to talk. I wanted your kisses, and your arms around me."

He wanted that, too; he dreamed of that! "Then you shall have them, all of them, for as long as I have breath. Only come back to me." He saw her move out of the corner of his eye. "Nerida. Please. The night is growing short. Must we fight and waste what little time we have?"

She tossed her head and held it high as she strode past him. "It is time to go."

Fine. Jakin swung himself up on the horse behind her. They would go. He would wait for her to calm down. He couldn't make sense of her. His heart pounded partly in fury and partly in disappointment. This had not gone the way he'd wanted, either. He'd apparently have to prove himself trustworthy before she let him into her life.

The moon had returned to normal size and sat high in the sky, shedding its light on the water below. They flew just above the surface, every now and then tipping to allow Marinna to feel the water between her fingers. Not him. There was no way he was letting go.

"The sea! I love it, Jakin. This is one thing you can know about me. I belong here near the water. I can feel its ebb and flow in my veins."

Ah, this was a start! He was pleased with this small chink in her armor.

Marinna had just lifted her fingers from the water when she gasped. "Look, there they are! Jakin, look!"

He leaned over perilously far and saw faces. It so startled him he would have fallen if Nerida hadn't caught him. They flew above a dozen beautiful faces, mermaids and mermen, all gazing at them with alluring eyes, their hair streaming behind them like seaweed in the current, their fish tails pumping hard to keep up with them. One female raised her arms and with a strong stoke broke the surface.

"Neridaaaaa!" she cried in a long wail. "Come back to us. Come back!"

Marinna screamed and kicked Conquest hard in the ribs and they shot away, the faces below fading as they went.

Jakin had his arms around her and could feel her sobbing. Come back to us? What could that possibly mean? He was familiar with siren tales; what sailor wasn't? They were magical creatures, dangerously seductive—catching unsuspecting human partners and luring them into the water where they were never seen again. But, certainly Nerida couldn't be a siren! Though she may well have bewitched him with her enticements, instead of luring him into the water, she'd fled from it. What then? He didn't understand at all. And he wouldn't risk asking any more questions.

The moon set an hour before dawn and in the utter

blackness, Marinna pecked him on the cheek and clipped a good-bye, leaving him on the shore by his boat before he could even respond. He rowed to the ship and collapsed into his bunk, the scent of her hair bewitching his dreams.

Chapter 21: Catkin's Crown

Rory couldn't hide her anger. Her very own friends had invited that vile creature who'd stolen her feather into the castle. Her castle. And they'd brought another nasty ghillie as well, grossly deformed. She kept her distance, unwilling to get anywhere near them, lest they somehow steal her necklace or Gram's feather.

"Give us a little room to breathe!" Spike requested as the others pressed around the table to watch. He had been elected to apply the tennifel to Catkin's head since his miniscule fingers could massage around the tight band without hurting her.

"Of course," Kalvara said, straightening a little. She held a vial of tennifel oil in her hand. "Just dip your finger into the oil, Spike."

"Ah, yes, exactly my plan," he said studying Catkin who sat in front of him. He turned her head to make eye contact and spoke to her soberly. "What will you do with the ring after it is off? Surely you will never wear it, again."

"Throw it as far away as I can!" Catkin pledged. "That's what I get for my greed. Worse'n the dragon, hisself."

"The dragon!" Rory exclaimed, before she could stop herself. "What do you know about the dragon?"

Dew bounded up on the table. "Leave 'er alone; cain't ye see she's outta her mind with pain."

Rory seethed.

Spike touched the oil and held his glossy finger in the air. All eyes were on him. He spoke to the ghillies with authority.

"Dew and Catkin. We are pleased to be able to relieve you of this terrible condition. But it comes with a price. We will hear of this dragon before we begin, and we will keep the ring after it is off. These are our conditions. Would you like me to proceed?"

"Let's go, Cat!" Dew grabbed her arm and began to pull her away.

"No!" she cried in pain.

Dew hesitated and Catkin dissolved in tears.

"What does it matter, Dew, if they hear about the dragon? If I tell 'em about the lair we found this accursed ring in? We don't want it n'more—it just brings bad luck. It's nearly killed me, Dew!"

Dew shook for a moment, so upset. Then his shoulders slumped. "Cat, me love. I guess ye're right. No matter at all. We'll never go back there, and they'll never see it. I'd like t'keep the ring, though, I would. We could hang it in our tree and watch it catch the light."

Catkin swooned, and Dew caught her just before her head hit the table.

"We will not proceed until you agree to our terms," Spike spoke firmly, the healing oil glistening on his fingertip.

Dew reluctantly sat down with Catkin, gently positioning her head on his lap. "Last I saw ye—at least some of ye," he eyed Finn and Rory, "I was grabbed by that Roc and carried away t'the dragon king and his queen."

"That was after you'd stolen my feather," Rory accused.

Dew shrugged. "It was me only hope of finding me love, and it did bring me t'her. She was a captive there in the Queen's courtroom, locked up in a cage right there near the throne."

Rory hadn't realized the feather had worked its magic for Dew! It had taken him where he'd envisioned—to Catkin. Wow, that was something. And they'd been in Marinna's throne room as well as in the dragon's lair! She listened, hoping she could learn something.

He sighed and started talking. "Here's the short of it. We escaped, me and Cat, and sneaked through the accursed tunnels all the way t'the dragon's lair. 'Tis a huge cave that opens t'the mountains outside and 'e comes an' goes in and out. It'd been a long time since we'd smelled fresh air and we jus' followed the scent of it and there we were. On our way through the cave, though, we stalled a bit, gawkin' at the hoard o' loot he had. Cat loved this ring and we were playin' with it, pretendin' it was a crown, when the dragon came back, hurt bad and bloody." Catkin moaned and Dew finished quickly. "We barely made it out alive but here we are." He glared at Spike. "Now git busy with that oil!"

"And do you agree that we will keep the ring in payment for saving Catkin's life?" Spike persisted.

Dew crossed his arms across his chest. "Can't ye see she's dying? Git on with it!"

Spike waited.

Catkin moaned.

"We agree," Dew sputtered. "The accursed ring is yours."

Spike applied fingertip after fingertip of the tennifel oil, rubbing it gently around the gold band and over the swollen part of her head. She closed her eyes and relaxed. When he was done, Spike touched her hand. "There now, Catkin. We will wait here with you as the healing oil works. You just rest there on your Dew's lap."

Catkin soon fell into a deep sleep and Dew, himself, dropped off, snoring gently, his head bobbing over hers, his green hair a wispy curtain fluttering as they breathed.

Rory moved closer to observe them. They loved each other, that was plain to see. Gruff as he was and mean as he acted, he had a soft spot for his girl. And little Cat adored her wild-haired beau. They were pretty cute as they slept. A small smile played at the corners of her mouth. Her feather had done this. Reunited these two creatures. In the long run, no harm had been done. *Floxx, are you upset? The only time I saw you angry was when Dew stole the feather.* She thought about how it'd turned out and decided that if Floxx would forgive this little creature, she would, too. She heard her answer deep inside. "Of course, you should forgive him, Rory. That's exactly what I've done."

Two hours passed, and the swelling had decreased by half. Dew woke from his nap, but Cat slept on, cradled on his lap. Spike applied another oil massage, this time able to work a bit under the band.

In another hour, Catkin stirred and rubbed her head. She sat straight up. "Oh! My head is much better! Oh, Dew, the terrible pain is gone!" She threw her arms around him, then turned to Spike. "It's workin' and we thank ye!" She tried to wiggle the band and it did move just a little. "Could ye put a bit more o'that oil around the band please?"

Spike obliged.

Catkin wiggled and lifted, and slowly, gently maneuvered her crown off her swollen head.

Dew grabbed the ring. "There now! How d'ye feel, me love?"

"So much better, Dew! Me head's not throbbing n'more and I don't feel sick at all."

Dew took her hand. "Well then, Cat, 'tis time for us t'leave." He grabbed her hand and leapt from the table, clutching the red ring as they ran. But she was hit from behind by a ball of thorns that knocked her over.

"Ow, stop that!" Cat cried, and Dew spun to see Spike crouched on her stomach, his thorns extended just enough to hurt.

"You choose, Dew," Spike challenged. "Either Catkin or the ring stays here. You can't have both."

Catkin, trapped by the prickly creature, glared at Dew. "We gave our word, Dew. What're ye trying t'do, dishonor the name o' ghillies? We're better'n that. Give 'em the accursed ring."

Dew begrudgingly handed it to Spike. "Now, git off 'er!" Spike jumped off, and Dew and Catkin bounded out of sight.

"Not even a thank you!" Rory scoffed. "Wretched creatures!"

"Well done, Spike!" Finn exclaimed. "You've made her better and procured a valuable gem besides!"

Spike jumped to Finn's outstretched hand. "Not just any gem, Finn. This one had been hidden in the dragon's lair, perhaps for ages. I have a hunch about this ring, Finn. It has the look of ancient days and this red stone is truly exceptional. You don't suppose...."

"The red stone!" Aric hooted. "Could it be the red stone for the crown, Finn? That's what you mean, isn't it, Spike?"

"It is, indeed."

Finn walked to a window to examine it in the light. The others followed, each taking a turn. The Queen brought some polish and cleaned the ring, bringing the gold and the gem to a brilliant shine. They scrutinized it.

"How would we know?" Finn asked.

"I don't think we can know," Rory answered, studying the ballad she'd written down. "But Floxx would know for sure." She laughed. "Can you believe it! We may have found two of the three stones that go into the ancient crown! And in just a few days! If this is the red King Stone, Eldurrin is for sure hurrying us along!"

"I wonder why the rush?" Finn murmured.

"I don't recall any urgency in the ballad," Kalvara commented.

"Not in the ballad, exactly," Rory said, "but Floxx did make a big deal out of my returning at exactly the right time. She mentioned it more than once. So, maybe we are being driven along a deliberate timeline without even realizing it."

She paused, considering. "And Draegin has clearly been on a mission to annihilate us and remove any possibility of me fulfilling the prophecy. It's obvious he's thinks it's urgent." Rory's voice caught, and no one said anything as she wiped her eyes.

Well into the evening, they relived the events of the day.

"The ring is stunning, Finn. Where will we keep it?" Kalvara asked.

"I think Finn should wear it," Rory said, surprising everyone.

"In plain sight?" Finn exclaimed.

"Well, no, not in plain sight. While it might not be anything more than a beautiful ring, if it is the King Stone, it belongs on you—you're the King the ballad refers to!"

"Of course!" the Queen agreed with her daughter. "You wouldn't have to wear it as a ring; it's too large anyway. But you could wear it around your neck. I have a heavy gold chain that was Merek's that would do nicely."

And so, it was settled. Rory clasped the chain around Finn's neck. It was long enough to hide the ring under his tunic. But, for now, they just admired it.

"It's perfect for you!" Rory whispered, grasping his hand, and seeing him a little more as the King the ballad spoke of.

Rory tossed and turned that night, fighting her dreams. Marinna appeared on the horizon, a speck in the sky. But, instead of flying out of sight, this time, the Queen turned and flew straight at her, riding not the Pegasus, but a lance. Rory barely had time to duck when she roared by, the rush of wind nearly knocking her off. Off what? She realized it was a tennin she was on and her fingers felt fur. Uriel! She had no time to think before the Queen attacked from the side. Uriel swerved at the last minute, looping downward at dizzying speed and Rory lost her grip on him, falling helplessly to a certain death. She screamed.

Her mother was shaking her when she woke. Realizing it had been a dream, Rory burst into tears and hugged her mother until the terror left her. When she'd found a measure of composure, she told her about seeing the woman on a Pegasus. She was sure it had been Draegin's daughter.

"Marinna?" Raewyn shuddered.

"I'm so sorry I haven't told you. I meant to do it first thing, truly I did, mother. But with all the excitement, I forgot. But this horrible dream reminded me."

"What do you think the dream means?"

"I think it's another warning. Queen Marinna intends to kill me."

At breakfast, Rory tried to hide her fatigue. She'd not slept after mother had gone back to bed. Her friends cast concerned glances her way as she yawned behind her hand.

Finn whispered to her. "Good morning. You look terrible."

"Thanks," she answered with a frown. "How thoughtful of you to say so."

"No offense intended," he touched her hand under the table. "But, can you tell me why?"

The sudden silence of the others betrayed their listening ears.

She sighed and spoke aloud. "Yes. I need to tell everyone." She took a sip of sweet, hot tea, appreciative of its comfort. "You need to know, and I've pushed it from my mind. Maybe even tried to convince myself it didn't happen."

Kalvara waited, an apple poised midway to her mouth.

"I had a nightmare last night that brought the frightening incident back. Finn knows, and now Mother does, too."

Kalvara pulled Aric's hand away from the plate of iced cookies, shaking her head in a subtle way the boy understood. Spike climbed up her arm and sat on her apple, crossing his twig legs and leaning forward so as not to miss a word.

"I've seen who I think is Queen Marinna—you know, Draegin's daughter and heir to his kingdom. I've never actually seen her before, but mother has and says she fits the description."

Her friends waited. In the silence, Kalvara absently bit the apple, sending Spike into a string of reprimands as he leapt onto Aric's shoulder.

Rory grinned and continued. "We were at Werner's farm, testing the airplane and I'd circled to a good height over Werner's field when I saw a dark spot near the mountains. Too big to be a bird for sure. As I watched, the thought hit me that it was the dragon. I started to descend, keeping a close eye on it. It flew closer and I could see it didn't have a dragon tail. But it did have a rider. A woman! Her black hair swept out behind her as did the tail of the creature she rode. It was a horse! A flying horse—a Pegasus! Its wings were outstretched and flying toward a mountain. But the woman must have heard the airplane; she was staring at it and I saw her recoil when she saw me flying it. Our eyes met for a second before she disappeared behind a ridge."

Kalvara stood so suddenly, she knocked her chair over. "Rory! I started to tell you and never got back to it. We've seen her, too. And her Pegasus. Close up. They were on the island and she was talking with Jakin when we came Topside. But her name isn't Marinna. Jakin called her Nerida.

Chapter 22: Attacked

Finn stood awkwardly as Rory hugged her mother for the third time, reaching up to wipe her wet cheeks. "It's not good-bye forever, mother. I'll miss you, for sure, but we'll see each other again."

Raewyn drew a steadying breath. "Of course, we will. I can see now how much Finn needs you. How he needs all of you." She smiled at Finn, Kalvara, Aric and Spike.

Finn took the Queen's hand. "Thank you for all you have done for us over these past few weeks. The rest and refreshment were sorely needed. I hope we weren't a burden."

"Don't be silly, Finn." The Queen patted his hand. "You are always welcome. All of you. Anytime."

"Eldurrin has called us to this task," Finn assured her, "and he will take care of us."

"Yes, I can see that he will." She glanced at the blue orb over Rory's head. "As he always has."

They were leaving. The problem was they didn't know where they were going. Finn chafed at the uncertainty but resigned himself to the impossibility of the task he'd been given. Eldurrin wouldn't let them down. Floxx would help them. Each of their packs was crammed with food, a new change of clothes, and a heavy blanket was tied underneath. Raewyn had also given them wool cloaks, thick and warm.

"Might be cold where you're going," she'd insisted when Finn had started to object. They were bulky, and too warm for here, but Finn conceded. She was right. He had to be prepared.

"I'll keep your airplane safe!" Raewyn called as they started down the long castle road.

"Bye, mother!" Rory waved, then turned to take Finn's hand. He loved that she did it so naturally, as if there was no doubt in her mind they belonged together.

They turned away from Masirika and headed west, eventually coming to the shore of Changeling Lake. They heard the distant roar of the two great rivers, the Caladrius and the Tennidrow, knowing they'd met before spilling over a cliff into the lake. But here the water was calm, and a thin stand of trees would keep the dew off.

"Let's camp here tonight," Finn said. Though it was several hours before dark, they had no way to cross the lake, and he had no idea if they should, so they might as well make a fire and stay.

"Where are we going?" Kalvara asked as they gathered dead wood to burn.

"Not sure, really. I'm hoping for some direction from Floxx." The uncertainty was unnerving. He was confident in the authenticity of the blue Stone of Valor; he trusted Uriel, and the fact it had been so elaborately hidden and protected. But did they really have the red King Stone? And how was he supposed to know where to look for the last gem, the yellow Eldur Stone? And then what? It was overwhelming to think about recreating the ancient crown. How could he begin to do that? What did it even look like? He reminded himself that, of course, he couldn't. But Eldurrin could.

Before long, a half dozen fat birds sizzled over the fire. They ate their fill with two birds left over.

"Well done, Aric!" Finn enthused, licking grease off his fingers.

"You're amazing," Rory agreed, ruffling the boy's hair as he dashed by.

"Where are you off to now?" she called to him as he ran to the water with Kalvara.

"Going to look for tennifel," he shouted.

Rory tore a handful of bread from a loaf and sat down beside Finn.

He moved close to her, liking the feel of her nearness. He tossed a stick into the fire. "I don't know what to do or where to go now. Maybe we should have stayed at the castle till we had a plan." He looked at her, apologetically and added, "But, I couldn't stand it any longer."

"That's okay." Rory nudged his foot with hers. "It was time to go. I was getting really wrapped up there, helping Mother. It's just as well we made a break for it."

They sat in comfortable silence for many minutes. Rory leaned back on her elbows and started humming.

"That's the tune of the ballad."

"Yes. I guess I've been thinking about it. I'll never forget how Floxx sang it so beautifully. Haunting." Rory sat up. "Do you remember the song she sang the next night—just before the tennins appeared?"

"Hmmm, a little. It's kind of overshadowed by everything else that night. I remember it had a lot of Falala." He laughed and tossed another stick.

"Finn, I've just realized it's about you! You! I remember a little of it—The king will reign, fa lei, fa la. No one can stand against him. The battle rages through the ages. Tis the plan of Eldurrin."

Spike appeared from a pile of branches and leapt onto Finn's knee, singing it loud and clapping his hands like Floxx had.

"That's it!" Rory laughed, jumping to her feet and clapping with him.

Spike sang all the verses, bringing Finn to his feet.

A mighty King, an elven son
Then rose to give him fight.
With pow'r from Eldurrin's throne
Tore down the beast with might.
Upon his head, the Eldur Crown,
His sword a fearsome blade
Forged by elves with skill renowned
From the fire Eldurrin made.

The three of them sang loud, clapping and dancing near the fire, sending sparks into the growing dusk. Finn felt his own spirit rise. He was this Elven King. It wasn't his plan; it was Eldurrin's. It didn't depend on him, not really. If he just stayed true, focused, faithful to the quest, he couldn't fail. Eldurrin would do the rest.

As the last notes faded, the same heaviness he'd felt at the Pool of Tennindrow began to settle on him. He took Rory's hand and they sat down. His spine tingled. The tennins! Were they here? What was happening? Rory had a death grip on his hand; clearly, she felt it, too. They waited. But no army of tennins appeared. Instead, a sweet voice drifted from a distance, lifting a song of worship in the way that only Floxx could. Suddenly, she was there, standing near them, facing the lake, her arms and voice lifted in heart-rending worship to the One she loved. Eldurrin. The familiar invisible weight settled on Finn and he surrendered to it, trusting that somehow this was The One Who Made Everything touching him, restoring him, loving him. He raised his own arms and began to sing words of love and praise to this One who cared so deeply. He could hear Rory singing as well, caught in the rapture of the moment, responding to the touch of someone eternal.

In a few moments the heaviness lifted and there was Floxx, laughing and suffocating them with hugs. "Here you are! I've missed you both so much! What a delight to see you face to face!"

Kalvara and Aric came running with armfuls of tennifel. "Floxx! We heard you singing and came as fast as we could." Aric jumped into her arms and squeezed her tight. Kalvara stood her distance, uncertain and shy. Finn wondered what she was thinking.

But Floxx wasn't about to be put off. In a few quick strides, she'd wrapped Kalvara in a strong embrace. "How very wonderful to see you, my dear friend!"

They talked and laughed for hours after the sun had set, bringing Floxx up to date on everything that had happened.

"Why were you gone so long, Floxx?" Aric asked, scooting next to her. Finn had wondered the same thing, though he hadn't had the nerve to ask her outright.

"I've had much to do in a distant place," she said, a smile in her voice as she pulled him onto her lap.

"Do you have to go back right away?"

"Not right away. I'll be with you for a while."

"Ah! That's great news!" Finn blurted.

"I thought perhaps we could go to your house, Finn."

He was shocked. "My house?" He hadn't even thought of that. It wasn't terribly far, but it was on the other side of the lake and the hike around would take days.

"Yes. I could use a couple of days in a cottage in the woods. There's nothing so refreshing."

"Of course. You'd be most welcome," he said, suddenly remembering his manners.

"And, I've had a craving for apple pie, and I've heard yours is the best in Gamloden."

He laughed. "Well now, I'd give the credit to the Tomitarn apple tree and the dwarf-made stove!"

Finn hardly slept that night, thinking about going home. What would Rory think of his tiny cottage? She was used to a castle now and even the servants' quarters were far grander than his house. And where would they sleep? Oh my. If Rory wouldn't mind, she could share his parents' bed with Kalvara, and Aric could sleep on the floor near them. Floxx could have his bed in the corner of the main room. He'd curl up on Da's chair. It could work.

Finn was up at dawn and joined Floxx at the edge of the lake. The sun was rising behind them and already was painting the lake with color.

"Pretty, isn't it?" Floxx whispered.

"Sure is." Finn savored the delicate colors and the orchestra of bird song as the feathered creatures greeted the day. Cheerful. Hopeful.

"It draws my mind to things bigger than me," he whispered.

"Exactly. It's a sweet reminder of Eldurrin and his goodness."

Aric broke the spell of the moment as he called to them. "Morning, Finn! Morning, Floxx. I'm going to get us some breakfast!"

"Be careful and quick about it," Kalvara mumbled in a scratchy morning voice.

Between Aric's morning hunt, and some not-too-stale bread they'd taken from the castle kitchen, they'd soon eaten their fill.

"Best pack up and get going," Finn said, brushing crumbs off his lap. It's a long walk around the lake. Probably take us a couple of days."

"Walk?" Floxx laughed. "Why walk when we can fly?"

Finn felt the heat rise to his face. He hadn't even thought of that. Did Floxx think she could carry them?

"What did you have in mind?" he asked. "We're too heavy for you."

"Of course, you are! But I can take Aric and Spike."

The boy let out a whoop and threw his arms around her.

"And, Uriel can bring the rest of you."

Uriel! Of course!

Right on cue, the orb exploded into Uriel, and stood towering over them. "I could take all three of you at once, but it might not be comfortable for you."

"Wow, that's great Uriel!" Rory laughed. "But, um, could you take Kalvara first, then Finn and I can ride together. That way no one is left here alone."

"Great idea!" Finn said. She was right. She thought of everything.

"Kalvara, can you keep this safe?" Uriel opened his huge paw to reveal the blue stone.

She tucked it into her belt pocket. "I'll guard it with my life!"

Uriel left with Kalvara, and Floxx flew with him. Finn laughed at Aric's shouts. He loved to fly! Kalvara gripped Uriel tensely, clearly not as comfortable as the boy! In a short time, Uriel returned.

"Floxx stayed with them," he said, as he bent low for Finn and Rory to climb on. Rory sat in front, her arms around Uriel's neck, and Finn settled in behind her, his arms around her.

"I could get used to this!" he whispered in her ear.

Uriel spread his huge wings and leapt into the air.

Finn couldn't keep himself from whooping like Aric had. Rory threw her arms out and laughed. They flew low over the water and he was surprised at how clear the lake was. He could see the rocky bottom in the shallow places, and silver fish darting through the sunlit water. The center of the lake was a deep blue, the color of the Stone of Valor. He was mesmerized with it when he caught a flash of movement reflected on its surface. He sat up and scanned the sky. Something black was speeding toward them.

"Uriel!" he yelled, panic in his voice.

Rory stiffened. "Marinna!" Uriel shot upwards as the Pegasus rushed beneath them. A near miss! Rory screamed.

Finn tried to keep track of Marinna, but Uriel shouted for him to keep down. *Floxx, help!* He locked one arm around Rory and clutched Uriel with the other. They crouched low on the tennin's back, trying to move as one with him. Uriel swerved and dove against the second attack, and Finn nearly lost his grip. *Floxx, we need you!* And then he saw her —a flash of white. He had his face pressed sideways on Rory's back watching the Firebird and Marinna. Floxx outmaneuvered the Pegasus and she dove at the rider, her wings nearly knocking Marinna off. Somehow, though, she held on, screaming words Finn could not understand. Floxx circled and dove, driving her beak into the horse's neck. The stallion screamed and fled for its life. Marinna glared at the Firebird and then, at him and Rory. She wasn't finished yet. She thrust one arm toward them, and he burned as if on fire. Rory screamed, again, slapping at invisible flames as best she could without letting go of Uriel. Marinna's laughter drifted away as she and the Pegasus retreated.

Uriel moved just above the water, slowing his pace. The coolness of the air and his diminished speed reduced the horrible heat. "Swim," he growled, and they slipped into the cool water. Just a dip was all they needed to feel instant relief. They climbed back on him and he took them to the opposite shore.

"My dream—it was like my nightmare!" Rory declared as she slid from the tennin's back.

Finn spun her around to see if she suffered any burns. There was no mark on her.

"How is it possible we are not terribly burned?" he wondered aloud.

"It was dark magic," Uriel rumbled, "but no match for the power of Eldurrin. He shielded us. We felt the heat, but it couldn't burn us."

The Firebird landed. "You're all right!"

Rory burst into tears. "She wants to kill me, Floxx. She's determined. I'm putting all of you in danger, again."

Floxx held her tight for several minutes, reassuring her it would be okay.

Kalvara and Aric arrived breathless and relieved to see no one was hurt. Aric jumped into Uriel's arms. "That was a close one," he called to the wolf-headed giant.

When Rory had calmed, Floxx held her at arm's length. "Rory, we've been with you since you set foot in Gamloden. We are well aware of Draegin and Marinna's raging lust for power and their focus on killing you. But we face their attacks together."

"Right," Finn said. "Just like on our trek to the castle, we will have your back." He put his hand on her shoulder and squeezed.

Rory took a steadying breath. "Okay. Thanks. I shouldn't have panicked; of course, we should expect attacks—maybe more now that we are closing in on your quest, Finn."

He nodded in solemn agreement. "Let's get going. My home is just a few miles from here."

Chapter 23: Finn's House

Finn was not expecting the rush of emotion he felt when he saw his home. He sighed remembering his mother and Da and covered his heart with his hand. They edged through the overgrown opening in the row of ancient hollies, their once prickly leaves now smooth, their branches heavy with red berries, and there, set back in a small clearing, guarded from behind by a stalwart line of gigantic Douglas Firs, was his family's small stone cottage.

He led the way up the steps, brushing cobwebs from the doorframe, and welcomed his friends inside. They moved past the bedroom on the left, into the small main room of the house, part kitchen and part sitting room. He lit the lamp on the rough kitchen table and grabbed some kindling left on the hearth to start a fire. He gestured for his friends to have a seat, saying it would warm up in just a few minutes, but no one sat. Rory took a cloth and tackled the substantial layer of dust that had settled over the everything. Kalvara and Aric went outside with a bucket for some water and proceeded to mop the stone floor. Floxx found some apples in the cellar and a wheel of cheese and carried them up to the kitchen. Uriel had transformed back to the blue orb and hovered at the window. Within a couple of hours, they'd cleaned his rustic home, and dined on cheese and fried bread, followed by warm apple pie. They shoved their chairs from the table, relaxed and satisfied.

"To tell you the truth," Floxx confided, "I'd kind of doubted Ardith and Werner's raving about your apple pie! But, it's completely true; yours is the best I've ever eaten, Finn! Truly remarkable! Better even than theirs, perhaps because of your special stove; you baked theirs in their own kitchen, right?"

"Right," Finn said, blushing a little, and clearly pleased. "And, thanks."

Finn followed Floxx's gaze to his wolf-headed walking staff. "Zithreh made that for your father, right?"

Finn was a little surprised. "Of course, you'd know that."

She walked over and retrieved it, handing it to him. "This is a most wondrous piece of craftsmanship."

"It's a wolf head!" Aric squealed, leaning on Finn's knees for a close look.

"Mmm, hmm, it is. Da was famous for killing Forsneer, the leader of the Amarok pack of wolves!"

Aric's mouth dropped open, for once at a loss for words.

Finn laughed. "He lost three toes in the wolf fight, though, and needed this staff to help him walk.

"Wow!" Rory leaned over Aric. "What a story! And such a beautiful staff."

"Zad's father, Zithreh, and my father, were very close friends. Zithreh was quite an artist and he made this, partly to celebrate the victory and partly to encourage Da, who got really sad after the war and his debilitating injury.

Finn turned it over in his hands. "I've never seen anything like it. Zithreh was very clever."

The wolf-head handle was carved from marbled green jade, and Zithreh had captured its hostile expression. Slanted yellow topaz eyes glared at them and its snarling jaw revealed the sharp black teeth unique to the Amarok wolves.

"Onyx? Rory questioned, pointing to the teeth.

"I believe so." Finn studied the band of gold that strengthened the joint where the jade handle met the amber staff, running his fingers over the green gems that studded the band. The gold was engraved. Finn read the words out loud. "It waits for one who is foreseen, child of nobility." He looked at Floxx. "Why would Zithreh carve these words into Da's staff?"

"I asked him to," she said.

"What?" He was shocked. "You were there when Zithreh made this?"

"I stopped in from time to time. We were close, Zithreh and I. And I knew the staff would one day be yours, Finn."

"Did Da ever suspect the child was me?"

"Not as far as I know. To him, the words just referred to a dusty prophecy. But he knew his friend, Zithreh, believed the old words, and so it was sentimental for him."

Finn's heart leapt. Zithreh had believed in Eldurrin! How he wished he was still alive to talk to. "Look," he ran his hand down the length of the staff's base, holding it for all to see. "This is resinite. Amber resinite. Fossilized tree resin that Zithreh said was likely from ancient times!"

"Seriously?" Rory studied it.

"Look here." Finn pointed a few inches below the place where the length of the staff was joined to its jade handle.

Rory stared. "Is that a cocoon?"

Finn laughed. "Sure is! And look, there's something else; see if you see it!" He handed the staff to Rory as Aric and Kalvara huddled close, peering.

Aric spotted it first. "A butterfly! A tiny white butterfly!" He jumped up and spun around a few times laughing. "How'd it get in there?"

Finn grinned and ruffled the boy's hair. "We think it had just emerged from the cocoon and spread its new wings to fly when it was caught in the dripping resin and preserved forever. See, this bubble between the cocoon and the butterfly is the space it left as it struggled to get free."

"Ohhh, the poor thing!" Rory moaned. "What terrible luck!"

"Trapped like we were, right Kalvara?" Aric touched her hand. She was staring at the poor creature. "Just like us," she said softly. "Only we got out."

Finn was long past feeling bad for the creature. A smile played on his face. "I remember Zad pestering me with this staff, poking me when no one was looking."

Rory laughed. "I can picture that."

"One morning I woke to Zad holding the wolf head over my face, snarling. I embarrassed myself by screaming and he teased me about it for years." He chuckled, then had a sobering thought. "So, Zithreh made a little speech when he gave this to my father."

"And you remember it?" Rory leaned closer.

"Some of it, yes. First of all, Zithreh was emotional. I'd never seen him like that, gruff as he usually was. 'Freddy, my dearest friend,' he said, 'this is to help you walk. But it's also a reminder about new beginnings and second chances. In the butterfly, Eldurrin shows us his desire to bring life out of death, joy out of sadness.' Zithreh then handed him the staff and said, 'Be encouraged, my friend; trust Eldurrin. There is life and joy ahead.'"

Kalvara smiled. "Those are good thoughts."

"And, there's a secret, as well."

"Really?" Aric jumped into Finn's lap. "What secret?"

Spike sat on the boy's head, listening intently.

"Well, that's just it. Because it was their secret, I never knew what it was. Just that late that night when they thought I was asleep, I heard Zithreh tell my father it was their secret now. And to guard it with his life. No one must ever know, he emphasized."

"Know what?" Aric touched Finn's cheek.

178

"No one must ever know their secret. And, unfortunately, my father never told me."

Aric bounded down and took the staff to the fire for the best light. He studied it from its wolf handle to its base. "Spike! Come help me. There's a secret in here!"

"Keep it away from the heat!" Spike cautioned, catching himself on the boy's shoulder.

"Finn," Rory murmured, "what happened to your parents?"

"Mother and Da both died a few years later in the Second Amarok War. I was 12. I went to live with Werner and Ardith, though I've often visited this house."

Rory squeezed his hand. "I'm so sorry."

In the morning, Finn woke early, started a fire and mixed up some dough. Aric, always an early riser, watched him as he shaped the round loaves.

"I'll help you wash up!" Aric called and dragged a chair over to the sink. Finn's red ring necklace was hanging from a hook near the sink, shining in the morning light.

"It really sparkles!" he said, reaching for it as he waited for Finn to pour the hot water into the sink.

"Sure does! I was admiring it earlier." Finn grabbed the pot of water off the stove and poured it quickly over the dishes. Some of it splashed on Aric's hands.

"Oh! Ow!" Aric yelled and jerked his hands away, wiping them on his tunic. "That's really hot!"

"I'm so sorry, Aric! You okay?" Finn checked his hands for burns.

"I'm fine. Just startled me. I dropped the ring in the sink, though. Sorry." He fished for the necklace and pulled it out, rinsing the bubbles off.

"Look how much more it sparkles when it's wet!"

Finn stood behind him. "That's truly amazing!" As they admired it together, Finn saw something new. "Let me see it for a minute, Aric." Finn studied the ring, dipping it in the water, again. "Will you look at this!"

Aric bent to see. "It's engraved!"

"Yes! I can't believe we never noticed it before. I don't understand the words though." He turned it this way and that, wetting it as he studied. "It's some language I can't read."

"I'll bet Spike'll know!" Aric ran off to find his friend.

Finn slid the chain over his head and tucked the ring away, chastising himself for being so careless as to leave it hanging on a hook.

The others soon stumbled in to enjoy the morning comforts of fresh baked bread and tea.

"So, here we are!" Rory yawned, holding her hot cup with both hands. "In your lovely home. What are we doing today?"

"We found a secret about Finn's ring!" Aric blurted.

She put her cup down and stared at the boy. "A secret?"

"Yes!" Aric shot out of his chair and jumped on Finn's lap, pulling the chain out from under his tunic. "It has a message!"

"I was going to tell you, of course," Finn said, elbowing Aric. "But I wanted to let you wake up first."

Rory slid her chair next to him. He loved feeling her close. "Let's see," she murmured. She turned the ring over and over, shaking her head. "I don't see anything unusual."

"It has to be wet," Aric advised, wrenching it over Finn's head.

"Aric!" Kalvara chastised. "Give that right back," she commanded.

He did. "Sorry, Finn." He hung his head. "I was just excited."

"It's all right. No damage done. Go ahead and dunk it in the water."

Aric grinned and got it wet. "Look!" He handed it to Rory.

She saw the markings right away. "No kidding!" She studied it. "How odd. Do you have any idea what they mean?"

"None."

Kalvara took a turn. "It's probably some strange language, maybe really old."

"That's what I thought, too," Finn agreed.

Spike had jumped on Kalvara's shoulder, clinging to her hair to peer at the ring. "Ah! I see! Yes!" he muttered, "it's a very old language."

"Can you read it, Spike?" Aric asked.

"Perhaps. But I'll need to study it awhile. Someone write the words down as I figure them out." Rory jumped for the paper and pencil in her pack.

"Round," Spike began. "Hmmm, this isn't making too much sense."

"Keep at it," Finn encouraged.

Spike studied and thought, scratching his head absently with a thorny finger. "Elven door!" he shouted abruptly. "Elven door!"

Aric let out a whoop and all the others stared.

"What about an elven door?" Finn asked cautiously. This was what they needed. Exactly what they needed. To find a way to the elves, whom he hoped were alive somewhere. The elves might be the only ones capable of recreating the Eldur Crown.

"And something about an island," Spike said, shaking his head.

"Maybe the island where we met?" Aric suggested.

"Oh." Rory's face fell. "Well, if it is, we can't go back there."

"Anyway," Kalvara said, "I doubt those elves have any secret, except the blue stone that was hidden there."

"Which we found," Aric added.

Spike studied on, though the others sat back, discouraged.

"So, this ring probably has the clue as to where to find the blue stone." Rory stated the obvious.

"Makes perfect sense," Finn mumbled, trying to stay optimistic. "Of course. It's brilliant, actually."

She read her notes out loud. "Round. Elven door. Island."

Kalvara reflected. "There were a lot of doors to tall ones' homes under the island, but none of them was ever called an elven door."

"Maybe not called that, but they all actually were elven doors." Rory sighed.

"Wait!" Spike shouted. "I think I've got it now."

Finn was skeptical. "Uh, okay, let's have it."

"The word is not round, it's circle. *The circle under the isle hides the elven door.*"

Finn's heart leapt! He stood and picked up the ring, looking at the runes and repeating what Spike had said. "The circle under the isle hides the elven door?"

"That's it!" Spike said, jumping on Aric's shoulder as the boy let out a whoop.

"The circle, Kalvara!" the boy shouted. "You know, the beautiful circle in the center of the garden."

Kalvara stared, not understanding.

"Remember, Kalvara? Under the glass dome?" Aric prodded.

Then, it hit her. "Of course! That must be it! Why else would they go to so much trouble to make the gorgeous light dome? They are hiding something underneath and turning everyone's attention upward to the dome, so whatever they're hiding isn't noticed! How entirely clever!"

"But if there's really a door to another elven world, why would they hide it? Are they protecting it? Or blocking it?" Rory wondered aloud.

Kalvara pondered. "My opinion is they are blocking it. That they fear the people who may be down there. That they don't want to be surprised should someone try to invade Underside from that portal."

Finn stood, amazed. "You think there are people living underneath the Underside?"

Kalvara shrugged. "It's a long shot," she admitted.

"But if it was true, where could this portal possibly be?" Rory prodded. "Aric, as you played, did you notice anything unusual in the surrounding gardens? You know, like a tree with a door in it?"

"No. And I explored them a lot."

"I wonder if it could be a trap door," Finn mused. "Built into the ground and opening to a tunnel."

"But that could be anywhere!" Kalvara shook her head.

"It could. Or maybe it's in full view." Finn leaned toward her. "Think, Kalvara. Put yourself on that circular bench directly under the dome."

She closed her eyes.

"What was on the ground where the benches sat?"

"Stone. Surrounded by flowers and bushes."

"Yes. Describe the benches, please."

"They were just seats, no backs, and made of polished rock. Very pretty. They were crescent shaped—two half circles set around a low round table. The Tall King often used the space for meetings."

"What was the table made of?"

"Wood. With a beautiful top of tiny multi-colored stones fitted together in a lovely design. The tabletop sat on a wide pedestal, which I think was also made of rock like the benches."

"And what was under the table?"

Kalvara paused for a long while. Finally, she sighed. "I can't remember anything remarkable under the table. It just sat on the stone courtyard."

Finn kept drilling. "Did you ever see the table moved?"

"No. It was very heavy, much too heavy to move. It stayed there, like the benches."

"So, servants just cleaned under it."

"Yes, that's right." She raised her eyebrows. "What are you thinking?"

"It's just a hunch. But what if the table was sitting directly on top of the underground entrance, hiding it from view and preventing any access?"

"Floxx?" Finn asked. "What do you think?"

He turned to her but found her chair was empty. "Where'd she go?"

"No idea!" Kalvara said.

"I saw her go outside a while ago," Rory said. "I thought to get more firewood or something, but I don't think she ever came back in."

Finn walked to the window but didn't see her. He opened the door. "Floxx!" he called. Then a second time. There was no answer.

"Do you think she left, again?" Aric moaned. "I really wish she'd stay with us."

"I think she's gone," Finn said, seeing no sign of her. He noticed his father's staff was also gone. The secret! Of course, she would know the secret!

He told the others and disappointment settled on all of them. "Oh well," he consoled the others, "we know she is doing what's most important. She must have thought we could handle things on our own."

"I wonder why she came back at all?" Rory grumbled.

"Maybe she just wanted that staff," Finn mused. "She sure was interested in it last night." He sighed and brightened. "Well, let's carry on. I think we've found something significant. The writing on the ring leads us to an island. We can't be sure it's the pearl island, but it may well be. I think it's worth following the clue. What do you think?"

Aric ran to Kalvara. "But what if we meet Nizat, again? If he catches us, we'll be taken to the Tall King and killed."

"It's true." Kalvara brushed the hair from his eyes. "But we will be very careful. And remember, Eldurrin is with us."

"Rory? Do you agree?" Finn asked. "The risk is high."

She didn't hesitate. "Yes. It is. But I will trust Eldurrin to lead us. And Floxx to keep us safe."

"Let's pack up, then, and head back to the island. We can plan our strategies along the way!"

"Let's hope we don't meet Marinna, again!" Rory worried aloud.

Finn squeezed her shoulder. "It will be all right, Rory. Like you said, Eldurrin promised and I don't believe he will let us down."

Chapter 24: Island Castle

Marinna raked her fingernails over the two dragon's heads that formed her throne's arm rests. Back and forth she went, over the jeweled scales, sliding over the emeralds, digging into the crevices. *Rory.* She seethed. *Why didn't my attack succeed? She wasn't even singed! What powers does she have to defend herself against my diabolical fire?* She exhaled, trying to clear her mind and think. *Humans have no power. They are weak creatures, pitiful and simple. That tennin and Floxx must be protecting her. But they are no match for me! Surely, I can exploit them!* She focused on their weaknesses. Rory! Of course! She was their common weakness. She'd use the girl to get at her protectors and when she'd disarmed them, she'd kill her. Only when pain shot through Marinna's hands, did she realize she'd broken all her beautiful nails. Her fingertips were bleeding. Her anger spiked. *Rory will not survive. I will make sure of it. No one can stand between me and world domination. It is my rightful heritage and I'll not be defeated. I will destroy her and her allies once and for all and will rule just as it is prophesied.* She stood, her heart hammering. She must calm down, get a grip on her rage so she could think clearly. She strode across the throne room, gulping deep breaths, setting her mind on pleasurable thoughts.

Jakin. The moment his face flashed in her mind, she felt giddy. A thrill rushed through her limbs, lighting every nerve. She cared for him. A lot. She'd never cared for any living being, except perhaps her father in a love/hate kind of way. Her stomach clenched. What was happening to her? Why had she let him grip her like this? This was supposed to have been a fling; an amusement to break her boredom, spice up her life, expand her horizons. She'd never been kissed before. But now, it was all she wanted. His nearness haunted her, his arms around her, stubble scratching her cheeks, hungry lips finding hers. Her face heated at the thought. She wanted to see him, again. She wanted to see him every day, every night. Her own heart had betrayed her! And it must stop. She was Queen! She was going to rule the world. Ruthless, strong, cold. That's who she was; that's who she must be. She had no room for love.

And yet, she couldn't shake her desire for him. Nor did she really want to. What harm could it bring to indulge just a little longer. He brought her great pleasure. Jakin the giant killer. Raised by dwarves. Owner of a pearl-trading ship. Imagine Prince Tozar's shock if he knew she was seeing his heroic kin. She could cut the prince out, really, and get her pearls directly from Jakin. But, no, that would give away their secret. No one knew; just the two of them shared this delight. She should ride it till the end. Once she ruled, she might never be able to indulge in romance again.

"I'll be with my steed," she clipped to the Inozak on duty as she brushed past him. But first, she walked the long corridor to her father's quarters and checked on him. His attendants shook their heads; he hadn't awakened in several days. His breathing was greatly slowed, though he lived still. She wondered if his body had entered some sort of reptilian state of hibernation, allowing it to conserve as much energy as possible as it tried to heal. She looked in on him to see for herself. She drew a sharp gasp. He already looked dead! His face was ashen and skeletal. What would she do without him? How could she possibly rule if he was not there to guide her? Follow your heart, he'd told her. You have the insight of both magician and siren. You will know what to do.

She sat by his bed and took his hand. Cold. Scaly. She shuddered and set it down, covering it with an inappropriately cheerful quilt.

"What will I do?" she asked him. "When you are gone, how will I rule?" She sat in silence for a few minutes, considering. "I do not want to reign from this isolated palace. Grand, though it is, father, I dislike it. I yearn for the water, for the warmth of the sun and its sparkle on the sea's surface." She touched the quilt and felt the hand it hid. "It's my mother's heritage I'm feeling. Surely, you would understand, father. I have your wisdom and her yearnings. Together they make me different from you."

She squeezed his fingers, suddenly knowing what she must do. Of course! It made perfect sense. "Father, I'm going to rule, just as you said. But I'm going to rule from the island. I'm going to build my castle there, amid the blue-leafed trees, overlooking the Syrean Sea. That's exactly where I belong! Near the water; near my people; near the desire of my heart." She stopped short, wondering whether she meant the sirens or Jakin. What did it matter in the long run? She would rule from a seaside throne. It was exactly what her heart was telling her, and she would take her father's advice and follow it.

"Good-bye, Father," she whispered, bending to kiss him on the forehead, recoiling as his parietal eye quivered at her touch. She wiped her lips. "I will be on the Pearl Isle laying plans to rule. If you ever awake, I would like to show you, and I hope you will be pleased."

Conquest snorted as she fitted him with gear, pawing impatiently at the ground. "You're ready, too, aren't you? Ready to leave this mountain prison and fly free. Ready to choose your own way. Ready to listen to your heart. You and me, Conquest. We have a royal destiny to fulfill."

The sunset was waning as they took off. The darkening sky was calm and clear of storms, though a cloud cover hid most of the stars. They flew down the valley, feeling protected by the rock spines on either side, then once clear, cut a straight course for the sea. Marinna's heart leapt as they neared. She knew its shape even in shadow, and she savored its salty smell. They kept their distance from Syrea, not willing to risk a sighting. A woman on a Pegasus would stir a lot of commotion. Her time had not yet come. Let them wait. Let them wonder. Let them tremble at the castle that would rise to tower over the sea. She felt her destiny with a new strength of purpose; a strong sense of authority. She was made for this. Great powers were hers, father had said, and she had a premonition she was about to discover them.

Over the water, broken clouds allowed the moon to show; its half circle brightening the sky. After a while, she spotted Pearl Isle and, as they got closer, she scoured the shoreline. Where was Jakin's ship? She flew around the entire island and it was not there! Her heart sank with such despair, it unnerved her. Pull yourself together, she chided. What did it matter if he was here or not? She wasn't asking his opinion; she didn't need his approval. She had made up her mind. Well then, whether he ever returned or not, she knew she would proceed with her plans.

Conquest landed on a remote beach, splashing down in shallow water. They sauntered into the center of the island where the leafy canopy was so thick, it blocked out the moon, and Marinna suspected, most of the sun during the day. Consistent with what she'd observed from above the island seemed completely deserted. No one lived here. Perfect! She could build her empire unnoticed until the top of her castle stood above the trees. Even then, only a few seafaring vessels would see it. And she'd commission a fleet of her own ships to protect it. She envisioned her private quarters high above the treetops, overlooking the blue waters. She laughed, delighted at the thought.

She found herself strolling on the shore where Jakin often tied his dinghy. It was deserted. Night creatures skittered and squeaked as she walked, and the eyes of their predators gleamed from the trees. Wanting to keep her feet dry, she settled a few yards from the sea on a flat rock under a crooked tree. Its leaves leaned over the water as if yearning for a drink. Moonlit rocks of all shapes and sizes sparkled on the shore. They were beautiful. She would use island rocks to build.

But who would oversee the work? She wondered if the artisans who'd built her mountain palace still lived. Surely, they weren't Inozak—those fearsome warriors were bred to destroy, not to create. She couldn't remember her father ever saying what workers he'd drafted. But then it hit her! Dwarves! His alliance with them must have started then. They were excellent stonemasons. Of course! The dwarves had done the work, right down to her gem encrusted throne. Well, wasn't that perfect! She'd conscribe crews of dwarves, bringing them from Orizin on ships. They would comply or face deadly consequences. Prince Tozar already bowed to her; he'd be the perfect one to oversee the royal commission.

The wind came up, gusty and cool, so Marinna pulled her cape around her and returned to the shelter of the forest. She felt little wind on the ground, though the leafy tops swung wildly above. Conquest wasn't bothered by it at all; he was grazing, lifting his head to whinny as she returned. She found a comfortable nook and settled down to sleep.

The next day, Marinna explored the island in earnest. Though she saw no signs of anyone living there, she was perplexed as to where Jakin's crew lived. Did they stay on the ship? Surely at least some of them had families and homes. She'd ask him about it when he returned. If he returned. Oh, she hoped he would! The wind persisted, and Marinna found it too cold to do more exploring. She settled at the base of a tree where she was protected from the gale. She'd just rest a few minutes, she told herself as she closed her eyes.

She fell asleep thinking about her castle. She wanted a large cupola, winding staircases, domed ceilings, each room decorated with nautical themes, sea life, sirens, shells and driftwood. She sank into a deep slumber, drifting into a fantastic dream. In the dream, a path opened from the shore to the castle site. Rocks of all sizes and colors tumbled along it and piled themselves into a heap. Rock by rock, the stone foundation appeared, then a grand first story; its pillars sculpted with mermaids. Oh, they were beautiful and strong; they looked almost alive! She walked inside to see a huge military complex, Inozak coming and going from it.

An instant later, she floated up a winding staircase to the second floor and entered her throne room! A polished stone floor gleamed under her feet, seashell mosaics adorned the walls, and driftwood sculptures graced the room's perimeter. She caught her breath at the sight of her throne, overlaid with mother-of-pearl, its ivory sheen glowing in the soft dream light. Gems in blues and greens spiraled along its curved edges, reminiscent of sea grasses undulating in the current. The salty, tangy scent of the sea filled her senses. Shells and pearls marched across the throne's arched back, embedding themselves in a beautiful pattern. She was irresistibly drawn to it. She ran her fingers over the sea-colored jewels trimming its edge. Taking a deep breath, she turned and sat, regal and proud. Queen! She was Queen of the land and the sea!

Her exultation grew as a merman approached her, tall and striking, elegant and proud. He bowed, giving her honor, calling her Your Majesty. He presented his request on behalf of all the sirens. Yes, she would aid them; yes, they would be allies. Of course, she would maintain peace between them and the sailors who ravished the sea's resources. She knew what to say; wise words rose to her lips from deep inside her. The sea belonged to them all, she proclaimed, and those who threatened peace would answer to her. He touched his heart in allegiance and vanished.

Suddenly, she was swept up to a breezy cupola that topped the castle and peeked above the forest canopy. It was night; the room flickered with candlelight. The shutters were thrown open, the air perfumed with the fragrances of salt and sea. Leafy shadows danced on the walls and the breaking surf beat its rhythm on the shore. What a refuge! This would be her sanctuary, where she came each night to rest, to renew her energy. Here she would free herself to love. Her body heated at the thought of Jakin and the light in the room flickered red as she dreamt.

Moonlight shone on an oversized hammock hanging from the center of the cupola, woven from island leaves and piled with pillows and blankets. Mother-of-pearl benches sat beneath each of the four open windows, reflecting the stars outside. She rested on one of them enthralled with this magnificent chamber. She gazed out the window at the clusters of constellations brighter than she'd ever seen them, close enough, it seemed, to touch. She had a sudden yearning to bring the stars inside, so she waved her arm and starlight scattered on the ceiling and walls! She leapt and spun in circles, laughing out loud that even the stars obeyed her! And why shouldn't they? Never had so grand a Queen come to power in Gamloden! Giddiness overtook her and she tumbled into the hammock, and Jakin materialized there. She reached for his embrace as the room began to spin, slowly at first, then tighter and stronger, circling with such force she couldn't move. She gasped for breath and jolted awake in the woods, curled in the nook of a tree, hugging a bulging root.

Chapter 25: Forgiveness

The birds in port were ravenous; Jakin wondered whether they'd eaten since the last time he'd fed them. After they'd finally left the island, they'd spent a few days at sea—the fishing had been unprecedented, and they'd crammed the ship so full it was in danger of sinking. But they'd made it to port, sitting lower in the water than ever before. After all that, Jakin had misjudged the market; they'd brought way more to Syrea than he could sell, though he'd make a tidy sum even so. With a lot of surplus fish, he'd spent the morning tossing them to the birds, amazed they were never sated. Squawking and diving, they swarmed the ship, swooping and squealing for more, an incessant greedy cacophony.

"That's it. That's all I got," he said, turning the last barrel upside down and batting at a few low flyers. "Go away!" he yelled. "Come back next time."

He jumped into his dinghy and headed for shore. The dwarves had already loaded the crates of pearls into his wagon and he snapped the reins, heading for the city. He'd meet his uncle in their designated place, hoping he wouldn't be too irritated the shipment was so late. Weather. He'd blame it on weather. What did it matter if Tozar doubted him? He'd make the same choice, again. Nerida. His heart lurched at the thought of her. Such a beauty. The thought of touching her sent heat flashing through him. But she was hiding something; perhaps many things. He wondered what she was so afraid of? Whatever it was wouldn't keep him from loving her. It would bring them closer; he was sure of it. She just needed to trust him, and he would cherish her, protect her, shield her from criticism or whatever she was afraid of. He glanced at the sea as he drove and let his mind remember. That night! That flight! Her skimming the water with her fingers. The strength of the steed beneath him. Mermen and mermaids beckoning to her. He shuddered, remembering the keening of the one siren: Neridaaaaaaa! Who was she? He was determined to know.

Prince Tozar was waiting at the appointed spot, a small boarding home on the outskirts of town frequented by sailors, many of whom Jakin knew from Orizin. In fact, Tozar's prosperous sea trade was the reason they were all there; the pay was handsome, though Jakin worried at how much longer he'd be employed.

"Where've ye been?" Tozar strode out to meet the wagon.

"Weather, Tozar. Terrible weather. It couldn't be avoided."

"Your crew says different," Tozar fumed. "Each day costs me money. Each day makes the Queen angry at the delay of her pearls."

Jakin took a step back, out of striking range.

"I don't need ye, Jakin. I can buy you out and find another first mate, no problem. One more stunt like this and I'll do just that."

Jakin nodded briefly, gritting his teeth. "I understand." He wheeled on his heel to unload the cargo.

Later that night, he sat on the ship's deck, sulking. He didn't need this job, this hassle. He didn't need to answer to Tozar or to anyone. He threw his knife at the wooden rail and it stuck. He should just leave. Move on. Find someone who respected him. Let Tozar try to find a first mate as good as him. Who? Nizat? One of the other dwarves? Ha! They'd drink away half the profits. One of the tall ones? They'd be late every time. They didn't need to work, didn't need the money. They were spies, that's all, keeping an eye on the world for their reclusive Tall King. He crossed to the rail and pulled his knife out, wiped it off and slipped it back in his pocket.

The sky was clear, the moon hung low on the horizon, a slender crescent. Nerida. What was she doing right now? Was she thinking of him? Those kisses she wanted? He was dying to give them to her. He'd do anything for her, even hang on to the ship and keep working for another chance to meet her on the island.

The next several days were a holiday for his crew. Normally, they got two days in port, but they'd demanded five, due to the long delay on the island. Jakin hated Syrea, the crush of the crowds all day, the drunken brawls at night. What was he going to do for five days? He was already fidgeting, wishing he was back on the island where there was at least the hope of seeing his love. He strolled down the seaside road, away from the noise and found a quiet spot on the shore. He settled on the rocks, watching the lazy waves and listening to the cries of birds. The warmth of the sun made him drowsy and he laid back and closed his eyes.

He must have dozed a long while; when he woke, the afternoon was getting on. He lay there, sleepily realizing he'd just dreamt about Rory. Rory! He hadn't thought of her in many weeks, since she and Finn had snuck onto his ship in the night, thinking he didn't know they were there. He'd seen them all right; he'd almost thrown them off, still feeling vindictive after the fight Finn had picked with him in Syrea. But they'd looked terrified. Something had happened. Something bad. And he knew what that felt like. So, he figured he'd just look the other way and give them a ride to

Syrea. It was no big deal for him, really, the least he could do in light of all the grief he'd caused. Just a small step toward making it right.

He cherished his friendship with Finn, all the years he and Zad had been so close. He'd hoped he could talk with them before they disembarked; if nothing else, he wanted to apologize. But, as soon as they'd reached port, Rory and Finn had run. He wished he could somehow make things right. But could they ever forgive him? He'd stolen his best friend's girl and her father had died because of it. He'd wrecked everything and there was no undoing it. Why was he thinking of her, anyway? Then he heard faint voices and he had his answer.

"We need to find a way back to the island."

A woman's voice. Rory! He'd know it anywhere.

Someone groaned. "No dwarves. We couldn't risk another capture!"

Finn! That was Finn!

"And no tall ones!" a child chimed in.

Aric!

Jakin raised his head and spotted them, sitting on the edge of the road not far from where he was laying. What were they doing here? Had he heard right? They wanted a ride to the island—the one they'd just fled from?

He stood and approached. Finn, startled at his sudden appearance jumped up, his hands fisted. Jakin held his own hands out in a gesture of peace and called, "Finn. Please. I just saw you there and wanted to say hello."

Finn eyed him, frowning, but said nothing.

Jakin walked as close as he dared. "What are you doing here?"

"I might ask the same of you."

"Me? We just brought the ship in from the island. I took a walk and fell asleep over there." He motioned to the spot. "The crew is in the city, but I can't stand it there."

"Ah. Yep. I'm the same way with cities." Finn unclenched his hands. After an uncomfortable moment, he continued, "Kalvara told us how you helped Aric and her get off the island and brought them here."

Jakin shrugged. "It was nothin'. The least I could do for all the heartache I've caused."

"Well, thanks. We are all grateful." Finn glanced at Kalvara and Aric sitting with Rory. They still hadn't stood but were watching warily.

"You know, I saw you and Rory." He hesitated at the confusion on Finn's face. "The night you snuck on!"

"Oh!" Finn's face reddened. "Right. We did sneak on. Because the last time we'd seen you, it hadn't gone well."

"I figured that was it. Look, Finn, Kalvara told me some of what happened to you. I had no idea about Nizat! Kidnapping you all—the scum! I never trusted that dwarf." He scuffed his boot in the dirt. "And the Tall King—I had no idea there was a city down there. You all were so lucky t'get out alive. Where'd you meet up?" Jakin gestured toward the others.

"Back at the castle."

Jakin's face burned with regret, remembering his last visit to the castle where he'd shamed King Merek, his uncle, at his memorial service.

"Look, Finn, I'm so sorry about," Jakin's voice cracked, "well, about everything. Rory. The bracelet. The King."

Finn took a step closer. "What's done is done."

"Can you ever forgive me?"

Silence. Then, "I think so." Finn hesitated. "At least I can. But," he glanced at Rory, "You should apologize to her, personally." He waved Rory over.

"Hello, Jakin," she said coolly, grabbing Finn's hand.

"Rory."

She shifted her weight to the other leg but said no more.

"Look Rory, I'm so glad to see you. All of you."

Rory stared at the ground.

"Um. I've made such a mess of everything. The bracelet—though I swear I didn't know what it was—and the horrible things it brought. Your father." His voice broke again. "I was telling Finn how sorry I am for everything. I had no idea, didn't mean…. I'm so sorry the King died. And the way I acted at the funeral, well, it was crass and hurtful and unpardonable; I was just so angry but that's no excuse. I don't deserve your friendship at all, but could you, possibly, um, do you think you could ever forgive me?"

Rory stared at him.

"I wouldn't blame you if you turned and walked away right now. But maybe you could at least consider it?"

"Wow," Rory said, looking from Jakin to Finn. "I wasn't expecting this at all."

"I think he's truly sorry," Finn murmured. "I think maybe Jakin was as much a victim of Draegin as you were."

Jakin scuffed his boot, again. "It was my own fault. At least at first. I was just so jealous about you two and I let it fester. When I met that specter in the woods, I didn't know who it was, but I was terrified. I never meant for anyone to get hurt. It got way, way out of hand. I'm so sorry, Rory."

She crossed her arms, not exactly warming up. Then she surprised him. "Okay, Jakin. You were a good friend of Finn's for a lot of years. If he thinks he can trust you, I'll go along with it. I forgive you."

"Oh." Jakin was at a loss for words. "I'm so glad." His voice was husky with emotion.

Rory's voice took on an edge. "But you hurt a lot of people, and there's someone I love who is still devastated. I think you know who I mean."

He was afraid he did. "My aunt?"

"Yes. Mother was nearly shattered by the whole horrible nightmare. And when you insulted the memory of her husband…." Rory huffed and shook her head. "You need to apologize. To. Her. Face."

He hadn't counted on this. "But I hardly know her," he stammered. "She probably wouldn't even see me."

"Doesn't matter. You owe it to her to try."

He sighed. Maybe she was right.

"And one more thing." Rory's voice was icy. I belong with Finn. And I don't want any misunderstanding about that ever again."

"Got it," Jakin said. His heart belonged to someone else now anyway. No problem. She'd forgiven him and that was huge. Maybe the ice would melt; maybe they could eventually be friends, again, but for now, having Finn's friendship back was enough.

Jakin shifted his weight, putting his hands on his hips. "So, I overheard you say you need to get to the island?

Finn nodded.

"I could take you. I've got five days and nothing to do."

"How soon?" Finn asked, grinning.

"Sun-up tomorrow. And you can camp on the ship tonight."

Rory looked uneasy.

"Just a skeleton crew, Rory," Jakin assured her. "I can round up a few sailors I trust. Promise."

She glanced at Finn. "Okay then. We're in."

They slept on the deck under the stars, not wanting to take the remotest chance of being trapped below. At dawn the crew hoisted the ropes and set sail. A prevailing headwind really slowed their progress and the one-day trip stretched to two. They were forced to drop anchor in the middle of the choppy sea, three-quarters of the way there. Again, they stayed on the deck under the stars, sharing stories to keep their mind off the choppy sea. Finn and Rory rehashed all the details they could remember about the Night of the Tennins, which Jakin had missed. Kalvara and Aric had been there, but she'd just tried to kill Finn and had been tied to a tree on the edge of their camp. She recalled very little besides her rage.

Spike came out of hiding and perched on Aric's shoulder to hear all about it. Jakin laughed when he met the stick man, shaking his head at the creatures right there on the island that he'd never even known existed. He shared his ghoulish experience of meeting Draegin in the woods, how he thought he'd barely escaped with his life, though now he realized it was all a trick, a set up, so Draegin could slip him that bracelet and trap them with his dark magic.

"So, tell me, again, Rory," Jakin said at the end of his story, "why Draegin wants to kill you so bad?"

She squirmed. "It's complicated." She leaned against Finn. "But the simple truth is he feels I threaten his throne."

"What about you?" Jakin said, looking at Finn. "He doesn't want to kill you?"

Finn shrugged. "He doesn't know about me. Somehow, he's overlooked my heritage."

"So, Rory, you're actually taking the fall for Finn?" Jakin was astonished.

"It seems so. But Floxx has always been there to protect me. She and the tennins."

"Wow," Jakin said, "I never realized that. I mean, that's crazy. A raging dragon and his insane Queen out to kill you because they think you threaten them when the real threat has been Finn all along!"

"Well, strictly speaking, my heritage actually is a threat. I mean, I am a princess. But Finn's the one Eldurrin has chosen and Draegin is oblivious to the fact he even exists."

"A brilliant tactic, for sure!" Kalvara added.

Jakin took a deep breath. He didn't know what to make of this revelation, but he was grateful to have his friends back. He was glad to be on their side, again. He'd rather face Draegin together with them than on his own. But later, a doubt niggled at him as he stared at the stars. Would Floxx protect him like she protected them? He remembered Zad's death, and feared he, too, might be considered expendable.

Morning dawned, cool and breezy. There had been no storm, just a lot of wind and choppy water. Jakin had dozed fitfully, his mind vacillating from the weather to the ship and then flipping to Draegin and his friends. They ate smoked fish and some bread Jakin had picked up in town and pulled up anchor. Jakin was at the wheel, studying the surf and deciding how close to bring the ship. His friends stood at the rail, staring at the island, murmuring to each other in voices just low enough he couldn't understand.

Suddenly Rory called, "Who's that?" She pointed to a person on the beach. "No, this can't be; it's not possible! I'm going below!" And she flew down the ladder, Kalvara hurrying after her.

Jakin stared. The figure was unmistakable even from this distance. Her long black hair blew wild in the wind. Nerida! What was she doing here? And why was Rory so frightened?

Chapter 26: Back Under

Rory trembled on the narrow bunk below deck, staring out the small porthole. They were closer now, and she could see the woman clearly. Her long black hair shone in the sun and her beauty was apparent. The blood had drained from Rory's face. She turned to Kalvara. "This is terrible. That's Marinna, I'm sure of it. She's exactly as mother described. What is she doing here? Has she been tracking me all this time? How would she even know I'd come here?"

Kalvara scooted closer. "Rory, calm down. Think. She could not know you'd ever been here, and she'd have no reason to expect you'd come. This is an isolated place; a tiny speck on the sea, known to very few."

"Well then, I don't get it. Why is she here?"

"My guess is she's waiting for Jakin."

Rory stared at Kalvara, confused. "Waiting for Jakin? Not me?"

"Remember? Aric and I saw her and Jakin together the night we escaped."

"Right, you did tell us that."

"They acted awfully friendly; seemed like things were a little steamy."

"That is totally gross. And terrifying. We have to warn him. He has no idea who he is dealing with. She will kill him."

Aric swung himself down the short ladder. "It's Nerida!" he shouted. "Or maybe her name's Marinna—Finn and Jakin are arguing about that."

"Shhhh." Kalvara hushed him. "We know. That's why we are down here. We don't want her to see us."

The boy climbed on the bunk, squeezing between them, and stared out the porthole. "She sure is pretty."

"Don't be fooled by her looks!" Kalvara whispered. "She's as deadly as her father. Never forget Droome, Aric."

Jakin and Finn soon clambered down the ladder. "I know, I know. It's Marinna. As in Queen Marinna! I can't believe it. She told me her name was Nerida. And I promise I had no idea. I mean, why would Queen Marinna be flying around on a Pegasus way out here?"

"That's exactly what we'd like to know!" Kalvara stated. "And we wonder what else she's lied to you about. You know, Aric and I saw you with her here, just before she and her flying horse left. The same night we escaped on your ship."

"Oh." Jakin blushed. "I can't believe this." He turned and stormed up the ladder.

"And I can't believe it's taken him this long to figure out who she is!" Rory whispered, moving close to Finn. "What do we do now?"

"We wait. We find out what she's doing here before we make a move. Uriel is already floating among the trees watching and listening."

The day dragged. The crew had gone ashore and Rory and the others alternated between napping and pacing in the dim, cramped space below deck.

"We need Floxx," Rory complained. "Where in the world did she go? I can't believe she'd leave us in this mess!"

Finn tried to encourage her. "Eldurrin is not surprised by anything that's happened, Rory. He knows exactly where we are and where Floxx is."

She nodded, an involuntary shudder coursing through her.

"I'm sure he called her away for a good reason. Let's just keep our minds on him and his promise to always help us." He nudged her playfully. "I think he's good for his word."

"Right," she said, wishing she had half the confidence he did. As soon as night settled, they climbed to the deck. Rory inhaled the sea air, clean and cool on her face, and regained some of her optimism. The stars flooded the sky and reflected on the calm water's surface. "It's so beautiful!"

"Where's Jakin?" Kalvara asked.

Finn peered over the side of the ship. "The dingy's gone. He must have gone to find Marinna."

"Bad idea," Kalvara scoffed. "Let's hope he didn't do that."

Rory couldn't believe the mess they were in. It just kept getting worse. She tore a piece of bread off a loaf and passed it around, then a chunk of cheese, saying nothing as she reached out silently for Eldurrin. *I'm trusting you. I could get killed here; you know that. We could all get killed. One of her fireballs could take out this ship. But you promised to help us. You promised to do what was impossible. And fighting her is impossible.* That familiar presence began to stir inside her. *And really, we aren't here to face her, anyway. That actually might be easy, compared to what we have to do to find the elven tunnel. Do you really want us to go back Underside? The Tall King will kill us on sight; he'll take no more prisoners, I'm pretty sure of that.*

She glanced at Finn. He'd stretched out on the deck, hands behind his head, studying the stars. The red ring had slid from under his tunic and dangled openly. *Are we right,*

Eldurrin? Should we head for the center of the garden? Or do the runes mean something different? A breeze ruffled her hair and she waited. But she heard nothing. She felt nothing more. With a sigh, she settled down next to Finn. *You won't let us down, right?*

They took turns standing watch through the night. Kalvara and Aric took the first shift, then Finn, and finally, Rory. When Finn nudged her awake for her watch, she jolted, disoriented for a moment. "Oh. Wow. I really slept hard." She sat up rubbing her eyes. "Anything of interest happen?" She yawned.

"Not a thing. The stars paraded across the sky uneventfully."

"Good to know."

He helped her to her feet, pulling her close for a kiss before he collapsed in the spot she'd vacated. "Mmmm, still warm," he whispered, then curled on his side and immediately dozed off.

Her heart swelled with affection as she gazed at him. *He'll make a great king. Strong and gentle. Smart and sensitive. His faith in Eldurrin is growing stronger each day as he gives himself to the daunting task he's been called to accomplish. He's right. Eldurrin is good for his word. No need to worry.*

She took a seat behind the ship's wheel, running her hands over its polished spokes. She'd never have guessed Jakin would captain a ship; he'd never mentioned any special love for the sea during their time together. What a mess he was. First falling prey to Draegin's bracelet scheme, and now hooked into a romance with Marinna. She felt sorry for him, desperately needing love but never finding it. He'd been so hurt that his uncle had abandoned him to the dwarves. Why had Father done that? She realized it must have been devastating for him when she'd been kidnapped, and then her mother succumbing to that horrible sick trance. But she would have thought caring for his nephew might have brought the King a great deal of joy. If only he'd tried, the links in the chain of horrors that had taken his life would likely have been broken. She was so engrossed in her thoughts she didn't notice the soft paddling on the water.

Jakin appeared suddenly on the ship and she squeaked. "Oh my gosh! You startled me!"

"Some watchman you are," he said without a hint of a smile.

"Where have you been? We've been so worried about you."

"Really? As if you care."

"We do, Jakin." She crossed her arms. "What happened?"

He squeezed his eyes shut. Then his shoulders sagged, and when he finally looked at her, she could see the pain in his eyes.

"You went to see Marinna."

He nodded.

"And?"

"And she's lied to me. It's all been a lie. Her mother's name was Nerida, not hers. Why couldn't she just tell me her own name?"

"I'm sure she thought you'd realize she was Draegin's daughter!"

He didn't respond.

"And what is she doing here?"

"She plans to rule from here, protected by the sea. She wants to build a castle."

"Rule? She thinks she can rule from here? Rule what?" Her heart pounded for her mother and the citizens of Byerman.

Jakin shrugged. "Everyone. Everything."

"Why did she leave her mountain palace? Is Draegin dead?"

"She said it didn't concern me." He slapped his fist into his palm, angry, and then shook his head ever so subtly as if he'd made up his mind. He moved a step closer. "She's seen

you, Rory," he whispered. "All of you. I told her you were part of the crew, but I don't think she bought it. You have to leave the ship. Now. She might already be on her way here."

Rory woke the others. In a few hurried minutes they grabbed their gear and slipped into the dinghy. Jakin kept to the shadows and rowed them to a wooded part of the shore, not far from the tunnel entrance.

Finn was the last to climb out; Rory fidgeting as she waited, her heart hammering. He hesitated a moment, touching Jakin's shoulder. "Take care of yourself, okay?"

"Sure. You, too."

"Come on!" Rory hissed. In a moment, he grabbed her hand and they sprinted into the tunnel. Kalvara and Aric were already there, holding the bellasol to light the way. And she was thrilled to see Uriel zip in just behind them. It was quiet in the tunnel. Most of the dwarves were in Syrea; theirs had been the only ship anchored near the island. Rory hoped they could pass through without meeting anyone. Her senses were on high alert, listening for any sound, any indication Nizat might be patrolling this passageway. But she heard nothing.

They came to a branch in the tunnel and Finn questioned Aric who was familiar with the route. The boy pointed left.

"What's down that way?" he whispered, nodding right.

"Don't know. Never been."

"Uriel?" Finn pointed down the right tunnel branch. "Could you take a look?"

He's brilliant, Rory thought. She'd never thought of sending Uriel ahead to scout.

They waited in silence. Kalvara tapped the bellasol off as their eyes adjusted to the dimness. When Uriel returned, he blinked and led the way to the right. Finn winked at Rory, took her hand and followed the blue light. They descended in a curve and were startled when they splashed into water. Uriel blinked on the other side, urging them to follow.

Rory was the last. "Okay, okay," she whispered, tucking the hem of her dress into her waistband. "What I'd give for my jeans," she muttered, taking off her shoes and socks and slogging through the dark water. In a half dozen steps, she was on solid ground that appeared to rise gradually as it curved to the left. Aric was the only one who got through dry, riding on Finn's shoulders. Soon the tunnel leveled out and they walked for a long time. When the air grew warmer, she guessed they were near the exit and she was right. Uriel poked out first, flitting one way then the other, then zooming back to blink an all-clear at them.

They emerged in a field. It was mostly weeds but even so, she was amazed so much growth could survive in the dim light. Water gurgled in the distance and they crept toward it. Someone was laughing. A splash. More laughter. Shushing. The voices were too far away for Rory to make out what they were saying.

"I know that voice," Kalvara whispered. "It's Riza; she was my bath maid. So nice. Very gentle."

"So, we must be opposite the baths," Finn deduced. "This stream must feed them."

"I wonder where the water comes from," Rory said.

"Wet tunnels," Kalvara told her. "Riza told me about them when I asked her the same question. Apparently, water drips through some of the tunnels and feeds the streams."

"Like the one we just walked through."

"Right. That explains why we met no one. The Tall King forbids trekking through the wet tunnels, wanting to keep the water clean."

"Smart."

"And useful information for safe passage." Finn grinned.

"So, now what?" Rory looked at him.

"We wait on Eldurrin. Cause I sure don't have a clue."

Chapter 27: A Fish and a Fly

Jakin remained tense as Marinna stormed his ship bow to aft. "So where is this crew you told me about?"

He shrugged. "Home, I guess. Having dinner with their families."

"And where, exactly, do they live?" she hissed.

He shrugged. "Somewhere out there, I guess." He actually didn't know—he'd always stayed on his ship when he was here. His crew kept their distance from him; he'd had no idea Underside existed until Kalvara had told him. He didn't dare tell Marinna. No way. As angry as she was, who knew what she might do. He'd seen her father's fury and presumed she had inherited some of it. He'd leave her alone until she calmed down. He walked away from her.

"Where are you going?" she demanded.

"Fishing. In my dinghy," he snapped. He glared at her and saw a heat aura blooming around her. He'd better not make her any angrier. "Look, Marinna," he said, palms open in a gesture of peace. "I'm hungry. I'm going fishing. You're welcome to join me, but let's not fight. Please. I'll take you back to shore if you don't want to come."

She turned her back on him and pouted.

He dropped gingerly into the rocking dinghy and waited. In a few minutes, she stepped stiffly down the ladder and sat down with a thump.

"I'll come," she clipped.

Jakin headed for open water and unloosed the sail hoping the breeze would cool her off. He sailed for an hour in silence, glancing at her from time to time. Once the shoreline disappeared, she visibly relaxed, leaning against the port side. As hurt as he was with her deception, he couldn't keep his eyes off her. Her expression of rage slowly changed. If he didn't know better, he'd call it joy. She liked sailing! When she broke a smile, he figured it was safe to talk.

"First time sailing?"

"Yes."

"Fun, isn't it?"

"Yes."

Hmmm. One-word answers. She wasn't cutting him any slack. He slowed as he neared his favorite fishing spot and lowered a small net. Just a few fish would be more than enough.

Her expression was priceless. She'd clearly never been fishing. Eyebrows raised, she watched everything he did, but was too proud to ask any questions.

He stretched out on the boat, propping his feet near her. "Beautiful day," he said, eyeing the soft clouds. He put his hands behind his head, rocking with the ship.

"We just wait?"

"Yes."

"You don't have to watch the net?"

"No."

"Jakin!" she walked over to him, exasperated. "Talk to me. You haven't said a word since we left."

He patted the space beside him, inviting her to settle in. She stood too quickly, nearly capsizing the boat.

"Easy, easy!" Jakin grabbed her arm. "Just be still a moment."

They waited until the craft settled.

"Move slowly and keep your balance."

She warily crept toward him and sat.

"Comfortable?"

"Yes."

That heat he'd seen around her earlier began to bloom in him. He leaned over, an inch from her face. "What did you want to talk about?" he asked just before he kissed her.

It was several minutes later before she got around to answering. She ran her finger down his cheek. "Jakin," she whispered, "I want to talk about us."

"Okay."

"Now you know who I am."

"I do."

"Are you afraid? Draegin's daughter?"

"Mmm hmm. Yes. Well, I'd say cautious. On guard. You know what I mean?"

"I do."

He chuckled at her mimicking him. "Tell me honestly, Marinna. Do you care for me?"

"Isn't it obvious?"

"Well, yes and no."

"What does that mean?" Her icy tone was returning. Too many questions.

"When we are together, we sizzle."

She laughed.

"But we are not together very often."

"I was hoping that would change with me on the island."

"So, wanting to rule from a seaside castle isn't your only reason for being on the island?"

"What do you think?" She nuzzled his neck. "Now, that's enough talking."

A few minutes later, something hit the side of the boat. Jakin jumped. "The net!" he hollered, reaching over to see it crammed with fish. "Look at these beauties! We'll eat good for a week, Marinna!"

She shrieked, pulling her feet and her gown up onto the bench as he sloshed the wriggling net into the boat. She peered down at the fish. "Oh my. So that's how it's done! They really flop around!"

"Not for long. But let's head back and cook a few of them. I'm starved."

"I am, too. But, since we're out here, Jakin, could we sail a little more? See if we can find those mermaids, again?"

"The one that called you Nerida?"

"Mmm hmm."

"Why did she call you your mother's name?"

"I was as surprised as you were. But I'm guessing I look a lot like her."

"You're guessing? Don't you know?"

"No, I've never seen my mother." She hesitated. "She died giving birth to me."

"Oh. I'm sorry," he said lamely. Great. Way to ruin a nice moment. He really didn't want to spend more time on the water—he was very hungry—but now he didn't have the heart to say no; besides, mermaids and mermen fascinated him. Maybe she'd talk a little, too, about why they would know her mother.

They tacked in every direction possible, searching for a couple of hours. Nothing. Finally, Jakin headed back to the island. They sailed in silence. She was crestfallen.

"We can come, again, and look for them. No problem," he encouraged.

Hope lit her eyes. "I would like that."

Later, under the trees, Jakin licked his fingers, his stomach finally full. He'd eaten two big roasted fish and a handful of berries Marinna had provided. She'd polished a whole fish off, herself. He settled back and ventured a question, hoping it wouldn't shut her down. "So, that mermaid mistook you for your mother?"

She held her finger over her lips. "Not now, Jakin. Not out in the open. Who knows if dwarves are listening." She moved closer to him. The feel of her body set him ablaze. He kissed her. She responded with a passion that turned him to putty. He was barely able to keep his desire for her under control. His conscience screamed for him to stop. To get up, move away. He should not let his lust rule. But, did it really matter? Clearly, she had no inhibitions, no boundaries, so why should he? Nevertheless, he found the strength to pull away, putting a few inches between them.

She moved seductively closer. "Jakin," she whispered in his ear. Her warm breath made his skin tingle.

He heard his name again, "Jakin." Wait. That was not Marinna's voice. Spike. It was Spike. He couldn't believe it. The stick man was here? Did he have no privacy at all? He ignored the bramble, kissing Marinna again and again, lingering on her cheek, her neck.

"Jakin." Spike was insistent.

Jakin groaned and sat up.

"Not again! Do I bore you?" Marinna hissed, insulted.

"Of course not, love. I need to, well, you know," he looked sheepish and disappeared into the woods.

"What?" he hissed at Spike, trying to brush him off his shoulder, but the bramble was hidden in a fold of his cloak.

"Watch out for her."

"You interrupted us to tell me that?"

"Jakin, listen to me. She is a fish and you are a fly. Get it?"

He shook his head and relieved himself. However, when he returned to her, he sat, leaning against a tree trunk. "Come, love. Sit by me. Please."

She did. He put his arm around her, pulling her close.

She exhaled a sigh of disappointment. "You don't want me."

"Don't be ridiculous. I'm dying with desire. That's why it's safer if we sit," he teased.

She pouted.

"There are no dwarves around. If we whisper, will you answer my question?"

She looked at him blankly.

"The mermaid who called you Nerida. Why would she know your mother?"

Marinna stiffened and turned so she could see him.

Jakin put it as bluntly as he could. "Did your mother know mermaids?"

Marinna suddenly burst into hysterics, laughing so long, she gave herself hiccups.

What was so funny? Had he missed something important? Said something really stupid? He frowned and folded his arms across his chest.

Marinna took his hand. "Jakin," she murmured, lifting his fingers to her lips and kissing them, her eyes lingering on his lips. Heat shot through him like lightening, but Spike's warning had made him wary. Even so, it took all his willpower not to sweep her into his arms and lose himself in her. He caught a flicker of surprise in her eyes at his resistance and it made his resolve stronger. He could resist— he had the strength— though she was full of powerful charms, like her father.

She appraised him. "You are relentless with your questions." She raised one perfectly arched eyebrow. "But I suppose it wouldn't hurt anything if you knew."

He held his breath.

"My mother was a mermaid. A siren."

"Your mother was a siren?" he repeated, slack jawed.

She hiccupped, trying desperately to swallow a laugh.

"So, you are half siren?" Well, that explained her intense seductive powers.

"Tell me what you know about sirens," she teased, running her eyes slowly up and down his body.

His mind fogged under her erotic gaze. He struggled to even speak. "Uh, what do I know. Sirens can live on land or underwater. They beguile lovers into the sea with them where the unfortunate paramours drown." He met her eyes. Deadly. Sirens were deadly. He broke her gaze and stood. The evening was breezy, the blue leaf canopy gently swaying. He exhaled. That was that. She was a fish and he was a fly. He wasn't going to play her game. He couldn't. He thought of all he had to live for. His friends. He had his friends back. He realized how much they meant to him. Finn and Rory. Marinna would destroy him first, then go after each of them. Just like her father. He had to leave, break off the relationship. But before he did, he'd find out a little more.

He turned to face her. "But your siren mother didn't beguile your father into the water."

"No. His magic was stronger. I've often wondered if she was shocked at the strength of his enchantments." She stared past him, unfocused, and whispered, "and how much she knew of who he really was."

"Does your father ever speak of her?"

"Briefly. He told me they'd met in Syrea on the beach. I have no details, except that she was beautiful. He emphasized her exceptional beauty."

Jakin gazed at her. She must, indeed, resemble her mother.

"They fell in love and were married—two magical creatures, terribly unsuited for each other. Who knows if their love was genuine or contrived by enchantment? I like to think it was real. The fact that they conceived a child is outlandish, a fluke, a bizarre twist of the impossible. Yet, here I am, their improbable progeny, one that cost mother her life." Marinna's voice cracked, snapping her back to the moment. The small window into her life slammed shut. "That's about all I know," she said, her icy voice returning as she stood. "I do regret not knowing her."

Jakin considered her in a new light. Half siren. What might that mean? "So, when you disappear for weeks, do you go under the water?"

215

Another spurt of laughter escaped before she could catch it. "No, Jakin. I'm only part siren. Apparently, just the part that lives on land." She gazed through the trees. "But I do love the sea. It ebbs and flows in my veins." She beckoned Conquest. "I think I'll go for a ride." She did not invite him to come. "Good-night, Jakin."

He was being dismissed. No problem; he wanted to leave anyway. "Good-night, Marinna," he said and walked back to his ship, kicking at stones along the way. Half siren. Of all the bad luck. What a doomed lover he was. And what about the other half of her? He couldn't imagine what Draegin's heritage was. Master sorcerer. Enchanted shape shifter. Ancient and deadly, that much he knew. It suddenly struck him that Marinna had no human blood at all. Nor any sense of right or wrong, no loyalty, no genuine affection. Was she even capable of love, real love, the kind that cared about the other person? Or was it just about touch? Did her feelings for him even remotely resemble his feelings for her? Or were hers only about pleasure, control, power? He'd been an unwitting pawn before. But not this time.

Chapter 28: Riza

Riza was moving across the river toward them, quiet, stealthy, whispering to someone. Kalvara could not quite make out what she said. She motioned for the others to move back far enough to be hidden. But she kept Aric with her, warning him to be silent. Soon, weeds on the shore began to sway and Riza's soft voice was clear.

"There now. We're back. You're safe. I loved seeing you. I have to go to work, now, but here. Some food for you. Stay warm, love. And don't be afraid. I'll come for you after dark, as always." Then they heard her splashing softly, again. Kalvara and Aric waited for many minutes until Riza's companion emerged from the tall weeds.

"It's a girl!" Aric blurted, stunned at the appearance of a child. She was about the same height as him, with dark eyes and matted coarse brown hair. She had Riza's face, that was certain, but not her body. Riza was short and stocky the way all dwarves were. But the girl was lean and lanky.

The child screamed and bolted, and Aric chased her, yelling, "Hey, wait! I won't hurt you. I just want to meet you."

Noisy splashing in the water warned Kalvara that Riza had heard the commotion and was hurrying back. In a few moments, she plunged through the weeds, terror on her face. She saw Kalvara and stopped, staring at her, terrified.

"Hello, Riza."

"I thought ye were…dead." She snapped back to the moment. "Where is Zenna?"

"We startled her, and she ran off that way," Kalvara pointed. "Aric chased after her."

They could hear the children talking in the distance. "I guess they are okay now." Kalvara chuckled.

Relief flooded Riza's face. "Kalvara. I can't believe it. It really is you. And Aric. Whatever are ye doing here? Ye were dead. I mean, the King held a death dirge for ye both. Poisoned by those cursed berries. He was broken-hearted over it."

"Ah. Well, here we are. Hale and hearty."

"It was all a lie? Why would the Tall King do that?"

There were a lot of reasons, but Kalvara picked one she'd understand. "Probably to cover up our escape."

"Ye escaped?" Riza was skeptical. "But ye are still here."

"Well, it's a long story. Aric and I came back. With them." Kalvara waved to Rory and Finn, and they came out of hiding.

Riza gasped. "I remember them! That day in the arena!"

"Mother!" Zenna ran to Riza. "Why are ye here? Won't ye be late?" The girl seemed worried.

"I heard all the noise," Riza soothed. "And, yes, I do have to leave, or they will notice me missing." She frowned.

"Riza," Kalvara said, eyeing the children together. "Does Zenna come here often?"

"Yes." Her voice dropped to a whisper. "But she must keep quiet."

"I see." What was going on? Was Zenna in danger? Hiding? Was this part of the island watched? "Well, she can certainly stay here today, even though we are here, too. We will all be very quiet. Do you understand, Aric?"

"Yes. I'll whisper."

"And only when necessary," Kalvara warned. "Perhaps we are in more danger here than we thought."

"Okay, then," Riza kissed her daughter. "Today, ye will have friends to keep ye company. But, shhhh."

Zenna grinned at Aric, as her mother turned and disappeared through the weeds.

Kalvara smiled as the children played. They'd invented a game of hide and seek and stayed within the boundaries she'd set. When one was found, the seeker would tap the hider on the head and giggle, but other than that, they made little noise. They were both stealthy, a fact that surprised Kalvara since dwarves were notoriously clumsy. Must be from hiding all the time, she reasoned, watching Zenna glide as gracefully over the rough ground as Aric did. What tragedy had befallen her young life to plunge her into fear and hiding? She'd once thought escape from the tunnels of Droome would bring carefree happiness all of her days, but she was wiser now. Trouble lurked everywhere. Evil drank joy like water. Was no one ever safe? Could Finn really fulfill the prophecy and bring the peace the world so desperately needed?

It was well past dark when Riza returned. Kalvara and the others were waiting with Zenna by the river, near where they'd met that morning. Riza offered no spoken greeting, just waved her arm at them as she strode past, beckoning them to follow. She led them into the wet tunnel, waded through the water matter-of-factly, and made a sudden right turn into an opening they hadn't seen. Then, a left, and a right and they found themselves in a small cave. Riza lifted a torch from the wall and lit it. So, this was Zenna's hideaway! How smart of the girl not to have given it away.

Riza smiled. "There now. We are all friends. Friends in hiding, that is."

"What are you hiding from, Zenna?" Aric whispered.

"The K---," Zenna started to say, but was quickly interrupted by her mother.

"Sit. Please."

They sat in a circle and Riza pulled food from her satchel, handing each item to Kalvara to distribute. A dozen small dried fish, a few blocks of cheese, two round loaves of bread. Finn pulled a few apples from his pack, cut them into pieces and passed them around to share. A bounty.

They devoured it all in silence, Aric and Zenna sitting close together as if they were the best of friends. Finally, Riza spoke. "Thank ye all for being so kind to Zenna today. She has no friends and, well, Aric, you've made her day very special."

The boy laughed. "For me, too!"

"But it isn't safe here. You must leave tonight when Zenna and I do. I overheard a guard mention hearing some noise over here. They are likely to swarm the area at daybreak; they would have already, but today was a holiday, and no one, not even Nizat, wanted to miss the food."

"Thank you for letting us know, Riza," Finn said. "We will definitely leave whenever you say."

She studied them openly. "So, you all escaped. And yet, you came back, knowing the danger you would face. What could be so important?"

Finn smiled. "It would take too long to tell you the whole story. But we can give you the short version."

Kalvara wondered how much Finn would say. Surely, he wouldn't give away much. She saw the glint of the gold chain on his neck, thankful the priceless ring was tucked away.

Finn picked up a stick and doodled in the dirt. "We have reason to believe there may be an underground tunnel, beneath us. You know, under the Underside, odd as that sounds." He laughed.

Riza stared at him.

Whoa. That was more information than Kalvara would have shared. But, now that he'd told her, she decided to jump in. "Have you ever heard of such a thing?"

Riza didn't reply at once but took her time appraising Finn.

"How is it ye know of this when few in Underside have heard of it?"

"So, it's true then?" Finn avoided answering her question.

Riza started to get up, but Kalvara reached out to stop her. "Riza. Dear Riza. You know we mean you and Zenna absolutely no harm. Please stay a little longer. We, also, fear for our lives here, and for good reason. But we are risking them for a very great hope, a dream that if it can possibly be fulfilled would bring an end to all the strife and fear we face every day. Peace. It would bring peace. This tunnel Finn mentioned is key to finding that peace."

Riza looked at her in disbelief.

Kalvara waved off her skepticism and plowed on. "Look, we have little time, so I'm going to shoot straight. We suspect it may be in the very center of the courtyard, but we have no way of exploring without risking our lives."

Riza gasped. "A tunnel? In the courtyard?"

"Under the round table where the Tall King sits and holds his meetings. Right under the dome."

Riza stood, laughing. "Surely, you're kidding! There's nothing under that table."

"Oh," Kalvara couldn't keep the disappointment from her voice. "You sound quite sure."

"Indeed I am. I've cleaned under that table on my hands and knees. There's not a crack in the stone anywhere. It's just a floor, nothing else."

"Has the table ever been moved?" Rory asked.

"Yes, on rare occasions, though it takes six of us to shove it. It's actually moved right now; we cleared the patio for the feast today. Tomorrow, though, it goes back."

Kalvara furrowed her brow and said nothing more.

Rory took advantage of the temporary lull. "So, Riza, what do you know about the tunnel?"

"Probably no more'n you. Everyone's heard the tales. But that's all they are. Tales. Made up stories that mean nothing."

"What tales," she prodded.

Riza eyed them warily. "If ye don't know the tales, how do ye know of the tunnel? There's more to this than ye are saying."

"There's a lot more," Finn agreed. "But we lack the time to tell you."

She shrugged. "It's just a tale anyway, so what does it matter," she said, more to herself than anyone, then spoke candidly. "There's more of em. The tale says there's more of the tall ones that escaped ages ago."

"Through a tunnel?" Rory asked.

"That's right. But no one's ever seen any sign o' them or a tunnel. Make of it what ye like. We're leaving now." She took Zenna by the hand, pausing to speak to Kalvara. "They're not nice, ye know."

"Who?"

"The tall ones, like ye."

Zenna raced over to Aric and hugged him.

"But," Riza smiled, "I guess you two might be the exceptions."

"Here," Zenna said, so softly even Aric barely heard her, as she handed him something. He held it up. It was a crescent-shaped stone, about as big as his thumb. "I found it in the tunnel."

"Thanks! It's great!" Aric dug in his pockets and pulled out a pearl. "Found this in the street in Syrea. Came from the sea, though."

"Oh, it's pretty! Thanks!"

They gathered their things, put out the torch, and filed out.

"Wait," Aric whispered after a few steps. "I forgot my slingshot." Rory and Finn waited with Kalvara until Aric returned with his prized possession. Riza and Zenna were a good way ahead, and as they followed, they heard Zenna scream.

"No!" Riza shouted. "Give her back!"

"Shut yer trap!" a gruff voice rebuked.

Nizat! Finn stopped in mid-step. Kalvara tapped the bellasol off. They listened to the brief volatile encounter.

Nizat gloated. "Two fer the price 'o one. Wait'll the Tall King sees yer runt. His runt. She'll clean up to be a pretty little plaything for 'im."

A scuffle ensued and they heard a hard slap. "Try that again and ye won't live to see yer filthy spawn another day."

"Riza," Kalvara whispered to herself. "Stop. He'll kill you."

But Riza didn't stop. She screamed and wept, fighting with everything she had. Finally, they heard her shriek, then a sickening thud as she fell. "I told ye t' shut up. Ye shoulda listened."

"Mother!" Zenna sobbed.

"Leave 'er."

Zenna screamed for help.

"Scream all ye want, waif. There's none t'hear for miles around." They scuffled briefly, but soon his footsteps faded away.

Finn and the others rushed for Riza, finding her crumpled against a dark wall. "Let's get her back to her cave," he directed, and they did. They laid her down gently. By the light of the bellasol, they could see she was bleeding.

"He stabbed her," Rory confirmed. "Right here." She pointed to Riza's right side. She and Finn staunched the bleeding while Kalvara and Aric ran to get some water. Before long, they'd cleaned the wound and bandaged it, tearing cloth from Riza's underskirt.

Chapter 29: Crescent Stone

"You stay with her," Finn told Kalvara and Aric. "Rory and I are going after Zenna." He chastised himself as they flew through the tunnel. Even though their weapons were back in the woods, why hadn't he defended Riza? He could have fought, but, no, he just let that scumbag stab her. And kidnap the child. His mental tirade left him ashamed and chagrined. He was determined to make it right. When they emerged from the tunnel, they headed for the water. But there were no footprints in the soft earth, no sign that Nizat had come by boat. They backtracked in the dark and stood at the tunnel entrance.

"He came over land? Alone? That seems so odd." Rory frowned.

"It's possible he's been spying on them for some time. He knew his way through the tunnel and was coming intentionally for them. And coming alone would mean no one would hold him accountable for his actions."

"So, am I understanding Zenna is the Tall King's daughter?"

Finn sighed. "So it seems."

"And Nizat, I suspect, has been stalking them, like he did us, for another gift for the King."

Finn studied the shadows, looking for a clue, broken twigs, crushed weeds, something, anything. He walked several yards in all directions and finally, off to their right, heading into some woods, he found something.

"Rory," he murmured. "The pearl."

Together they headed into the woods, following a path of crushed undergrowth. Nizat hadn't bothered to cover his trail, in fact, it looked as if he'd been using it a while, coming and going, waiting for his chance at the child. Zenna had ripped leaves from the trees and strewn them behind her as she was carried, leaving a wobbly trail to follow.

"She's as smart as Aric."

They'd walked about a half hour at a steady pace, listening for any sign of them. Nizat was deadly, and they wanted every advantage on their side. Soon enough, they heard a slap. Then crying. They peeked through the trees to see Zenna cowering against a tree and Nizat glowering over her.

"Where is it? I know ye have it. I seen ye playing with it."

She checked her pockets. "I don't know. I must have lost it."

He slapped her, again, and she wailed, shielding her head with her arms. He yanked her to her feet, ripping a shoulder of her tunic. He leaned down eye level and shook her hard. "I'll ask ye one more time. The crescent stone. Where is it? Ye had it a few days ago when the moon was the same shape. I watched ye hold it up to the sky, playing with it."

Zenna was horrified. "Ye watched me?"

"Course I did. I 'ave me ways o'stayin' quiet." Nizat leered at her. "I guess I'll 'ave t' search ye, myself." And he ripped the rest of her tunic.

Finn flew at him in a blaze of fury. "Oh no, you don't, you filthy bag of garbage." He tackled Nizat, bashing him hard into a tree.

Rory grabbed Zenna and they raced away, back down the trail.

Nizat caught his breath, glaring at Finn. "Why if it isn't the rat, come back to die in the dark." In a blur of motion, he threw something at him.

Finn ducked in the nick of time and heard the dwarf's knife stick in the dirt inches from him. He grabbed it and lunged.

Nizat rolled away and Finn slammed into the tree, losing his grip on the knife.

"I got ye now, ye slimeball."

He choked for air as Nizat's fingers pressed against his throat. Finn gasped and struggled, trying to breathe. Was he going to die here? No! He mustn't. *Eldurrin, help me! Save me!*

Finn was barely breathing when Nizat screamed, loosened his grip, and grabbed his eye. "Ahhh, get off! Stop, I tell ye!" The dwarf spun round and round, clawing at his face, wailing in agony.

Finn grabbed the knife, tense and ready to use it.

Nizat dug at his eye and finally pulled out a thorny bramble, cursing and crushing it in his fist. In one furious move, he reached into his tunic and flung a dagger at Finn, and in reflex, Finn flung the knife he held at Nizat. The dwarf missed Finn by a foot, his one-eyed aim badly off. However, the knife Finn threw hit its mark, sticking Nizat squarely in the chest. The dwarf stared in shock for an instant before he collapsed in a heap.

Finn rushed over and pried opened his hairy fist and there was Spike, broken beyond repair. He lifted the bramble to his face. "You saved my life, Spike. Again. Thank you. Thank you for everything. You've made such a huge difference." He wrapped him gently in a leaf and tucked him in his pocket, hoping somehow to hold a fitting send off for their wondrous little friend. Finn cleaned off the knife and the dagger, and checked Nizat for other weapons, but found none. Deep in the dwarf's pocket, though, he found a small skin, rolled and tied with a piece of vine. He opened it and saw a crude map burned on its smooth side! He studied it a moment and couldn't make sense of the location, but he recognized a crescent-shaped symbol. He wondered if this was why he'd wanted Zenna's stone. What had Nizat been up to? Was he looking for a treasure of some kind? He tied it, again, and dropped it in his own pocket and headed back to the tunnel.

Finn entered the cave without a sound. Rory and Zenna were there. He knelt by Riza's side; she was breathing normally. Her daughter had curled next to her and fallen asleep.

"How are they?"

"Riza will be okay, I think," Kalvara answered. "I made a poultice of tennifel and it seems to be working." She studied Zenna. "The child, though." She shook her head. "I've seen a lot of childhood trauma. Some never recover."

"She was brave," Finn said simply. "And she's strong. Nizat is dead. There'll be no more threats from him. Let's try to get some rest." He settled down next to the wall, covered himself with his cape, and was asleep instantly. When he woke, Riza was sitting up, eating.

"Well, isn't this a happy sight!" he said, sitting next to her.

"Hungry?" Zenna asked him, holding a blue leaf out for him, filled with berries.

"Zenna! You're looking very well!" He eyed the berries. "Where did you get those?"

"Aric knows. We went together. The circle of berry trees isn't too far from here."

"The poison berries?" Finn questioned, looking from mother to daughter.

"Most dwarves know they are not poisonous, in spite of what the tall ones believe. No one eats them much, though, as we definitely prefer meat." She popped one into her mouth. "But they are way better than starving!"

Finn ate a handful, relishing the burst of flavor. He motioned for Rory and the others to join them.

"We ate already," she said smiling. "You slept late and the long rest was well deserved, Finn. We are all relieved Nizat is dead."

Then Finn remembered. He frowned and lifted their broken bramble friend from his pocket. "But, not without great cost." He opened his palm for them to see.

"Spike!" Aric wailed. "Finn, can we fix him? Will he be okay?"

Finn's eyes held the sad answer. "No, Aric. I'm afraid not. He saved my life but lost his own in the saving." Finn told them about the fight. "I'm not sure how Spike found me, but he was so courageous!"

Aric was inconsolable. "We need to bury him," he lamented.

"Yes. How should we do it, Aric? What would be most fitting for a bramble sprite?"

He sniffed and thought about it. "Well, it should be windy. Spike loved the wind."

"Okay."

"And by those berry trees he lived in."

"That's a good idea. Should we try to go Topside?"

"No, it's too dangerous. But I don't think Spike would mind if we buried him by the berry trees down here. They're not far." The boy perked up at the thought.

"When would you like to do this?" Finn asked the boy.

"As soon as Riza is up for the walk."

Chapter 30: Circle under the Isle

Two days later, they headed for the circle of trees to hold Spike's funeral. Aric and Zenna ran ahead and were well up in a berry tree by the time the others arrived.

"Can you find us?" Aric called to them, ducking behind a large leaf and winking at Zenna. She was a good climber. He could tell she wasn't used to it, panting and all, but she could climb for sure. That must be her elf half, he figured, smiling at the thought.

"No, we can't!" Kalvara whispered back. "Come down and shhhh!"

They'd waited until dusk, wanting to avoid the dwarves who watered those trees each day. Aric gathered everyone in the center of the grove of trees. Riza and Zenna stood by Kalvara, and Finn held Rory's hand, their attention on Aric. He clutched Spike's remains close to his heart. His eyes suddenly pooled with tears.

"We will miss you, Spike," he whispered. "You saved us all more than once. Thank you for everything. I hope you will be happy here, even though it's not Topside." He nodded to Zenna. She laid the perfect blue leaf they'd brought from the tree on the ground. Aric placed the broken bramble between two plump berries on the leaf. They stood for a few minutes in silence.

Aric continued. "Not only were you a friend, and so much fun, but you were smart. You knew all kinds of stuff and we won't forget what you taught us. Especially the old songs. And the runes. *The circle under the isle hides the elven door.* We'll find it, Spike; I promise we will."

At those words, the blue orb floated to the leaf and touched it, blinking once.

"See, Spike, how Uriel loved you. We all did. We'll never forget…"

But before Aric could finish, several dwarves jumped from the foliage and rushed them.

"Gotcha!" one yelled, grabbing Zenna. Aric leapt away and shimmied up a tree, out of reach. The dwarf who had Zenna was carrying her off, but Aric fired a rock at him, hitting him hard in the back of the head. He screamed and dropped the girl, who scrambled up the nearest tree to safety. Her attacker ran off, clutching his bleeding skull.

Two dwarves wrestled with Rory—Aric recognized them as the two who had watered the trees. She kicked and screamed, making it hard for them to tie her. Kalvara had her bow and shot both the attackers, killing one and sending the other running. Riza was screaming as the one remaining dwarf hoisted her over his shoulder. Finn drilled an arrow into him, and he fell forward, dropping Riza hard in the dirt. She shrieked in pain.

As fast as it had started, it was over. Two dwarves lay dead and blood was splattered everywhere. Aric dropped from the tree and called Zenna down. She jumped from a great height and landed lightly on her feet. His eyes widened; she could almost fly!

"Mother," she cried, sobbing. "Are you okay?"

"Shhh, yes," Riza said through gritted teeth. "I'll be fine."

Zenna helped her mother sit, brushing the dirt and debris out of her hair. "I landed on something sharp," Riza said, rubbing her side and looking for whatever had nearly impaled her.

"There!" Aric said, scooting behind her to point out a jagged rock protruding through the jumble of undergrowth. It was the oddest thing, like a small stalagmite, growing straight up from the forest floor. He brushed away the dirt to have a closer look. "It's growing out of a big flat rock."

Zenna took a close look. "If you'd landed straight on it, it could have killed you, mother."

"I guess I just grazed it. But it sure hurts; hit me right near the wound." Riza rubbed her ribs.

Aric spotted the blue leaf on which he'd laid Spike, now crushed and sticky with dirt and berry juice. "They wrecked it!" he wailed. He clutched it to his heart, sobbing. "I'm so sorry, Spike." He hated this place, the dwarves, the tall ones, the darkness. His grief flashed to anger, and he kicked the pointed rock over and over, venting his fury on it.

Rory and Kalvara tended to Riza, staunching the new bleeding, and tightening the bandage to try to ease her pain. Zenna clung to her mother, watching Aric fume.

"That's enough, Aric," Kalvara reprimanded, squatting next to the boy. "Spike would understand the situation. And he'd be very glad none of us were hurt. It could have been much worse, you know."

Aric wiped his wet face. "I just wanted it to be perfect for him," he whimpered. "And now, he's all squished." He launched a last kick at the nub and heard it crack. Good. He'd broken it.

"You sure showed that rock a thing or two!" Kalvara teased, tousling the boy's hair. But suddenly, they felt a strange rumble under their feet and backed away. The ground shook. Before their eyes, the forest floor caved in, creating a hole big enough to fall through.

Once the shaking stopped, Aric lay on his belly, sticking his arms down the opening. "It's deep!" he called to the others. "I can't feel the bottom."

Kalvara knelt beside him, shining the bellasol into the opening.

He peered in, hanging over it enough that Kalvara gripped him with her free hand. "It slopes like a slide and goes on forever," he called into the hollow, then let out a "oooooh" just to hear the echo. He was so excited, he stood and whooped, forgetting all the trauma and angst of a few moments earlier. "Can I slide down?" he asked Kalvara.

"Absolutely not," she said, pulling him away.

"It's probably not very deep. Who'd dig a tunnel around here anyw--?" He stopped and looked up, turning full circle and found he was standing exactly in the center of the blue-leafed berry trees. "The circle under the isle hides the elven door," he said aloud. "This is it!" He exploded with laughter and pulled on Kalvara's hand. "The trees are the circle, not the dome! That's what the rune on the ring means. Right here—this hole is the elven door!"

The others stared at him. "It's possible," Rory said. "But, boy, we sure would have been on a cold trail, thinking it was under the glass dome."

"And probably dead," Finn added.

"There's nothing under the dome, anyway. I'm sure of it," Riza assured them.

"Well," Kalvara said slowly. "Maybe the Tall King was protecting more than the blue stone. Maybe he didn't want anyone to discover this."

"If he even knew about it," Aric said, shaking his head.

A twig broke in the distance, then another. Someone was coming.

"You first," Finn said to Kalvara, pointing to the hole. "And hurry!"

Uriel blinked into the hole just before Aric and Kalvara disappeared behind the orb, followed by Riza and Zenna, then Rory and finally Finn, who had the presence of mind to pull a leafy branch over the opening.

They slid for a terrifyingly long time, careening through loose rocks and gravel, kicking up a blinding cloud of dust. Then, one by one, they screamed as they tumbled from a great height into a pool of deep water. Aric nearly landed on Kalvara and clung to her as she managed to pull each one out of the way before the next one hit.

"It's deep!" Aric gurgled, "and dark. I can't swim very well!"

Zenna was at his side in a couple of strokes. "Hold on to me; I'm a really good swimmer."

Aric lunged at her.

She pushed him away. "Don't drown me!" She reached out her arm to grab his. "Just kick your feet and move your other arm like this." And she showed him how to paddle to the rocky shore.

Riza followed her daughter's example, with Kalvara's help; and Rory and Finn helped each other, though neither of them had much experience swimming. Two by two, they floundered their way to the shallow water, pulling themselves up on a rocky ledge to catch their breath.

"What a ride!" Aric burst into laughter.

Kalvara held up her hand in silent warning, pointing up.

"Whoever was coming may well follow us into the hole," she whispered. "We'd best get moving."

Finn and Kalvara took the lead, their eyes sharpest in the dim light. Kalvara held the bellasol and headed uphill.

"If it's like Droome, Kalvara, we should go down to get out, not up," Aric argued from behind.

She turned and knelt to his height. "The tunnels are similar, but Droome was high in the mountains, so we went down to get out. Here, Aric, we are deep underground, so we want to go up to get to the surface."

He grabbed her hand. "Oh. That's right. You're smart, Kalvara!"

They hadn't gone far when Aric pointed out a path that wandered away from the pool.

"All right," Finn said. "Let's take it. It'd be good to be out of sight should an angry dwarf plunge into the water."

An hour later, they came to a large cave, or more accurately, a series of caves, filled with long stalagmites and stalactites. The air was moist, and they could hear water, though they couldn't see it. Aric took the bellasol from Kalvara and shined it on the dagger-like protrusions.

"Whoa! Look at those spikes. Like the tiny one I broke only way, way bigger." These were several times the height of the boy, giant daggers protruding from both the floor and ceiling of the caves.

"The colors!" Rory whispered. The formations were striated with greens and blues and yellows that sparkled even in the dim light.

Aric turned full circle with the bellasol, pointing it in every direction. "Even the walls are shiny with starlight! What is it?"

Riza laughed. "Those are minerals, Aric, flecks of special rocks that shine. They come in a lot of different colors."

"We didn't see these in Droome, did we, Kalvara?"

"No, Droome was heavily mined for its minerals and gems. They were mostly gone before you were born." Her hand was warm on his shoulder. He was suddenly grateful and threw his arms around her. "You saved me, didn't you? I'd still be there without you."

She hugged him back in silence.

Riza found a flat rock and sat. "I'm so sorry, everyone," she groaned. "I'm in a lot of pain. Could we rest a while?"

"Absolutely," Finn said.

"Great!" Aric exclaimed, grabbing Zenna and climbing to a wide ledge.

"We are resting, Aric," Kalvara warned. "Not exploring, though perhaps there will be time for that later."

"We won't wander," Zenna assured her.

"Promise," Aric agreed. "We'll stay up here right near you."

Once everyone was settled, Kalvara flicked off the bellasol, plunging them into darkness.

"Sleep if you can," Finn whispered. "We will need our strength soon enough."

Chapter 31: Siren

"Weak," Marinna said aloud. "And ridiculously innocent." She scoffed and fussed, striding back and forth, eyeing the whitecaps frothing their way to shore. "And yet, he resists me. How is that possible? Where does he get the strength to reign in the heat of his passion?"

She hadn't seen Jakin in several days. She thought perhaps he'd left the island, sailed back to Syrea, but she'd seen him coming back from one of his fishing trips. She'd supposed he'd gone fishing, again, today. But it was getting late, well past the time he should have returned, and there was no sign of him. Well, then, perhaps he'd left her, once and for all. Fine. She didn't need him. He stirred something powerful inside her, that was certain, but no matter. There were plenty of other men.

That night the moon rose full and bright, and a stiff breeze tousled the big leaves overhead, allowing her glimpses of it. Marinna tossed restlessly in the hammock. Finally, she gave up trying sleep; she wasn't tired. A midnight ride, that's what she needed! She readied Conquest.

The wind was tricky to fly in, and they bucked updrafts and downdrafts, but Conquest eventually found an altitude that was relatively smooth. He turned so the wind was at their backs and let the tailwind speed them across the sky.

This was glorious! Wondrous! She exulted in the rush of speed; the thrill erupting in a great burst of laughter. Conquest neighed and she hugged his neck, patting him and cooing her thanks. They flew for a long time before the stallion descended, flying just a few feet above the surface of the sea. The moon grinned at them from beneath the water, its face rippled with froth. Marinna was studying the reflection so intently she didn't see them approach. Before she could react, an enormous merman jumped out of the water and snatched her off her horse. She screamed and splashed into the sea, dragged under by the ferocious strength of the siren.

She was going to die. What a fool she'd been to fly so close to the surface. Her shallow lungful of air was quickly running out. She was dizzy. She needed to breathe. Another 30 seconds passed. Still, he held her in an iron grip; she had no strength to fight him. She had to breathe. Now. She opened her mouth, gulping water, knowing she would die in moments. His powerful tail propelled them ever further down, down, into the depths of the watery world. As she blacked out, the irony was not lost on her: one siren drowned by another.

Marinna woke in a pool of bubbles. Had she died? She took a deep breath. Apparently not—she was very much alive! How was this possible? She saw she was alone in an underwater alcove of sea grass. The water was full of bubbles. She marveled as she realized it was the grass that made the bubbles. Air bubbles. And she was breathing them. How? Why? She shifted her position and found it was soft underneath. Sand. She raked it with her nails and found the sensation immensely pleasurable. She raised her head and laughed, delighting in the feel of water on her skin, sand under her nails. Her hair flowed around her, a black curtain swaying with her every move.

And suddenly, she was not alone. Her captor darted in through the grasses and embraced her.

"Ah, Nerida! You live! I am so glad to see you!"

She shoved him away. "I beg your pardon!" She stood but found her feet were gone, replaced by a thick fish tail. And her top half was bare naked. She instinctively covered herself with her arms.

The merman was angry. "Do you not recognize me?"

"No."

He extended his muscular arms. "Nerida, it's me. Adrian."

Adrian? This merman had known her mother?

"Adrian," Marinna said, with as much dignity as she could muster. "I am not Nerida."

"Ah, but surely you are! You haven't changed a bit!"

"No," she insisted. "Nerida was my mother. I am Marinna."

Adrian stared. He swam a full circle scrutinizing her. "Is this true? Nerida had a child?"

"I can assure you it is true."

He shot out of the grass enclave and back in, angry, again. "And who, exactly, is your father?"

"Draegin. He is not a merman."

"Who is he, then?" Adrian challenged.

"A great Thaumaturge. Shape-shifter. Half dragon."

Adrian was stunned. "Half dragon? But, if you are her daughter, as you say, you look exactly like her. It's as if your mother disappeared for 20 years and has come back. Where is she then?" he demanded. "Where is Nerida?"

Marinna sighed. "Gone, Adrian. Dead. She died the day I was born."

He thrashed his great tail, whipping the grasses in frenzy. "King Llyr's granddaughter is dead?" She saw grief in his eyes. He said nothing for a few moments but studied her intently.

"Your hair. Hers was the same. Black as night, long and straight. Your nose and your mouth. Hers exactly. But your eyes are different. I hadn't noticed before. Hers were as blue as the sea on a cloudless day. But yours have a yellow in them that makes them green."

Draegin's eyes were yellow. She shuddered with the thought of her parents loving each other. Distasteful. Disgusting perhaps. But her green eyes testified to the truth of it.

"Adrian, I don't understand how I am alive. I am only half-siren. How is it that I breathe?"

"Why, with gills, of course." He whisked around to her side, pointing out the obvious.

"But I've never had gills before."

"Well, perhaps you did and didn't know. You've no use for them on land. But you surely didn't grow them on your way down here!" He laughed as if he'd made a great joke.

She felt the sides of her neck. There they were. Gills. There'd never been a slit, never a bump, not a sign that gills lived just under the skin of her neck.

"And my feet?" Dismay laced her voice as she swished her fish tail. "When I go back to land, will I have them, again?"

Adrian laughed, again. "Of course. If you go back. It is the way of all sirens. We adapt. And we love. Both on land and in the water. Come, beautiful daughter of Nerida. Let me introduce you."

They emerged from the grassy nook to the gasps of dozens of mermaids and mermen.

"Nerida!" they exclaimed, "You've come back!" They were clearly shocked, but soon laughed and applauded. "We have missed you for too long!" They formed a circle around the two of them.

Adrian raised his arms for quiet, then said, "This, my friends, is not my Nerida. I am very sorry to say that Nerida is dead. But she did leave some of herself with us. Please share my joy in meeting Nerida's daughter, Marinna!"

There was a momentary hush, and in that instant, a distinguished silver-haired merman swam slowly toward her. He wore a crown of black and green pearls and carried a trident, which he handed to Adrian to hold.

"Marinna!" He placed a hand on each of her shoulders and inclined his head. "I am honored to meet you. I am your great grandfather, King Llyr. I am very, very sorry to hear of your mother's death."

She bowed as best she could in the water, hoping he knew she meant respect. "The honor is all mine," she replied.

His expression reflected the truth of his sadness. "I loved my granddaughter very much, though, I fumed when she left. She was so young." He frowned, remembering. "She would not listen to me or anyone else. It seemed she was charmed somehow, entranced by a power she could not resist. Very few sirens ever leave, and of those who have, none have returned. It's terribly tragic. I hope we do not have the same misfortune with you, Marinna. We welcome you to our family and trust you will stay."

Stay? Oh, she could not stay! She'd never consider it. Still, she smiled at the King, but he wasn't fooled.

"Three times, Marinna. Three times and you will be ours." He retrieved his trident and swam away, his thick tail propelling him slowly through the water.

Is that a threat? Three times? What does that mean? Well, I'm not staying, so what does it matter. I never meant to be here at all and once is definitely enough.

Once the King had left, the younger sirens murmured among themselves. Marinna caught snatches of conversation, questions about who her father was, where she'd lived for so long, how her mother had died. Adrian, with much patience, answered them all.

"Come, then," a pretty mermaid said, "It's time to go. Come with us and meet some others."

Marinna swam with a dozen mermaids and mermen swooping along the sea floor, scattering formations of fish into glittering fragments and watching them reform after they'd passed. She touched purple and orange flowers, so gorgeous. They laughed and talked and cavorted, gliding under and sliding over each other in erotic moves. She loved all of them, but one merman, in particular, made her heart throb. Orkha. Raw desire gripped her.

"Come, my beauty," he teased. "Swim with me. Let's leave these lovers to themselves."

She couldn't say no. She had no willpower to refuse him. She would follow him to the greatest depths, the roughest waters, the dirtiest seas. She took his hand and they swam gracefully away from the group. He led her to a quiet cove, a good distance away, near the shore in shallow water. There they explored the coastline together, winding in and out of reefs, picking their favorite shells, frolicking in the rushes. He brought her to a bed of water lilies, dozens of them blooming yellow and orange, vibrant against their verdant leaves. There they embraced. His kisses were like poison to her, a delicious, powerful poison, rendering her weak. She responded with a passion that would have killed Jakin, unleashing the full strength of her desire on Orkha.

"You are gorgeous, Marinna," he murmured when their passion subsided. "The most beautiful siren under the sea." He strung a delicate necklace of white cowrie shells, streaks of yellows and oranges swirling across their smooth curves.

"For you, my princess," he said, as he tied it around her neck.

Marinna jolted. Princess! She already was a princess! She was to be Queen. Rule the world. Draegin! She remembered she was his daughter. She had a destiny. She had to go back to the land. She struggled to leave Orkha, but he held her tight.

"Oh no, my love. You cannot leave. You are mine now."
She wrenched with all of her might, but he was too strong
for her. He would not let her go. She must get away! She had
a kingdom to rule. A castle to build on the island. Her father
was counting on her. And her beautiful mother was, too. She
fought with him, her anger rising. Still, he prevailed, twisting
her arms to her side, preventing her escape. In a burst of fury,
she wrenched away, throwing a wave of heat at him that
scalded the water, hotter and hotter, bubbling, boiling, and
finally erupting in a blistering geyser. Orkha fled and
Marinna raced for shore, crawling with her last bit of
strength out of the water.

She woke on her stomach, laying on the rocks by the
shore. What a nightmare! She rubbed her eyes and they stung
with salt. She was so groggy; her body felt leaden. Then she
felt the water on her feet. Wait, had that been real? She
bolted up, ready to run from Orkha. But he was nowhere to
be seen. She collapsed on the rocks, again, damp and
drained, clutching her knees to her chest. It all flooded back
to her. She'd been a siren! She felt her neck for gills, but they
were gone. No matter, she knew they'd been there! Her hair
was matted with seaweed and sand; her long red fingernails,
which had just grown back, were all broken, again. She
remembered fighting Orkha. He would have kept her forever
as his lover. Perhaps that would have been a great honor for
another siren. But not for her. She'd have no kingdom to
rule, no conquests to make, no castle, no Pegasus. She
shuddered at the thought of what she'd nearly lost, never
before appreciating the privilege of her destiny.

She understood now why her mother had chosen Draegin.
Perhaps she had been enchanted as King Llyr had suggested,
but Marinna doubted it. She'd just craved a different life.
One full of adventure and challenge and risk. Draegin hadn't
forced her to leave the sea or tricked her into it; she had
chosen. He'd offered her the chance of a better life, and she'd
taken it. Marinna smiled, understanding her mother far more

than before. She'd redeem her mother's sacrifice, make her proud.

She stood, and it was only then she realized she wore only Orkha's string of shells. She dashed into the trees, lifting the necklace over her head to toss it on the ground, but hesitated. No, she'd keep it in memory of her mother, a reminder that life under the sea, as glorious as it was for some, was not for them. She straightened her shoulders, lifted her chin high. She was both siren and sorceress. She had daunting challenges ahead, a world to conquer, a kingdom to rule. Father had said so. He'd promised she would be Queen. Her mother had died to give her the chance. She determined she would never look back.

Chapter 32: Mera and Toad

Rory slept fitfully, running from nightmares she couldn't escape and waking in panic. She decided to sit up and wait for the others to wake. If she happened to doze, fine. She moved as close to Finn as she could, careful not to wake him with a brush of her touch. She knew how lightly he slept. Her eyes had fully adjusted to the dark and the caves shimmered in nuances of shadow. In the silence she could hear water dripping but the echo made it impossible to tell where the source was. There must be water in many places, seeping through the rock, slowly carving this maze for ages. Did the elusive elves live here deep in these caves? Had they settled in darkness like the eldrows in Droome, adapting to the environment? Maybe these were kin to Kalvara and Aric, not the tall ones they'd grown to distrust. She peered until her eyes watered but saw nothing new. She listened but heard nothing except the distant dripping. The soft patter lulled her back to a dreamless, exhausted sleep.

She woke to the sound of Riza rustling in her pack. Finn was at her side as she opened her eyes.

"Good morning, sleepy head," he ran his thumb down her cheek. "I'm so glad you slept."

"I guess I did," she mumbled, stretching.

He leaned over and kissed her soundly on her mouth.

Affection for him bloomed, warming her from the inside. She sat up to take the food he offered—a chunk of damp bread and some cheese—and leaned contentedly against him, munching. She was relieved to be away from Underside. Nothing good was there, and they'd managed to escape unscathed. If they'd truly found where the elves of old lived, they'd be so much closer to getting the crown restored. If they ever found them. If they didn't kill them on sight. If the elves remembered the old ways and if they'd even cooperate. The odds were so slim. Impossible.

She stopped, her bread halfway to her mouth. Yes, impossible! That's what the Firebird had said at the Pool of Tennindrow. The words floated through her mind, as if whispered in her ear. *Finian, these are feats far beyond your own capability, impossible to accomplish in just your own strength, and yet Eldurrin has called you to do this. Therefore, he, himself, will go with you....* And hadn't he done that? Here they were, two gems found, and exploring what they hoped were the elven caves. *Thank you, Eldurrin! Thanks for guiding our steps and protecting us. Please help us finish this charge you've put before Finn.* That peace she hadn't felt in a while settled in her, the certainty that all would end as Eldurrin said. She encouraged Finn with her thoughts.

Aric burst into their quiet moments, running toward them with several small fish dangling on a line. "We found a pool! And it's got waterfalls and fish!" Kalvara and Zenna followed behind him. Even in the dusk, Rory could see their smiles.

Kalvara had found some nuts she was familiar with, and some pale berries. "Butter nuts we called them in Droome. If you crush them, you can spread the paste on bread. The berries we called pinks, and they grew everywhere in the caves wherever there was water. Same here." She laughed, dumping them out on a rock. "We won't starve."

"These are fabulous," Finn said, grabbing a second handful of butter nuts. "Want to move to the pool? We could roast the fish there and have water and food nearby."

The pool and waterfalls were gorgeous, but a very long walk. Rory was tired by the time they arrived, though everyone else seemed undaunted. What was wrong with her? She yawned and couldn't shake the heaviness. Maybe it was just the letdown from days of running, watching, being always on guard.

"Finn, I'm going to find a spot over there and rest." She indicated a few small nooks within sight.

She could see his worry. "I'm fine, I think. Just super tired. I actually was up much of the night."

He walked her over to the crannies, like little bedrooms off a main room. He shone the bellasol around each of them, checking for lurking creatures, but found none. "These seem safe enough," he said, satisfied. He took off his cloak and spread it out on the hard ground. She curled up on it and he covered her with its edges. "Sleep well, love," he whispered.

Rory watched the others from her little cocoon—setting up camp and searching for twigs to burn. But soon, her eyelids refused to stay open, and she fell into a deep slumber. The heaviness that weighed her down was a great pillow, cushioning all sensation. It grew cold and she burrowed tighter into Finn's cloak, his scent a comfort. She inhaled deeply and drifted. She felt as if she was being dragged, and she gave in to the feeling, allowing herself to float away. She dove deeper into the rich, thick sleep, engulfed in its embrace, unaware of any noise or movement. The silence padded her senses and she curled into it. Many hours later, she had no idea how many, she felt herself rising to the surface. She stretched, her muscles shaking after being limp in one position for so long. She yawned hugely several times and listened. She relished this in-between time, not wanting to open her eyes just yet. She heard nothing. Where was everyone? Had she slept hard all day and they were now asleep near her? She cracked one eye open and jolted. A pair of yellow eyes stared back at her, curious and unblinking. She bolted back, pulling her knees to her chest.

"It's awake," the creature called and another one approached.

"You slept long," it said, offering her a cup of something hot.

Was she dreaming? She pinched herself and it hurt. Where were Finn and the others? She was not in the same cave, though it wasn't all that different from the one she'd fallen asleep in. She took the cup but set it on the ground.

"Who are you?"

"Meratibulidina, dear," the bigger one said. "Just Mera will do. And this is Toad."

"Toad," she repeated.

Mera nodded. She was bigger than Toad but still no more than three feet tall. Had her hunched back been straight, she would have been closer to four feet. Her head was disproportionately large, perhaps a quarter of her height, in contrast to her small, shriveled body. Her wrinkled skin suggested she was very old. Her fingers were long and thick pointed fingernails curled from the end of each. Ten bear-like claws. White hair sprouted from her head in patches, hanging ragged around her long face, and her eyes, bright with intelligence gleamed yellow, like Toad's.

He was smaller by a foot, and judging by his smooth skin, much younger than Mera. A child, perhaps. He sat on his haunches, the size of a one-year-old human, studying Rory, nibbling meat off a small bone until it was clean. He picked up the rest of the animal, tore off another leg, and Rory understood how Toad had gotten his name. In a gesture of kindness, he held the mangled amphibian out to her.

"No thanks, Toad."

Rory studied them. Not hostile as far as she could tell. But what reason did they have for bringing her there? "How did I get here?" She tried to keep the quaver out of her voice. "And where, exactly are we?"

A soft gurgle came from Mera, which Rory thought might be laughter. Mera's gaze flickered over Rory, landing on her neck for a long second.

"She asks two questions at once, Toad."

His gurgles confirmed her suspicion. They were laughing at her. This was not funny. Time to go. She stood, banging her head hard on the top of the cave, yelled, and fell back on her bottom.

"Hasty, hasty, fair one," Mera crooned, nudging the cup closer to her. "We won't hurt you; not us. We saved you from it." Her gaze darted from Rory's face to her neck.

"You saved me from what?" Rory touched her neck and felt her necklace. The star sapphire was hanging in full view.

Mera bowed her head, then lifted her gaze, regarding Rory with wonder.

"Floxx," she said simply, eyeing the necklace.

"Yes. Floxx gave it to me."

Mera bowed, again.

"We saw it and had to save you."

"Save me from what, Mera?"

Mera's eyes shadowed with fear. "Skrack," she whispered.

"Skrack? What is that?"

But neither would answer.

"What about the others?"

They looked at her blankly. "No others. You slept alone."

Oh no! She had to warn her friends.

Mera wandered away but Toad stayed, watching her with unblinking eyes, licking frog juice from his fingers.

Rory considered them. A child. And an old woman who knew Floxx. Some kind of elven folk, ancient perhaps.

Her stomach growled. She wished she'd eaten some of Aric's fish before she'd slept. She glanced at Mera, who was bent over some rocks, and realized she was cooking. Her mouth began to water.

"Help me, Toad," Mera called and he immediately went to see what she needed.

They carried over two roasted toads and several small fish. Toad went back for a large bowl of something that sloshed as he walked. They set it all before Rory.

"Eat," Mera said simply, reaching for a fish of her own. Toad grabbed another toad. Rory tasted a fish and found it delicious. She ate two more before she was done. Toad spilled out the contents of her cup and ladled fresh liquid into it before handing it back. She tasted it. Water. She felt ridiculous for being so wary. Mera returned to the cooking pit, deftly pulled out something from deep inside and set it on a flat piece of slate. Bread. She had an oven over there!

Rory ate two big chunks of it, hot, crusty and delicious. "Thank you, Mera. That was really good."

Mera tipped her long chin in response.

"Are there more of you? More family? Friends?"

She shrugged. "Not here."

"What happened to them?"

"Skrack," she said, a deep sadness pooling in her eyes.

What monster lurked in these caves? She asked them twice, but they refused to say more. Mera banked the fire and the two curled up to sleep in a nook Rory hadn't noticed.

Great. It was nighttime, again. She was definitely upside down in her sleeping pattern. She listened, hoping to hear the distant voices of her friends. But it was dead quiet, too quiet. Almost like they were in a soundproof room. In spite of her misgivings, Rory relaxed, wrapping in Finn's cloak and inhaling his familiar scent. *I'm okay, love. I hope you are, too.* She must have nodded off, but a distant buzzing woke her. What was that? It rose and fell like the screech of summer insects, vaguely familiar to her. She thought dully about the bloom of bugs in Alaska. Swarms of them to be sure, and they stung and bit, but they didn't screech like this. Then she remembered the monstrous little bugs she and Finn had faced in the arena. They sounded just like this! Was it possible? Did they live down here? Maybe they bred down here and somehow found their way to the Underside? She sat up, horrified, remembering they were omnivorous—they ate everything: vegetation and flesh. She remembered they'd eaten one of the tall one's children. Were her friends all right? Had they been attacked? She ran over and shook Mera awake.

"Listen!" Rory urged the terrified creature.

Mera covered her ears in terror.

Rory pulled her hands away. "What is that noise?"

"Skrack," Mera wailed. "Skraaaack." She shielded her ears and curled over Toad, refusing to say more.

Rory was in full flung panic, crawling through the cave, pressing against the shadows, searching frantically for the passageway through which she'd been dragged. Finally, on the far side of the cave she saw a puddle of darkness and rushed to it. A tunnel! So low, she had to crawl through it. The screeching was louder here. She started down it, banging her head in her haste and ducking lower, hoping she wouldn't blunder into a nest of the insects. She was scrambling as fast as she could, when she saw a familiar blue light speeding toward her. She started to call, "Uri---" when suddenly she was tackled. Strong hands clamped over her mouth, for only for a split second.

"Rory!" Finn whispered. "It's you! Oh, we've found you!" And he hugged her so fiercely, she had to pull away to breathe. Kalvara was there with the others, shining the bellasol on her.

"The bugs," Rory stammered. "Did you see them?"

"We didn't see them, but we heard them. And we turned down the first tunnel we could find. We've been searching for you, checking every nook in the cave for any sign of you." He hugged her again. "What are you doing here? Why did you crawl away?"

"I didn't crawl; I was dragged." She told him about her dream and that she'd been so deep in sleep she hadn't awoken. "They dragged me here, two tiny people. Kind of elvish, I guess. They say they saved me from the bugs. Skrack they call them.

"They saved you?" He chuckled.

Rory grinned. "So they say. They're harmless, I think. Actually, super sweet. And very short; I'm sure they just walk through here." She pointed at the low ceiling. "Come on, I'll take you to meet them."

Chapter 33: Freezing

Finn would not let her out of his sight and Rory relished his attention. He'd almost lost her, he said, desperation in his eyes, though truth be told, she'd never been in danger with Mera and Toad. He insisted on going with her to get water; and accompanied her berry picking, holding the sack as she picked, doting on her with obvious affection.

"You know," he said, "we've found two of the three gems, but you, Rory, are my greatest treasure." Her heart swelled with fondness for him. They needed each other, she was becoming more and more convinced of that; and not just because of their growing love. She was a part of his calling; she was certain of it. She had a part to play and she had no idea what it was. She was sure of one thing: Eldurrin had led them this far. He would show them what to do. And she would wait, she really had no other choice.

He busied himself where he could see her, watching her work with Mera, baking the day's bread. She smiled at him and turned her attention to the wizened little woman, blushing at Mera's knowing wink. Rory studied Mera's cooking pit. It was roughly rectangular, two or three feet deep in the center where it always glowed red. It sloped upward on the sides with several built-in ledges for cooking at different temperatures.

"You made this oven?"

Mera nodded.

"It's brilliant! Your bread always comes out perfect!"

"Bread. This one." She pointed to a side shelf.

Rory smiled as Mera slid the dough into the indicated shelf.

"We wait for the right smell."

Rory laughed. She looked around for wood or debris or whatever Mera used for fuel. There was nothing. Puzzled, she asked, "What keeps the fire going?"

Mera shrugged.

"You know, wood or coal, what is it you burn?

Mera chortled. "Nothing to burn." She gestured at the rocky cave.

Rory was dumbfounded. "Then what keeps the fire burning?"

Mera hesitated, not meeting Rory's gaze.

Was this some magic she had? Some ancient knowledge?

Then Mera caught sight of the star sapphire and met Rory's eyes. "Floxx. She made the fire. It always burns."

"Floxx was here?" Rory touched Mera's hand. "When, Mera?" This was fabulous news!

"Long time. Far past. I was small, like Toad."

Rory stared at her, speechless. Floxx had been here in the distant past! In this very cave? And she'd given Mera fire that never went out!

Before she could ask any more questions, Mera turned away, taking her water skin, and ambled toward the stream.

Toad had taught Aric how to catch his namesake amphibians, and Aric had made slingshots for his new friend and for Zenna to shoot fish. Once they understood how water bends the location of what's underneath, they caught an abundance of fish. Mera's hideout was a refuge for sure, an inner sanctum. The old woman had been standoffish at first, reclusive by nature, and suspicious by necessity. Recognizing Floxx's necklace helped, and after Aric and

Zenna had hit it off with Toad, she began to soften toward the others. Rory and Finn shared their story of fighting the bug tree in the arena, and she'd been horrified. A whole tree of Skrack! Aric told how Spike and the brambles had saved them. Mera was thrilled. Her face split into a wide smile and she laughed deep and long. Rory loved the sound of it.

"So, Mera," Rory said, touching her sapphire necklace, "how do you know Floxx?"

Mera took Rory's hand. "Long time ago, when Skrack attacked our tribe, she bring me here. 'Stay safe,' she said. "Wait."

"Only you? There were no other survivors?"

The sadness in her eyes held the answer.

"What about Toad?"

"Find in stream. Wee one."

Aric couldn't contain his excitement over this bit of news. "He just floated by one day?"

Mera nodded.

He ribbed Toad with his elbows. "Like a toad, even then!" And they all laughed.

"So, there must be more like you somewhere if Toad was born!" Kalvara exclaimed. "Have you looked for them?"

Mera shook her head. "Floxx say wait. Stay by fire."

"Wait for what, Mera?"

She shrugged. "Floxx will show me."

"Mera," Kalvara asked timidly, "what are your lovely people called?"

"Shrives. We are shrives, though only two."

Rory squeezed her hand. "I'm glad to know you. Thank you for saving me from Skrack."

Mera pointed to the necklace. "For Floxx. She save us and we save you."

Once it was clear the shrives were not a threat, Finn settled down and got busy with the children, helping them fish and explore the labyrinth of caves. Rory was pretty good with wild Alaskan plants, but she knew nothing about cave growth. So, Kalvara showed her the edibles that grew by the stream. They found butternuts, ground them, and spread the paste on Mera's warm bread every morning and evening. It was delicious, similar to peanut butter. A little further upstream, they discovered another type of berry, whose leaves were also good for brewing for tea.

"We had similar fruit in Droome," Kalvara said as they picked. "I was always amazed it grew in the dark."

Rory loved watching tall, young Kalvara and tiny, wrinkled Mera together. Their affection for each other was sweet, like granddaughter and grandmother cherishing each other. Mera questioned her endlessly about Droome, and Rory learned much about the struggles there. How Kalvara had survived was astonishing, and the fact she'd escaped with Aric, a miracle. Her admiration for her eldrow friend grew into a deep respect. One day, Kalvara found a certain large rock, flat on the bottom, rounded on top and very heavy. The two of them half rolled, half carried it back to Mera. It took hours, and Rory smashed her fingers more than once.

"Aren't there other rocks like this a lot closer?" she complained.

"Not that I've seen."

Rory sucked her swollen finger, reluctant to continue the effort.

"You'll see, it'll be worth it. I had one like this in our cave to boil water in."

When they got within shouting distance, their calls brought the others to help. Kalvara spent several days chiseling a deep bowl in the rock's center. It took three of them to lift it to the edge of the cooking area where it would get some heat but not be in the way. They filled the hollow with water and soon had hot water for cleaning and bathing. As Rory washed her face that night, she had to admit the hard work had been totally worth it.

They'd lost track of time; it was impossible to tell day from night in the perpetual dusk, but Rory guessed they'd been with the shrives a couple of weeks. She and Finn and Kalvara and Aric were restless to move on. Riza and Zenna had decided to stay on with Mera and Toad. Though Riza's wound was healing, she needed more time to regain her full strength and mobility. She and Zenna wanted to return to Underside; Riza felt confident they could find their way back. She even had a workable plan to access the tunnel from the pool of water they'd fallen into. They'd face whatever awaited them when they returned; but she and her daughter wanted to go home.

Rory and the others made plans to leave. They questioned Mera on several occasions about other creatures. Had she ever seen any elves similar to Kalvara?

"Yes," she remembered. "Long ago. But no more." Most had died in the devastating Skrack attack. Some, perhaps, had escaped, like her and Toad; she had no way to know. She squeezed Kalvara's hand. "But you are special. You survived even worse! I will never forget you."

Rory and Kalvara had stuffed their packs with nuts, berries, and dried fish. Mera had added several loaves of bread. They were ready to leave early the next morning. That night, they enjoyed a last meal together.

"Mera," Rory said, taking the small wrinkled hand in her own. "I can never thank you enough for rescuing me, for saving me from the bugs." Mera ducked her head, suddenly shy.

"You tell Floxx," Mera managed to say, tapping her own neck and glancing at the star sapphire.

"I certainly will."

Aric presented both Toad and Zenna with smooth rocks for their slingshots. Toad had made Aric a bone necklace from the dried frog legs he'd saved.

"I still have your pearl," Zenna whispered to Aric as they hugged good-bye. "I'm so glad we found it again."

"And I've got your crescent rock. I'll cherish it always."

Rory and the others turned in for the night, planning to be gone before anyone stirred. Finn and Kalvara had scouted the caves and found a long tunnel that cut for a great distance. They'd already explored its first few miles. The elves were there somewhere, they hoped. It occurred to them that maybe their elven magic was advanced enough to keep them hidden, to shield them from discovery. What if elves could be right next to them and they wouldn't know. They hoped it wasn't so.

The tunnel was dark, way darker than the open caves had been and they used the bellasol during all their waking hours. At night, the presence of Uriel's glow gave them much comfort. They wound slightly upward, then down, for what seemed like days.

After three sleeps, however many days that was, Rory decided to ask the obvious question. "So, are you as surprised as me that this tunnel hasn't run into any more caves?"

"Totally," Finn answered. "I expected it would."

"It doesn't seem natural," Rory said.

"What do you mean?"

"Well, the other caves and tunnels meander into each other, the way water moves over land. This tunnel was carved. Like a road. A way to get from one location to the next in the least amount of time."

"But we're not getting anywhere," Kalvara observed dryly.

"We will. And who knows what will be waiting."

"What are you saying?" Finn gave Rory his full attention.

"If this is the main passageway between Underside and the elves' hideaway, don't you think it's watched? And trespassers quickly dispatched, if you get my meaning. They've managed to stay undiscovered for eons of time."

"That's just it," Finn said, thoughtfully. "If this is what you suggest—the main passageway—no doubt it was watched a long, long time ago, but I can't imagine they waste their time watching it still."

"Well, okay, I'll give you that. But their ancient traps may still lie undisturbed. I'm just thinking this too easy; we should be more careful traipsing through the dark."

"Well said! Of course, you're right!"

Kalvara teased. "Wouldn't want to go careening off a ledge, now would we?"

"Let's hope you are far from the truth," Finn said soberly. "Aric, it's important you stay closer to Kalvara. No more running ahead or lagging behind. Rory and I will do the same."

Two more sleeps passed. They had used up all their water. "It's okay." Finn tried to encourage them. The ground is damp, can't you feel it? We'll find water soon."

Rory's feet were sinking into softer earth, that was true. It felt more like dirt than rocks. But she wondered about water. There was no sound of it, no trickles, no drips. And it was getting colder. Last night, she'd felt her breath freezing as she talked.

On what Rory figured to be their sixth day, they walked steeply uphill and realized the tunnel was widening. Eventually, it opened into a massive, freezing cold cave. And they found their water. The problem was it was frozen. The stalactites had been replaced by a frozen waterfall, its long icicles dangling on the far side of the cave.

"Let's see if we can scrounge something to make a fire." Rory suggested. She knew cold weather survival and it always involved making a fire first and keeping it going.

"Okay," Kalvara said. "Let me take the light and go search. The rest of you huddle together and stay warm, since you can't wander around in the dark." And before anyone could object, Kalvara headed off, taking the bellasol with her.

Finn put his arms around Rory, sandwiching Aric between them. "It's going to be okay," he encouraged.

"It smells familiar," Rory said. "Like snow. We had a lot of it in Alaska."

"I smell wet and cold," Aric said.

"Yep, that's it!" She tousled his hair just as Kalvara screamed.

They grabbed Aric's hand and stumbled toward her voice, shouting as they went.

"Help," she yelled. "But go slow. There's a ledge and I've fallen off."

The three of them got on their hands and knees and crawled toward her voice.

"Keep talking, Kalvara. We're almost there."

"I've caught myself on a branch. But, it's not real strong."

Rory and Finn felt air beneath their hands at the same moment.

"Stop," Rory yelled. "Back up!"

"Kalvara," Finn called. We are at the edge of the cliff. Any idea how far down you are?"

"I'm guessing 20 or 30 feet," she called. "Hurry! This shrub is giving way!"

Finn pulled rope from his pack and tied it first to Rory, then to himself. They backed up several feet from the ledge, and Aric tossed the loose end in.

"Got it!" Kalvara called, her voice wavering in panic. "I'm tying it around my waist. Are you ready? Can I climb up?"

"Ready!" Finn and Rory called together, leaning back to offset her weight.

Within moments, she surfaced, struggling to hold back tears. "I can't believe it. I actually fell off a cliff—it's what I was joking about. I'm so glad you were close!" She was trembling when Rory hugged her.

They moved away from the ledge, away from the frozen wall of water, going slow and holding onto one another. There were no scrub bushes, nothing to burn as far as they could tell. Just frozen dirt and rock. They settled into a cranny that didn't seem quite as cold as the open area and huddled together for warmth.

Kalvara blew on her fingers. "I'm so cold," she said.

No one spoke anymore, conserving their energy. The nook was just big enough for three of them to sit shoulder to shoulder, knees to their chest. Aric wedged himself on Kalvara's lap. But Rory knew they couldn't continue in bitter cold like this. They had no fire, no water, and lightweight clothing. Hypothermia wasn't far off. Kalvara already was shivering, though it was less severe than it had been. Rory was afraid they'd all fall asleep and their body temperatures would drop so low, they'd never wake up. Finn was already whiffling on her one side and Kalvara's head hung limp over Aric. She looked for Uriel; his protection was so comforting, but she couldn't see him with all the frozen fog their breath was making in their nook.

Floxx! Eldurrin! Rory reached out silently. *We need you. We need help. Please! We're in a long, frozen tunnel. It's very dark and there's a deadly drop off ahead. We don't see any way to get around it. We're out of water and have no fire. Help us, please, we're freezing to death!* She must have dozed off in spite of her efforts to stay awake. When she woke, the hair around her face was covered with frost. She shook Finn and he didn't respond.

"Wake up!" she yelled at him. His eyebrows and eyelashes were frosty. She straightened his knees and crawled over his lap, blowing warm air on his cheeks, kissing him, covering the tips of his ears with her hands.

"Wake up, Finn! We have to move." He stirred. She kissed him hard on the mouth. His eyes flew open. "Get up! We have to move, maybe run in place or something. We're freezing to death!"

Finn groaned and Rory helped him stand.

"I can't feel my feet," he said. "Or my fingers."

Kalvara heard them and reluctantly lowered her knees, waking Aric. "Let's walk a little," she said to him. "To get our blood moving, again."

They ran in place. Rory taught them jumping jacks. They did warm up and were encouraged. Kalvara pulled four smoked fish from her pack. "Wish we had water, but fish will have to do," she said, passing one to each of them. They had to gnaw them, frozen as they were, and after a short time, they gave up trying.

Then they squished together for another nap. In two hours, Rory woke them again and they repeated their routine. She wasn't sure how much longer they could do this. Their food was not edible in its frozen state, and they had no water. They should turn back after one more rest. She hoped they would listen to her.

But she didn't wake up the third time. No one woke.

Chapter 34: Letter

Jakin shaded his eyes against the morning sun, searching for the drunken crew he could hear. There they were, on the shore, arguing about who would row the dinghy to the ship. He'd been waiting for them all night; they were supposed to have sailed at dawn. They'd wanted work and so he'd given it to them, making three trips in just two weeks, each one crammed to overflowing with cargo. He was back in Tozar's good graces. A few weeks ago, the crew had whined they weren't working enough; now they complained it was too hard.

"Shay, bosh, we're back," the captain slurred as he climbed onto the deck and staggered toward him. "Thanksh for the night off."

"You're late, all of you," Jakin reprimanded. "I gave you the night off, but not for an all-night drinking spree. We were to sail at dawn and I shoulda just left you. Shoulda picked up another crew; there's lots of sailors lookin' for work and you know it's true." He glanced at the captain, who was swaying dangerously on the steady deck.

"Ye're right," the captain slurred, looking contrite. "Let's get goin' then."

Jakin scolded. "Not a chance I'd give you the wheel. If you can't walk straight, you sure can't steer straight. Below deck, all of you. Sleep it off. You'll wake in the sea, and we'll get t'fishing first, then pearling. You've got at least a day t'make up."

One of the dwarves took a swing at him, as he staggered by, missing him by several feet. "Don't tell ush what t'do. It's our cap'n we lishen to, not ye."

"Let'sh go, boysh," the captain waved them to the ladder. "Shleep it off. I could use a lil shut eye anyway."

"Bah," Jakin scoffed, and strode to the captain's chair. He'd counted six crew, all drunk, the captain and five sailors, two of them new to his ship, though he'd seen them crewing others. Fine. He'd break 'em in. Lucky for them he was sober and had slept most of the night. Well, maybe not slept. More like rested.

The truth was he'd been brooding. His mind had wandered, thinking back on all that had happened since Rory had shown up. He was still fond of her, no doubt about that. But Finn loved her, really loved her. And she'd made it clear she loved Finn back. He remembered when he'd thought she loved him like that, but it had only been the magic. The moment she'd slipped that bracelet off, her feelings for him had fallen away, too. But the three of them truly were friends and they'd been big enough to forgive him. He didn't count that lightly; good friends were scarce.

He'd been sailing a couple of hours, nearing that fishing spot he'd taken Marinna to. What a day that had been—she'd loved it. And she'd been charming, nice, fun to be with. The sea brought out the best in her. He didn't understand then, but now he knew why. He shook his head. Half siren. He had to stay away from her. She was toxic. He was actually a little surprised she hadn't come around looking for him, but it was just as well. He could barely resist her. Maybe she didn't realize the effect she had on him, and he for sure wasn't going to let her know.

He reached his fishing spot, so he slowed and dropped a net on each side of the ship. The sun was high, and it was warming up. Once he had the nets secured and the boat stable, he swung into the hammock, studying the occasional clouds. He wanted a girl who wanted him. Who liked him for who he was. Someone who would love him back. Trouble was he didn't know any girls like that; he actually didn't know many girls at all, not human ones at least. Anyway, no one would want him now that he'd ruined everything.

He must be the laughingstock of Byerman and probably Orizin as well. What a mess he'd made of everything. He wanted to go back; he didn't want to live as an exile all his life. Finn and Rory had forgiven him. He wondered if others could, too. He thought about Queen Raewyn. He had no idea what she was like, but according to Rory, he'd hurt her bad. Of course, he had. Her husband had been killed and he was to blame. And then, he'd insulted his memory in front of her friends and family, embarrassing and infuriating her. Rory had insisted he apologize to her mother, but he doubted the queen would allow him anywhere near the castle.

The hammock swayed and he considered. Apologizing to the queen had seemed really important to Rory. And Finn had agreed. Maybe he should do it. At least try. He really did regret everything. He'd been such a fool, self-centered and heart-broken, and Draegin had played him for the pawn he was. He was lucky he hadn't been killed himself, though most everyone probably wished he had. Life wasn't fair. Others had suffered for what he'd done. And he'd run away, coward that he was. He sighed. What did he have to lose besides the tiny bit of pride he had left? He could try it. He could go to Masirika and seek an appointment with Queen Raewyn. But what if she misunderstood his motives? What if she had him captured and thrown into prison? He couldn't deny he deserved it. Suddenly, he had an idea. He'd write her a letter of apology and have it delivered. Then, he'd show up at the castle to see her in person and hope for the best.

By the time the crew shuffled above, squinting and moaning, the nets were full. The captain took over, grouchy as he'd ever been. "Get them nets and hurry up. Haul 'em in. Let's go. Get them fish in the hole. We got t' do a pearl run yet, 'fore the sun sets."

They worked for three days solid, sleeping only briefly, pearling the coast and fishing the deep. Jakin didn't want to dock on the island. Didn't want to give Marinna an opportunity. So, he drove the crew to exhaustion. The boat sat low in the water under its heavy load as it lumbered toward Syrea. They tied up at dock. Jakin took the captain aside. "Nice work, you and the crew. But I got news. I'll deliver this load and then the ship's all yours. I'm leaving and it might be awhile before I'm back.

Jakin had worked hard on the letter to the queen, writing several drafts before finally deciding short and sincere was better than long and flowery. As soon as he got to his meeting place with Tozar, he handed him the parchment explaining it was to be delivered to Queen Raewyn. Tozar raised his eyebrows and refused to take it.

"I've written an apology."

Tozar didn't believe him.

"Fine," Jakin said, exasperated. Did no one trust him at all? "Open it and read it for yourself."

Tozar slid the parchment from its leather carrier. He scanned it. "I see," he stroked his beard, glancing at Jakin. "You really mean it, don't you?"

"I feel terrible about everything that happened."

"As we all do, of course," he mumbled. He read it, again, from top to bottom, shaking his head and muttering into his beard. "Yes, this is good."

Most Honored Queen Raewyn,
I am ashamed to even write to you, and yet I feel I must. I hope you find it in you to read this rather than toss it into the fire. I've been terribly wrong in much that I've done. Although my choices were self-centered and born of self-interest, I am sincere in saying I had no malicious intent. Certainly, I never imagined the nightmare that happened. It is true, I was terribly angry when I realized my relationship to you and the King had gone unacknowledged all my life. I thought marrying Rory and taking her away from you would be a sweet revenge. I was the fool. Thoughtless. Mean-hearted. Short-sighted.
I want to apologize to you in person, if you would allow me the opportunity. I have already apologized to Rory and Finn and they have graciously extended forgiveness. I pray against all odds that you might find it within yourself to do the same. I should very much like to acquaint myself with you on better terms, that I might honor you in a way I never did my Uncle. I am sincere and Tozar is witness to the truth of it. I will follow in person a few days after this letter.
Jakin

Tozar re-rolled it and slipped it into its pouch, then considered Jakin. "You might make a good diplomat after all," he smiled thinly. "All right, I will deliver this personally."

Jakin left Syrea on foot soon after Tozar did, wanting to avoid the crew and a lot of questions. He headed for the forest trail, hunting small game to eat along the way, though he had little appetite. The woods were beautiful, rich with color, vibrant with birdsong, abundant with life. He'd not noticed when he'd passed through the first time; his anger had blinded him. He'd walked through all of this splendor, oblivious to it; a captive of his own dark soul, bitter, mean, hurting. He thought about Zad and all the time they'd spent in the woods together. Zad would've been horrified with his behavior. He'd really let him down, even if it was just his memory. And Tishkit, he'd disappointed her. And Zirena. He'd shamed them all. Then left them to deal with the damage he'd caused. His family—he ones who'd raised him, fed him, cared for him, taught him, loved him—were holding the broken pieces of the dream he'd shattered.

It occurred to him as he sat alone in the woods that he had a choice. He didn't have to be bitter. His emotions didn't have to rule his life. It's true his human family relationships had been tragic. His parents killed, his uncle abandoning him and dying a horrible death. It'd been easy to run. To try to forget. Move on to the next thing. Make his own life. Trouble was, he hadn't forgotten. He couldn't. He didn't want to. He loved them, though he'd never thought much about it until he'd lost them all. But, he could do better than his uncle, King Merek, had. He could do the hard thing. He could reach out to his aunt and, perhaps, begin a new relationship with her. He could return to Orizin and restore his relationship with his dwarf family. They might laugh at him, tell him to get lost. But it was worth a try.

Chapter 35: Luminest

Rory was warm. Weightless. And wet. Her eyes flew open. Green, everything was green. She jolted and slipped, trying to get her footing; panicking briefly until she realized the water was shallow. Finn, Kalvara, and Aric were near, sprawled half in and half out of the pond, sleeping. Steam curled over the water's surface. She stood, felt the sting of chilly air, and sank back in, closing her eyes. If this was some kind of dream, she'd hold onto it as long as she could.

"I thought I saw her move," a deep voice growled.

She snapped awake. She knew that voice! Uriel! She stumbled out of the water and threw herself on him, dripping everywhere. "You brought us here?"

"Me and Floxx."

Rory turned and there she was, beaming at her. "Oh! I am so glad to see you!" And she rushed to embrace the silver-haired woman.

"What happened?"

"I heard you call me, and I came," Floxx said simply. "We flew you over the great cavern and brought you here."

"You saved us all!" Rory hugged her, again.

Finn stirred, and Rory laughed as he gasped and floundered, just as she had.

"Floxx! Uriel!" He splashed out and embraced each of them. "We nearly died, didn't we? Froze to death."

"Almost," Uriel rumbled.

Aric woke before Kalvara and rubbed water on her face. "Wake up!" he whispered. "You won't believe this!"

They all laughed.

Rory looked past the lush vegetation around the pool. Rocks. Nothing but rocks. They were still underground, though it was much brighter here. The ceiling was high, and the cave-like area was huge and devoid of stalactites, stalagmites, or icicles. But now that she was out of the water, she was cold. She remembered visiting hot springs in Alaska. The water was wonderfully warm, hot even, and it had been a lot of fun to swim in sub-zero temperatures— until she had to get out!

"I brought dry clothes for all of you." Floxx pointed to a pile of tunics and cloaks tossed over a scrub bush. Rory picked a dark blue tunic and a purple cloak, marveling at the exquisite material and the excellent workmanship. Finn chose a tan tunic and a brown cloak woven through with gold flecks of thread.

"Where'd you get these? They're fit for a King," he said.

Kalvara's clothing fit her well, cut extra-long, and in shades of green, just as she liked. Aric's ensemble was gray and fit him perfectly.

"Where did these come from?" Rory repeated Finn's question in wonder. The clothes were really beautiful.

"Friends," Floxx answered mysteriously.

After they'd changed, they ate, Floxx providing a bounty of bread, berries, and cheese.

"This food is absolutely delicious!" Rory said between mouthfuls.

Floxx smiled. "From the same friends."

Finn laughed. "Can we meet them?"

"Of course. They are waiting for you."

Rory felt better than she had in a very long time. They gathered their things, eager to meet their benefactors. Uriel walked in front beside Floxx, treading on his wolf paws. This was very odd; he rarely stayed in his tennin form. Her skin prickled. Something was up. Something big. The others must have felt it, too, because no one asked any more questions; they just followed their two leaders in awe.

The light grew brighter and soon shrubs and trees flourished.

"Listen!" Aric whispered. "You hear that? Birds!"

Rory strained but heard nothing until they'd walked further. The vegetation grew thick and Floxx followed a path through it.

"It's like the gardens in Underside!" Aric said, skipping ahead.

"Wait!" Floxx called him back. "Stay with Kalvara. Take her hand. We are almost there."

Two more curves in the path and they arrived in an enormous open area. Trees edged the circumference and flowers grew in small gardens, vibrant reds and yellows, here, and cooler shades of blue over there. It was definitely brighter than any place they'd been in the caves. Aric was right; this was a lot like Underside. The focal point was a raised circular platform, built of stone with stairs on two sides. The platform was empty, except for an elevated dais in the center. No one was there. No one was anywhere at all. The area was completely empty and silent except for the birds; beautiful birds and their wondrous, joyous trilling.

Floxx and Uriel headed straight for the platform, glancing back to motion for the others to follow. They climbed the steps; Floxx ascended the dais, itself. Uriel stayed on the platform, standing a few feet below Floxx. Rory and Finn stood on one side of the tennin, Kalvara and Aric on the other. Floxx raised her arms and began to sing as Rory had seen her do many times. Her voice spun a mysterious mood, its melody beckoning images of shadows and secrets. Uriel joined her, his deep bass in perfect harmony. Soon another voice, light and melodic joined. It seemed disembodied; who was singing? Then another and another, until a chorus of voices surrounded them.

As the sound grew in volume and intensity, shapes emerged from the air. It was actually their lights Rory saw first, and the forms slowly manifested around the lights. As the singing increased, the lights brightened, and the figures became clearly visible. They were tall and clothed in long trailing robes. Rory gaped. She couldn't believe it! Who were these beings? Where had they come from? How did they appear from nowhere! They surrounded the platform— she could hear them behind her, but she didn't dare turn to look. They were tall and lean like eldrows, but their skin was different, their inner light gave them a golden tone. Their hair shone like burnished bronze, a rich brown, shiny with strands of gold and red. Most of them were tall, about Kalvara's height, though some were shorter—children, perhaps. They gathered around the platform, their voices filling Rory's heart with an ache, a yearning, mystery, hope, joy.

The throng parted for a very tall figure, his hair not bronze, but silver. It hung in a braid down the length of his back. He wore a crown; a simple circlet made of gold. He held the hand of a woman, whose silver hair hung loose to her waist. Slightly shorter and frail, she wore a similar crown. Those they passed, bowed, creating an elegant ripple through the throng, lovely to watch.

Finn squeezed Rory's hand and she stole a glance at him. His face was radiant; she'd never seen his smile so big.

Floxx brought the singing to an end. She extended her hands outward in welcome as the two silver-haired beings gracefully climbed the stairs.

"Trummarius." She grasped the hands of the man. "And dear Ellisa." She hugged the woman, a full foot taller than she was. "It is time."

The two ascended the dais, on either side of Floxx, and turned to face Rory and the others. Finn's gripped her hand so hard her fingers grew numb. Trummarius! She couldn't believe it! They'd found them! They did live! These were the ancient high elves. Finn's ancestors. Family. Their royal blood ran in his veins. A lineage of kings.

Floxx introduced them. "High Elf Trummarius and Queen Ellisa, it is my great honor to introduce you to Finian, son of Frederick, son of Tillary, son of Thatcher, who is your son, Trummarius. Finian has been called by Eldurrin to restore the Eldur Crown and bring peace to Gamloden for the ages to come."

"Finian," Floxx beckoned.

He stepped forward and bowed before them. The red ring slipped from his tunic, dangling in plain sight, but he dared not tuck it away at that moment.

"We welcome you to Luminest," Trummarius proclaimed for all to hear, his eyes flitting from Finn's face to the ring. He reached toward Finn, lifted the chain over his head and kissed the ring, then returned it to Finn's neck, leaving it exposed.

"The Red King Stone," Floxx cried in a loud voice, turning Finn in a circle for all to see it.

The elves murmured in low voices.

"The Blue Stone of Valor," Uriel rumbled, holding the gem high in the air.

Louder now, the elves cheered, elated with seeing the two stones. Rory was sure they understood their significance.

"The Yellow Eldur Stone," Queen Ellisa proclaimed, lifting high a clear gem, larger than the other two and sparkling like a star.

Rory cried, "Oh!" before she could stop herself. Had the elves had it all this time?

Applause and laughter broke out freely; it seemed to Rory even the birds sang louder. Instruments appeared in the hands of dozens of elves, flutes and fiddles and horns of all kinds. The music was spontaneous, a lively, joyous ensemble to mark a momentous occasion in history. All three of the missing stones had been found and were together here with Floxx. Eldurrin must be celebrating, too, with all of his tennins in ways she could only imagine.

Trummarius took his Queen's hand and raising her arm with his, declared, "We are thrilled and honored to see this day, to be close to fulfilling the ancient prophecy. Floxx has spoken with us, along with Uriel, a tennin of highest honor. We have agreed to do our part to restore the Eldur Crown. We must uncover the ancient fires and revive the forgotten artistry of gemology. It is my wish that we begin at once."

Those gathered cheered and hugged and clapped. As the applause dwindled, the music picked up. Nymphs and sprites and fairy-like creatures sprang into sight, dancing and frolicking. Many were tiny, lit from within with tiny lights that cast shadows on their lacy wings as they frisked through the air. Others were larger. Rory spotted a small group on the fringe of the festivities that reminded her of Mera and Toad, their large heads swaying in rhythm to the music. They had to be shrives! Mera probably had no idea they existed! She noticed they stuck close together. In fact, there was little intermingling as far as Rory could see, each celebrating with their own kind. Rory gasped when she saw two felinexes, leaping around each other, cavorting with great merriment, their tails entwined, their color shifting to blend with their background every time they moved. She pulled on Finn's sleeve, but he was intrigued by something on the other side, and when she looked back, the felinexes were gone.

"Ghillies, Rory," he whispered. "Did you see them? Had that crazy green hair, just like Dew."

The elves wandered off in groups and the music moved into the forest. The brilliance dimmed as they left.

"The light is actually in them!" Rory whispered to Finn. "See how it darkens as they move away."

"It's wondrous to be sure."

Out of the corner of her eye, Rory saw Kalvara frown. What was wrong? She didn't like these elves? Had she seen something to make her distrustful?

"Shall we?" Floxx said, gesturing for them to follow. "They've prepared a great feast. I wouldn't be surprised if the celebration continues for many days."

"I should hope so," Ellisa commented. "It is only fitting for such a significant occasion."

They wandered into the woods and meandered through the merriment. Food was everywhere! Fruit hung from great vines and nests filled with nuts perched in the elbows of nearly every tree. Laughter rang in all directions as friends gathered to eat and drink. Rory noticed they hushed, though, as they passed, not bowing exactly, but tipping their heads in respect. Trummarius led them deep into the forest, away from the others. Rory heard water and sure enough, the forest opened to a breathtaking view. Similar to the Pool of Tennindrow, but underground, waterfalls cascaded from openings high in the rocks, splashing into the stream before them. Flowers grew in profusion in wild, chaotic bunches.

"Look, tennifel!" Kalvara whispered to Aric, pointing.

Hundreds of tiny winged creatures flew in the mist, their lights casting miniature bows of color on the water and the rocks.

Aric laughed out loud. "Look!" he pulled on Rory's arm, pointing to Finn and Kalvara. Little prisms of color danced on their faces.

"Is it on me, too?"

"It is!" Rory told him, laughing, as he spun in a circle of prisms.

They walked along the rocky shore for a while before they came to a rope bridge that spanned the river.

"After you," Trummarius gestured to them. They were the first words he'd spoken since they'd left the dais. Why the silence? Rory thought it odd. She and Finn and Aric and Kalvara stopped in the center of the bridge, lingering to watch the fish in the stream, their scales flashing with reds and golds.

Aric was thrilled and pulled out his sling. "Look at them all!" he exulted. "I'll get us dinner!"

"Not now," Kalvara told him discreetly. "I'm sure there's plenty of food."

The boy was disappointed but tucked his sling away.

Trummarius and Ellisa waited silently with Floxx and Uriel until they had completely reached the other side. Rory studied them as they came across. What was causing that light within them? They could turn it up or down like a dimmer switch in a modern house in Alaska. How was that possible? How could they appear and disappear at will? Mysterious and wondrous. Elegant. The elusive high elves. It seemed odd that no one talked. Were they telepathic? Maybe they were talking in their minds to each other. She smiled at the thought; she'd give anything to hear their conversation. Once they'd crossed the bridge, Trummarius and Elissa took the lead. They turned away from the stream and wound along a rocky path, ducked behind a waterfall and into the mouth of a high-ceilinged cave that the falls had curtained from view.

"Welcome to our home!" Ellisa said stiffly. "Please. Make yourself comfortable."

Several large trees grew inside the cave and served as separate rooms would in a house. They were ushered to the first of the trees, its stooping branches formed gnarled steps to a leafy alcove. They settled on the pillowed platform around a low table. Fascinated, Rory studied the three other trees. Two were clearly sleeping quarters, their vine curtains parted to reveal plush bedding nestled in high branches. The other was a kitchen. She could see a bounty of fruit, nuts, and waterskins stored in the branches. Two shrives crouched over something in the floor. As they stood, Rory saw it was a cooking oven like Mera's. She wondered if it, too, had a fire that never went out. The shrives turned in their direction, laden with food and drink. One was stooped and wrinkled, very much like dear Mera; the other younger, a slenderer version of Toad, a girl maybe. The fruit and bread were similar to Mera's. Rory really wanted to talk with Floxx about this, but everyone was eating in silence, so she ate quietly.

Finally, Ellisa spoke, her voice surprisingly strong for her frail demeanor. "Finian, we have pondered Eldurrin's prophecy for ages, wondering who the King it speaks of might be. And now here you are, kept a secret to all but Floxx." She paused, eyeing him. "She has told us much about you."

"I hope I am not a disappointment to you," Finn replied. Seeing her raised eyebrow, he cleared his throat and straightened. "It is true that I am no one special, and yet Eldurrin has called me to this great purpose. He has assured me the task is impossible." He chuckled. "But he promised that he, himself, will bring it to pass as long as I do what he tells me to do."

Rory's heart swelled with admiration for him. What a great King he would be. Humble. Strong in his faith in Eldurrin. Solid in his commitment to his calling. She esteemed him highly.

Elissa's haughty expression said more than words could. She was looking down her nose at Finn! Had her elven grandeur gone to her head? Had she envisioned one of their own—a purebred elf—fulfilling the prophecy? Well, Finn was one of their own; they'd just have to accept that. Even with as little as she knew about these high elves, Rory could see their abilities were superior to any other beings—at least any she was aware of—with the exception of Floxx and the tennins. But Eldurrin apparently didn't choose his ruler based on abilities. He'd said the task was impossible and was looking for someone who would trust him—the One Who Made Everything—to make the impossible happen. Floxx had proclaimed Finn's elvish lineage to one and all; that could not be disputed. Rory hoped the high elves were above jealousy; and that they'd recover from disappointment if that was the issue. Equally important, she hoped they would welcome Finn into their company in far more than an official capacity.

If Ellisa's coolness bothered Finn, he didn't show it. He turned to Floxx and asked bluntly, "Where was the Eldur Stone?"

She laughed her merry laugh, bringing much warmth to the chilly luncheon. "In your father's staff, Finn. I had Zithreh hide it there when he crafted it."

"Where in the staff?" Rory and Kalvara asked at the same time, causing them to laugh.

"Wait. I think I know," Finn said before Floxx could answer. "The bubble. The big yellow bubble. It wasn't a bubble at all, was it? It was the gem."

"Perceptive," Trummarius stated, his unexpected one-word contribution to the conversation, jarring. Rory hoped he had more to say; surely, he'd been involved in extracting the gem from the staff. They waited a second or two, but he retreated back into stony silence.

Cold. More than that. They were icy. Whatever their grievances were, they needed to get over them. They'd publicly committed to recreating the Eldur Crown, and frankly, Rory now wondered how Floxx had managed to persuade them. She hoped they'd honor their promise. These elves alone held the knowledge of ancient metallurgy. They were the only ones who could forge the Eldur Crown. The fulfillment of the prophecy hinged on them.

Chapter 36: Apology

Jakin entered Masirika from the outskirts avoiding as many people as he could. He didn't want to be bullied or hassled before he saw the Queen—if she would even agree to meet with him. It was early in the morning and he stood, dusty, tired, and apprehensive at the end of the very long road that led to the courtyard. He could see Rory's airplane in the distance, near the castle and he wondered how it had gotten there. There was so much he'd missed. Two troops spotted him and approached on horseback. His heart pounded as he waited, surrendering his fate with a desperate plea. *Eldurrin. If you hear me, I'm sorry. I've made a terrible mess of everything. If you let me live, I'll do right. I promise you that.* He had no more time to think as the two guards swung off the horses. They rushed him, bending his arms behind his back.

"Well if it ain't Jakin, the deceiver, traitor, murderer." While one tied his hands, the other circled, taunting him. "Come to insult the dead King, again? Your uncle knew what he was doin', avoiding you all those years. Look at the havoc you wreaked in just a few months." He spit on him and the other guard laughed. They tied his wrists to one of the saddle horns and mounted the horses, moving fast enough that Jakin had to run alongside or risk being trampled.

They yelled as they approached the courtyard. "Hey everyone, look who we found. It's Jakin the giantkiller, come back to give us more grief. Ain't it enough we lost dozens o'loved ones t' the dragon?" The soldier hit his horse on the rump and the steed jolted sideways, knocking Jakin down.

Onlookers jeered and taunted.

"You lookin' for that magic bracelet?"

"Rory'd eat him alive if she were here!"

"Swine. Filthy, no good swine. That's what he is."

"I can't believe he'd show his face after insulting our good King like 'e did."

"Murderer. The Queen'll hold him accountable for King Merek's death."

"As it should be."

The Commander strode through the growing crowd. "Stand down," he growled at the two soldiers and they backed away. He calmed the steed, then in one smooth motion, cut the rope attached to the saddle.

Jakin scrambled to his feet, wary.

"The Queen says you're here on official business. Follow me." He turned and strode toward the castle, Jakin following.

"I'll deal with you two later," the Commander hissed at the two soldiers.

Jakin had only been in one section of the castle, the large alcove where the treasury was, where he'd claimed Rory as his reward for slaying Morfyn; the same alcove where King Merek's body had been laid out. He followed the soldier through a different entrance and up a wide and lavish staircase. The hallway, itself, was gorgeous with its hanging tapestries, and he gawked all the way to the throne room entrance. The Commander left Jakin in the care of two guards while he entered the room. He returned shortly.

"The Queen wishes to see you."

Jakin was terrified. Would she even give him a chance to apologize? If her opinion of him was as hateful as her troops, he'd be lucky to get away alive.

He was led to the circle on the floor situated in front of the throne. Jakin was stunned at the beautiful room; the gold and blue flags and finery, the troops at attention, the tapestries, the throne, itself. And there was the Queen, his aunt, sitting regally, regarding him.

The Commander announced, "Jakin, the giant killer."

Jakin had the sense to bow.

"Thank you, Commander. You may leave," she said in a confident voice. A pause as his footsteps retreated, then, "You may rise, Jakin."

He stood before her, ashamed and trembling. She could have him imprisoned for insulting the King's memory. She could implicate him in the King's death, and there would be much truth to the charge. She must loathe him. First, he threatened to take Rory away, their lost daughter who had only just returned to them. He hadn't thought about that, then; how precious that restored relationship must have been to the Queen, how close she and Rory probably had become, and what heartbreak she'd likely suffered at his insistence on taking his bride to live in Orizin.

He realized he'd been staring at the floor. He focused on the Queen. She was pretty, he realized. Rory clearly resembled her.

"Jakin," she said, finally breaking the uncomfortable silence.

"Your Highness," he replied. "Thank you for granting me an audience."

She nodded.

As the silence became awkward, Jakin thought maybe she was waiting for him to talk. "I came to apologize," he blurted. "I know it's perhaps a trite gesture in light of the horrific events that have transpired, but I felt I must do this, at the very least."

She said nothing, just sat perfectly still.

"Your Majesty, I deeply regret so much that has happened. The bloodshed and death that I contributed to. The hate that ruled my life. How I resented both you and my uncle when I found out who you were. How angry I was at you for abandoning me after Morfyn killed my parents. Perhaps if I'd forgiven you when I'd had the chance, things would have turned out differently."

The Queen did not move, didn't even blink. It was as if she was made of stone.

Jakin sighed at her lack of response and figured he may as well finish his long list of regrets. "I am so sorry for how I hurt Rory—all of you and my family as well—in everything concerning our engagement. What I did in giving Rory that bracelet was wrong, and yet, truly I hope you believe me when I say I was unaware of the capability of its powerful magic. Though it is true a specter gave it to me, and true that I was a fool to pass it to Rory, I'd no idea that the specter was Draegin, himself, or that he intended the bracelet as a tool to bring about a bloody massacre. 'It will make her love you,' he'd said simply, and in my foolish desperation, I tried it."

He saw his aunt flinch at the word massacre. He was doing this all wrong. Making it worse.

She exhaled, and he wondered if she'd been holding her breath for all that time. But still she remained silent.

He continued. "There's more. A lot more. I am truly sorry for venting my rage at the King's memorial service, insulting and angering you and the others. It was terribly mean of me, self-centered. And besides, much of what I said was false. Though the King did not choose to have a relationship with me, he was a man of highest integrity and character. He was fair and good to his countrymen and to the neighboring citizens of Orizin. This I know, of course, from being close to Zirena and Tozar."

The Queen stood. Jakin stopped talking. Was he being dismissed? Taken captive? She descended the steps from her throne and walked toward him slowly, the troops on high alert. She stood in front of him, her countenance sad. But her eyes held something unexpected. He'd been anticipating judgment. Condemnation. Rejection. Hate. But her expression was one of compassion. While he'd dreamt of reconciliation, he'd not dared put much hope in it.

She touched each of his shoulders. "Jakin, my nephew. I forgive you."

It took a moment for her words to sink in.

"You forgive me?" he repeated. His throat constricted. "I don't deserve it," he said, his voice husky.

"Perhaps not," the Queen said. "But I offer it anyway." She peered at him with a mix of empathy and curiosity. "I'd like to start over with you. We hardly know each other." She paused. "I would like a nephew."

"And I would like an aunt." He dared not say more for fear he'd break down and sob. The Queen embraced him. He kept an eye on the guards as he hugged her back.

"Follow me," she said and led him to the side dining room. "Please join me for lunch and we can talk further."

He hadn't realized how hungry he was; he ate three bowls of stew and half a loaf of bread, a huge helping of berries, two lemon tarts, a dozen iced cookies, and washed it all down with a pitcher of ale.

"Zad would have loved this," he said, setting his mug on the table.

"As Zirena and Tozar do," the Queen smiled.

"Yes, they do, indeed!" Jakin sat back. "I saw Rory and Finn a fortnight ago in Syrea."

"Tell me," the Queen said, and he did, describing the city, the ship, the sea, the island. He left Marinna out of it but did say Rory and Finn had apparently gone underground where a population of tall elvish people lived. His aunt was fascinated, and wanted all the details, asking lots of questions as he talked.

"I have a council meeting in a few minutes," she finally said, bringing the luncheon to a close. "Can you stay with us for a few days?"

He was thrilled and he didn't try to suppress a smile. "Yes, Your Majesty, I would be honored to stay a while. When I do leave, I am planning to go to Orizin to try to make amends to those I've hurt there."

"That would be a very good thing to do." She stood but had another thought. "Jakin, when it's just us like this, would you call me Aunt Raewyn. I would like that."

He smiled. "I would like that, too. Thank you, Aunt Raewyn."

The next morning, Jakin entered the Queen's private suite at her invitation. They planned to eat breakfast there and go riding afterwards. After the meal, his aunt sat back and appraised him.

"What?" he asked, now comfortable enough in her presence to be candid. "Have I got egg on my face?"

"Not today," she teased but grew instantly serious. "I don't know how much you know about me, but I wanted to tell you what happened so there would be no more doubt."

Jakin braced himself.

She told him about discovering the horrible creature in Rory's cradle the morning of her disappearance, and how she'd been so shocked she'd fallen and hit her head.

"I was recovering all right, I suppose," she confided, "though I was suffocating with such grief it is hard to know. It had been very difficult for us to conceive a child; we'd nearly given up hope and it was improbable we'd have another. I couldn't bear the sorrow. I just wanted to be alone, to curl in a ball, to stare out the window and not think. It was all too painful to deal with. But there were visitors. So many of them. At first, I refused to see anyone, but your uncle insisted we see a few: relatives and important political connections. One day Queen Marinna visited."

Jakin jolted in his chair.

"Queen Marinna?" He was incredulous.

"Yes. From Droome. At the time, we had a tenuous relationship with her and her father, Draegin. No trade, but no open hostility either. This was before we had any idea how diabolic they were."

Jakin leaned forward. *She thinks Marinna is diabolic?*

"I was feeling unwell that day, not so sick I had to be in bed, but weak. Marinna had brought a bird with her. A gift, she'd said. A Caladrius. Do you know what they are?"

"Yes. Beautiful and rare. Big white birds said to have healing powers."

"Exactly. It was a lovely and very fitting gift." She hesitated. "Marinna had covered the bird's head; she said it kept it from panicking, and we believed her. The Commander had interrupted our meeting and Merek had stepped out of the room to take care of whatever was so urgent. While he was gone, Marinna uncovered the bird."

Aunt Raewyn's hand fluttered at her throat, and she took a long drink of water before continuing. "That bird glared at me with the reddest, angriest, most hostile eyes I've ever seen. A bolt of pain pierced my head and I screamed in agony. I saw your uncle rush in just before I fainted. Marinna apparently had covered the bird, again—Merek thought it odd she hadn't yet given it to me—and feigning distress at my condition, left with the creature while the doctors fussed over me. She'd brought that bird to kill me, though I fainted before I felt its full effect."

Jakin was horrified. Marinna had tried to kill his aunt?

"It was so clever of her to bring a curse under the guise of a blessing. We never even suspected. That event had a life-changing impact on my life—and yours, too, Jakin. It left me in a stupor for sixteen years. I was awake but unaware of who or where I was. My dire condition was the reason you did not come to live with us when you lost your parents."

Oh. Oh no. His aunt really had been sick; terribly sick the entire time Tishkit and her family were raising him. No wonder his uncle had asked for their help. The King had tried to tell him, but he'd refused to listen. His heart twisted with remorse.

"We realized, after Rory returned and after I was healed, that Marinna and her father were on a rampage to kill any and all royal families. You know, of course, Draegin has tried many times to kill Rory?"

He stared, trying to put the pieces together.

"Jakin?"

He snapped back to the moment. "I'm so sorry. Please, what did you say?"

She looked at him curiously and repeated her question.

"Yes, I know that, Aunt Raewyn. I escorted Rory with the others when we left Tomitarn to bring her here. We faced wolves and Inozak and the dragon, himself, along the way. It's, um, it's how Zad was killed."

"Of course. Yes, forgive me for my blunder in not remembering that. Zad was a hero. Rory told me how he'd fought for her life and been slayed so brutally by the dragon. She described his grand funeral, and mentioned you'd stayed behind in Orizin while they'd continued here."

Jakin nodded. "That's right." He couldn't concentrate on the conversation. Marinna had tried to kill his aunt. She and her father sought to kill royal families? Had they been responsible for Rory's infant abduction? Was Marinna still chasing Rory now? His mind reeled. How old was Marinna, anyway, if she'd been an adult when Rory was born? Was she, in fact, diabolic like her father?

"Are you all right, dear," his aunt asked.

"I, uh, I'm feeling poorly. If you don't mind, I'd like to delay our ride. Could we possibly go this afternoon, instead?"

"Certainly, Jakin. I do hope you feel better."

Chapter 37: Time to Conquer

Marinna flew along the dark shoreline of Pearl Isle. This had become a nightly routine; Conquest needed the exercise and she never grew tired of exploring the many inlets and coves. She had lingered on the island far longer than she'd intended, reluctant to leave the sea she'd come to love. She was careful to stay away from the deeper water since her encounter with Orkha. She touched the shell necklace he'd given her and smiled. Though they'd fought, she'd never feared; she was stronger than any siren. She had the strength of a dragon and the cunning of a sorcerer in her blood. He hadn't stood a chance, she realized now, though at the time, she'd been shaken. Her body heated remembering the moments they'd shared, the feel of his body against hers, the softness of the water, the thrill of her senses. She hungered for more. No, she told herself. Not now. But she smiled. Perhaps one day. Perhaps when she was Queen. When Orkha bowed to her. When all sirens bowed to her. She remembered the merman in her dream. She would command their respect, their allegiance, their obedience. She would never again allow her authority to be challenged.

Conquest shattered the night with a cry, snapping her back to the moment. He climbed hard and fast, relishing the thrill. She wrapped her arms around his neck, feeling him strain, gripping his sides with her knees. When he was high enough, he frolicked, tumbling through a few thin clouds, spinning beneath the starlight. She moved with him, entwining her fingers in his thick mane, giving him full freedom.

"It's been a while since you've played, hasn't it?" she crooned.

He nickered in response, climbing higher, then diving to skim the surface of the shallows. She abandoned herself to the wild ride, soaring and plummeting at his whim. When he tired, they landed in a cove. It was still very dark; the moon had not yet risen. Marinna slid off, exhausted, allowing him to graze freely. She wrapped her arms around herself and dozed against a rock.

When she awoke, the moon was up, a bright half circle lighting the night. A last quarter moon! It had been the same the night she'd left Droome. She'd been gone from her palace an entire moon cycle! What had happened in her absence? Had Draegin returned to consciousness and asked for her? What if he'd died? She was gripped with foreboding. She must go see him! She'd been away too long.

She called Conquest and leapt on his back, whispering Droome in his ear. She felt him tense; he hated it there, loathed his mountain corral. It was just for a little while, she assured him, stroking the side of his neck. And she would leave the gates open so he could fly whenever he liked. They took off, skimming the water's surface, and turned on course for Droome.

Several hours later, Conquest strained as he climbed the last few miles of the steep mountain heights. The frigid air, so different from the tropical weather they'd grown used to, froze her nose and stung her skin. She hurried him to the entrance closest to her throne room, rather than to his corral, slid off his back and gave him some time to graze and cool down. She strode through the door and into her palace. Her throne room was cold and dark. She nodded at the Inozak on duty, snapping at him to light the sconces, and headed straight for Draegin. She brushed past the guard at her father's door and marched into the room. The bed where he'd lain unconscious for so many months was empty.

She spun around to the guard. "Where is he?" Had her father died while she'd been cavorting with sirens? Guilt squeezed her stricken heart.

"Out, Your Highness," the Inozak grunted.

"Out?" She was incredulous. "Out where?"

The guard stared straight ahead. "I do not know. He left several days ago to hunt and has not returned."

"To hunt?" She released the breath she'd been holding. "He has recovered, then?"

"Yes, Your Highness. He is well."

"And when did this happen?"

"Not long after you left."

He'd been well for weeks! Had he been searching for her? She was suddenly afraid. He would be angry she'd left the palace. How would she explain her long absence? What wrath would she face when he returned? A shudder wracked through her, and she hoped the Inozak hadn't seen.

She lifted her chin and stormed back to her throne room. She was Queen! She answered to no one. No one except her father. Draegin, the great Thaumaturge. Dragon. Sorcerer. Master of darkness. Would his love for her protect her from his rage? Though she held her head high, inside she trembled like a child. She took her seat and called for a report. A court official, an intelligent eldrow, approached, wary. She had never spoken to him; always depending on her father for news and for direction.

"What has happened in the weeks of my absence?"

"We have had reports of unrest in Syrea."

"What sort of unrest?"

"The ships, Your Highness, that supply us with food and pearls, are behind schedule. Sailors complaining about lazy captains. Skirmishes in the saloons. Minor violence."

"I see." She wondered if Jakin was involved. How many other trade ships supplied the mainland with pearls? She knew little about it.

"Other news? About Draegin. How is it he is well?"

"His Highness woke one morning a fortnight ago, feeling well. The infection in his chest had healed. After a few days of weakness, he regained full strength."

"I see. And did he inquire as to my whereabouts?"

"He did, Your Highness."

"And what was he told?"

"That you had ridden away on the Pegasus, Your Highness, and had not returned." The eldrow hesitated.

"Is there more?"

"I'm told he set out searching for you, fearing to find you injured or worse."

"I see. Thank you."

He stood, waiting.

"Leave me," she snapped.

Her heart hammered. He was probably checking every mountain crevice, every valley, for her and Conquest, not knowing if they were dead or alive. He could smell blood a mile away and his keen vision cut through daylight and dark equally well. While he would be initially relieved to see her, she would certainly face his wrath. Perhaps she should leave, again, and send word to him. Warn him she was returning. Give him time to fume and cool off. Yes, that's what she must do. Manage his wrath. Protect herself and the Pegasus.

She walked outside and swung onto Conquest. They took off and headed south, down the narrow valley. A few minutes later, a dark shadow flittered overhead. The dragon! She'd recognize the shape of that silhouette anywhere. She watched it pivot and turn in pursuit. Conquest screamed and she urged him to land in a small flat space on the edge of a cliff. While her father in his human form was capable of mercy, or at least of intelligent thought, she feared the dragon was not. Her only hope was that he would shift back to Thaumaturge. The Pegasus landed hard in a very small space, jolting them both. Marinna guided him behind a rock protrusion where he folded his trembling wings. The dragon roared. It had seen them. Would it circle and burn them alive? How much control of his dragon nature did her father have? They didn't have long to wait to find out. She could see it approaching. The horse trembled but stood steady. In spite of her fear, she admired the dragon's two-footed landing in such limited space. It fell to all four, tucked its wings in, then shuddered and disappeared. In its place, stood the tall pale silhouette of her father. He did not approach her.

"Come out," he commanded.

She dared not disobey and risk fueling his wrath. She strode out, alone. "Father," she cried, walking swiftly to him and bowing her head in respect. "You are well! I am so glad."

"Are you now?"

"Of course." She stood to her full height. "Had I known you'd revived I'd have returned immediately." He made no move to touch her, take her hand, embrace her. His eyes, usually warm with affection for her, were cold. His rage had always terrified her, but this time a sudden strength bloomed in her; a confidence she'd not experienced before. *Charm him. Gentle him as you did Conquest. Captivate him with tenderness.*

"Where have you been?"

Suppressing her fear, she mustered an expression of love, and gazed at her father with affection. "Syrea." Her soul responded to the challenge with rising passion, her voice honeyed to an alluring, mysterious tone. Her father's gaze moved from her eyes to her lips. "I went to Syrea in search of memories of mother."

His expression softened. Was it because of her mother or because of her? What did it matter? They were both sirens.

"And what did you find?"

"I found I am much like her."

His gaze flickered for an instant, then hardened, again. *Do not let up. Win him. Pull him to you.*

"Foolish!" he blurted. "The sirensss would kill you."

Marinna kept her voice even and met his gaze with bewitching eyes. "You speak truth, father. They would kill me. They tried."

His yellow eyes flashed, then softened, then flashed, again, betraying his inner struggle.

The edges of her perfect lips curled up. "But my father's nature also lives in me. I am the daughter of a mighty sorcerer. I am stronger than the sirens; I survived, and I fear them no longer." She brushed the tip of his cold fingers with her own.

His face split into a grin. "I must hear more of thisss. Come, let usss go back to the palace."

Relief flooded her. She'd faced her father and won! Charm had defeated rage! The power of manipulation! She called Conquest and he emerged, skittish at the sight of Draegin.

Marinna reached for the reins, speaking words of encouragement to the horse. Draegin stood very still, watching the steed. She gentled Conquest, stroking the side of his face. "He will not hurt you, my Prince. I promise," she cooed. The horse took a few uncertain steps toward Draegin. Marinna reached for her father's hand and placed it on Conquest's face. The horse screamed and reared. Marinna pulled his rein, speaking firmly. "Settle. Settle. He will not hurt you. You have my word." She shot a warning glance at her father. He did not move, just watched intently.

Conquest twisted, clearly uneasy about Draegin, as though he sensed the deadly power of the Thaumaturge. Marinna persisted with calm whispers, making eye contact with the stallion as often as he would allow. She stroked his long cheek. The stallion slowly regained his composure, though his ears stood straight, all senses alert.

"Father." She held out her hand for him, again. He took it. But she did not place it on Conquest. She just let the horse see them touch each other. The stallion neighed and skittered away. She stuck to his side and in one swift, fluid motion, both she and her father mounted. Conquest screamed and reared, but they held on.

"Droome," Marinna commanded, and the Pegasus reluctantly turned his face to the mountaintop.

Later, Marinna met with her father in her throne room, captivating him with stories of the island, the sea, the mermen. Her confidence grew with each story and every approving nod. She showed him the long strings of pearls for Conquest's bridle and he marveled to hear they were strung with eldrow veins. How perfect! She described the dream she'd had of her castle on Pearl Isle, recalling the details vividly, and sweeping him into the vision as if it were real. He sighed in satisfaction when she'd finished, and though he made no comment, his eyes held approval. Bolstered by his encouragement, she found the nerve to tell him what she held closest to her heart—her transformation to mermaid. His eyes widened in shock. Tell me everything, he'd said, leaning forward. She described it all, being mistaken for Nerida, meeting King Llyr, falling for Orkha, then realizing her mistake and fighting to escape. Never before had she opened her heart to her father. She hoped her secrets were safe with him. However, she held one thing close; she did not mention her affection for Jakin. Finally, she stopped talking, and gave him a chance to respond.

He was silent for several minutes, staring vacantly as if she'd cast a lingering spell on him. Tenderness softened his reptilian eyes. Perhaps he was thinking of mother, the only one who'd ever cracked his tyrannical shell and pierced his malevolent heart with warmth. The only one, that is, until now. She swallowed a laugh and that gurgle brought him back to the present.

"I was fearful for your life, Marinna. Your mother and I have risked everything for you, and I feared it was for naught. And when I spotted you, today, I was both relieved and furiousss." His nostrils flared. He leaned forward and glared at her and it took all her strength to avoid flinching. But she did not look away. He finally broke eye contact and sighed. "You have matured more quickly than I'd ever imagined." He turned his head away and she thought she detected a smile at the corners of his mouth. Was he amused with her? Didn't he realize the power she had over him? Anger threatened to ruin her composure. Or, a troublesome thought niggled at her—had he played her with his own wiles; had he been goading her all along? Her confidence faltered.

He turned back to her, smiling widely this time. "I'm proud of you, Marinna. Taming the Pegasus. Exploring Syrea. Discovering your siren heritage and escaping their captivity. Planning to rule from a seaside castle! Well done, my daughter. Well done, all of it."

He was pleased! More than that, he was thrilled! As she struggled to contain her volatile emotions, he confided how he'd hoped for her powers to bloom though he'd not been sure how or when. He'd sensed greatness in her from childhood. Well of course he had. He'd always told her so. Had he not really known? She responded with her most captivating smile, but her poise faltered. Could he tell? Who was manipulating who, she wondered.

If he sensed her unease, he didn't show it. He changed the subject. "Tell me, though. Why do you not like it here inside the mountain?"

"I despise the cold and dark, father."

He eyed the glittering throne, sadness shadowing his face. "I had hoped you would rule from here." He met her gaze. "But that was a father'sss dream."

She masked her expression, not wanting him to see her joy that he would not stand in the way of her leaving.

He crossed his arms over his chest. "Tell me, Marinna, in your travelsss have you heard anything of the royal family? King Merek? His queen or the princesss?"

His casual posture did not fool her; she saw his forehead quivering. She shook her head. "I have traveled covertly and spoken with few, staying hidden as much as possible, knowing my time had not yet come."

"You are wise beyond your yearsss."

"But I do have some news about King Merek from Prince Tozar, who supplies me with pearls."

Draegin waited, his forehead pulsing.

"The king is dead. Hundreds were injured or killed at the ball, though the queen and the princess still live."

His parietal eye flew open. Marinna did flinch this time; unable to hide her revulsion. Her father was furious; the eye raged.

She turned her back and feigned a cough, walking a few steps away, giving him time to regain his composure. "When you are stronger, father, we shall attack them together. They will be unable to deflect a double assault."

"Yesss. Yesss, that is a good strategy," he murmured from the darkness of his head covering. After the eyelid had closed, Draegin approached and she turned to see his hands outstretched as if in explanation. "It was a foolproof plan. The boy, Jakin, was an easy target, vulnerable, weak-minded, easily influenced. He did just what I wanted; a puppet in my hand. It nearly worked. I should never have removed the bracelet from Rory'sss wrist. Itsss enchantment caused her to love him. Marrying him would have forfeited her right to rule. Then they both would have been mine. Clay in my handsss. Easy to crush."

Jakin? Marinna was stunned. Her father knew Jakin? How was that possible? Jakin, her Jakin, had nearly married the princess? Her heart thumped unevenly; her skin grew clammy.

"Marinna." Draegin leaned closer. "Are you unwell? Is something wrong?"

She jolted to the present, dropping her composure into place. "Oh. No, father, forgive me. I, ah, was contemplating the brilliance of your ruse."

He considered her, and she shifted uncomfortably as his eyes lingered on hers. "The princess is no match for us," she said, again, in an effort to divert his attention. "We will take our time and conceive a plan that is infallible."

"That we will," he said decisively. "Now, about the island castle. Perhaps, it is time. Yesss, I can see that it isss. Time to come out of hiding. Time to raise our flag, release our troopsss, set the prophecy in motion. Time to let the nationsss tremble as they observe usss, the dragon and the queen, establishing our power. The castle you saw in your dream? I believe it was more than a dream, Marinna. It was a stirring of power in you. A vision of what is to come. We shall build it just as you described. It is time to conquer."

Chapter 38: Two Years

"They're hiding something," Rory whispered to Finn as they walked alone by the river the next morning.

He looked at her, surprised. "You think so?"

"Um hmm."

"What do you think it is?"

"No idea." She shrugged. "They just aren't convincing. They were so sincere at the formal announcement of the restoration of the Eldur Crown, yet they've been sullen and silent ever since."

"Maybe that's just how they are."

"Maybe." She doubted it but dropped the subject. No use upsetting Finn when he didn't seem alarmed at all. She even felt a little guilty for raining on his sunshine. He adored Trummarius and Ellisa! She could see reverence in his eyes as he watched them. His elven heritage had come to life! He was so thrilled; these were the heroes of his dreams! Unfortunately, she couldn't shake the uneasy feeling she had about them. For creatures of light, of joy and merriment, those two were sour. She'd keep an eye on them.

They'd walked for a long time beside the river, enjoying the birds and the bursts of colorful flowers. Suddenly Rory realized the light was different. Thinner somehow.

"We don't have to be back for anything, do we?" she asked Finn.

"Not as far as I know." He grinned at her. "Isn't it beautiful here?"

"Truly it is." She squeezed his hand. "Cold though."

Finn stopped and laughed. "It is cold! You know, I'm so caught up in the magic of this place, I didn't even notice!"

He put his arm around her, pulling her close and they walked on in silence. She guessed they'd walked a few miles. The elven gardens were long behind them, but scrub greenery was prolific. The ground sloped uphill, so gradually, she hadn't noticed until now. The cave's ceiling was very high, and the rock walls spread wide apart. Something on the ground caught her eye and she bent to pick it up.

"Whatch'a got?" Finn asked leaning close to see.

Rory didn't answer and Finn saw an odd expression on her face.

"What is it, Rory?"

"This arrowhead. It's familiar. Look closely, Finn. Can you see any writing on it?"

Finn held it up to the light, turning it this way and that. "Yes. Yes, actually, I do. Very tiny letters. It's hard to make out what they say."

"Rosie's mother had a few of these. She'd been reluctant to show me, saying they were the arrowheads belonging to the little people, blamed for murders and kidnappings in Alaskan lore. She was truly terrified. This looks like the same thing."

"Why is it here in the caves?" Finn asked, confused.

"That's my question, exactly! I wonder if elves still hunt with these arrowheads?"

"Well, even if they do, why would Rosie's mother have found them near her home?"

"I have a crazy hunch!" Rory grinned. She sniffed the air and started jogging.

"What's your hunch?" Finn asked, jogging to keep pace.

"That smell. Reminds me of Alaska in winter. Snow and deep woods."

"Mmmm." He sniffed. "I like it."

She inhaled deeply and let it out. "You know, I guess it's my overactive imagination, but I'm pretty sure I smell wood smoke, too. Oh my, Finn. I'm so homesick."

"Well, it's probably time to turn back anyway. Maybe the walk back will cheer you up."

Rory didn't move. She studied the light, sniffing the air again and again.

Finn chuckled and reached over to smooth her hair. "What are you thinking?" He looked at her with those dewy eyes she found so hard to resist. He leaned down and kissed her, but even that didn't distract her from her thoughts.

"So, I'm wondering why it's so bright here. Unless we have a cadre of elves following us and making light, it should be dark."

"Okaaay."

"Do you think it could possibly be sunlight?"

His face showed his shock. "Sunlight! Are you thinking we might be at the end of the tunnels?"

She grabbed his arm, excited. "Maybe! Let keep going! Maybe we are close to the fresh air. Maybe it's not my imagination. Maybe all this light is actually from the sun!" She broke into a run.

"Rory! Wait for me!" He sped after her.

The smell of smoke was undeniable. Short spindly spruce trees grew amid the scrub bush. Rory raced toward the light. It wasn't long before shadows dappled the greenery. Long, low sun rays stretched their fingers. The air was colder but fresh, bursting with familiar fragrances. Fresh snow, spruce, wood smoke. Breathless, they sprinted the last quarter mile and came to the mouth of the cave.

Rory stopped, stunned. She looked out on a familiar scene. A forest of skinny spruce trees stood before her; their boughs white with several inches of freshly fallen snow. Thin tendrils of smoke hung in the biting air. The silence was stunning, like a heavy blanket over the world. Rory took Finn's hand. "I can't believe it!" Her voice trembled with excitement. "Finn, I think I recognize these woods! Come on!" They ran out of the cave and Rory turned full circle looking around. "This way!" She turned right and dashed through the trees; Finn fast on her heels. Rory skidded to a stop. "There it is!" she gasped.

"What?" Finn asked looking quickly around.

She was panting so hard it was difficult to talk. "Boat." She pointed and grabbed his hand, walking toward it as she caught her breath. "This boat, Finn. I know this boat." She glanced at him, seeing both confusion and curiosity in his face. She brushed the snow off the upside-down rowboat and sat on the hull, patting a place beside her. He sat. She looked hard around her. "There's a big river just there," she said pointing. "Under the snow. I know where we are, Finn! I've been here lots of times. We are in Rosie's village in Alaska!" She turned to face him. "Eeeeee!" she squealed. "The tunnel leads here, right here to Alaska!" She leapt up and grabbed his shoulders. "Finn, do you know what this means?"

He looked at her, eyebrows raised.

"Our worlds are connected! We can travel back and forth! Anyone could."

"Rory. Calm down. Take a deep breath. Think about how hard it was, how dangerous. I mean we nearly died."

"So, it's not exactly a walk in the park. But there's a passage. A real passage. Oh. My. Gosh!" She strode away, calling to him. "Finn, come on. We have to go find Rosie! Wait till she meets you! Wait till she hears this!"

They tramped as fast as they could toward the village, wrapping themselves in their hooded cloaks, leaning into the wind.

"It's really, really cold," Finn said, tucking his hands under his crossed arms.

"It's winter. Alaska is super cold in winter. And it gets dark early." She eyed the sun low on the horizon. She'd guess it was late February, maybe early March, hopefully the same day she'd left. Rosie wouldn't realize she'd been gone, again. She'd have some explaining to do, but her friend would catch on quick. Especially with Finn there—proof positive she was telling the truth! A thrill bubbled inside her at the thought of Rosie meeting him.

As they drew close to the edge of the village, she sensed something was off. No one, absolutely no one, was outside. This was very odd. Kids were always out playing, even in weather like this. Three skinny dogs shot from behind a cabin, snapping and snarling. Where was everyone? It didn't feel right.

"Finn," she said uncertainly. "I'm not sure you should come with me. Not until I figure things out."

"What things?" He stomped his frozen feet.

She led him away from the village, hoping no one had actually seen them. Dogs barked all the time at wildlife; maybe no one had bothered to glance out the window.

"Here. Come in here out of the wind." She led him into a stand of trees.

"Ahhh. This is better." He rubbed his hands together. "I guess it's the wind that bites so much."

"Will you wait here for me? I want to go to Rosie's house first. Just to make sure everything's okay."

"Only if you promise to explain to me what might be wrong?"

"I will, I promise." She turned and ran off. "When I get back!" she called.

"Rory, wait! I meant now!"

She kept running until she reached the homes on the edge of the village, then she stopped and watched. It was still and silent. When they saw her, the dogs picked up their barking, again. She stole through the snow-covered street, sure she was being watched, though no faces showed in any windows. The back of her neck prickled.

Rosie's house was just ahead to the right. It looked normal. Same snow machine outside. Same rusty bike propped against the crooked shed. She knocked on Rosie's door. No one answered. The dogs had followed her down the street, making a racket. The whole village must know she was there. Suddenly, she realized how she must look—a hooded, caped figure no one had ever seen before, showing up from out of nowhere. No airplane had brought her; she hadn't come by snow machine on the river. She threw her hood back and shook her hair out.

"Rosie!" she called. "It's Rory! Rosie, are you in there? Open the door!" She thought she saw a face in the window but when she looked, again, it was gone. In another second, the door opened an inch.

"Rory?"

"Rosie! Yes, it's me!"

Rosie opened the door wide and threw herself into Rory's arms weeping. Rory was shocked. What was going on?

Rory hugged her friend. "Can I come inside? It's freezing out here!"

Rosie giggled through her tears. "Of course! Come in."

It wasn't very warm in the house, either, but it was better than outdoors. Rory took her cape off and hung it on a hook where it could drip.

Rosie was staring at her clothes, her long dress and high shoes.

Rory shrugged with a grin. "It's the way they dress in Gamloden. Jeans to them are totally weird."

"You've been in Gamloden all this time?"

"All what time? How long have I been gone?"

"Two years, Rory, last month. We all thought you were dead."

"Oh!" Rory squeaked. "I'm not dead. I mean, I must have messed up the time transfer somehow. I'm so, so sorry to have frightened you." She paused. "So, two years? Wait. I'm 18 now?"

Rosie laughed. "You and me both!"

Rory gasped as she thought about her family. "Dad and Gram—they think I'm dead, too?"

Rosie nodded, then burst into tears and crushed her with another hug. "I'm so glad to see you," she mumbled, wiping her runny nose with a dirty dishcloth.

Rory glanced around. The kitchen was a wreck; piles of crusty dishes filled the counter, garbage overflowed in the corner. Rory looked into the other room. Clothes were strewn everywhere. Whiskey bottles lay on the floor. She'd never seen Rosie's home like this.

"What's happened, Rosie? Where's your mother?"

"She died last year," Rosie's voice broke. "I've barely managed to keep it together; you know, stay warm and eat."

"Oh Rosie! Why didn't you send word to my dad? He would've come to get you!"

"With him thinking he'd lost you, well, I couldn't do that to him." She looked down and shrugged. "It's been hard."

Rory didn't know what to say, but Rosie continued before she had to think of something. "My father got out of jail. He thinks he can live here now."

Anger flushed Rory's face. "No way."

"I leave when he's around. There are a lot of homes I can stay in." Rory noticed the dark circles under Rosie's eyes. She was exhausted. Skinny. And maybe sick.

She suddenly remembered Finn. "Rosie, grab your jacket. You have to meet Finn!"

"Finn? The elf? Are you kidding me!"

A laugh lit up her friend's face, and Rory was so encouraged to see it.

"Here, Rory, put on my mother's coat. You really looked like a weirdo walking around with that hooded cloak."

She slipped into the coat, a size too big, but at least it was from the right century. "Um, Rosie, you don't have a man's jacket around, do you? And a hat?"

"Yup, sure do." She grabbed a blue ski jacket off the floor and a black ski cap.

"Any gloves?"

Rosie sighed. "Still the same Rory! So needy." They both laughed and searched through a drawer of gloves and mittens until they found a pair for Rory and a pair for Finn.

"Okay, let's go!" Rory said, grabbing her cloak and throwing open the door. She screamed. Rosie's father was swaying on the other side, a half-empty bottle poised inches from his mouth.

"Excuse us," Rory said loudly. "We were just leaving."

"I don't shink sho," he slurred, leering.

Rosie was cowering behind her; Rory'd have to be bold enough for both of them.

"Let us pass," Rory demanded.

"You are free to go. But Rosie shtays here with me."

Rory looked past him and let horror fill her face. When he spun around to look, she shoved him hard, sending him sprawling in the snow. She and Rosie jumped over him as he floundered to get up and were halfway across the village before he hollered at them. "Hey, that's my blue shacket!" This time, faces filled the windows. A few doors opened and both kids and adults laughed. Some clapped.

"Run," a woman shouted.

"See ya later!" a child yelled.

They ran past the last house and instead of following the river, Rory pulled her friend into the woods. A few minutes later, she introduced her to Finn. They stared at each other, momentarily at a loss for words, before Finn suddenly bowed. "Rosie! How very lovely to meet you!"

Rosie giggled. "Finn, I'm so glad to meet you as well!"

"Finn," Rory said. "I'd like to take Rosie with us back to Luminest. She needs a safe place to stay for a while."

Finn looked uneasy.

"She's in danger here. We have to get her away."

"I see." He quickly made up his mind. "Right. Off we go, then," he said, putting on the jacket and gloves and pulling the black cap over his ears. "That's so much better! Thank you!" He beamed at Rosie. "Follow me!"

Chapter 39: Connected Worlds

Floxx greeted Rosie warmly, making up for the high elves' coolness. "Welcome to Luminest, Rosie!" she said, hugging her when they were introduced.

"Thank you," Rosie replied, stealing glances at the bizarre creatures in the cave. Shrives and elves, flitting fairies blinking in the shadows—she was beside herself with wonder. She clenched Rory's arm, not willing to let go even to take off her coat.

"Hello," a deep voice growled behind her.

Rosie turned and screamed when she saw Uriel's wolf head towering above her.

"It's okay, Rosie. Meet Uriel. He's our protector. Remember that blue ball of light that used to glide above Cue's head?"

Rosie nodded, not taking her eyes off him, her free hand over her mouth.

"It was him."

Rosie glanced sideways at Rory like she was crazy.

Uriel rumbled in mirth and Rory and Floxx burst out laughing. Even Elissa suppressed a smile.

"You hungry?" Rory asked, changing the subject. "It's about time for dinner." She led her friend up into the tree where she could stare at the creatures surreptitiously.

Rosie studied the shrives as they cooked and dished up the food. "Little people!" she whispered, enamored with them. "I can't believe it!" Rosie ate well, complimenting the shrives on their delicious cooking. The edges of their mouths turned up at the compliments from the new human.

"Such nice manners," one whispered to the other as they descended the steps. Rory warmed in appreciation for the kindnesses that bound all creatures together.

It was odd no one asked Rosie who she was or why she was there. Trummarius and Elissa said nothing. They ate in total silence. Finn and Rosie chatted, and Rory stole a glance at Floxx, raising her eyebrows in question about the high elves. Floxx subtly shook her head, so Rory didn't pursue it. She wondered if Floxx also had concerns about them.

Not long after dinner, Rosie stifled a yawn and Floxx graciously offered to get them settled. "Come with me. It's late and you're tired. I'll show you where Rosie can sleep."

"Next to me, please," Rory whispered.

"Of course."

"Good night, Rory." Finn stopped her to grab a kiss.

"Night, Finn." She patted his cheek. "See you in the morning."

"Good night, Rosie," he called to her. "It's nice to have you with us."

"Thanks. I'm beyond happy to be here!"

Rory would have talked half the night with Rosie, but her friend burrowed under the covers and fell asleep within minutes. She swallowed her disappointment, realizing this might be the most secure sleep Rosie had had in a very long time.

Early the next morning before Rosie stirred, Rory crawled out of bed. Just the shrives were up, laboring silently over their oven. She tip-toed to the mouth of the cave and leaned against the rocks enjoying the mist from the waterfall on her face. The river gurgled and she stared downstream trying to absorb the fact the tunnel led to Alaska.

"Morning," Finn whispered, surprising her with a kiss on the top of her head.

She wrapped her arms around him. "Morning!" She loved hearing his heartbeat and closed her eyes, relishing the moment.

"What are you thinking?" Finn whispered.

"About you and me and the fact that our worlds connect. We can move between them at will, without magic, gems, or feathers." She pulled back and looked up at him. "This changes everything!"

"Well, I suppose in a way it does. What a trek, though. And actually, nothing's really changed; I mean, it's been like this for eons. We just never knew."

"Hmm, I never thought about it that way." They stood quietly for a few minutes. "Finn," she pulled away to look at him. "My family thinks I'm dead. I have to let them know I'm okay."

"Of course. I was thinking about that, too. So, you want to go back to Alaska? Are they near Rosie's village?"

"Not too far from there. I've been trying to figure out how to contact them." The village had cell service and she could charge her phone there, but there was no service at Gram's cabin. She'd always called Rosie from the airplane. It wasn't worth trying to explain all that to Finn; phones, electricity, and pretty much all things in the modern world were going to amaze him.

"Can we walk there?"

"It's possible, I guess, but it would take days and it's too cold. I've always traveled from my house to hers by airplane."

"Ah. I see." He frowned, seeing the challenge.

"I think I can call flight service and leave a message there. Dad always calls them to check the weather."

"All right." Finn looked dubious.

"We'd have to stay in the village and wait for a return call."

"Stay for how long?"

"That's just it, Finn. I don't know. Could be just a day. Could be a couple weeks if he's out on a long trip."

Finn brushed a strand of hair out of her face. "Let's do it. Whatever it takes. I know I wouldn't want to be mourning your loss when you were alive and close by!"

After breakfast, they pulled Floxx, Uriel, and Rosie aside to explain what they'd like to do. Uriel glanced at Floxx and a nearly imperceptible nod passed between them. What were they up to?

"Rory," the great wolf rumbled, "I can take you both."

Of course! Why hadn't she thought of that!

Finn squeezed her hand. "I get to meet your family!"

"I've told them all about you!" she teased.

"Will you come?" Rory asked Floxx.

"I will be with you as always. I'll hear you if you call. But I think I should stay here with Rosie."

"Rosie? You okay with this?"

"I think so. It's all so amazing, and so crazy. But I feel safe with Floxx. I trust her already."

"There's no one you can trust more!" Rory assured her.

They left after the mid-day meal, Rory and Finn walking, and Uriel, a blue orb bobbing above. It was dark when they reached the woods, early evening, Rory guessed. Uriel immediately shape-shifted.

"You know the way?" she asked him.

"Rory, I spent 16 years with you here. I definitely know the way."

"Right." Her face heated. How had she not put that together?

It seemed to her the flight took much longer than it had in an airplane, but finally, they spotted the cabin. Smoke curled from the chimney. Someone was home! She hoped their arrival didn't scare them too badly. Uriel landed on the snowy runway and as soon as Rory and Finn were off his back, he shifted back to an orb, blinking at them.

"Gram and Dad are used to seeing him like that," she explained to Finn. "He floated over Cue's head all of my childhood. I never knew he was Uriel until the Night of the Tennins."

"Ah," Finn said, self-consciously pulling his cap over his ears.

"They'll love you, Finn. Elf ears and all."

"Maybe it's best if they discover my ears after we've had a chance to visit awhile."

"Sure," she said smiling. "Come on!"

They ran up the path toward the cabin. Home! She was home! Happy tears ran down her cheeks. "Gram! Dad!" she yelled as they neared. "It's Rory! I'm home!" Someone moved behind the curtain. "Gram! Dad!" she yelled, again.

The door flew open and there was her grandmother, looking frailer than she remembered. She rushed to hug her, careful not to squeeze too tight.

"Rory?" Gram pulled away to look at her. "Oh, Rory!" she said, tears filling her eyes. "It is you! It really is you!" She held her, again, for a long minute. "Come in out of the cold. Your father's out back, splitting firewood. I'll call him."

"No, let me! We'll be right back! Come on, Finn!" Rory raced around the house to the woodshed. "Dad!" she cried, "Dad!"

He dropped the axe and spun around.

Rory ran into the lamp light and threw herself into his arms, not caring if she knocked him over in the snow. But his reflexes were quick, and he caught her.

Stunned, it took him a moment to realize what had happened. "Rory?" He peered at her teary face. "Rory!" He crushed her with a bear hug. "You're alive!" He was sobbing. He clung to her as he wept, eventually able to choke out a few words. "Thank God you're back!"

"I'm so glad to be here; it's so good to see you!" She loosened herself from his grip and swiped at her wet cheeks. "I messed up the time thing, really bad; I'm so sorry, Dad. I had no idea two years had gone by. Rosie told me. Oh my gosh, I have so much to tell you!" She turned around looking for Finn. "But Dad, I brought someone—my friend, Finn; I've told you about him." She motioned for him to come out of the shadows. "Dad, this is Finn. And Finn, this is my fa…."

But Dad didn't give her time to finish. He pulled Finn into a bear hug that Rory could see had taken him by complete surprise. "Thank you, Finn, for caring for my daughter. For protecting her. For keeping her safe and bringing her home." He was close to breaking down, again.

Finn's cheek was pinned so hard against Dad's shoulder he could barely talk. "Yeth, isth a great privileth to know her." He pulled away, tugging his crooked hat over his ears. "And also, a privilege to meet you." Then, he bowed.

This was awkward.

Dad managed to suppress a laugh as he clapped Finn on the shoulder.

"Gram's waiting, Dad. We met her at the front door a few minutes ago."

"Right! And you are just in time for dinner! She's probably rushing to make something special for dessert! Let's go."

Finn helped him load the chopped wood into the wagon and jumped as the snow machine engine roared.

Rory grinned. "Welcome to my world!" she teased, reaching inside the shed to flip the light off.

An hour later, they were stuffed with chicken and dumplings, smothered in Gram's thick gravy, followed by a warm blueberry crisp with whipped cream.

"That was delicious, ma'am!" Finn said, pushing back from the table. "Very, very, delicious!"

"Well, thank you, Finn!" Gram smiled and Rory could tell she liked him. "I'm so glad you enjoyed it!" She made no move to clear the table, just followed Finn's lead and sat back.

"So?" Dad raised just one eyebrow, which meant this was important. "Two years? That was a long time. We'd pretty much lost hope of seeing you, again. What happened Rory? Tell us everything."

She and Finn talked about the island, Spike, the Underside and their escape. Gram made a pot of tea and they went on to describe the airplane repairs Werner and the dwarves had made.

"They are amazing craftsmen, Dad!"

"Ah, well, that explains something I've wondered about. The Cessna disappeared the same night you did. We considered reporting it stolen, but decided it was too much of a coincidence."

"Right! That makes sense! I didn't think it could be in two places at once!" She described the test flight and spotting Marinna and the Pegasus.

"A Pegasus!" Gram murmured. "I hadn't imagined that!" She pumped Rory for details that led to some background on Draegin, which Rory had actually hoped to avoid. She didn't want to terrify her family.

Finn jumped in, changing the subject, to describe the thrill of their flight to the castle, their reunion with her birth mother, and how well the Queen was managing affairs after the King's death. He let Rory carry most of the conversation, though; he was very distracted, scrutinizing everything in the cabin. It was definitely backwoods compared to more modern homes in Fairbanks, but he was amazed with all things electric—the lights, the oven, the hand mixer Gram had used to whip the cream. He'd seen the kitchen faucet turned on and off several times, and expressed his wonder that water flowed on demand, both hot and cold. It was a lot for him to contemplate!

By midnight, they were all exhausted and promised to talk more in the morning. Gram bedded Finn down on the couch by the wood stove, fussing over him like he was her own grandson. Though there was still so much to tell them, especially the astounding fact that their two worlds were connected by an underground labyrinth, for now, for this one night, Rory wanted to cherish the moment. She climbed to the loft and snuggled under the blankets in her childhood bed. Seeing the knots on the ceiling, she realized their story had, in fact, unfolded—she had flown away. As a child she'd thought they told the whole story, but now she knew they depicted only the beginning.

Her time in Gamloden flashed before her: Floxx, Finn, the prophecy; her birth parents and all their heartbreak; Draegin and Marinna's murderous attacks on her and their obsession to rule, obliterate freedom and replace it with tyranny. She shuddered at the horrors they would inflict if they succeeded, crushing Gamloden with oppression, despair, and grief.

Finn carried a daunting challenge. Though Eldurrin and Floxx and the tennins, along with all of Finn's allies would fight with him, it wouldn't happen unless he fulfilled the whole prophecy, somehow forging the crown and taking his place as the long-awaited Eldur King. The stakes were impossibly high, and Rory dared not think about the cost. Zad and her birth father had already died facing the dragon. Would there be others? A terrible war seemed inevitable. What tragedies would it bring? And how would it end?

About the Author

Kathleen King and her husband, Dwayne, are missionaries with Kingdom Air Corps, a non-profit organization based in Alaska that trains missionary pilots to operate in the remotest areas of the world. Kathleen was a technical writer for the Aircraft Owners and Pilots Association (AOPA) for 30 years. Also an English professor, she taught writing classes at Shippensburg University for 10 years. She holds a Master of Fine Arts in Creative Writing and a Master of Business Administration.

This is the second of three young adult, fantasy fiction books in the Firebird series. Please consider leaving a review of this book at Amazon.com.

Read more about the author on her website, www.kathleen-king.com.

Made in the USA
Middletown, DE
21 May 2021